A
CURSE
IN
DARKNESS

PROLOGUE

Willow

I DIDN'T SCREAM when Azel made the final slice in my back. After hours of torture, I had nothing left to give—until the sick, twisted fallen angel began broadcasting horrific images of my family directly into my mind. I screamed then, and something inside me shattered so thoroughly I knew that if I survived this, I'd never be the same again.

He leaned over me. "Do you see, witch, what I will do to them if you don't let me into that fucking compound."

My body was jostled roughly as the grasping hands of his demon followers carried me to the warded gates of the knight's compound. A ward that I'd created.

The knights of Hell protected this city from the demons who resided here, and their compound sheltered those most vulnerable to attack.

They'd trusted *me* to help them do that.

Azel had held my friend Luna and her brother Ronan captive

most of their lives, but they'd gotten away. Now Luna was here, finally safe and mated to one of the knights. But Azel wanted Luna back, and I was currently the thing standing in his way.

The demons dropped me. I hit the ground hard, and stared blankly at the massive iron gates blocking our path. Azel crouched beside me, his mind twisting deeper into mine, attacking, stabbing, breaking me from the inside out now. He'd found my weakness, my family. And I wasn't sure how much longer I could withstand this torture.

Everything went dark. He'd taken my sight, so all I could see were those images; my family, bleeding, screaming. Suffering.

I cried out, suddenly not sure what was real and what wasn't, if it was actually happening or just a horror show of his own making playing in my head.

"You can make it stop, witch," he said, his hot breath on my neck. "Drop the ward or I will tear the skin from their flesh, starting with your sisters."

I couldn't think—the pain, my family...I couldn't let him hurt them, I couldn't...

"Now!" he roared.

Tears stung my eyes as their blood-covered faces contorted in agony in my mind, as he continued his relentless onslaught. I wouldn't let him hurt them, I couldn't. He would kill them if I didn't do this, and he would make them suffer when he did it.

A sob was torn from my raw throat as I held out a trembling hand, palm down, fingers spread, and I choked out the words that would drop the ward.

Azel laughed, the chilling sound, lifting goosebumps all over my battered body.

Still blind, I could only hear what followed, the gate exploding open, fighting, yelling, screaming, the heat of flames on my skin, until consciousness was too much of a struggle—then there was nothing.

When I woke next, my sight had returned, and Grace, one of

the knight's mates, was crouched beside me. I struggled, trying to get up, to search for the rest of my friends.

"It's okay. Azel's dead, he can't hurt you now," Grace said as her mate Chaos, and leader of the knights, strode toward us.

I couldn't face him, I couldn't face any of them. I'd failed them all.

But before Chaos could reach us, Warrick, alpha of the hell-hounds was beside me. The huge male growled, raw violence and molten rage radiating from him as he carefully lifted me and held me protectively to him.

"I've got her," he snarled at Chaos.

"Willow?" Grace said, asking me if going with the alpha was what I wanted.

"Warrick will take care of me," I rasped. We weren't friends, he and I, I didn't really know what we were, but he made me feel safe. And I desperately needed to feel safe. My gaze slid to Chaos. "I'm sorry. I tried to stop him. He was...he was just too strong."

"You did nothing wrong," Chaos said. "Jesus, we should have done more to protect you."

"No shit," Warrick barked, then he turned and carried me away.

I squeezed my eyes closed and focused on the heavy beat of his heart, and tried to force those awful images from my mind.

Warrick pressed his mouth to the top of my head. "No one will ever hurt you again, dove, I promise you that."

CHAPTER 1

Willow

AN ICY BREEZE brushed over my bare skin, and I shivered as a steady stream of blood ran from my thigh, down my leg, to soak into the soil where I'd dug my bare foot.

An owl hooted in the distance, and I searched the shadows surrounding me.

Oldwood Forest was at the southernmost end of the larger Roxburgh State Forest, just beyond the city itself, and a hangout for all manner of creatures, mainly the unpleasant kind. So, standing here, completely naked, wasn't my idea of a good time. Unfortunately, I didn't have a choice.

Reluctantly, I tossed my dagger onto the pile of clothes I'd recently shed, drew in a deep breath, and closed my eyes.

Clearing my mind, I allowed the warmth of the soil to soak in, heating the soles of my feet. It vibrated, like the earth was *humming* softly beneath me.

The autumn breeze grew stronger, shifting my long, out-of-control red hair against my bare shoulders. Closing my eyes, I lifted my arms, tilting my head to the moonlight, its glow a welcome caress. "Guide me, old ones. I am your servant, the Keeper chosen to fulfill the rite of Coven Thornheart." The wind blew around me faster, dried leaves brushing past, small twigs and sticks scraping my skin as they whipped around my naked body. "I'm here to accept my task. Whatever you ask, I will undertake."

The air suddenly stilled, and cold, dark dread arrowed up my spine, shooting into the base of my skull. I gasped as silence engulfed the wood. Even the owl was silenced, not wanting to draw notice from the creature I'd summoned from its slumber.

Something oily scraped my leg, the tickle of a forked tongue tasting my blood. Then it came, the rattle, like a plastic bottle filled with dried beans.

I opened my eyes and the enormous serpent lifted its massive head, its glossy black eyes staring into mine. Dark and light, terrifying magic flowed from her, surrounding me.

The magic of my coven, of others like it.

Mother Nature, the Great Goddess, the Creatress of all life—or Mother, as she liked to be called by the witches who worshipped her—was not some beautiful maiden; she had no corporeal form at all.

But when she needed one, she chose to inhabit her pet serpent. At least thirty yards long and as thick as the ancient oak behind my aunt Else's house, she was a terror to behold. I held my ground. Any sudden movement would prove I was unworthy, and my life would more than likely come to a brutal and swift end.

The Goddess didn't play. She may create life, but she wasn't averse to taking it either.

Being the Keeper of one's coven was an incredible honor. If I were given a choice, though, it would have been a hard pass from me. But we didn't get a choice. And I'd rather it be me than someone else I loved, especially one of my sisters.

The mother's voice filled my head with the same words she'd

the middle of the road, no longer in his beast form but as a man, huge and naked. And judging by the glowing red eyes, pissed off.

"I thought you were going to talk to him?" Ren said. "Just because the guy has the ability to know where you are at all times, doesn't mean it's cool to act like a stalker. And he just messed up my freaking car."

"I'll get it fixed, and I've tried, believe me." The alpha did whatever the hell he wanted. I'd turned him down every way it was possible to turn someone down, but since hellhounds could *see* where a person was by their scent, he always knew where I was. And he wasn't giving up.

Ren gripped the wheel tighter and scowled. "I don't care about the car...I'll talk to him."

Lord, spare me from overprotective males. Between Ren and Warrick—and the half angel, demon hunter knights of Hell, who also happened to be my good friends—I was up to my neck in a serious amount of testosterone.

I glanced at him. "And what are you going to say?"

"I'll tell him to stay the hell away from you."

Closing my eyes, I rubbed my throbbing temples. "If you go to the clubhouse, *his den*, he'll see it as a challenge, like you're making some claim over me, and he'll hurt you."

"I'm your familiar; I do have a claim over you." His expression turned mulish. "I'm not afraid of him, you know. I've been training."

I held back my bark of disbelief, because the last thing I wanted was to hurt his pride. "Warrick is an alpha. He's huge, unreasonable, aggressive, and has lived a *very long* life, most of that in Hell, among the kind of violence we can't even imagine. He got to the position he's in now by killing and maiming anyone who dared challenge him."

Ren's cheeks flushed pink. "You think I'm weak."

Teenage boys. *Sheesh*. "No, Ren. I think he's really freaking strong. You're also still young; he's hundreds of years old, maybe more." I reached over and gave his arm a squeeze. "He's just had more practice, that's all."

My sweet fourteen-year-old shadow was now a surly nineteen-year-old man-boy, and his drive to protect me was messing with him. The danger I'd been in lately was bringing out a side of him that should never have been. Which was another reason I had been keeping things from him.

Familiars, animal or shifter, got themselves killed doing all kinds of stupid shit trying to protect their witches. I would not let Ren take on an opponent he had not a shit show of beating in a million years. My gran and great aunt had both suffered through the loss of their familiars. The grief had haunted my gran until the day she died, mere months ago. I wasn't letting anything happen to Ren. There was not a single chance in hell I was going to willingly involve him in this mess I found myself in, at least not until he was a lot older, a lot stronger, and a whole lot wiser.

The rest of the ride to my great aunt Else's house was quiet, besides the angsty 80s grunge music Ren turned up while he brooded.

So I closed my eyes, exhaustion washing over me, and let myself drift off.

CHAPTER 2

Willow

THE NEXT TIME I opened my eyes, Ren was shaking my shoulder. "We're here."

Rubbing my hands over my face, I tried to wipe away the grogginess and glanced out the window. Our family home was a two-story gothic Victorian made of black stone. It had arched windows, a blood red door, a curved turret, and a peaked roof—it was the witch's house in every fairy-tale storybook. My aunt, and Gran, when she'd been alive, had thought it was hilarious.

I groaned.

Everyone was here.

Magnolia should be in her room studying, and Iris was supposed to be on a date with her boyfriend, Brody. Instead, she was currently peering out the kitchen window at me. Rose was probably sitting at the kitchen table waiting for me as well. My sisters were protective.

I glanced at myself in the rearview mirror. I looked like shit, skin pale, dark rings under my bloodshot eyes, and my limbs still felt like overcooked noodles. It'd take a few days for the effects of the venom to dissipate. Good times.

I seriously hated my family seeing me like this.

"Let's get this over with." I shoved my door open and somehow made it inside on unsteady legs, while mentally preparing myself for the onslaught to come.

Yes, they drove me crazy sometimes, but I loved every one of them more than anything. Their faith in me, that our magic was safe in my hands, that I could save us from ruin, was humbling... and utterly terrifying. If I didn't complete the task set by the mother, then win against another witch in a magical combat trial, we could lose everything.

My life included.

Witches sometimes died during the trials—which was something we chose not to talk about. But a coven only kept the powers gifted to them by proving themselves every two hundred years, and not doing this, and failing my entire coven, wasn't an option.

I already knew what it was to let down those who relied on me, to feel weak and defeated, to fail the people you'd promised to keep safe. I couldn't go through that again, and not with the people I loved most in this world.

The cold, ugly grip of evil had clawed at me, marked me, beaten me, and if I wasn't strong enough to defeat whatever came at me this time, I'd never forgive myself.

Some nights it weighed so heavily, I woke in a cold sweat.

That couldn't happen again.

I wouldn't let it.

Shoving those dark thoughts aside, I walked down the hall to the kitchen.

Magnolia exploded out of her seat. "You're bleeding."

"It's not my blood," I said quickly. "A demon tried to get in our way."

She let out a breath and dropped back into her seat around the huge, scarred wooden table. "Okay, next question...dude, where are your pants?" Bram, Magnolia's familiar, bobbed his feathered head from his spot on her shoulder. Bram was a crow shifter, and in his human form—let's just say he'd scared the shit out of me several times, lurking around the place like a massive, dark shadow.

Mags was eighteen, the baby of the family, and in her final year of high school. She also worked part-time with our great aunt, making herbal remedies, potions, and tonics that I sold in my shop, The Cauldron.

"I didn't have time to put them on," I muttered and plonked into the chair closest.

"I hope you've got undies on or we'll have to bleach that," Iris said, passing me a mug of coffee while rubbing Nia's head. Nia was Iris's familiar, a German Shepherd, not a shifter, and we all loved on her regularly.

"Nope, not bare-assed," I said and would have rolled my eyes if I'd had the energy. Iris was twenty-three, the second eldest, after me, and three years younger. She could be reckless, especially when it came to protecting her family, and she was also a neat freak. I lost sleep over her regularly.

"Bunch of prudes," Else said, limping into the room. Elswyth Thornheart was seventy-two, our great aunt, and the most sarcastic being I'd ever encountered. Her name meant "elf from the willow tree," which was where my name came from, a gesture from my mother since Else didn't have any children of her own. My sisters were named after flowers, just like my mother and grandmother had been.

Else put her hand to my forehead and shoved a thermometer in my mouth. "You look like shit."

"Gee thanks." Her familiar had been killed protecting her a long time ago. She'd lost a leg during the incident. We didn't know exactly what happened, she wouldn't talk about it, but it had to have been pretty bad.

"Are you feeling okay?" Rose asked from her seat beside me, giving me a sympathetic look. Roe was twenty-one, and honestly, the only one of us that wasn't a bit of an asshole. I mean, my family was awesome, but we'd inherited our sense of humor from Gran and Else. The only person in this family who gave anyone sympathy was Roe.

My stomach tightened at how tired she looked this morning. For witches, three was a power number, the most important number. My mom had four kids, throwing the balance off when Magnolia was born, and for some reason, Rose was the one paying the price. That was what we assumed, anyway. Her illness was a complete mystery, and none of us knew what to do to make her better.

Which was another reason I was determined to complete my task and win my final trial. More power meant more to go around, right?

A coven that didn't grow in strength over the centuries became a target for those that did. No way was I letting that happen.

Roe also didn't have a familiar. We'd tried to tell her they were out there somewhere, that they'd find her, but none of us believed that, not anymore. Now we made a point not to talk about it because it hurt her when we did.

I gave Roe's hand a squeeze and forced a smile. "I'm fine, Roe."

"Keep your mouth shut. It won't be accurate if your jaw's flapping the whole time," Else said, pushing the thermometer deeper into my mouth. "Last time you got that wicked fever. I've come up with an elixir that should knock it on the head."

I shut my mouth and sat there while she watched the clock.

Finally, she slid the old-school thermometer from my mouth and looked down at it. "Huh?"

"What?"

"It's normal."

"Why do you look so disappointed?"

She shrugged. "I was looking forward to trying out the elixir. Me and Mags worked on it most of the day."

Magnolia hid her grin behind her mug.

"Your concern over my health is heartwarming, truly." I glanced at Iris. The traitor was smirking as well.

"*He* was there," Ren said, scowling.

"Ren," I warned.

"Who?" my mother asked as she walked in, Arthur right behind her. Arthur was mom's familiar, an owl shifter that preferred his human form. He was middle-aged with dark brown skin, cropped hair, and kind brown eyes. He wasn't much of a talker, but he loved us all. And puttering around the cemetery gardens with Mom was his most favorite thing to do in the world. It had also become obvious a long time ago that he was completely in love with Mom. I had no idea if she felt that same way, but the longing in his eyes when he looked at her was torture to watch sometimes.

"Warrick," Ren announced, ignoring my warning completely.

My mother brightened. Daisy Thornheart was a hopeless romantic, hopeless being the operative word, which wasn't surprising, considering our history. Our shitty luck with men was first documented around the 1400s. Back then, they used local place names, occupations, or sometimes nicknames to create what became a family's surnames. Ours came from the jilted lover of one of my ancestors. He yelled at the top of his lungs that she had a heart of thorns. It caught on. Eventually, it became Thornheart, and here we are.

And that shitty luck carried on down the line. In fact, Iris, Mags, Roe, and I all had different fathers because our mom tended to fall for any loser who gave her a second look. All four of our sperm donors were complete and utter losers. We were pretty sure Arthur had finally cracked and gotten rid of Mag's father himself. Mom had hidden it, but the fucker had been verbally abusive until it became more. He hurt Mom so badly he put her in the hospital.

The prick vanished after that.

One day he was here terrorizing us, the next there was a large patch of freshly turned earth in the far corner of the backyard. No one questioned it.

If Art hadn't done something, Gran or Else would have. I didn't care who did it; I was just glad he'd gotten what he more than deserved.

"God, Mom, I can actually see hearts floating around your head like a cartoon character," Iris said and fed Nia a doggy treat.

Mom held out her hand to me, and when I took it, she tugged me out of my seat. "Couldn't get a better protector than a hellhound, and my baby needs all the protection she can get."

Ren flushed, and his jaw got tight. "She doesn't need him. She has me."

"Mom," I growled out under my breath. "I'm more than capable of looking after myself."

She waved a hand. "Ren knows what I mean." She dropped a kiss to the top of his head and cupped his whiskered jaw. "Look at this face. This is not the face of a cold-hearted killer."

Ren flushed hotter, and I winced. *Jesus.* I gave her a look that I hoped expressed the need for her to stop talking.

She was right, though. Even covered in demon blood, Ren was the kind of good-looking that stopped people in the street. My fox was utterly gorgeous. He'd been a beautiful boy at fourteen, and I'd always known he'd be a heartbreaker when he became a man. He had dark russet hair and chiseled features that were perfectly proportioned. Add in the thick lashes and those great lips—man, I was jealous of those lips—and he was every teenage girl's fantasy. His square jaw, now covered in a short beard, stopped him from heading too far into pretty territory.

"Warrick scares the hell out of me," Rose said.

Mom glanced at her. "He's just man, Roe, like any other."

If only that were true. If he was just like every other man, then maybe I'd know how to deal with him.

Roe scoffed. "A man whose eyes glow red."

Mom shrugged. "Only sometimes." Then she grabbed the bottom of my sweater and tugged it up.

"Mom!" I tried to wrestle it from her. I lost.

"Pish. We've seen it all before."

Ren averted his gaze. Just because he was used to nudity didn't mean it was okay to stare at a naked woman being ogled by her entire family.

"Let's see the new ink," Mags said, moving closer. Bram bobbed on her shoulder and looked away as well. "Oh wow, that one's seriously awesome."

"It's big," Iris said. "Does it curl around your nip, or start under your boob."

I sighed. "It starts under my boob and will join up with the one on my hip."

"You know, I've been thinking," Mags said. "You're the new Keeper of an untried branch of the coven, what if this isn't your last task? What if the mother makes you do another one to prove we're not a bunch of duds of something?"

I rolled my eyes even as something unhappy curled in my gut. Mags had been getting "feelings" about things since she was little, and they'd become more accurate as she'd gotten older. But when it came to Magnolia, you didn't know which thoughts were just her highly active imagination and which were a developing sixth sense. "That won't happen." I turned to Mom. "Right?"

She chewed her lip, something she and Magnolia both did when they were feeling unsure.

"Mom?"

She waved her hand again. "No, I'm sure that won't happen."

"Imagine if the next one pops up in the middle of your forehead," Mags said and snorted, then her eyes widened. "Holy shit, she'd have to bite your head."

"Anything could happen, we're in uncharted territory here," Else said. "And Selene had one covering the entire right side of her face."

"You're joking." She better be goddamn joking.

"You've seen the painting in the library, kiddo."

Shit. I had seen the painting. Selene was a past Keeper of our coven and also Iris's doppelgänger. The two weren't just alike; they were scarily identical. "I thought that was something else. Painted or drawn on for a ritual or a spell..."

"Nope, the mother gave it to her." Else shrugged her narrow shoulders. "Not sure why you're worried. Selene looked badass."

Mags threw her head back and howled with laughter so hard I thought she was going to rupture something. Iris joined in.

Rose offered me a sympathetic look. "It might not happen."

CHAPTER 3

Willow

Business was slow today, and I wandered around my shop mindlessly straightening products on the shelves. Everything I sold at the front of the store was harmless. I stored Else's potions and elixirs out back. When someone came in looking for help, I treated them like a doctor would a patient. They needed a consultation first. You couldn't just hand that shit out willy-nilly without all the relevant information, or things could go seriously awry.

The bell jingled above the door, and I smiled at the woman who walked in. She averted her eyes and headed to one of the shelves.

"Can I help you with anything?"

She shook her head, her hair a little wild, her hands shaking as she picked up bottles and sightlessly stared at labels.

Something was off.

I waited for my blade to warn me. It remained still.

When a witch turned thirteen and they begin to learn more

complicated magic, they are given a dagger. Especially witches who use blood to spell. Not all did, but our coven, which was made up of close and extended family, scattered all over the country, frequently used blood magic. When I became the Keeper, one of the gifts I received from the mother was making my dagger more useful, as well as the nice boost in power she'd given us.

Now it warned me of danger, and the strength of that warning correlated with the scale of the threat. It also increased my ability to fight, passing on the skills and knowledge of Keepers past.

It was an extremely cool gift, and I'd been more than grateful for it many times over the last year.

Although my ancestors had some serious moves, I'd been training as well, taking advanced fighting classes. I needed to be unstoppable. No one would hurt me again. But more importantly, no one would hurt my family or someone else I cared about.

I glanced at the woman again. Her eyes were wide, and there was no missing the look of desperation. "Are you sure you don't need some help?"

She eyed me from the other side of the room. "Are we alone?"

Still no warning from my blade. "Yes, is everything all right?"

A tingling sensation danced over my ribs. It started gently at first, the tattoo-like vines growing warm in a familiar way under my skin.

My task.

Whatever this woman was about to tell me, I had to help her.

"You're a witch, aren't you? I mean, you sell all this...witchy stuff, and you look like..." She motioned to me, waving her hand about. "*That*. I don't believe in any of this bullshit...well, I didn't." She shoved her fingers through her graying dark hair, and she was shaking, badly. "I've been to our church, and they think I've lost my mind, and I...I didn't know where else to go. Witches, they can perform exorcisms, right? I googled it and that's what it said..."

I lifted my hands to get her to slow down. She flinched. "You have nothing to fear from me." I motioned to the door. "I'm going to close the shop, and we're going to have a cup of tea and a chat. Whatever is worrying you, maybe I can help, okay?"

She nodded and took a big step away from me as I walked to the door to flick the lock and flip the sign to *closed*. Then I led her to my kitchen behind the shop. I lived back here most of the time, but lately I'd been staying with my family, in my old bedroom, since things were so volatile.

I turned on the kettle and pulled a chair out from the table. "Take a seat while I make the tea."

She perched on the edge of the chair as if coming into contact with too much of it might give her witch cooties. Or maybe she thought it's where I chopped up my eye of newt, frog's toes, and bat's wings? They weren't actual ingredients we used. Of course, I'd chopped up a few other things on that table that were pretty disgusting, including harvesting demon organs from a fucker who broke into my shop. But she didn't need to know that.

I steeped the tea, adding a few extra herbs to hers that would help her calm down, added a little honey and a squeeze of lemon, and slid it across the table, making sure not to get too close. The last thing I wanted was to spook her and have her run off.

I sat as well and took a sip of my tea first, showing her that I hadn't poisoned it, and no, she wouldn't turn into a toad or something if she drank it, and waited for her to do the same. She watched me, then finally lifted the cup shakily to her lips and sipped. Surprise crossed her face. Yes, my tea was good, really good. After a few more sips, she'd visibly calmed.

"Sorry, I didn't catch your name?" I said and smiled.

She blinked a couple of times, studying me, still wary.

"I'm Willow," I offered, still trying to put her at ease.

She took another sip of her drink. "Rebecca."

"Okay, Rebecca, why don't you tell me what brought you here today?"

Gripping the cup with both hands, she drew in a shaky

breath. "My daughter Jane has been acting...odd. She's always been a bit of a problem child, acting out, headstrong, willful... but lately she's been hanging around with a bad crowd, and I think..." Her lips quivered. "I think they're devil worshippers. I think they've been doing terrible rituals...and...and I don't know what."

Okay, not what I was expecting. "What makes you think that?"

Her hold on the cup tightened. "She's been dressing differently, wearing a lot of black." She paused, her gaze moving over me and my almost entirely black outfit.

I was starting to get the feeling that Rebecca was somewhat judgmental and I kind of felt bad for Jane. "Black clothes don't really point to devil worship," I said, needing her to be more specific. Whatever this task was, I needed all the details I could get.

"No, of course not. But it's more than that...fishnet stockings, lots of black eyeliner, and...and slutty underwear."

Was this woman for real? Slutty underwear? *Jesus Christ.* I would have told her I couldn't help her and sent her on her way if it wasn't for the way those tingles at my side had increased. "Is there anything else?"

She nodded vigorously. "I saw her walking to her room the other morning, she'd just showered and was only wearing a towel, and there were these marks, wounds, almost healed...but it looked like a bite mark on her shoulder."

My mind started spinning. Demon? Shifter? Vamp? There were numerous *others* who liked to bite while they were getting busy. Or just as a way to feed.

"Right, and what did your daughter say?"

She bit her lip. "That she was bitten by a dog."

A dog? A weird feeling curled in my belly. "You don't believe her?"

"There were no other marks on her that I could see. Just on

her shoulder. Wouldn't there be others, and scratches if she was attacked by some dog?"

"Maybe she was telling the truth?" Or maybe it was a shifter gone rogue?

Then why is your side tingling?

She shook her head. "No...that's not it."

"Is there anything else? You mentioned exorcism."

Rebecca wrapped her arms around herself. "This morning, I went to check on her. She was with her friends again last night and didn't get home until seven a.m. She wouldn't wake and was breathing oddly, heavily. I shook her, and when she opened her eyes, they were black. Her entire eye was black." She gripped the small gold cross hanging around her neck. "And her voice...it wasn't hers."

Perhaps she should have opened with that instead of slutty underwear. "Where is she now, Rebecca?"

"She ran off before I could do anything. She threatened me and pushed me over, and then she ran. I think she's gone back to her new friends."

My stomach sank deeper, because I knew what she was going to say. Somehow, I just knew. "Do you know their names, her new friends? Where they live?"

"They live in Linville, and they're a motorcycle gang...a gang of thugs. They call themselves the Devil Dogs."

Hellhounds.

Awesome. Just freaking wonderful.

"Can you help me?" Rebecca asked, voice full of fear. "Please."

"Of course." It wasn't like I had any other choice.

It was a thirty-minute drive from Roxburgh to Linville, New Jersey. The town was small, just over three thousand people resided there, and of course, the hellhounds.

I drove up to the entrance of their clubhouse. The gates were closed; they were always closed, and the huge chain-link fence butted up against an old brick building, a dive bar, one of the two businesses they owned and operated. The other was a garage. The bar was shut for the day and would open later. The garage beside it was fairly busy, the wide roller doors up, several hellhounds inside working on cars and bikes for the unsuspecting people of the town.

Only invited guests of the hellhounds were allowed past those imposing iron gates and into their clubhouse. Except me. I could come and go as I pleased. Warrick's orders. Not that I took him up on the offer all that often. The male had staked some claim over me more than a year ago, for some reason known only to him, and I didn't think encouraging him was wise.

I didn't belong to anyone.

We hadn't dated...if hellhounds even did date, and we sure as heck hadn't slept together, so I wasn't sure why he was so possessive of me. He'd told me we had a *special bond*, whatever the hell that meant.

Being around the guy unnerved me. He was overwhelming, and kind of terrifying at times. He was blunt and rude and demanding. He was also the sexiest male I had ever encountered. He took that rough around the edges thing some males had and cranked it all the way up to high. I won't lie, it worked. Oh, he pissed me off more than anyone else in existence, but yeah, it seriously worked for him.

And unfortunately for me, he'd been the one to come to my rescue—more than once. He knew I could take care of myself, he just didn't seem to care, and for some reason, had appointed himself my personal bodyguard.

Dragging in a steadying breath, I shored up my defenses and climbed out of my Morris Minor truck. It may be old, the blue paint faded and chipped, but I took good care of her. I'd had a few modifications done over the years—a bigger, faster engine, for one. It had once belonged to Gran, and she'd given it to me when I got my driver's license. I loved it, even when occasionally it wouldn't start on cold mornings.

Fender, one of the lower-ranking hellhounds, was working on his bike next to the clubhouse and spotted me first. I waved, and he straightened and slowly cleaned the grease from his hands before finally swaggering my way. He had long hair and a beard, like most of the hounds seemed to, was well over six and a half feet, and exuded cockiness and aggression with every breath, which was also something they seemed to have in common. Fender's hair was a deep red and his eyes were light amber.

They studied me as he gripped the chain-link with thick fingers. "What you doing here, Wills?"

"I need to speak with your alpha," I said and plastered a smile on my face.

"War's busy at the moment."

War was a fitting nickname for the hellhound alpha. The way he fought, the male was a one-male army, or maybe a tank. "I'm sure he'll want to see me."

Fender's lips twisted. He was not pleased. "You should go."

This was new. They always let me right in. "Did Warrick ask you to turn me away?"

He shook his head.

"He'll be pissed if he finds out I came here and you told me to leave."

Fender growled under his breath. Then, after long seconds, he finally unchained the gate and motioned for me to come in.

The fact I'd turned down their alpha was obviously becoming a sore spot. Great, that's all I needed. More hellhounds pissed at me.

I drove through the gates and up to the clubhouse, parking beside the long line of bikes. To people living in Linville, the place looked like a human motorcycle club. It worked for them. They had a hierarchy, a roughness, and most definitely a lawlessness that suited that whole vibe. They also loved bikes. Hounds like the wind blowing through all that hair—they preferred that in their hellhound forms, on all fours, running through the woods— but riding a bike was the next best thing, or so I'd been told.

There were other hounds milling around and music was playing. The clubhouse, or den as Warrick sometimes called it, was an old factory and had their MC name, the Devil Dogs, painted on the side.

The music got louder.

Awesome.

They were having a party.

I strode through the doors and braced. Anything could be happening in the main room when they partied. Fucking, fighting...fucking *and* fighting. I'd seen it all. Things I wished I could unsee but were now imprinted on my brain forever.

I tried not to look into the dark corners, but there were several human females around the room, wearing little to nothing. No sign of Warrick, though, and the guy was hard to miss. He was the tallest of the hellhounds and radiated so much menace and violence he set off my fight-or-flight instincts whenever we were in the same room.

Without my say-so, an imprint of the way he held me after I'd been hurt a year ago had my skin tingling like a phantom caress, something else that often happened when we were together. He'd carried me away from the fear, from the guilt, from the scene of my failure, promising to protect me from ever being hurt again. That menace, that incredible violence that rolled off him, it'd made me feel safe then. And I'd needed that more than anything.

I didn't need it anymore, though.

You sure about that?

I shut that voice down even as my belly gripped tight at the memory and the urge to run the hell out became almost more than I could resist.

Maybe I wouldn't even have to see him? Lothar leaned against the wall, drinking a beer and surveying the room, seemingly oblivious to the woman clinging to him and all but dry humping his thigh. Lovely.

"Hey, Lothar," I called over the music.

He turned to me and raised a dark brow.

A man of few words was Lothar. "I just want to ask your friend something."

I tapped the woman's shoulder, and she turned, scowling at me. "Go find your own guy."

Lothar smirked, and I rolled my eyes. "I can assure you I don't want..."

His eyes narrowed.

"Um...as wonderful as he is, he's all yours." The big male's mouth twitched. Okay, the hound wasn't totally humorless. "I'm actually looking for someone. Do you know Jane? She comes here sometimes."

She shrugged as she dragged her hand down Lothar's chest, over his stomach, and grabbed his dick through his jeans. Lothar remained completely unmoved. "Last I saw, she was with Maddox."

"Right, thanks." I turned, about to head to the doors across the room, the ones that led to the rooms where they took their females to bump uglies. There was also a door that took you to the lower levels, tunnels the hounds had dug out, vast and complicated, and where they lived and slept most of the time. They never took humans down there, keeping it hidden. I'd been down there, though, several times.

Lothar grabbed my arm, stopping me, and shook his head.

"I need to find this girl," I said.

He shook his head again. "You wait until Maddox is finished with her."

Delightful.

"I wouldn't usually do this, but it's important." Goddammit, I was going to have to find Warrick. "Is your alpha here? I need to talk to him."

Lothar's nostrils flared and his eyes narrowed again, then he tipped his head down. I assumed it meant he was in his room below. "You can wait until War's finished as well."

I froze.

He was with someone?

Something unhappy squirmed in my belly, and for some reason my face flushed hot. "This can't wait."

"Yeah, it can."

I don't know what came over me, but an urgency slammed me in the gut, and I was on the move before I knew what my feet were doing, pushing through the hounds and their women, making my way to the door that led to the tunnels. I punched in the code to open it and shoved the door open, slamming it behind me.

Shadows closed in, firelight flickering from the torches that lined the passageways. It looked medieval down here, the way these guys liked it. Warrick's room was the closest to the exit. As alpha, he put himself in the most vulnerable position of the pack, making himself their first defense. Something else he'd told me the last time I was here. I'd been recuperating after my first task. One of the times he'd found me injured and I'd been forced to share more with him than I'd been comfortable with.

His door was shut, and my fist was up and banging on it before I could think better of it.

No answer.

Visions of him and some other woman filled my head. It should be a deterrent, but it wasn't. This couldn't wait, that was the only reason I was pounding on his door, there was no other reason.

Keep telling yourself that.

I put more heft behind it.

The heavy, scarred wood swung open, and my knees literally

went weak. Warrick filled the opening, close to seven feet tall, long, thick, black hair hanging past his shoulders, beard in need of a trim, and his tattooed, monster chest, bare and on full display under his leather vest. All the hounds wore them, with the Devil Dogs emblem on the front. Warrick's said President, fully leaning into the whole motorcycle club ruse.

He also had more than a dusting of chest hair, they all did, and his carried on *down*, thinning into one of those trails, dipping below the waistband of his faded jeans.

His pale, gold eyes locked on me, and I had to force myself to breathe normally.

Pull your shit together.

"Dove," he growled out in that incredibly deep, impossibly rough voice, something else the hounds had in common. But Warrick's was the roughest, as if he were more beast than man.

"Don't call me that." I ignored the way my belly flipped and pushed on. "Now tell your plaything to leave, I have something important to discuss with you." Maybe I should tone down the attitude a few thousand notches, but for some reason, I was having serious trouble doing that. I guess I could have waited until he'd finished fucking whoever he had in there with him, and I didn't want to think about why I insisted on busting in on his private party, but there was nothing to be done about either of those things now.

Warrick stared down at me, his gaze locked on mine. "Jag, we're done here for now." He didn't break eye contact.

"Jag?" I said stupidly.

He nodded.

"I thought...I assumed, because Lothar said..." I bit my lip. *Shut up.*

"What did Lothar say?" Warrick asked, crossing his heavily muscled arms, causing the chunky silver rings he often wore, one a skull, another engraved with a language I didn't recognize, to glint under the torchlight.

Jagger, Warrick's lieutenant, strode up behind his alpha, and he didn't look impressed.

My gaze slid back to Warrick. "He just...well, he implied..." Goddammit, my face was getting hot again.

"That I was fucking?"

I didn't reply because I'd come down here all hot under the collar for reasons unknown and...god, he was loving this. "You can screw who you like, Warrick."

His jaw hardened. "I know I can."

Jagger slipped past without a word and walked away.

"Right." My face grew even hotter.

We stood there, eyeing each other for long, overwhelming seconds, and my flight instincts were kicking in. "Well, are you going to let me in?" I asked, ignoring them completely.

He stepped back, making space for me to pass, and I entered his private quarters.

I looked around the big room. A massive bed, he'd made himself out of logs, that I was sure he'd torn out of the ground and split with his bare hands, sat against the far wall. There was also a fire burning in the hearth on the opposite wall and animal furs on the floor.

I'd woken up in that humongous bed after my last combat trial...with a sleeping, *naked* Warrick plastered against me—

The sound of female voices came through the door across the room. It opened to a staircase that led directly to the main room aboveground. I guess so he didn't have to bring humans through the tunnels.

Someone knocked.

"Busy," he barked.

"It's Molly, can I come in?" a female voice called.

"No."

Another knock. "It's Diane, what about me?"

"Fuck off," he said, his expression unchanged.

I snorted. "Seriously? Women stand outside that door and wait for you to let them in?"

He dipped his chin.

"That's pathetic," I said, way too bitterly. "And here I thought we had a 'special bond,'" I said, adding air quotes. I had no idea why I was goading him. And yes, sarcasm was dripping from my voice, along with a good dose of bitterness.

"What do you want me to do, Willow? Sit around with my dick in my hand, drawing love hearts and listening to Coldplay while I wait for you?"

My mouth opened, closed. "No, of course not..."

He took a step closer, so close the heat of his body soaked through my clothes. Warrick was always hot, his skin like a furnace. "They like the way I fuck, dove. I guarantee you would too."

A rush of heat pulsed through me, because I suspected he was right about that.

"Say it," he growled out.

"What?" Again, I was pushing him like a goddamned fool. I knew better.

"Yes."

His deep voice reverberated through me. I gritted my teeth.

"Say yes," he commanded, *ordering* me to submit, to give myself to him.

I shook my head, because suddenly my mouth was too dry to speak.

"Female, if you gave yourself to me, I wouldn't put my dick in anyone else ever again, only you," he said just as growly.

I swallowed, trying to get moisture back into my mouth. "Such a romantic."

His brows lowered and he snarled a warning. Anyone else would know they were on thin ice. I lacked self-preservation, and honestly, common sense around this male. My self-control wasn't

35

great either, which was one of the reasons I'd been staying the hell away from him lately.

"You ran from me the other night in the clearing. I smelled your blood." His expression darkened. "And I smelled the fox."

"You know why I was there. I have my new task..." I straightened. "And apparently, it involves you."

CHAPTER 4

Warrick

WILLOW FOLLOWED me up the stairs, and her scent reached out to me. I breathed her down deep, and like always, being anywhere near my dove drove the beast closer to the surface.

I bit back a possessive snarl. If anyone else had banged on my door the way she had, spitting fire and attitude, I would have kicked them the fuck out. But that was the last thing I wanted. I liked her fire. It made my dick hard. She'd tried to hide it, but she didn't like the idea of me fucking other females, and I liked that too. Maybe it would get her to stop fighting what she truly wanted and give herself to me.

Or at least stop her from running.

I gritted my teeth when another wave of her scent reached me—the shampoo she used, mixed with an oil she favored, a flower of some kind, along with the natural scent of her skin... and her cunt. I sucked it down like an addict, taking a desperately needed hit. I wanted to bury my face against the sweet spot just below her ear and my cock between her thighs, and fucking live there, breathing her in and fucking her for the rest of eternity.

I'd been waiting for her to come to me, to finally work out she was mine, and the fact that she was here over some bullshit involving my brother and his female, pissed me the hell off. I'd hoped that when she came to me again, it would be to ask me to service her tight little body, not disturb my brother while he rutted with his mate.

As we walked down the hall, we passed rooms, some with their doors shut, others wide open. Most of them were occupied. The sounds of fucking, of females getting off, and getting off good, filled the narrow space.

Willow snorted.

I glanced back, brow raised.

She rolled her eyes. "They're faking it, or at least some of them are."

I shook my head.

Her lips curled in a smirk. "You're in denial, alpha."

I turned to her. "You think they come here to chitchat? Our dicks are big, and we know what to do with them. And they curve." I held out my hand, bending my fingers up slightly, giving her a demonstration. "We also love eating pussy."

My dove froze, blinking up at me.

I took enjoyment from her shocked expression, then noticed how the pulse at the base of her throat fluttered faster—and the scent of her cunt grew heavier. My dove was turned on, and whether she would admit it or not, it was my job to ease that need. "Say it," I said again, closing the space between us as need and possessiveness pulsed through me. "Say, yes. You know you want to."

"Pass," she said, the color of her cheeks darkening.

I was about to offer my mouth to ease her obvious need when another scent hit me. I tilted my head back and sniffed, scenting the air. *Fuck*. I ran down the hall to the end room and kicked the door open.

My growl tore through the small space.

Dove rushed in behind me and cried out in alarm.

Maddox's female, Jane, lay draped over the bed, and she was sliced down the middle, through her sternum and down her belly, her innards spilling over the covers. Maddox stood naked by the bed, his massive chest heaving.

He spun toward us. Blood coated his face and hands, and his usually bright green eyes were black, completely devoid of color.

He snarled.

I'd never seen anything like that, not among my brothers. "Maddox," I said, filling my voice with dominance, trying to get through to him.

Maddox bared his teeth, his gaze sliding to my dove.

"Mad," I growled again, trying to get him to focus on me.

Willow slid her blade free. "He's possessed by something or someone," she said, her blade ready to fly when it became obvious Maddox was about to attack. "He won't listen to you."

With a roar, Maddox ran at her.

I charged, taking him down, the both of us crashing to the floor and plowed my fist into his face, once, twice, a third time, trying to snap him the fuck out of whatever this was, whatever had him in its grip. Instead, Maddox grinned up at me, baring bloody teeth, and laughed. The thunder of boots echoed down the hall, then the room was filled with my brothers.

I dragged Mad off the floor and passed him off. "Chain him below." I didn't know what the fuck was going on, but I didn't want this shit in my den. I didn't want whatever evil this was corrupting my brothers.

They lifted Maddox without question as he struggled, spitting and cursing, and carried him off.

Dove watched them take him away. "Whatever was possessing Jane, it moved to Maddox."

"What the fuck was that?" Jagger said, expression fierce.

I filled my lieutenant in with everything Willow had told me when she got here. I hadn't really believed it. Hellhounds were strong, powerful; we were not easily defeated or fooled. I didn't know how to fight this. "Make sure Maddox is secure."

Jagger gave me a sharp nod, turned, and strode out of the room, and I walked to the side of the bed, where my dove now stood looking down at Maddox's dead female.

"How did this happen?" I asked her.

She turned to me, her beautiful green eyes wide. "I have no idea, but I think it's my job to find out."

Willow

Jane had been pretty, young, her whole life ahead of her. She'd come here looking for some fun and wound up dead. I had no idea how this involved my task. Maybe I'd just failed it? I didn't know what this meant, but now, somehow, I had to explain her death to her mother.

I had to take her mangled and mutilated body home and try to explain what the hell happened here.

Her eyes were still wide open and filled with the shock of her last moments. I'd sent a quick text to Chaos while Warrick spoke to Jagger. The leader of the knights of Hell was an expert when it came to demons. I didn't know if this was what we were dealing with, but if we were, the knights needed to know.

His reply had come a few seconds later. They were on their way.

"I've never seen this before," Warrick said.

"I contacted the knights. They'll be here soon. Maybe they'll know something," I said.

"Which knight did you contact?" he gritted out.

The hellhound alpha didn't much care for Chaos, especially after he discovered the leader of the knights and I used to hook up from time to time. It felt like a lifetime ago now. Our feelings for each other had never been any deeper than friendship. Never mind that Chaos was now mated and completely besotted with his female, Grace, who also happened to be a good friend of mine.

"You need to get over it. Chaos and I are friends, nothing more." And why the hell was I explaining myself?

Warrick snarled. "He left you unprotected, he's the reason Azel got to you—"

"That wasn't Chaos's fault." That was no one's fault but my own.

He crowded me, until my back met the wall, and he dipped his head. "And that fucking knight has had what I want. He's been inside you. He's heard you come. He's tasted your cunt. So, no, dove, I won't get over it. You belong to me. I want to kill every male who has ever touched you."

I stared up at him in shock. "Are you serious?"

The muscle in his jaw ticked.

He was serious.

He wanted me, yes, but once he was done with me, he'd move on to his next obsession, and I'd be left feeling like a fool. I wouldn't allow myself to be another one of his conquests. Just another woman to warm his bed. He spoke of wanting me, never of feelings. The hellhound alpha didn't know what they were. He didn't care about me, he felt territorial over me for some messed up reason. That's all.

"I'm not yours, Warrick. I'm not a possession you get to claim. And a lot of guys have touched me, so if you're going on a killing spree, I'd suggest adding some rosemary to your Wheaties in the morning for an extra energy boost."

His nostrils flared, and he leaned closer, his features changing, blending with his hound, a grizzly mask transforming his face.

"Don't push me. You tease and you taunt and I allow it. You are the only one I let do that. Anyone else I would punish. Right now Mad is chained to the floor belowground, trying to tear his own face off. I'm not in my right mind, dove, and if you carry on snapping at me, I might bite back. You don't want that."

I blinked up at him, my heart pounding, fear pulsing through me, but not the bad kind. It quickly turned to something else, something dark and unwanted, a yearning that I could never, would never, give in to.

I loved my mother, but she was an excellent example of why a relationship wasn't something you jumped into, why you didn't let lust rule your actions, and I had enough on my plate as it was.

I definitely didn't need to throw a controlling alpha into the mix, or my bed, no matter how much the thought of reaching up and brushing my thumb over those snarling lips called to me, and no matter how much that wildness inside him drew me.

I didn't do relationships. I kept my heart guarded, but there was something about Warrick, something that fascinated me, tantalized me, and that was reason enough not to get tangled up with him.

The casual relationships I'd had in the past...there'd been no risk, no feelings beyond friendship. Warrick and I weren't even friends. I didn't know what we were, but I was finding it harder and harder to resist him.

"You're right. No, I don't want that. I'm sorry," I said and lowered my gaze. Challenging this male in any way right now was the seriously wrong move.

He growled again, dipping lower, his gaze searching mine. His eyes flashed red. "Don't," he said harshly.

I looked back up. "Don't what?"

"Be scared of me."

I couldn't promise him that. He scared me in a multitude of ways, but physical harm was the lowest on the list. "Step back," I said, making sure not to touch him.

He bared his teeth; his incisors had extended. "Dove..."

"Please, step back."

The thunder of boots hitting the stone and packed earth floor echoed outside the door a moment before it was shoved open. "War, it's Edric. Whatever's going on with Maddox, it's got him too. He almost took Fender's head off then ran."

"Fuck," Warrick ground out.

This was not good. Not at all.

A short time later, after Warrick had sent any remaining women home, and some of his brothers after Edric, we were informed that the knights had arrived.

As if tensions weren't already through the roof.

Four massive males were standing on the other side of the main gate when I walked out. Chaos, Rocco, Gunner, and Zenon. Roc lifted a hand, waving when he saw me.

I strode up to the gate. "Hey."

"What's up, Wills?" Roc asked.

"More than I know what to do with," I said and turned, waiting for someone to let them in.

Warrick was just emerging from the clubhouse, ducking to fit under the doorframe, then took his sweet time striding our way, and with more arrogance than any one being had a right to.

Chaos muttered a curse.

Warrick finally reached us, and he gave the knights a chin lift. There were muttered greetings all around.

"Can you let them in? We need to know if it's a demon we're dealing with."

"Make this quick," Warrick said to Chaos. "We don't want you here longer than necessary."

God, the male was difficult.

"Fair enough," Chaos said. "Let's get this over with then."

They were allies, but they'd never exactly been bosom buddies.

Warrick's arm hooked around my waist and he tugged me aside as he opened the gate, like he actually thought one of them would try to snatch me away or something.

I pushed out of his hold and scowled at him. Warrick scowled back, but finally he led the way inside. The sooner I got the hell away from here, the better. He took the stairs, leading the knights below, something he wouldn't normally do, but there was no other option.

We heard the snarling and cursing, the twisted words filled with hate and violence, as we approached the end of one of the tunnels. Warrick pushed the door open and we filed in.

Maddox was on the stone floor, bleeding from deep scratches over his face and neck. His head snapped our way, black eyes locking on us. "Let me free," a distorted voice said. "I won't hurt anyone, I promise." Its empty gaze slid to me, and Maddox licked his lips.

Chaos moved in then, crouching down, concentration transforming his features. Finally, he lifted his head. "This isn't demon. This is human. A human soul. Zen?"

Zenon nodded. "Definitely human." The others nodded their agreement.

Shit. "You can't help us then?"

Chaos crossed his arms over his wide chest and shook his head. "How did the spirit get into the clubhouse?"

"A human female," Warrick said.

"Yeah, we can't meddle in human business. The fact this soul is possessing a hound makes no difference. The angels would lose their shit if we got involved with this. There would be consequences, bad ones. I'm sorry."

"It's fine." This was my task, unless, of course, keeping Jane alive had been part of it. If that were true, then I'd already failed. Though, I kind of thought something would've happened by now if that were the case. There's been no sign from the mother. So, I'd carry on until I knew otherwise.

But I'd had to check with the knights first, otherwise things could have gotten complicated. So now I knew for sure—the scary evil spirit was all mine. *Goodie.*

I took a small bag from my satchel, our family's own special mix—rock salt, cemetery dirty, and a few other carefully selected herbs—and lay a thick line of it from wall to wall. "Don't break this line, and don't cross it. It will contain the spirit and stop it from moving to someone else."

The hounds nodded. Then the knights left and I headed back to the room where Jane's body still lay. What the hell was I going to do with her? I could call Ren. His family didn't usually work with humans, but I needed a way to get her out of here, and they had a hearse.

"You can't take her home," Warrick said, like he could read my mind as he moved up behind me.

"Her mother should get to say goodbye to her daughter." Jane looked small all of a sudden, fragile. Just an insignificant human in this shitty, fucked-up world filled with monsters.

"You take her home like that, you'll bring human police here to the clubhouse. It will end in more death."

I turned to him. "I can't leave Rebecca wondering for the rest of her life what happened to her kid. That's cruel, Warrick."

"That's how it has to be," he said, expression cold, unmoved.

"Seriously?"

"Yes."

"Is your heart made of stone?"

He took a step closer, his gaze searching mine. "Lucifer gave us the ability to understand emotions, dove, but we were created fully formed, full-grown warriors. Emotions of our own weren't necessary or wanted. Tender emotions are a hindrance in battle and are especially unnecessary, and not something we were exposed to. But loyalty and courage, he gave us a deeper knowledge of, and we seemed to have developed the ability to feel them over time, along with anger. So, to answer your question, probably."

Not something he was exposed to? A life without love or tenderness? I didn't want to imagine what that was like, and I hated the idea that Warrick had never experienced it.

And if there was ever a reason not to let myself give in to this thing between Warrick and me, he'd just given it to me. The male was as cold as ice, but I'd been right, he wasn't entirely emotionless. I'd sure as hell felt and seen his anger. "So what about Jane?"

"We may be soulless, but we aren't total monsters. We want Jane to be with her family as well. She deserves that respect. We'll move the body, take her to Roxburgh, away from Linville. She'll be discovered there."

Soulless? Jesus. The revelations just kept on coming. "Thank you. I appreciate that," I said, feeling unsteady. I felt every emotion, acutely, and seeing Jane like that...it was affecting me. Deeply. I couldn't imagine looking at a scene like this and feeling nothing. Did she have siblings? Sisters? Brothers? I thought of my mom, of what something like this would do to her.

Warrick's thick, calloused fingers slid under my chin, surprising me. He tilted my head back and brushed his thumb across the apple of my cheek. "You have dark circles under your eyes, dove, and you look pale. You took a lot of venom?"

I pulled away and took a step back before I did something stupid like lean into that touch. "I'm fine." He knew about the tasks and the trials I had to complete, because the last one had required blood, mine, a lot of it. I hadn't told my family about the trial, I hadn't wanted them to see me hurt if I lost. I'd battled the witch chosen for me by the witches' council, and I'd won, but I'd passed out afterward, and he'd found me by my truck before Ren could get to me. Thankfully, I hadn't passed out in the woods.

He'd brought me here and hadn't let me leave his room until I told him what was going on and where the thorn-covered-vine tattoos on my arm had come from.

He eyed me now, not believing my bullshit one bit, and suddenly, I would have given anything for a hug. For Warrick to wrap those massive arms around me and hold me against his massive, solid body, to hold me up like he had when I'd been hurt. Because I was scared, and that made me feel so fucking weak.

This task was going to take me places I didn't want to go, that I wasn't sure I could go, but had to anyway. And I was terrified I'd fail.

Stop it.

I mentally kicked my own ass. My family was depending on me to do this, to succeed. There was no time to indulge in self-pity. I didn't have that luxury.

And letting this male close would be a serious mistake. I couldn't afford any of those, or to lean on anyone. I had to do this myself.

I took a step back. "I'll contact Rebecca and tell her I couldn't find Jane, that the other girls said she'd stopped coming here. I don't know if she'll send the police here or not, but it's the best I can do."

"We'll make sure she can't be traced back to us."

I didn't know how he was going to swing that and I didn't really want to. With Warrick, that could mean anything. They were hellhounds, created by Lucifer, and as far as I could tell were completely without conscience. "I need to leave."

He moved back in, getting far too close. "Stay."

"Maddox and Edric are possessed by evil spirits and there's a dead girl on the bed beside us. I think you have your hands full right now," I said and took several steps toward the door.

His nostrils flared and his shoulders bunched like he was about to pounce, like he was going to chase me down if I tried to leave. "I'd rather they were full of you."

"Because you want to sleep with me, right?" I said because he didn't get it. He seemed to be incapable of getting it.

His gaze bore into me. "No, there would be no sleeping, only fucking."

"You're consistent, I'll give you that. As tempting as that wonderful offer is, again, I'll have to decline." I was starting to think that it wasn't that hellhounds were incapable of emotion, but more they were ruled by anger and lust, so much so, there didn't seem to be room for anything else.

"You're angry with me," he said, actually looking confused.

"Nope."

"You are. I don't like it."

"You'll get over it." I strode to the door. "Keep Maddox chained, and I'll get everything I need to perform an exorcism. And I recommend keeping the women out, the bar closed, and shutting down the garage until this is resolved. The spirits target you because you make excellent vessels, so keep to yourselves."

He nodded and licked his ridiculously tempting lips. "When will you be back?"

Too damn soon. "In the morning. It'll take me some time to gather everything."

His massive shoulders lost some of their tension. "I'll be waiting."

The way he said it almost sounded like a threat.

CHAPTER 5

Willow

"This place gives me the creeps," Magnolia said. Bram cawed, making the whole scene a hell of a lot more macabre, and flew over to perch on one of the headstones.

I, on the other hand, found this place peaceful, kind of comforting. I glanced at my sister. "I don't know why. Everyone here is family. And you didn't need to come. Ren and I could've handled it." Ren was already on the other side of the cemetery, looking for the items on my list.

She shrugged. "It's good for me to learn these things. Creating elixirs and potions is one thing, but harvesting our own ingredients is part of it. I need to desensitize myself."

"True. But you've been coming here since you were a baby, I'm not sure what has you so freaked out."

"Iris told me that Morag was a zombie and lay awake in her coffin, waiting for someone to come so she could drag them in with her 'cause she was lonely."

I spun on her. "What? Iris said that?"

Mags nodded and laughed her sweet musical laugh. "She was pissed at me after I put pepper on her pillow because I wanted to hear her sneeze."

Iris had this squeaky, high-pitched sneeze that cracked us all up. She was super embarrassed by it. I chuckled. "You were so asking for that."

"I know," Mags said, still grinning.

"Well, we can think of this as a field trip. And I'll protect you from Morag." Our family burial grounds were behind the house and a place of great power and plentiful resources. Every blade of grass, every pebble and flower petal, held magic. Our ancestors were buried here, and since magic never left us completely—even when one of us died—every crumbling bone continued to pump magic into the earth.

We harvested the dirt, flowers, rocks, and stones for spells and elixirs, to ward or hex, or unbind places or objects. The uses were limitless. If a coven had a nice burial ground, especially large and old like ours, they were considered formidable and not to be messed with. No other coven had one more powerful, more impressive than ours. Which was why it was warded to the gills. Only people we wanted here could pass through the cemetery gates.

A car door closed, and I glanced at our neighbor's house. Cora Cates had lived next door for ten years and was Else's bestie. Her grandson Brody, who had moved in with her a year ago, after he'd lost his mom, was dating Iris. They'd been hot and heavy for the last six months, and they were currently making out by the car, not realizing they had an audience.

"Gross," Mags bit out. "That guy is such a douchebag."

I raised a brow. Brody was a nice guy. He took care of his grandmother, worked several jobs to make sure she had everything she needed, and doted on our sister. "What can you possibly have against the guy?"

She shrugged.

"Is this what you're looking for?" Ren called.

Mags ran to him. "Ren found them!"

I headed over and, sure enough, there was a cluster of Calla lilies, just as Mom said there would be. We did a lot of planting here. Well, Mom and Art did, always making sure we had what we needed. Mom had a wicked green thumb and was never happier than when she was here puttering in the cemetery gardens, and yes, the reason she named her children after flowers and a tree was not just to carry on a tradition started by our great-great-grandmother.

Crouching down, I took out my sheers and cut the two I needed, making sure not to disturb the roots, and placed them carefully in my bag.

"What's next?" Mags asked.

"I need to fill this jar with dirt." I handed her the large mason jar and the trowel. "Over there by Beatrix. You'll need to offer blood first though."

Beatrix was our great-great-great-aunt and one of the most powerful witches in the history of our family.

"How much?" my sister asked, pulling out her small knife—we each had one, all different and beautiful in their own way, given to us by our mother when we were thirteen.

"A few drops will be fine." Most things here you couldn't remove without an offering. Some things like the flowers, herbs, and shrubs, things Mom planted, could be freely taken, but soil and stones, anything from the ancient trees here, even the grass, you needed to provide an offering. Blood was our coven's currency. We went through a lot of Band-Aids.

"Come help me, Ren," Mags said as she grabbed him by the wrist and dragged him across the cemetery.

The sight of Ren being manhandled by my baby sister would have usually had me laughing, but after my shitty day, I didn't have it in me. The conversation I'd had with Rebecca, telling her I'd found no trace of her daughter, had been awful.

If Warrick had done what he said he would, Jane's body would be somewhere in the city now. I hoped they made it look like an accident and not the brutal end she'd come to. But with the injuries she'd had, I wasn't sure that was possible. That was all I could think about while I'd talked to Rebecca. Right then, she still had hope, still believed her daughter was alive and out there somewhere. She had no clue she was already dead. Already gone.

My phone beeped, and I tugged it from my back pocket, and my stupid belly flipped. Speaking of the sex-obsessed alpha-hole himself.

Warrick: Maddox is foaming at the mouth and bleeding from the eyes.

I stared down at his message and imagined him stabbing at the screen with those massive, blunt, often motor oil-stained fingers.

Willow: That can happen. Just make sure he can't hurt himself or others. Any sign of Edric?

Warrick: No. What time you getting here in the morning?

Willow: Ten. I need to prepare. I'll do the exorcism at noon.

Warrick: Good.

I shoved my phone back in my pocket and tried not to think about tomorrow. So many things could go wrong, and I'd be in a room full of hellhounds who probably wouldn't love it if I accidentally killed one of them. Let's hope that didn't happen. I'd prefer to walk out of there in one piece tomorrow.

My hair was still damp from my shower when I walked downstairs and into the living room an hour later. There was a fire blazing, and Rose was sitting in front of the TV, a woolen blanket draped over her knees.

She smiled at me when I walked in. "How did it go at the cemetery?"

I sat and lifted her feet onto my lap and started rubbing them. Her feet were always so cold. "Good. I'm all set to vanquish an evil spirit tomorrow."

"You think that's it? That once it's gone, this task will be over?"

"I don't think so. There's Edric as well, another hound. He's still on the loose, but once they bring him in, I hope so."

"It's a shame Zinnia isn't in town," she said. "She could've used her magic to contact the sprits."

I wish that was an option. "Zinny's family and a member of our coven. I can't ask family for help, remember?"

"I hate that rule."

"Me too." Rose looked thinner, her wrists so painfully tiny. "You want a snack? I'm in the mood for some popcorn." We were always trying to feed her, but she had the appetite of a sparrow.

She shrugged her thin shoulders. "Sure."

"Be right back." I hit the kitchen and put a bag of popcorn in the microwave, closed my eyes, and drew in a calming breath.

"What's going on?" Iris asked, walking in.

"You just finished work?"

Iris picked up a plate someone had left on the table. "Yeah, it was quiet tonight. Jim let me leave early." She put it in the dishwasher, grabbed a cloth, and went back to wipe down the table. She couldn't help herself.

"Rose's in the living room. We were going to have some popcorn. Are you seeing Brody tonight or can you hang out with us?"

"Brody's working." Iris looked toward the muted light coming from the living room door. "How's she doing?"

The microwave beeped, and I took the popcorn out. "Tired."

"She's getting worse," Iris said, voice shaking.

My stomach churned. "Yes."

Iris looked down at her hands, and I watched as she crushed them into tight fists. When she looked up, her eyes were bright with fury. "Why is this happening to her, Wills? What if...what if she..."

"Don't," I said. Thinking the worst was hard enough, actually saying it, hearing the words out loud was unbearable. "I'm going to pass this task and kick ass in my final trial, the mother will gift us with more power, and Roe will be okay. She has to be."

Iris nodded and grabbed a bowl from the cabinet. I dumped in the popcorn, then watched as she drew a calming breath, picked it up, and carried it into the living room. I heard her greet Roe, teasing her, making light, joking. Forcing down her pain and fear for our sister.

I plastered a smile on my face as well and followed, taking my seat again at the end of the couch and pulled Roe's feet back onto my lap.

Mags walked in a short time later and sat on the floor at the other end of the couch, and Roe started playing with our baby sister's hair. Mags had the most beautiful thick, wavy, black hair, and we used to fight over who got to brush it in the mornings.

It'd been so long since we'd all hung out like this. That was partly my fault...no, it was all my fault. I'd been so caught up with this whole Keeper thing, with training, with making sure I was ready when the mother finally called me back, and I missed them so much. I missed this.

"Movie?" Iris asked.

Mags grabbed some popcorn and tossed it in her mouth. "Something dirty," she said and grinned.

Rose giggled, and then we were all laughing.

Iris scrolled through Netflix. "Something dirty coming up."

Three hours later, I woke with my neck bent at a weird angle and still on the couch. Mags was lying on the floor under a blanket. Iris was head back, mouth wide open, snoring, Nia at her feet, and Roe was curled up in a tiny ball. None of them stirred. That's when I felt it, the tingling at my side, like a million fire ants marching across my skin.

I quickly slid Roe's legs from my lap and climbed off the couch...and bit back a startled cry.

Bram sat across the room in an armchair. He was the same age as Ren, nineteen, and he was a big guy in his human form, lean but extremely tall and broad shouldered. He studied me now, glossy black hair hanging around his face, and those black as coal eyes aimed at me under a heavy brow. He was beautiful, but not in a classically handsome way. More striking. His nose was prominent, jaw square but with a bit of a point to it, and he had sharp cheekbones. Bram could also hover in a shadow form, a state between his human and crow form, and some of that shadow seemed to hover around him all the time.

He blended into dark places easily, and given his size and being the quiet guy he was, he had a tendency to scare the shit out of people.

"Sorry, Bram, didn't know you were there."

He shrugged a broad shoulder. "Okay?"

"Yep, all good," I lied. "But I have to head out." Then I rushed from the room before he could ask any more questions.

My keys were on the counter, and I scooped them up, along with my jacket and satchel, checked that my blade was still at my hip, and quietly slipped out the front door, pulling it shut behind me.

Something was telling me to get in my truck and drive into the city, and I knew after the last task, I had to go with these hunches. I winced as I started my old truck, praying I didn't wake everyone, and rolled down the driveway and onto the road.

The tingling feeling continued, growing in intensity the

farther I went, which I assumed had to mean I was heading in the right direction.

Twenty minutes later, I was almost in the city. Roxburgh was busy this time of night. Honestly, the city never slept, and it was also the hub of demon activity. Though things here had quieted down a little since Lucifer returned to Hell—a long story, but for a while he was locked out of Hell, and his evil son, Diemos, took over, doing all sorts of twisted evil things. I sure as shit wasn't the only one happy things had settled down around here.

My phone rang and I didn't need to check the screen to know who it was. Cursing, I hit the call button. "Yeah?"

"Where the fuck are you going?" Warrick's deep voice growled through the speakers.

I ground my teeth. "I have to say, I'm not a huge fan of you constantly tracking me, alpha."

"Tough shit. Where are you going?"

"No idea. I'll find out when I get there."

"Dove," he said, and the way he said it was obviously through gritted teeth.

This was getting ridiculous. I didn't get this obsession he had with me. And it wasn't like I could call the cops or put out a restraining order. He was a literal beast created in Hell by Lucifer, and he wanted me with a single-minded focus and relentless determination that was...yeah, more than a little intimidating.

"Why me?" I asked over the sound of his heavy breathing filling my car, and surprising myself.

"What?"

"You say you want me. You follow me. You track me. Why?"

"Because you are..."

"If you say because I'm yours, I will hang up and never answer another one of your phone calls again.

He made a rough sound. "Then because I want..."

"Same goes if you say you want me under you, or you want to fuck me. Or any variation of the same theme."

Silence.

Why did that sting? It shouldn't. I knew this already. It was an animal thing, a lust thing, and not a me thing. "That's what I thought."

"Hang on a minute—"

"You need to find someone else to focus all that horny energy on. It's wasted on me. I need to go."

"Dove," he snarled.

I disconnected and ignored the barrage of calls and text messages that followed. He was in Linville and I was in Roxburgh. He was fast, but it took thirty minutes by car, and a little less when he shifted and ran. With any luck, I'd be done with whatever this was and home again by the time he got here. Because there was no doubt in my mind that he was already on his way.

I turned left, then right, then left again, weaving through the streets, no idea where I was going, only that this was where I needed to be. I ended up in a fairly rough part of the city. There were a lot of dive bars around here, and this particular area was known for its frequent gang altercations and the odd semi-regular murder.

The tingling grew stronger, to the point it made me want to scratch at my skin. I pulled over, parking across from a bar, and it was like a siren going off in my head. Here. Whatever was about to happen, it was here.

The sign above the door was neon and lopsided, and there were a couple letters missing. I assumed it was supposed to be *Angus's Bar*. Instead, *Anus Bar* flashed unwelcomingly. *Tough break, Angus.*

Tingles danced across my scalp and down my spine. Yes, this was most definitely where I was supposed to be. I checked for my blade again and shoved the car door open. I'd taken two steps across the street when a thump from behind had me spinning around.

Ren was standing there, running his fingers through his wind-blown hair.

"What are you doing here? Were you hiding in the back of my truck?"

He closed the space between us. "I wasn't hiding, I was resting there in case you needed me. I was right."

Goddammit.

There was nothing I could do about it now. He was here, and I knew him well enough to know there was no way I could make him stay in the truck while I went into the bar. "You need to do as I say, Ren, I mean it." The prickling feeling at my side was so bad it was distracting as hell. "No heroics."

He muttered something.

"What was that?"

"I'm not a damned child, Willow."

Hmm. When I looked at him, I still saw the scrawny fourteen-year-old kid, the boy who followed me everywhere like an excited puppy.

"You said you've been training?"

He straightened. "Yes."

"With a weapon?"

His eyes widened slightly, more than likely realizing the full magnitude of this situation, then his jaw firmed and he shook his head and patted his jacket pocket. "But I have a knife."

I inwardly groaned. "I have no idea what's brought me here, but I know it's not good. You do not take that knife out of your pocket, do you hear me? Until you know how to use it, you're a danger to yourself and everyone else."

"Willow—"

"I don't have time for this, Ren. Either do as I say or go back to the truck."

His eyes flashed bright gold—his fox not cool with the way I was talking to him—but I couldn't be gentle right then. I needed him to understand how dangerous this could be. I couldn't lose him, he was too important to me, to all of us.

"Fine," he said low. "But there's no way I'm waiting in the goddamn truck."

I gave him a nod and he followed me across the street. I slipped my blade free as we approached the door, sliding it up under my sleeve. There were low-level vibrations radiating from it now, letting me know danger was close by, telling me to be ready.

The more I used the knife's gifts, the easier I could read its vibrations. But if there was imminent danger, it sounded an alarm in my body, in my mind, that was impossible to miss. It set my muscles in motion, adrenaline shooting through my veins, and the blade made a kind of shrieking sound that only I could hear. And when I threw it, as long as the range wasn't too far, I never missed.

We reached the door. Music was spilling out, classic rock, of course. There was a lot of other noise as well, and at first I thought what I was hearing was loud singing or maybe even fighting, but then I pushed the door open.

I was wrong.

It was screaming.

CHAPTER 6

Willow

IN THE CENTER of the room, a man stood laughing—he was covered in blood, and there were two mutilated bodies at his feet, both women. A third he held by her throat. She was bleeding and terrified.

Judging by his colorless eyes, twisted expression, and the way the vine markings on my side burned like actual fire, I'd say I'd just found another malevolent spirit.

If I didn't do something now, the woman he was holding was dead as well.

Fuck.

Swinging my satchel around to the front, I shoved my hand inside and grabbed a handful of salt from the side pocket. Usually, I'd use it to contain the soul, but right now my need was more immediate. I rushed him and tossed it in his eyes. He roared, dropping the woman.

Gripping her arm, I yanked her back toward Ren. He grabbed

her, dragging her away as I quickly took another bag of salt mixed with cemetery dirt—not something I usually carried, but this latest task had me stocking up—and stabbed it with my blade.

I ran in a tight circle around him before he realized what I was doing. He hissed, watching me with wide, revolting black eyes.

"Everyone out!" I yelled.

The people standing around in obvious shock had no idea what this was, but they scattered, a stampede of terrified humans running for the door. Ren crouched over the injured woman, pressing his hand to the deep wound across her stomach, trying to staunch the blood.

"What do I do?" he said, sounding terrified.

"Get her to the hospital."

The possessed man rushed forward and hissed when he came up against the barrier I'd created.

A siren wailed in the distance. "Someone's called an ambulance. Get her outside and wait."

"I'm not leaving you."

"Get her out of here, then bring me the bag from the front seat of my truck." I'd packed it to take to Warrick's in the morning, but it looked like I'd be performing an exorcism right now.

I spun to him when he didn't move. "Ren..."

"She's dead," he said, eyes huge.

"You're sure?"

He nodded shakily. "What do I do?"

"Put her down, and go get the bag from my truck, okay?"

He nodded, laid her down carefully, and quickly rushed out of the bar.

I turned back to the possessed man, doing my best to stay calm. "Who are you?"

"Your worst nightmare," he said.

I couldn't help it; I snorted. "First, that was embarrassingly unoriginal, and second, my nightmares are a lot worse than a creep like you."

"You want to play with me?" he asked. "I wonder if your insides are as pretty as your outsides?" He rushed me again, and this time he was shoved back by the salt barrier.

It'd hold him for a little while, but we couldn't hang out in this bar indefinitely. The cops were coming, for one thing.

"Where did you come from?" I tried again.

He moved forward, as close as he could, and I held my ground, my blade gripped tight in my hand while I reminded myself that the face this monster was wearing wasn't his own. This was some poor, unsuspecting human. He could have a wife or kids at home.

Killing had to be the last resort.

A crash came from the back of the bar, and I turned as Ren, in his fox form, my bag gripped in his mouth, rushed in. He made a chuffing sound, a warning.

"The cops?"

He yipped.

Shit.

He dropped the bag and I scooped it up, my heart racing. There wasn't time for this. It took time to mix the oils, to get in the zone, to prepare the room. My hands started to shake.

I was failing.

I was failing my family, and I was failing this man and the women the fucker possessing him had murdered.

The door crashed open, a gust of wind rushing in as an officer charged through it. A section of the salt circle was swept away, and the spirit charged me. Ren jumped up, flying at him. The man grabbed him by the ruff and flung him hard across the room. The cop fired off a shot, and the man dropped, the bullet hitting him in the shoulder.

Something hit me, an energy like forked lightning carried on molten wind, knocking me off my feet. I landed hard on the ground.

The cop was shoved aside by invisible hands, his shoulder hitting the wall, knocking him down as well.

The man screamed suddenly, his eyes wide and filled with horror, staring at the blood on his hands. The agonized cries he made as he scooped up one of the dead women lifted the hair on the back of my neck.

"What have I done?" he choked out in horror. "Why...why did I do this?"

The spirit had exited his body, leaving him with the living purgatory of remembering everything he'd done while he was possessed.

The cop by the door wasn't moving, but there were more police coming. And there was nothing I could do—for either of them.

I needed to get out of there now.

I ran to Ren. He was too big for me to lift and far too heavy. He may be a fox, but he was a shifter, which meant he was a lot bigger than one in the wild.

"Can you walk?"

He nodded, and we rushed out the back, ducking into an office when more police busted down the back door and ran into the bar. As soon as the coast was clear, we quickly left, sticking to the shadows in the parking lot. Pulling a scarf from my satchel, I tied it around Ren's neck and hoped like hell he'd pass for a dog. Just a random woman walking her dog at night.

We made it back to the truck, skirting the crowds gathering, and Ren jumped into the front with a yelp of pain. I fired the Morris to life and got the hell out of there before the street was cordoned off and we were stuck. Ren shifted back into his human form and opened the glove compartment where he kept a spare pair of shorts and slid them on.

I glanced over at him. "Okay?"

He nodded, but said nothing. He wasn't okay. And I wasn't just talking about the horrible gash in his side. He should be with a witch who could give him what he needed. The witch I used to be, full of fun and laughter. Having adventures that didn't involve him having a woman die in his arms and being attacked by a man possessed by an evil spirit.

Jesus, where had the spirits come from? I'd thought I was dealing with one rogue entity out to do harm, but I'd been wrong. There were at least three. One would be bad enough, but of course, it wasn't that easy. And now more humans were dying.

"I need to find out where the spirits came from. That was insane." I glanced over at my silent familiar. "Ren?"

His fingers were clenched into tight fists, and he was staring silently out the window. *Shit.* My sweet fox wasn't cut out for this, no fox was cut out for this. It just wasn't in their natures. I was hurting him, he was hurting himself, and I didn't know how to stop it, how to help him.

"I'm sorry," I said. "I never should have taken you in there with me." When he was a kid, he was always joking around, playing pranks—fun, cute things that made us crack up. He'd bring me gifts, too, all the time, things he'd made himself while he ran in the woods. His nature had been all fox, as it should be. I was turning him into something else.

"That won't happen again," he said, voice low, devoid of emotion.

"What?"

"I'll follow your orders, Willow, and I'll learn to fight, properly...how to handle a weapon."

I turned back to him. "No, Ren, I don't want you to do that. That's not you. I know it's hard, but I think...I think we need to..."

"No." His eyes were glowing gold in the dark cab of the truck. "You can't tell me to go, I won't do it. And you can't...you can't keep leaving me behind." He took in a shuddering breath. "Please."

My heart shattered in my chest. That's exactly what I was

thinking. Anything to prevent him from being hurt again. I loved him, he was my family, and seeing him like this was killing me. "But this situation, it isn't right for you."

The gold in his eyes flickered. "I was…" He cleared his throat. "I was born to be by your side, Willow. If I'm not your familiar, then I'm not…I'm not anything." His gaze turned wild. "Don't send me away. I'll do better. I can do better."

Pain arrowed through me, and I reached over and grabbed his shaking hand and squeezed. "I promise I won't send you away. I need you just as much as you need me." And it was the truth. The bond went both ways. I don't know what I'd do without him. But, yeah, I'd been pushing him away lately. My goal had been to protect him, instead I'd hurt him even more.

"Promise," he said.

I gave his fingers another squeeze. "Promise. You really want to learn to fight?"

Determination transformed his handsome face. "More than anything."

If he wanted to do this, I had to help him. He had to learn to protect himself or I'd lose him. I nodded. "Okay."

"Okay?"

"We'll dress your wound, and then you need to get a good night sleep, because you're coming to the hounds' clubhouse with me in the morning."

His brows lifted. "Really?"

"Yep."

He needed to know how to fight in both his human and animal forms, which meant he needed to learn from other shifters.

There was nothing else for it, I had to throw my sweet fox to a pack of hellhounds.

We pulled up at the house, and Mags and Iris ran out, Brody right behind them.

"Where did you go?" Mags said as she opened my door. Her gaze shot to Ren, only realizing in that moment that he was sitting beside me, and her eyes widened. "Ren, oh god, what happened to you?"

"I'm fine," he said and shoved his door open. He got out and Mags rushed around to help him.

"Inside," I said to him. "We need to take care of that wound, then you can crash on the couch."

He nodded and strode inside. He still seemed dejected, and I hoped taking him with me tomorrow wasn't a terrible idea. But honestly, I was out of options. I could ask Rocco for help, I guess, but though the knights shifted forms, they weren't "shifters" as such. No, I'd stick to my plan. It was the best I had right then, and I'd never forgive myself if Ren was hurt again because I let him come with me so completely and utterly unprepared like I had tonight.

"You need me to stick around?" Brody asked, looking concerned. His muscled arms were folded, blue gaze alert.

The last thing we needed was another overprotective male on our hands. "Thanks, Brody, but we have it covered."

"I'll give you a call in the morning," Iris said to him and gave him a quick kiss. He stared down at her for several long seconds, obviously reluctant to leave, but then nodded and gave her another kiss before striding back to his grandmother's house.

We headed inside. I was cleaning Ren's wound when Mom walked in.

"Doesn't anyone sleep in this house?" I muttered.

"Not when one of my girls vanishes in the middle of the night without even leaving a note," she said and moved closer to inspect me. Her gaze slid to Ren and the cut in his side. "You're not giving up, then?"

Ren's jaw got hard. "No."

She patted his shoulder and gave him a sympathetic look that was sure to make him feel even worse.

"How about everyone go to bed and we can talk about this in the morning?" I said, trying and failing to not sound as impatient as I felt. It wasn't that long ago I'd lived full time in the back of my shop. Mom had no idea what I was doing any given day or night, and considering I was twenty-six years old, that was exactly the way it should be.

"Speaking of notes," Iris said and put two pieces of paper in front of me.

I glanced down at the top one, more than a little surprised by the name I saw, and squashed the tiny flutter of my long-dead, school-girl heart. "Did he say what he wanted?"

Iris shook her head. "He called the house yesterday morning. I forgot all about it. He wanted your number. I said if he didn't already have it, it was because that's the way you wanted it."

I inwardly grinned. Iris was like me in a lot of ways.

Mags twisted to read the note. "Clayton Whitlock!" she shrieked. "Why is he calling you?"

"Wills dated him in high school," Mom said.

Mags spun to me, her eyes huge. "You dated Clayton Whitlock? *The* Clayton Whitlock?"

"Yes. It was a very long time ago."

"Holy hell, the guy is so freaking hot. Did he dump you or did you dump him?"

"I dumped him."

"Are you insane!" she cried. "I would kill to be with Clayton Whitlock. I can't believe no one ever told me about this!" She yanked her phone from her back pocket, tapped the screen, and turned it to me with a sigh. "He posted this today. Look at him. Look at those abs. Good god, just look at all that perfection."

He was by a hot tub, hair artfully tussled, grinning at the camera, his sculpted chest and tight abs on full display.

"Clayton Whitlock," Mags muttered. "I can't believe no one told me you dated him."

"Can you stop saying his whole name like that," Iris said. "You sound deranged."

Mags flipped her off, and I glanced down at his name and number written on a scrap of paper and scowled. I'd really liked him once. He'd been funny and sweet. Then he'd cheated on me with one of my friends. He broke my fledgling romantic heart, squashing my dreamy-eyed fantasies, and solidified my already strong feelings of distrust and relationships when it came to men —thanks to Mom and her many and varied asshole boyfriends.

He was a fairly powerful witch now, the Keeper of his own coven. The Whitlock's were nowhere near as strong as us, but they did okay. They were loaded, though, running several businesses, one of which was importing rare and highly sought-after ingredients for spells and potions, and other witchcraft related relics. He'd be in the midst of his final task now, like me.

Keeper or not, I had no idea why he'd call me. We had absolutely nothing to talk about. I hadn't seen or spoken to him in years.

"He said to ask you to call him, that it's important," Iris said.

I screwed up the paper and tossed it in the trash.

Mags shrieked. "What are you doing? You can't just throw Clayton Whitlock's number away!"

I shrugged. The other note, well, not a note, it was an invitation. Some ball, a gathering of the Keepers from each coven. *Pass.* I tossed that as well.

Iris snorted, then headed up to bed, Mags reluctantly following her when Mom gave her a shove toward the door.

"Your family doesn't think I can protect you," Ren said when we were alone again.

I covered the wound on his side with gauze and tore off a piece of tape. "I don't need you to protect me, you know that, right? I have all these magical fighting skills, and this wicked awesome knife," I said, patting the knife at my hip. "Being some-one's familiar isn't only about that."

His jaw worked. "I know, but you're a Keeper now. And it doesn't change the way I feel." His gaze turned hollow. "It doesn't change what I need. This tie to you is part of me, and every time I fail you, it...it tears me apart. I know I'm not what you need. You should have a familiar who is your equal. I'm not, not yet. So yeah, I know you don't *need* me. But I need to be needed by you, and right now I'm more of a hindrance than a help and it fucking sucks."

I moved around and cupped his sweet face. "I need you, Renny. You're my best friend, my family. Don't ever think I don't need you. Not ever."

His amber gaze met mine before he dipped his chin, and I could see that he didn't believe me and that killed me.

"I'm ready to train, Wills," he said, that determination hard-ening his beautiful face. "Whatever it takes, I'll make sure I'm worthy of being your familiar."

I wrapped my arms around him and squeezed him tight.

He already was. I only wished he realized it as well.

CHAPTER 7

Willow

As soon as the gates were opened and I drove in, Warrick appeared at the door of the clubhouse and strode toward us. His vibrant golden eyes slid to Ren sitting beside me, and his expression darkened.

Ren stiffened beside me. "You didn't tell him I was coming?"

"It'll be fine."

Ren shifted in his seat and cursed under his breath. I didn't blame him. Warrick was huge and imposing, and dominance radiated from him in hot, violent waves. I felt it and I wasn't any type of shifter. I couldn't imagine how it felt to Ren. I parked the Morris and Ren froze, his head dipping, gaze dropping as Warrick opened my door. His fox submitting instantly.

I pretended not to notice.

Warrick's gaze slid from me back to Ren. "Why is the pup here?"

"Wait here, Ren?"

He nodded and still didn't, or maybe couldn't, move.

I grabbed Warrick's arm and led him away, ignoring the instant tingles shooting up from where we touched. His gaze dropped to my hand on his arm when we stopped, the muscle flexing under my palm. He leaned closer, and more tingles danced across my skin.

I quickly let him go and shoved my hands in my pockets as I took a step back. "How's Maddox?"

His gaze ate me up for several long, intense seconds. "He broke his own wrist, then gnawed off his hand trying to get free."

Okay. Jesus. That was *really* not good. "That's awful."

Warrick kept that steady gaze locked on me. "It'll grow back."

"His hand?"

He dipped his chin.

"Well, that's...something, I guess. Still no word on Edric?"

"No. Something's wrong with his scent. Mad's is different as well. My brothers can't track him." He looked more than a little troubled.

"Shit." The hounds were the best trackers in existence. If they couldn't find Edric, no one could.

"You can get that evil fucker out of Mad?"

"Yes, and I was thinking that maybe I could go one better." There was no way I would ever ask for a favor from this male. Owing him was the worst possible case scenario for me, which meant I needed to offer a trade. "I can ward the perimeter of the clubhouse, which will stop any other spirits getting in, but..." I straightened my spine. "In exchange, I need you to do something for me."

His eyes flashed, and he was right in front of me a split second later. His fingers, hot and rough, curled around mine. "About time. Let's go."

I dug my heels in. "Go where?"

"To my room, I don't want anyone else seeing you naked—"

"What! No, that was not what I want from you. I'm not talking about sex." I tugged my hand from his.

His rough exhale came out more a low growl, and he took another step toward me.

I lifted my hands. "Stop." He wasn't trying to be threatening, but the beast in him seemed to be the dominant force more often than not.

And right then, I didn't want to think about the way my body instantly heated up in response.

"You're lying to yourself," he said.

Heat washed through me, embarrassment and anger, mainly because he wasn't completely wrong. "If you're that hard up, go fuck one of your groupies." I crossed my arms over my chest because the asshole threw me off balance with his sexy voice and outrageous arrogance. And goddess help me, it turned me on, all of it, and it *shouldn't*, and that pissed me off. What the hell was wrong with me?

"There are no females here, remember?" he said. "Not until this is over."

"Wow, how will you survive a day without screwing some random chick?" *Shut the hell up!*

"Jealous?"

"What? No, of course not." I kind of was, and that pissed me off as well.

"Don't worry, dove." His nostrils flared, and he prowled closer. "I have a hand...and an excellent imagination."

Do not think about it!

Too late. I was totally thinking about it.

Ugh.

"I don't want to know," I said, lying through my teeth, because I did. I really did.

He licked his lips. "You sure about that?"

"Yep." Time to move this conversation along. "Okay, so, if I ward this place, will you train Ren?"

He frowned, his chin jerking back before his gaze sliced to Ren, then returned to me. "To do what?"

I took several calming breaths. "He needs to learn to fight, in both his human and animal forms. He's young, and foxes aren't natural fighters. But with everything going on with me, and him being my familiar, he needs to know how to protect himself and take my back when necessary." Warrick didn't need to know the deep emotional pain Ren was going through. A male like him, devoid of any tender emotions entirely, wouldn't understand. But he would understand the need to protect, to fight.

"You need someone to take your back, I'll do it."

He said it completely serious, like it was obvious. Nope. No way. "Look, you don't understand how it works between a witch and her familiar. Ren has a need to...protect me, to the point that if he thinks I'm in danger, he will throw himself into a fight against someone who could kill him. It's instinct..."

"He wants you for himself," Warrick said, a whole lot of growl in his voice. "He wants to fuck you."

How was I even attracted to this guy? Seriously? "Nope, not even a little bit."

"Does he prefer males?"

I blinked up at him. Was he really saying that if a male didn't want me, it could only be because he was gay? I drew in a breath, trying to find patience. "The feelings we have for each other are like brother and sister."

His massive shoulders relaxed a little, but he didn't look completely convinced.

"So, do we have a deal?" I asked.

"How long will it take? The ward?"

"A night or two max."

"You stay here, and you sleep in my room, and until he's trained, I take your back, then we have a deal."

I ground my teeth. "Hang on, you don't get to add conditions."

"I just did."

His eyes seemed brighter, and my belly did a stupid little flip. "I'm not having sex with you."

"Maybe not, but that wasn't what I asked."

He knew how badly I wanted this, and he was using it to his advantage. "Fine."

Warrick glanced at Ren again, then whistled, like my best friend was a dog. Ren's head came up and Warrick crooked a finger at him. Ren was out of the truck in seconds, striding quickly toward the massive alpha, that gaze still dipped. He stopped in front of us. Warrick eyed him for long seconds, and it took everything in me not to tell him to stop being an asshole.

"You care about that pretty face, pup?" Warrick asked him.

Okay. Nope. "Now, hang on..."

Ren's gaze sliced to me, and he shut me up with a look. I was embarrassing him. Then his gaze slid to Warrick but stayed low, because he knew meeting Warrick's gaze would be a phenomenal mistake. He squared his shoulders, though. "The only thing I care about is being what Willow needs me to be."

"You want to fuck her?"

I shoved Warrick. "What the hell!" He didn't budge, not even half an inch.

Ren recoiled. "No. *God, no.* She's like my sister."

Warrick was quiet another few painfully long seconds, then he said, "Get inside. Ask for Lothar and tell him I sent you and why you're here."

Ren rushed off and Warrick strode to my truck without another word, grabbed out my bags, and headed inside. I took the broom I'd brought with me from the back as well and had no choice but to follow. I searched out Ren as soon as we walked in. Lothar was standing over him, several other hounds there as well, and Ren looked embarrassed, no...mortified. I couldn't do this. I couldn't let Ren do this. I changed course, about to go over there and get him, to tell him this was a terrible mistake, but Warrick grabbed my arm.

I spun to face him, and he shook his head.

"Let me go. I should never have brought him here."

He slid his blade free and offered it to me hilt first. "Want my knife to chop off his balls as well?"

I jerked back.

"The fox doesn't want to be a pup anymore, let him earn it. And no male wants a female to rescue him."

"You're a sexist pig," I bit out.

He shrugged.

"They're going to hurt him."

"Yes, but they won't kill him."

"That isn't very comforting."

"But he'll learn. No one likes to feel weak. He'll get bruised and he'll have some new scars, but when we're finished with him, he won't feel weak anymore."

It was black-and-white to him. Why were males like this? Why were feelings so damned terrifying?

Then again, that wasn't only a male thing, was it? It wasn't like I didn't actively avoid dealing with a whole lot of things I was feeling when it came to the trials, and Rose, or what happened at the knights compound a year ago. I shut down those thoughts quickly.

"Take me to Maddox. Let's get this over with."

He grunted, and I followed him across the room, down the stairs, and into the tunnels. We hadn't walked far down the stone passage, lit with flickering torches, when I heard the growls and howls. The hair on the back of my neck stood up.

Warrick shoved a door open, and we walked in. Maddox was still chained to the floor, only now, he had one of his arms free, and it ended with a bloody stump.

He stopped thrashing as soon as we entered and his neck twisted, black gaze locking on me.

"Hello, pretty," he said in a warped version of Maddox's voice.

This spirit needed to go back where he came from, or be sent to where it was meant to be. It was all about balance. I moved closer. "Tell me where you come from."

He laughed.

If a soul was here on Earth, it had either been here all along or someone had released it. Souls didn't just get out of Hell, or Heaven for that matter, and the darkness, the hatred, that came from this one had me thinking that Hell was exactly where it came from. If a soul was sent there, it stayed there. There was no mercy, no change of heart. No transfer to Heaven for good behavior or because some reaper made a clerical error.

"Why are you here?" I tried again.

He licked his lips. "Come here, little girl."

The voice sounded higher this time, sharper, more urgent.

Warrick moved up beside me. "Is Maddox still in there?"

"Yeah." But he wouldn't be the same after this asshole was gone, how could he be? Every sick evil thing this monster had done, past and present, would be in Maddox's head, every twisted thought seeping deeper and deeper into his consciousness—into his heart and soul.

I wasn't going to get anything from this spirit, though, and there was no way I could force him to share the information. There were ways to torture a soul, I'd heard of it before, but I didn't know the effect it would have on Maddox when we were done. And Maddox had been possessed for far too long as it was.

There were two other hounds in the room, standing behind the salt line that was now twice as thick since they'd been adding to it like I'd told them to.

They watched me closely as I took a silver urn from my satchel. I placed it on the stone floor along with more salt peppered with cemetery dirt, the lilies we'd gathered, some moss from one of the ancient oaks, a mortar and pestle, several different oils—Else's own special and highly potent mixes—and finally some more dirt, also from the cemetery.

I added the lilies to the mortar, crushed them, then added the oils, moss, and dirt.

"What are you doing?" Warrick asked.

"This mixture will act as a barrier when I get the soul out of Maddox. He'll be on the hunt for a new host and this oil mix will stop it from entering me. The salt across the doorway will keep it from leaving this room." I opened the lid on the urn. "The only thing available to him will be this dead rat. Silver is also a natural barrier, and this one is smelted with a whole lot of other goodies that will make it impossible for him to break free." Thankfully, the oil was fine to use *everywhere*. Gran had made sure of that, after years of using recipes that stung and left rashes in unmentionable places.

"Then what?"

"He'll possess the rat, and I'll keep it trapped in the urn until we work out how it got here—if it was summoned from Hell, or some other place, or if it's been in limbo. Whatever it is, I'll send it back to wherever it came from."

Warrick frowned. "Why can't you just do that now?"

"Because if I do the wrong ritual, things could get messy. We have to keep things balanced. Also, I want to know who unleashed them, if that's what happened. And if that was the case, we have an entirely different problem on our hands." I didn't want to think about that, not yet. One thing at a time.

When I had everything mixed, I stood and tugged off my jacket, then kicked off my shoes.

"What are you doing?" Warrick growled when I undid my pants.

"It's your lucky day." I winked. "Getting naked."

His gaze shot to the other two hounds. "Out," he barked.

They left quickly, and his gaze sliced back to me. "Why the fuck are you getting naked?"

"I need to rub that oil all over myself. Can't do that with my clothes on." I wasn't a shy person. I didn't get embarrassed. I was naked a lot—it was a witch thing. A lot of rituals and spells required it. "You should leave, or you'll be the next vessel."

"Not leaving you in here on your own with that fucker."

I tugged my shirt off, throwing it aside. His gaze dipped to my boobs and the deep purple bra I was wearing. He gritted his teeth before his gaze came back to mine and they were even more determined than before. "Not leaving, dove."

Shit. "Fine." This was *fine*. No big deal, right? Plus, I didn't have time to fight with him on this. "Then get your clothes off. I should have enough here for both of us." I turned away.

"What the fuck?" Warrick said, his voice filled with fury.

"What?" I started to turn, and he stopped me with a wide palm to the back of my neck, the other brushing my hair aside. Every muscle in me tensed as his finger traced the letters that had been carved into my skin, just below my shoulder blades over a year ago: WITCH.

"It's still there?" he said, voice vibrating with fury.

"Yes, he made sure of it," I said, keeping my voice as strong as I could.

Azel, that twisted fucking fallen angel, had chosen darkness over light. And my friends—mates of the knights of Hell—had almost died because of me, because I hadn't been strong enough to fight him. It'd been my protection spell warding their compound, and it was my fault that monster got through. A shudder moved through me at the memory.

"I didn't know," he said, deep, gruff.

My mouth went dry. After Warrick had carried me away, he'd cleaned me up. He'd wiped the blood from the letters carved into my back. I'd told him my aunt would make sure it didn't scar, but Azel had used salt, not only to cause pain but to make sure it scarred. Not even Else could fix that. Salt was one of the most powerful ingredients in our arsenal; it did a lot more than season food. So I'd lied to Warrick because he'd been so angry and there was no one left for him to punish. "It's fine…I'm fine. He's dead and gone. Never coming back."

He snarled. "It should have been me to end him. For you, I would have torn him to pieces with my bare hands."

My heart raced faster at his brutal declaration. "Just forget it's there. I do." It was a lie, of course. It was a constant reminder that I couldn't be weak ever again. That I wouldn't let anyone break me like that, and that I would do anything, *anything*, to protect the people who relied on me.

He grunted and finally released me, taking all that intense heat with him.

CHAPTER 8

Warrick

RAGE-FIRE RUSHED THROUGH MY VEINS. I hadn't been able to protect her a year ago, and it ate at me. The physical evidence of the pain that twisted fallen angel had inflicted on her had me roaring inside my head. The beast in me wanted that fucker alive again so I could tear him apart until he was nothing but bloody tatters at my feet.

Maddox thrashed, drawing my attention back to him and all the sick fucking shit he was saying about my dove. I opened the door. "Out in the hall," I said to her.

"I don't care what he says," she said.

"I do." Seeing those scars brought the memories back. Her body battered and bleeding, close to death. It had sunk its claws into my head. I couldn't listen to that fucker inside Maddox talk shit about her now, not if I wanted to maintain control.

She picked up the concoction she'd just made and strode out of the room. I followed and shut the door after us, then barked at Jagger, who was standing outside to keep everyone above ground.

My lieutenant rushed off to do as I said.

I didn't want any of my brothers seeing her naked. She was mine and I didn't share.

Gripping the back of my shirt, I tugged it off and tossed it aside, and the little breath Willow sucked in at the sight of my chest pleased me greatly. She tried not to look, but her pretty eyes kept darting back, watching me as I toed off my boots.

Then her gaze dropped, her small body freezing, when I tugged open the button of my jeans, and my satisfaction grew. She tried to deny what was between us, but she couldn't hide the way she reacted to me. Fuck, her scent alone would have been enough.

Her gaze darted up, and she realized she'd been caught staring and quickly looked away. She shoved down her pants, and I ate up the sight of her, freezing in place when her delicate fingers gripped the fabric of her panties. She pushed them down her legs and kicked them off as well. Her bra joined her pile of clothes next.

A snarl tried to crawl up my throat, and I bit it back. My dove was exquisite. Her skin smooth and golden, her hips wide and round, made to take a big male like me. Her breasts were full and heavy, big enough to fill my hands, and one day, they'd feed our pups.

I watched mesmerized as she scooped up some of the potent smelling oil and began rubbing it over her skin.

Mine.

My mate.

My dove.

The beast, the animal I was, the part of me that struggled to live by the rules of man, wanted to push her to the ground, wrap my jaws around the back of her neck, hoist her ass in the air, and claim her. But I was more than that; Lucifer had made it so. He had given the hellhounds he'd created control over their animal urges and instincts, tentative as it was, which meant I knew that was wrong. That my dove wouldn't like that. So I held myself back while she ran her oily hands all over her beautiful body.

Maybe if I slipped my hand between her thighs and played with her, readied her, she'd let me...

"Stop staring and start oiling," she said without turning around.

No, she wouldn't welcome that either. Still, I moved close, so close I could feel the heat of her bare skin and breathed in her scent. My arm brushed hers as I dipped my fingers into the oil. Still, she didn't turn like I desperately wanted her to, and instead worked at smearing oil over her shoulders.

I tried to focus, but there was no holding back my low growl when she smoothed it over her breasts and between the round cheeks of her luscious ass.

My cock was hard as steel, and when she finally dipped her fingers between her legs I hissed, wishing they were my fingers, that I could feel the slick heat there against my skin.

She still had her back to me, and I didn't like that. I wanted her eyes on me. I was strong and muscled. I had a big cock. Females enjoyed my skill in bed, they liked my body.

I wanted my dove to take pleasure from the sight of it, like I did hers. If she looked, she'd know I was capable of pleasuring her, of protecting her, that I would be the best choice for her to mate with.

The animal in me wanted her approval. Craved it.

Willow was intelligent and capable, smart and beautiful. My dove was tough. And she needed to be all of those things to be accepted by my brothers as my mate. We had enemies, and my female needed to be able to fight and protect herself and our pups if necessary.

But right then, more than anything else, I wanted her delicate hands on me. I needed her to touch me. "Need your help with my back, dove," I said.

Willow

Dammit. I didn't want to turn around. I wasn't sure I could do it and not ogle him like I'd already been caught doing.

"Just a second." I finished off my leg and foot, and when there was no other reason to delay, I took a fortifying breath, picked up the mortar, and made myself turn.

Holy shit.

He was turned away from me, giving me his wide muscled back, and I took advantage. It was impossible not to. Flames from the torches lining the hall flickered over his deeply tanned and tattooed skin. Some of the tattoos looked like script, but in a language possibly known to only him and his brothers, others were images that had to be from Hell, flames and demons, hounds in their beast form. His massive shoulders tapered down, but his waist was still thick, every part of him was thick and roped with muscle. His monster thighs, bulging calves, and his ass, now glistening with oil—I swallowed—good lord, that ass. You could bounce a quarter off it.

I bit my lip harder when what I wanted to do was drop to my knees and take a bite out of one of those muscled cheeks.

Instead, I resisted, closed the space between us, put the mortar by his feet, dipped my fingers in, and straightened. I lifted my hand and paused, almost afraid to touch him, because yeah, I wanted to so damned much.

"Dove?"

I pressed my hand to his smooth skin, the oil melting against his overheated flesh. He was always hot. Heat radiated from his body like he was a living furnace. I ran my hand over his shoulder, trying to keep my movements quick and efficient, trying to keep it as impersonal as possible and ignore the goose bumps lifting under my hand, all over his skin at my touch. When I was done, I stood back. "You got everywhere else?"

"Almost," he said and turned.

Do not look down. Don't you do it.

I kept my eyes up and he crouched, scooped the last of the oil with his fingers, and stood again. Then he dropped that big, rough-skinned hand to his groin and worked it over his balls and cock.

My eyes dipped without my say-so. *Holy shit.* My gaze shot back up to his, but he wasn't smirking like I expected. His gaze was intense, and he wasn't even trying to hide the fact that he was checking me out as well.

"You done playing with yourself?" I asked.

"You can take over if you want."

"I'm good, thanks." Somehow, I turned away from him and walked back into the room. I scooped up the urn and handed it to him. "Hold this, and when I brush a gap in the salt, take off the lid, okay?"

He nodded.

"As soon as the rat shows signs of life, jam on the lid."

His gaze slid to Maddox and he nodded again.

I grabbed more of my salt and dirt mix and laid a thick line of it in front of the door, then tossed the bag on the floor. Grabbing my broom, I walked up to the salt line between us and Maddox. Closing my eyes, I held my arms out on either side of me and started chanting the words to force the spirit out. A warm breeze moved through my hair, the mother's gift, an ancient one handed down to my coven by one of the first witches in our family to go through the trials.

The thorny vines on my skin heated, and I knew they were glowing as I said the words of the ancient spell, repeating them, slowly increasing in volume, in speed.

Maddox thrashed harder. I could hear his struggles, the spirit fighting against it, more than a little reluctant to leave such a strong host.

I continued to raise my voice until I was yelling the words that tumbled from my lips, words I felt as though I'd said before, but it wasn't my voice, it was the voices of generations past, witches who'd used this spell, their voices shadows, echoes of the past replaying like an old recording, adding power to mine, fuller, louder, stronger.

Maddox was roaring and growling, incoherent now.

I opened my eyes, and slamming my broom on the floor, swept away a section of the salt line and stepped back. A cold blast shot past me, and Warrick yanked the lid off the urn as I scooped up the bag of salt and threw down more, covering the gap again, sealing Maddox inside.

An icy wind filled the room, not like the last spirit, its frozen claws stinging as it passed by, the soul spinning around the room, rushing past us over and over again, desperate for a new host.

Then finally, with no other option, it slammed into the urn.

The dead rat shrieked.

Warrick slammed on the lid.

CHAPTER 9

Willow

MADDOX THRASHED against his chains and Warrick strode to him, his feet crunching over the salt, and crouched down. "Calm, brother," he said as he undid the shackles around Maddox's ankles and wrist. Maddox made an agonized sound and his hand came up, gripping his head.

Warrick loomed over him and said something deep and guttural, the words sounding brutal, harsh, in a language I'd never heard before.

Maddox shook his head, and his eyes flashed red.

"Get back," Warrick said to me.

He didn't need to warn me twice. I scrambled back as Maddox exploded into his hellhound form, enormous body, black shaggy fur, and terrifying red eyes. Warrick stood in front of him, still speaking in a different language. Maddox shook his head and made a sound that sent a shiver down my spine.

Maddox's boxy head turned to me, and there was horror in his red eyes.

"Brother," Warrick growled out.

He made that awful pain-filled sound once more and, with a burst of energy, Maddox smashed through the door and ran off.

The hellhound alpha strode to the hall, snatched his phone from his pile of clothes, and hit someone's number. "Maddox is coming, let him past then follow him. Don't let him out of your sight, but stay back."

I grabbed my clothes from the hall and shoved them on over the oily mess on my skin.

"What were you saying to him?" I asked Warrick when he walked back in carrying his jeans.

His expression was troubled as he pulled them on. "I told him it wasn't his fault."

"Of course it wasn't. That spirit latched on to him and there was nothing he could've done to stop it." I tugged my shirt over my head.

"He knows that. But when the spirit left and he shifted to his hound form, I could see what was in his head, and all I could see was the female he killed. His mind was filled with the memory of hurting her, of tearing her open."

This surprised me somewhat. "Sure, he's upset he killed Jane, of course he is, but why is he—"

Warrick growled. "We don't harm innocent females. Ever. Not human, not vampire or shifter..." His lids lowered, looking at me under thick, dark lashes. "Not witch."

The vehemence in his words and on his face surprised me as well. "What about demon?"

His expression remained intense. "Not all demons want to cause harm. There are good and bad among all species."

"Of course," I said, though I hadn't met any full-blooded demons that I'd like to be BFFs with lately. I began to gather my things.

"You think we could just kill an innocent without regret?"

"I don't know what you're capable of."

"Not that," he growled.

"Right."

Warrick grabbed my arm, pulling me back up. "Our kind don't have females, mating with other species is how we reproduce. Our sons are hellhound, our daughters take after their mothers, whatever that may be. We don't hurt females, we worship them."

I'd had no idea. "Are you telling me Jane and Maddox were *together?*"

Warrick's eyes flashed. "She was his mate. She carried his pup in her womb."

I blinked up at him, stunned. "Mate? I didn't realize." Now I felt like an asshole.

"We have many mated brothers. Two of them live here with their mates and pups. We have a family den deeper in the tunnels, larger quarters, where we can keep them safe."

This was news to me, and there was no hiding my surprise. "But only two live here? Where are the rest?"

"My brothers outlived their females, and any daughters they had."

His expression didn't change at that heartbreaking statement. "That's awful. And your sons?"

"They're immortal, like us. Relic is Lothar's son...and there are others."

"So does that mean your brothers took demon mates? You lived in Hell most of your life."

"Some. Like I said, not all demons are out to cause harm, and there aren't only demons in Hell."

Again, this was news to me. "Do you have children?" I asked, my curiosity getting the better of me.

"No." His gaze did not falter from mine. "Not until I claim my mate."

Okay, time to end this line of questioning. "So where would Maddox have gone?"

The muscles in his massive biceps flexed, and he shook his head. "Maddox has gone beast, he's taken to the woods. He needs time to come to terms with what happened."

Well, fuck. How did you come to terms with killing your mate and unborn child? I had no idea. Obviously, hounds weren't as completely heartless as I thought they were, or at least not all of them.

Warrick left to speak to his brothers, and I got to work warding the clubhouse. It was a long and repetitive process. Every two hours I had to walk the perimeter, reciting a spell that was long and complicated. It strengthened the ward with each pass, and with how many lived here, the more passes I could make, the better. Which was why I needed as much time as I did.

It was dark, and I was on my third walk around for the night when one of the hounds approached. I didn't know him, though I'd seen him here before, of course. And as he drew closer, my knife began to vibrate low against my hip. *Danger.* This male posed a threat to me.

This surprised me, honestly. My knife had never reacted to any of the hounds like this, not once since I'd been coming here. If they'd even contemplated hurting me, my blade would have picked up on it and warned me.

Hellhounds were, I assumed, like other wild animals—sudden movements weren't a great idea when they were in attack mode, so I stayed completely still. The level of vibration from my knife remained low. He didn't want to kill me, but he did want to hurt me in some way. I stopped what I was doing and slowly faced him completely, the hilt of my blade slipping into my hand. "What do you want?"

He glanced at my knife and growled, but kept coming.

The vibrations running through it stayed the same. He had no intention of stopping. I scanned his face, searching for any sign of possession, but there was nothing.

He wanted to scare me and that didn't justify me killing him. I stood my ground. "Stop."

He didn't.

"Don't make me cut you, asshole."

He advanced and grabbed my wrist. Despite my blade's warning, I was still shocked that one of Warrick's brothers would do this. The knife was gripped in the same fist, and he tugged me forward. "You could try, little female, but I'll make you bleed right back."

I didn't want to throw Warrick's name around, it would scream pathetic-weak-female to a male like this, but I would to stop this, whatever this was. With everything that was happening here at the clubhouse with Maddox and Edric, and locking the place down to keep more spirits out, some of the hounds were bound to be going through some stuff. How much had Warrick told them all? Maybe he thought I'd caused this? "I'm sorry about your brothers, but it has nothing to do with me."

"I know."

"Then what do you want?"

"To fuck you, right here on the ground," he said, his eyes now glowing red.

Again, I stood there stunned. Had he really just said that?

He squeezed my wrist tighter; the force making me wince, and if I didn't do something soon, he'd snap it. "You really want to risk pissing off your alpha?"

The hound barked out a gravelly laugh. "Warrick is weak. *You* weaken him. You turn him down in front of us. If I have you, they'll know I'm more of a male than he is." He dipped his head, his hot breath washing over my face. "He won't *take* you, but I will. I'll show him, I'll show all of my brothers who is alpha."

My free hand was pressed against his massive chest, trying to hold him off. "That logic is seriously messed up. And if you even try it, I will fucking end you." And I meant it with everything in me. Or I'd die trying.

"Your tiny knife won't do shit. I'll heal as soon as you pull it from my flesh."

I opened my mouth but never got the chance to curse him out. He swept my feet out from under me and threw me to the ground, his massive body coming down on top of me fast. So incredibly fast.

I slammed my hand against his ear, and when he reared back, I punched him in the throat.

He was ten times stronger than me, but I sure as fuck wasn't defenseless, and he was about to learn why he'd made a mistake coming for me. A thick branch lay at the base of a nearby tree. I called it to me, and it flew through the air and slammed into the side of his head. He roared and his grip loosened on my wrist. I tugged my hand free as his claws extended from the ends of his fingers and he shoved my legs apart with another roar of rage, those vicious claws slicing my inner thighs and tearing up my favorite jeans.

With a cry, I shoved my blade into his side, and he snarled, his face partially shifting into his hound, his jaws snapping, and thankfully missing my face. I stuck him again, and he sprang off me, shifted fully, and lowered his head, about to attack again.

"I throw this"—I held up my blade—"and you lose an eye."

He roared a third time, so loud and with such force, my hair blew back, then he turned and ran off.

Motherfucker.

I groaned and pushed myself up.

The scratches stung like hell and I wanted to go inside, take a shower, wash off the oil on my skin, and now the blood on my scratched-up thighs, but I had to finish spelling the perimeter. Stopping now would mean having to start from the beginning all over again.

It took half-an-hour longer than usual with me limping

around, while watching out in case that fucker came back, and when I walked inside the clubhouse, everyone was eating. There was a table laid out, groaning with food. I had two hours to eat, shower, and nap before I needed to go back out there and do it all over again, and right then the most pressing sensation I had, after pain, was hunger. So I hobbled to the table, grabbed a plate, and loaded it with steak, potatoes, and rolls.

"What the hell happened to you?" Ren said, suddenly at my side, gaze raking over me. "Was it the hound you exorcised?"

He looked kind of banged up as well, but not too bad, thankfully. I didn't have the energy to fight another one of these big bastards tonight. "Nope, but I'm fine. What happened to you?"

"Training."

"If you're having second thoughts..."

"I'm not. I want to keep training, and I'm more interested in why you're bruised and bleeding," Ren said, his expression growing more intense. No, pissed. This was his pissed-off face.

"It was just some asshole..."

Warrick was suddenly in front of me, growling, the sound vibrating through his wide chest. "You're bleeding. Why the fuck are you bleeding?" he said, lifting my wrist and checking out the fresh bruise there. I hadn't even noticed it. "Someone held you by the throat," he said with so much fury I winced. And only then realized it hurt there, too. I guess the fucker had grabbed my throat at some point.

"One of your brothers, with delusions of grandeur, thought it would be fun to try to force himself on me. Apparently, the fact that you haven't, makes you weak."

His gaze sliced down my body, taking in my tattered jeans stained with my blood, and he roared so loud the windows rattled. I froze, stunned at the violence of his reaction. Everyone in the room stopped what they were doing, silence filling the big space.

One of Warrick's massive hands cupped the back of my head

and he drew me against him, his nose dropping to my throat, pressing in and breathing deep. His head jerked back. "I will fucking kill him," he said. "I will make him bleed." He barked out words at Jagger in that same guttural language he had used with Maddox, then turned back to me.

"I stabbed him," I said, trying to calm things down. "I already made him bleed. He took off. I doubt he'll come anywhere near me again."

Warrick said nothing, grabbed my hand, and led me through the room. I limped behind him, trying to keep up, and as soon as we were out of sight of the rest of the hounds, he scooped me up in his arms and carried me down the stairs.

I wanted to tell him to put me down, that I didn't need him to carry me, but I realized in that moment, that I kind of did, and I appreciated that he waited until no one saw, so I didn't appear weak. At least he understood how important that was to me.

He shoved the door to his room open and kicked it shut behind us, then carried me into his bathroom. It was a nice bathroom. Surprisingly so for one built underground. The shower was massive and could easily fit several people, or two hounds, comfortably.

He lowered me to my feet, turned on the shower, and started stripping me. Again, I should tell him no, but honestly, I was tired. It'd been a big, stressful day, and I thought I might have lost a little more blood than I realized. And yeah, maybe I was experiencing a little shock from the whole attempted rape thing. I'd always felt safe here, physically, anyway, and now...not so much.

"I thought all hounds worshipped females," I said, my voice sounding different to my own ears.

"We do, which is why he's going to die." Each word was said with frigid precision, as if he were already imagining the act, and had ice slicing along my spine.

Warrick pressed his face to my hair and breathed in again,

then he propped me against the bathroom counter. He quickly shucked off his clothes and then helped me into the steaming water. We really needed to stop getting naked with each other like this. It wasn't normal. Friends didn't get naked together as often as we did, and we weren't even that.

But it did feel good, washing off the grime and the blood...the evil of the day. "I feel kind of...woozy."

"He clawed you. That you're still standing proves just how strong you are."

I grinned and thought it might look kind of loopy, but I didn't really care. "That's nice."

"Our claws are tipped with poison," he clarified and dropped to his knees in front of me.

"What are you doing?" I asked and shoved my fingers through his thick, dark hair. "You have great hair. Not coarse like your fur when you're in your hound form."

He ignored my idiotic comment about his hair and looked up at me. "I need to lick your wounds. It'll neutralize the poison and my saliva will speed up healing."

His voice sounded all deep and growly. "That's a neat trick." I could hear the words coming out of my mouth, words I would never say and couldn't stop it. *Neat? Gah.*

He moved me back so I was leaning against the wall. "Spread your legs for me, dove."

"You're loving this, aren't you?" I said and laughed, or more giggled. I never giggled. What kind of poison was this? I kind of liked the feeling.

"Not fucking loving that someone hurt you," he said with a lot of feeling behind it.

That was nice as well. "Okay, then. Get licking."

His eyes flashed red and he leaned in.

"Wait." I shoved at his forehead. "Do hounds like the taste of blood? You're not gonna get like bloodlust or something and eat me?"

He drew in a ragged breath. "No, I'm not going to eat you, not yet, and never in the way you mean. As for blood, I don't mind it, and yours is...delicious."

He'd said a whole lot of words, and it was like my brain had scrambled them all in my head. He lapped at my inner thigh and I burst out laughing. "*Oh god*, that tickles."

His massive hands banded my thighs, holding me still, then he licked some more, his wide, flat tongue rasping over every scratch and graze. I dug my fingers deeper into his hair, and as I watched him, the tickles quieted and something else started.

My belly was flippy and warm, and my limbs felt loose, and yeah, with every swipe of his tongue, my body heated more.

My mind began to clear as well.

I had the sudden urge to fist his thick hair more firmly and drag that tongue higher, to the part of me that was starting to throb, that was growing wet.

Thank god, I was standing under the water. As long as he didn't look *there*, maybe he wouldn't notice. He licked one of the deeper scratches and his lips sealed around it, sucking gently. It caused a deep pull in my lower belly and shot sparks down between my thighs.

Nose to my thigh, his wide, tattooed back expanded on a deep breath—

His eyes sliced up to me.

Oh hell. That look had the power to make me throw all common sense out the window. His eyes weren't red, they were bright gold and glowing. I'd never seen them like that, not ever. He sucked on my tender skin one more time, then he straightened a bit and pressed his face to my lower belly, drawing in another deep breath before letting it out on a growl.

"Dove," he said with a voice that sounded like someone had taken sandpaper to his vocal cords.

"Um..."

Slowly, he rose to his feet, and the hair on his monster chest brushed the very tips of my nipples. He was breathing hard when he loomed over me, with a look on his face that held the kind of pure unrestrained hunger that actually made my knees feel weak.

My hand had slipped from his hair to his shoulder, and I could have pushed him back as he leaned in. I should have, but I didn't. I blamed it on the poison, even though it was quickly leaving my system thanks to Warrick's...tongue.

I also could have told him no when he closed the gap between us, but I didn't do that either. His hands slid up to either side of my neck, thumbs brushing my jaw, and his eyes locked with mine before our lips touched. That's all, just lingering there waiting, waiting for me to do just that, to push him back. To tell him no. Again, I didn't, because I had thought about this, dreamed about it, fantasized about it more times than I would ever admit to anyone.

He huffed out a breath through his nose, and his fingers slid into my hair. He tilted my head back, gaze searching mine, then he said something I didn't understand. It was deep and low and in that same coarse language, more a series of harsh sounds than actual words, then he closed the gap with a snarl and *took* my mouth.

He kissed me like I knew he would if I'd ever let him. Like a warrior beast, a conqueror, like the alpha he was. His lips parted, his mouth opening wide, forcing mine to do the same, and his tongue swept deep, consuming me, putting every bit of pent-up lust into it.

It was the best kiss I had ever experienced, and I knew without doubt there would be no topping it. I didn't know it was possible to kiss like this.

His other arm hooked around my waist, and he hauled me off my feet, pressing me into the cool tile of the shower. My legs lifted instantly, scratches forgotten, and banded around his waist like they had a mind of their own.

His cock was *right there*, hard and hot. Huge. If I shifted a little to the right, he could thrust right into me—

Someone banged on the door to Warrick's quarters.

It was like a bucket of cold water being tossed in my face. I froze.

They knocked again with more force, and on the bathroom door this time.

"Fuck off," Warrick said.

I shoved at his shoulder, and his gaze sliced back to mine. The muscle in his jaw jumped, not missing my retreat, and he lowered me carefully to my feet but didn't release me or take a step back.

"Axton's back," Jagger called.

Now I wasn't being kissed senseless, and blood wasn't rushing through my ears, I had a silent freak-out at what I'd almost done, what I almost begged him to do.

"Who's Axton?" I asked.

"I have to go." He released me and took a step back. And no, there was no missing how much he wanted me. "Get into bed, get some sleep. I'll tell Ren to come wake you when it's time."

Then he climbed out of the shower and quickly dried himself off. I should have looked away, but I couldn't make myself do it. I was still blaming the poison from that asshole's scratches, even though it had completely gone thanks to Warrick's...help. He reached for the door—

"Warrick."

He stopped and turned back.

I almost asked him when he'd be back but stopped myself. Instead, I stupidly said, "Thanks."

His lips quirked up on one side. "Any time, dove."

He opened the door, and I realized how that sounded, like I was thanking him for kissing me. "I meant for licking me, not kissing me."

Jagger laughed in the other room and I flushed hot.

They left, and I dragged my tired, weirdly loose-limbed body out of the shower, and ignoring the *humm* of arousal still pulsing through my body, tugged on a shirt and climbed into Warrick's massive bed. This also wasn't a good idea, but I'd made a deal and I was too tired to find somewhere else to sleep.

A moment later, I was out.

CHAPTER 10

Willow

I YAWNED as I walked back into the clubhouse, Ren alert at my side after insisting on accompanying me. He'd stuck close most of the day. Thankfully, the perimeter walk and spell casting had gone without incident this time. No sign of the creep from earlier either.

I was tired but well fed since Warrick had sent a mountain of food to his room for me after he'd been called away by Jag. After he'd kissed me...

Yeah, best you don't think about that.

"Where're you bunking?" I asked Ren.

"They gave me my own room. Better than I expected, honestly."

"What did you tell your folks?" Ren lived in a small self-contained apartment in the basement of the funeral home where he worked with his parents. His parents lived in a house down the street.

"That I was staying with friends," he said. "You know them, they never ask too many questions."

I gave him a squeeze. "And you're sure you're cool to stay on here when I leave tomorrow?" I wanted to make sure he was really, truly okay and not just trying to prove something to me. "You don't have to."

He slid his hands into his jean pockets. "Believe it or not, I kind of like it here. I've only had a couple of lessons, but I leaned more in those few hours than all the other classes I've been taking combined."

"I'm glad you're getting something out of it, more than just the black eyes." I looked pointedly at his new shiner.

"It's nothing. Truly, I'm good. More than good." He smiled, and I could tell he meant it. "And Warrick told me he had you covered. My instincts tell me I can trust him to take care of you."

There was no missing the relief he felt about that.

My poor fox. I hated how much anxiety this whole situation had been causing him, and how it had messed with us and our friendship. I slung an arm around his waist and gave him a side hug. "We're gonna get through this, you know that, don't you? I'll be back at the shop, and you'll be back to working your way through Roxburgh's female population with gusto in no time."

He laughed, and it was genuine and so achingly familiar that it took me back to a time before the trials, before the fighting and the fear.

I hooked my arm through his. It was the middle of the night, but I was still surprised by how quiet the clubhouse was when we walked through the main room.

The quiet ended though as we headed down the stairs to the underground den.

A cheer echoed from somewhere deep in the caves, muffled and distant, but I knew where it was coming from almost immediately. The fighting pit.

The sound that reached us next had me pausing. Raw rage was

the only way to describe it, the kind of brutality that spelled only one thing—death.

I jumped into action, rushing toward it.

"What the hell was that?" Ren said, jogging beside me.

"It's coming from their fighting chamber. Someone's getting their ass handed to them." A weird feeling shifted through my belly. I didn't know what it was, only that a sense of urgency had surged through me, making me rush toward it. That terrifying sound was drawing me in a way I didn't understand.

I'd found the fighting pit once before in this maze of tunnels, but I'd still have trouble finding it again if it wasn't for the noise leading me there.

We rounded a bend and then turned right into a wide opening that led into a huge cavern. It was big enough that it could fit all the hounds and then some.

I knew from before what I'd find: a pit, several yards across, dug out in the middle of the floor, the pit walls blackened and charred. Hounds surrounded it now, their calls for blood lifting goose bumps across my skin and raising the hair on the back of my neck.

Ren stayed close to me as we pushed our way up beside Lothar and Jagger. Lothar saw me first and instantly stepped back so I could see what was going on, unmissable pride on his slightly terrifying face.

I looked down and stopped cold.

Standing in the pit in only a pair of bloodstained jeans was Warrick, and across from him was the guy who had attacked me. Axton, I assumed. The other male's face had taken a beating, but he hadn't gone down yet.

"What's going on here?" I yelled so Jagger could hear me.

"Axton attacked the alpha's female and instead of begging for his life he chose to challenge War for you and his position in the pack."

Lothar sneered. "Dumb fuck. He's always wanted what War has. This was a long time coming."

I'd seen Warrick fight a three-headed beast once, after it escaped Hell, but he'd been in his hellhound form then. I'd never seen him fight like this. I couldn't take my eyes off him as he stood there, steady, unmoving, barely a scratch on him as the other male cursed him out, posturing and feigning lunge after lunge.

Still, Warrick didn't move, didn't expend energy he didn't need to, and waited.

Finally, Axton rushed him, and Warrick stepped aside, delivering a devastating blow to the other male's kidney. He went down and Warrick advanced, fisted his hair, and dragged him to the edge of the pit, smashing his face into the charred packed earth wall. Axton dropped to his hands, and Warrick yanked his head back again.

The bravado had dropped from the prone male's face, and he shook his head. "No...please, alpha..."

Lothar growled under his breath. "Fucking coward."

"I'll leave...I'll never come back," he said, begging for his life.

Warrick looked into his eyes. "You attacked my female, you made her bleed, and then you dared to challenge me. The former alone is enough for me to put you to death, the latter you walked into willingly, knowing exactly what the consequences of defeat were."

"No...please..."

Warrick twisted his head with fierce brutality, snapping the hellhound's neck. Then he yanked a wicked-looking knife from his boot and hacked it off.

"Jesus," I said, watching in horror.

"If he doesn't take his head, he could survive. We heal from most injuries," Jagger said.

Then Warrick shoved the huge knife back in its sheath at his hip and strode to the edge of the pit. The hounds gathered around it, lifted their hands, palms up, and flames appeared, dancing across their skin, licking over their thick fingers.

I had no idea they could do that.

Warrick shook his head.

Silence filled the room.

I took in the faces of Warrick's brothers, their gazes lowering as they curled their fingers into fists, extinguishing their fire. "What's going on?"

"Burning him would send his soul back to Hell. Leaving his body to rot means his soul will be in eternal limbo."

Warrick meant business. You challenge him, and he will destroy you in every possible way. Why was I finding it hard to breathe all of a sudden?

Warrick looked at the males surrounding him, meeting their eyes, one by one. His chest heaved with his rage, his face contorted with the same. He was covered in blood, dominance rolling off him, saturating the room. "You lay your hands on my female, you dare touch what's mine, I will fucking end you. You challenge me for head of this pack, you enter the pit prepared to fight to the death. You'll get no mercy here."

Growls and grunts of approval echoed around them.

Then his eyes found me, and he drew in a ragged breath before moving my way.

Gripping the edge of the pit, he jumped out, grabbed my hand, and led me out after him.

My first instinct was to pull away, but that would be the absolute worst thing I could do in that moment. His heavy handedness may drive me nuts, but after that, I'd be humiliating him in front of his brothers, and even I wasn't that much of a bitch.

I glanced at him and bit my lip. My heart was beating too fast and my mouth was dry. "Did you really just sentence your brother to eternal limbo?" I asked.

"Yes," Warrick said. "And he ceased being my brother the moment he dared to lay hands on you."

I said no more as tingles shot up my arm from where his hand engulfed mine, hot and rough and covered in blood.

I sensed it probably wasn't the time for any kind of conversation about what he'd said, and where we stood, and why that declaration he just made in front of everyone was kind of...well, it was nuts.

Not after he just killed someone, brutally, in part for hurting me. So I shut my damned mouth and let him drag me back to his room.

I woke in Warrick's bed, the domineering male himself behind me, the intense heat of his body soaking right into my bones. We'd come in here last night, and he'd ordered me to get into bed. Then he'd walked into the bathroom and slammed the door. I'd still been standing by the bed, unsure of what to do, when he walked out, freshly showered and in only a towel.

His mood had still been volatile, but I knew he wouldn't hurt me, not that I needed the reassurance, but my blade had confirmed it. So when he lifted me, put me in the bed, and climbed in with me, I didn't fight him on it.

I had expected him to make some move, though. He hadn't. No, he'd wrapped his arm around my waist, hauled me in close, and gone to sleep. And again, I'd let him do it because, yeah, I'd just watched him kill someone then threaten to do the same to anyone else who hurt me.

The "don't fuck with me tonight, Willow," vibes had been intense, to say the least, and for once, I'd heeded them.

But now it was morning and I needed to do one more walk of the perimeter. Then I was going home to check on my family. I didn't like being away from them for too long, especially with Rose as unwell as she was.

Carefully, I wriggled out from under Warrick's arm, grabbed my bag, and hit the bathroom. I dragged off the shirt I'd slept in and pulled up short when I got a look at myself in the mirror. I was bruised, the discoloration at my wrists and throat now darker, but the claw marks on my thighs had healed pretty well thanks to Warrick and his magic tongue. A zap of electricity forked through my lower belly, and I traced one of the faded red marks with my finger. They'd been deep gouges last night.

I glanced at the shower. I'd almost given in to him.

It was getting harder to resist, and considering what happened last night, that shouldn't be the case. Sadly, seeing Warrick shirt-less and covered in blood was not as unappealing a sight as it should be.

I wasn't sure what kind of person that made me. Well, okay, probably just your typical Thornheart female. Another in a long line of women making terrible choices when it came to guys. But I didn't plan on looking too closely at that. As long as I stayed away from hellhound poison in the future, there shouldn't be any more reason for us to be naked in the shower with his mouth basically between my legs, or anywhere else for that matter.

Heat rushed through me.

Yep, that was my cue to get the hell out of here. I tugged on fresh jeans and was doing up my bra when Warrick walked in. He paused at the door as his gaze made a slow meandering tour of my body before locking with mine. Heat. So much heat in their depths. My reaction to that look was swift, tingles dancing over me. I ignored that as well.

"Do you mind? I'm getting dressed."

"I saw you naked yesterday, twice."

"You don't barge in on someone in the bathroom. What if I was on the toilet?"

He shrugged.

"You have no boundaries, do you?"

He closed in on me and I found myself backed up to the counter. His thickly muscled arms bracketed me and he leaned in. "No, not when it comes to you. They don't exist between a male and his female," he said in a gravelly, sleep-roughened voice.

"I'm not your female."

"Saying it over and over doesn't change facts."

I stared up at him, not sure what to say. "I don't understand you."

"You will, in time."

I studied the harsh lines of his handsome face, so incredibly rough, masculine, not of this world. You couldn't look at Warrick and not see he was more, more of everything. And I was starting to realize he truly meant every word of what he just said. I didn't know what to do with that. "Why did you leave Hell?" I asked, the question out before I knew I was going to ask. I'd wondered often. I mean, I knew some of the reason, but not all of it.

He blinked down at me. I'd surprised him. "Lucifer left," he said.

That was the part I knew. Lucifer enjoyed being above ground, and during one of his visits, his son, Diemos, had used some ancient magic to lock him out, setting off a whole shitty chain of events. "But why did you leave?"

"Diemos is a piece of shit. Lucifer created us, not his son. I didn't owe him my loyalty, and he sure as fuck never tried to earn it."

Diemos was most definitely a piece of shit, but Warrick had lived in Hell most of his life. "Do you miss it? Would you ever go back?"

"I don't miss it. But I'd return if Lucifer asked it of me. My loyalty is first and foremost to my king. My creator. He comes before anyone." His gaze dipped to the new thorny vines decorating my side, and then the tip of one long, thick finger dropped to trace it. Goose bumps lifted all over me. "Why are you out of bed?"

For some reason, I'd imagined him here, always. Still walking these tunnels long after I was gone. The thought of Warrick back in Hell, of never seeing or talking to him ever again—my belly clenched unhappily. "I need to do a final perimeter walk. I want the ward to be as strong as I can make it, then I'm going home to my family."

The muscles in his arms flexed, and those golden eyes were eclipsed by deep red. "You're leaving?"

"Yes. I've done all I can here." And I needed to get back to figuring out my task, and how it involved the souls running free in Roxburgh.

His gaze locked with mine and the muscle in his jaw jumped again.

"Are you angry with me?"

He pushed away, taking a step back, and I instantly felt the loss of that heat, that strength.

"Why would I be angry, dove?" he said, and it sounded like he actually wanted me to come up with an answer.

I didn't, because I didn't want to think about that too closely either. "Why do you call me that?"

He moved back in, so fast it was a blur, and I was bracketed between those strong arms again. And there was no mistaking that he was most definitely angry. No, he was *pissed*. "I call you that because you are small and fragile and I could break you with a mere flick of my wrist."

"Are you trying to scare me, Warrick?"

"Are you scared, dove?"

I'd be an idiot to underestimate this male. Part of him was animal, with animal urges. He'd been created by Lucifer himself. I didn't know how much of him was controlled by the beast, but I was pretty sure it was significant. I also knew he would never hurt me, not physically, anyway.

He leaned in, dragging his nose along my throat, breathing deep. "I can smell your fear like I could smell how wet you were for me yesterday."

"Do you want me to be scared of you?" I asked, ignoring the second part of that sentence and the way my heart was racing again. He was trying to punish me. I'd offended him. I wasn't exactly sure how, but he was lashing out because of it.

"No," he said through gritted teeth. "But you like it, don't you, dove? That fear, it turns you on. You allow yourself to feel it because it makes your heart race and your cunt wet, but you know I would never ever hurt you, so that fear, it's safe." His nostrils flared. "Maybe if you truly were scared, you'd stop running away from me."

I felt like he'd dumped all my darkest secrets at my feet. We stared at each other for long, tense seconds, and the tension between us was so electric, the hair on my arms lifted. Everything he said was true, wasn't it? He'd said out loud the thoughts I'd been too afraid to voice, thoughts that terrified me. "Just so you know, I'll never stop running. But try not to take it personally, I don't plan on stopping for anyone."

"Just so you know, dove, I'll never stop chasing."

My heart was beating funny, and my palms were sweaty. It took everything in me not to look at his mouth. "Look after Ren for me, he's my family. If anything happens to him, it won't just be me who will come after you."

His brow rose.

"He has more than one female completely and utterly in love with him." I'm not sure why I told him that, but I was desperate for a change of conversation. It was true, though. Ren wasn't some player, and he didn't lie to women, he didn't go out trolling to get laid, he was just his sweet, charming self and they fell at his feet like flies.

"Love isn't real, only animal need," Warrick said, gaze flat.

His words shouldn't surprise me, but they still managed to. He really and truly had limited emotions. "Right," I said, even as a weird, tight feeling grew in my chest. Why did that hurt? It shouldn't hurt. I'd already decided I wasn't going there with him. This was a good thing, it saved me from feeling guilty about rejecting him constantly. "Good thing I'm not an animal."

He snarled. "Stop fighting this. Give me what I want, what you want as well."

"I need to go." I shoved at his chest, and he didn't budge. I stared up at him silently, feeling like a lion tamer, afraid to make any sudden moves and risk getting my hand bitten off.

Then finally, after several long tense seconds, he stepped back and watched me broodily as I pulled on a long-sleeved black T-shirt.

"We have a deal," he said into the silence.

"I know."

"Do you?"

"Yes."

"If you break this deal, if you try to complete your task without using me as backup, I won't be happy."

I planted my hands on my hips. "Is that right?"

He flashed his teeth, giving me a terrifying smile as his canines had extended. "Don't test me. You have my number, make sure you fucking use it."

Slinging my bag over my shoulder, I walked out.

And I ignored him as he stood at the door to the clubhouse, watching me while I strengthened the ward, and then as I said goodbye to Ren.

I glanced in the rearview mirror.

He was still watching me as I drove out the gates.

Warrick

As my dove drove away, I growled, spun, and slammed my fist into the wall. Several of my brothers turned to me, then quickly looked away, going back to working on their bikes.

But not Jagger. No, my lieutenant headed my way, and I worked at calming the fuck down. It wasn't easy; the animal in me didn't understand why she kept leaving. Why didn't she feel as I did?

No, that was bullshit. She did feel it, I smelled it on her. I saw the way she looked at me. Her hunger was written all over her beautiful face. But she insisted on fighting it—on refusing me.

Jagger raised a brow at the hole I'd put in the wall. "Willow's left then?"

I grunted.

"What are you going to do, brother?"

I had no fucking clue. She watched me fight for her, kill for her. I proved my strength, showed her that I would protect her. That anyone who hurt her would get no mercy, and still she left me. "Fucked if I know."

"She's your mate, she'll come around. Like Elena did. She fought Dirk, but in the end, he won her over."

I grunted again. Elena was pregnant with Dirk's second pup now. Jag was right, she had fought him at the start, but she'd also given in quickly. They'd met and he'd instantly known Elena was his. Yes, she'd resisted him, but only a few months. My dove had kept me waiting over a year, with no end in sight.

An image of her in the shower, bleeding, bruised, filled my head. Naked and wet and vulnerable. She'd let me kiss her. *Fuck*. That kiss.

I thought letting her believe I was bedding other females would make her jealous, that she'd want to claim me as well, it hadn't worked. The truth was, I hadn't fucked anyone, not since I met her. Now I knew Willow existed, she was all I wanted. My dick didn't get hard for anyone else.

And it was getting more and more difficult to maintain my

control. Hounds fucked, a lot. And the way I wanted her...yeah, I was near losing my damned mind from the need that tormented me whenever she was near.

I glanced at Jag. "Where's her familiar?"

"Lothar's working with him now."

"Any good?"

Jag shrugged a big shoulder. "He's catching on quicker than I expected."

I stared out at the forest surrounding us and frustration slammed through me. "Any sign of Edric?"

"None."

"And Maddox?"

"We had eyes on him this morning. He's deep in the woods. Won't let anyone approach, though, and staying hound."

I nodded. "He needs time to deal with what happened. Have our brothers stay back, but I want a report on him every couple days."

"Done."

We were stretched thin between keeping tabs on Maddox and another team out searching for Edric. Maddox had been easy to find, with the spirit gone, his scent had returned to normal. Edric's scent was altered in a way that messed with our tracking powers. We couldn't see him anymore. It wasn't a feeling any of us liked, not one fucking bit.

I gave Jag a chin lift and headed for the den. I wanted to see for myself how Ren's training was going. Willow could take care of herself. But that wasn't enough for me. And if she kept resisting what was between us and kept me at arm's length, I wanted to make sure someone who knew what they were doing was at her back.

The pup wanted to learn to fight, I was going to make sure he was fucking deadly when he left here.

Willow

Rose was out in the garden when I got home. It was warm today and she was sitting on a wicker chair reading on her phone.

"Hey," she said when I got out of my truck.

I walked over and planted a kiss on the top of her blond head, choosing not to ask her how she was feeling because she'd only lie to me and I could see for myself how she was. Pain lined her delicate features, the kind that was bone deep. Seeing her like this broke me more and more each time. "What are you reading?"

She held up her phone, showing me the Nightscape App. Nightscape was a social media app used by mainly witches and shifters to share photos and other information and was magically hidden from humans. "I've been checking out the posts from everyone getting ready for the ball tonight."

"Already? It's still morning. The peacock parade isn't for hours."

Roe shook her head. "These things take time. What are you wearing tonight? Have you made appointments for your hair and nails?" Her gaze slid over me and she winced. "You look...kind of a mess, Wills."

That's what you got for having barely any sleep. "No way am I going to that shit show."

She bit her lip.

"What?"

"You might have to tell Mom that."

Ah, hell.

"Me and Iris will help, and you know how good Mags is with hair," Roe said, her face lighting up in a way I hadn't seen in a very long time.

She looked so excited by the idea, I didn't have the heart to say no. "Maybe?"

She smiled, her green eyes lighting up even more.

Shit. Just that smile and I was toast.

I left her to her phone and headed inside. Mom was in the kitchen. She was wearing shorts and a floral blouse, and there was already dirt under her nails. Then again, there was always dirt under her nails. Arthur was pouring them both tea. And the invitation to the ball was no longer in the trash but on the counter, right by the hook where I hung my keys.

"Morning, Wills," Mom said. "How did it go?"

"Tea?" Arthur enquired.

"Hey, Mom, and I'm good thanks, Art." I leaned against the doorframe. "I have the soul trapped, and the hound's clubhouse is warded. Unfortunately, there are at least two more souls on the loose."

Art took his usual seat at the kitchen table, and Mom sipped her drink. "You'll get them. I have complete faith in you, sweetheart." Then she eyed me over the rim of her mug before her gaze slid to that damn invitation. "You know you have to go, right?"

"I'd rather not," I said, which was the understatement of the century.

"All the other Keepers will be there. You need to network. Whether you like it or not, you're one of them now. A low profile isn't an option anymore. You'll also be fighting one of them soon. It's in your best interest to go. You need to know who won their first trial, who is failing their tasks, what their strengths and weaknesses are. Some will become allies, some enemies. We need to know who we can trust..."

"Okay, I get it. But I'm not sure how you expect me to find all that out in one evening." Mom was usually Ms. Easygoing. Honestly, I hadn't seen her like this before.

"You won't, obviously, but it's a start. Now we need to get you a dress."

I sighed. "I don't have time to go shopping, I need to open the store today." The store was our main source of income, and I had regular customers who expected us to be open. "Why don't you go ahead and pick something for me." I backed toward the door.

"Don't you dare walk out that door, Willow Juniper Thornheart."

I kept walking, despite her use of my middle name. "I'll be back in plenty of time." Then I bolted out the door and ignored my mother yelling at me to get back in the damned house.

CHAPTER 11

Willow

REBECCA WAS WAITING for me outside The Cauldron. I could see her through the window.

I hadn't seen or talked to her since I'd called her after Jane was killed, after I'd lied to her and told her I'd found no trace of her. I did my best to keep my expression neutral, but there was no controlling the churning in my stomach. I unlocked and opened the door. "Rebecca, hi." I barely got the words out before she collapsed into my arms, her thin frame quaking as huge sobs were wrenched from her.

Putting an arm around her narrow shoulders, I led her into the shop and locked the door after us.

"She's dead," Rebecca cried. "Jane's dead."

Pain for this woman, for her daughter, sliced through me. "I'm so sorry." And I meant that with everything in me. I had no hope of understanding what she was going through, but all the heart-break and horror poured off her. Her aura had been a dull, dense blue when she'd first come here several days ago, showcasing her disapproval of her daughter, and red, for the fear she was feeling. Now it was gray, as though her life, her vitality had been washed away with Jane's passing.

It hurt to look at.

She lifted her head, her eyes bloodshot and puffy, the skin beneath dark. Guilt grabbed me tightly by the throat. The truth, what really happened to Jane, was right there on the tip of my tongue. She'd already believed her daughter was possessed. It wasn't a stretch that she'd believe the rest of it. But telling Rebecca the truth would turn her world upside down—and expose ours.

Her world's already been shattered. The truth could give her some peace.

My phone vibrated in my pocket and I ignored it as I led her to the small kitchen at the back of the shop and sat her down, then put on the kettle. "What happened?" I asked, not wanting to know what gruesome story the human police believed but needing to know it all the same.

Her hands shook, and I took a box of tissues from the cupboard and put them in front of her. She grabbed a wad and blew her nose. "Someone murdered her, Willow. Someone mutilated my girl and left her body in the forest for wild animals to...to...*oh god...*"

I crossed my arms, curling my hands into fists. If this were me, one of my sisters—

The churning in my stomach increased.

Rebecca deserved the truth. "Where was she found?"

"J-just outside of the city...near Marsden."

Marsden was at the opposite side of Roxburgh. As far from the hounds' clubhouse as you could get. "Do the police have any idea what happened?"

She shook her head. "There were no prints, no DNA. Nothing. She must have been, oh god...*so scared*. So very scared." Her thin frame shuddered violently.

I felt sick.

"And there were...there were other bodies. I know you said you found nothing, but anything, no matter how small, might be a help to the police."

Other bodies? What the hell was going on? "I'm sorry, no. I didn't find anything. You said there were others?" I seriously hated myself right then.

My phone buzzed again, and I discreetly checked it in case it was one of my sisters. Several missed calls from Warrick. I ignored this one as well, put my phone on silent, and shoved it back in my pocket.

"They think she was targeted by a...a *serial killer*." She was shaking again, her voice filled with the horror those words conjured. "People...*monsters* like that..." she squeezed her eyes closed, her face bloodless. "They take pleasure in causing pain," she said, her voice growing panicked. "Oh god, how long did he hurt her, how long did he torture her..." She shuddered.

Seeing her like that and keeping my mouth shut, not telling her that Jane had been loved, or whatever the hellhound equivalent was, was so damn hard. Warrick and his brothers may not be capable of love as we know it, but Maddox was out there somewhere, suffering over the loss of his female and pup. He'd cared for her in his own way, deeply; there'd been no missing that.

If Jane were my daughter, I'd want to know that she'd been cared for, that it was a horrible accident, that Jane's death was quick, almost instant. That she wouldn't have suffered with the speed the hounds were capable of. One moment Jane would have been with the male she loved, then nothing.

Rebecca believed her daughter had suffered, had been tortured, terrified.

The truth, as hard as it would be to hear, would bring Rebecca some peace, and I wanted to give that to her so badly. "I can't imagine what you're feeling right now. I'm so sorry," I said again. Useless words, but I felt partly responsible and so incredibly guilty that I was keeping this from her.

"She was pregnant," she said. "She was carrying a baby and didn't even tell me. She hated me that much…"

"No," I said and covered her hand. "I don't believe that, Rebecca. She loved you. I fight with my mom, my sisters, but that doesn't diminish how much I love them. She loved you, she did."

Her eyes locked with mine, filled with utter heartbreak. "Why, Willow, why didn't she tell me? No one's come forward, there's no boyfriend that I know of. Don't they even care? Did some awful man get her pregnant and just leave her to deal with it alone? Maybe whoever she was seeing was the one who hurt her? She kept him hidden from me." She gripped her hair and shook her head. "Why would someone have done that to her? Why? Why did they hurt my baby?"

My resolve began to crack. I gave her hand a gentle squeeze. "She would have told you about the baby, she just didn't get the chance."

Rebecca crumpled and I stayed with her until she'd exhausted herself, then drove her home, feeling like the biggest asshole in existence.

I made her more tea after I helped her inside and put it on the coffee table in front of her. "I'm going to head off now, but if you need anything, please, just let me know."

She grabbed my hand. "You'll come to the funeral, won't you?"

"Are you sure you wouldn't prefer it to just be friends and family?"

"I know you didn't know her, but I don't really have anyone else…and I-I…" Her face dropped, devastation filling her eyes.

"Of course, I'll be there." And now I felt even more of a hypocrite.

She quickly wrote the details on a piece of paper and handed it to me. I shoved it in my pocket, made sure she was all set, and got the hell out of there before I caved and told her everything.

When I walked into our house later that afternoon, I didn't have time to dwell on the hurricane of emotions inside me, because I was swept up in the tornado that was my family.

Iris grabbed my hand, dragged me upstairs, and tossed me into the bathroom, going as far as turning on the shower before she left. "Make it quick," she called through the door.

Still feeling seriously unsettled after my day with Rebecca, I had to force myself to focus on something else. I couldn't go into that ballroom unprepared or off my game. Mom was right, the place was going to be full of sharks looking for easy prey, and I sure as hell wasn't going to swing my ass out for them to take a bite.

By the time I walked out, I'd made good progress at hardening my heart again, back to the way I preferred it these days. I was in my room and had covered the bruise around my neck with foundation so my family couldn't see it, when Mom burst in carrying a garment bag.

"Jesus, Mom, would it hurt you to knock?" I'd had enough people seeing me naked for a good long while. At least I'd put on underwear first, and thankfully, there were only faint red marks where I'd been scratched. If I stood with my legs together, no one should be able to see them. Thank the goddess for dim lighting.

She rolled her eyes and shrugged. "I've seen you naked a million times. Oh, and Rowena called earlier, she wanted to wish you luck for tonight."

Rowena was the head of our coven and Mom's second cousin. She'd been great since I was named Keeper, checking in, but not breathing down my neck, when I'm sure she wanted to. You know, since the entire future of our coven either strengthening our magic or losing everything was down to me.

Stop it. Don't think about that, not tonight.

Hustling to the closet, Mom hung the hanger from the top of the door and dragged down the bag's zipper. Emerald silk tumbled out.

"Where did that come from?"

Mom carefully slid the bag off and ran her hand down the liquid-smooth fabric. "It was Mom's. She looked amazing in green, like you, Wills. You got that gorgeous, wild auburn hair from your gran," she said, telling me something I already knew and loved.

I ran my hand over the fabric as well. It was exquisite. I'd loved color once, bright, fun clothes. I'd worn my hair wild, and always had lots of jewelry. After what happened at the knights' compound, being so close to losing my life, of almost causing the death of people I considered family, I hadn't felt like wearing bright colors anymore. A lot of things had changed for me that day. "Where did Gran wear this?"

"Her engagement party. My father's family had thrown them a lavish ball and everyone who was anyone attended." Mom sighed. "They'd been so in love. I'll have to show you the photos one day."

And then the Thornheart bad luck had kicked in and my grandfather had been run over by a garbage truck when Mom was just five years old. Gran had never remarried. "I'd love to see them...so what's the back of the dress like?" The last people I wanted seeing my scars were the witches in that ballroom.

"The back's not low," she said gently.

She didn't like being reminded of what happened to me a year ago. I tried to avoid ever bringing it up.

"Think of this dress as armor, Wills, when you're in that ballroom tonight. Your gran hated that part of her life growing up, and I know you don't want to do this, but you have just as much right to be there as the rest of them."

I was standing up for my entire coven, and the last thing I

wanted was to let them down. "Wearing this, it'll be like Gran's right there with me."

Mags burst through the door. "Why aren't you dressed? I need time to do your hair. All those uppity socialites will be going to top stylists, I need time to work my magic."

"We won't be long." Mom quickly helped me into the gown, and since the front dipped low, I had to forgo a bra. It was seriously risqué, and totally something I imagined Gran would have worn. Daisy Thornheart had most definitely not been a wallflower.

Mom handed me a pair of gold sandals from my closet. It felt like a million years ago now that I'd bought these. I'd worn them once. The heel was thin and delicate and added a good three inches to my height.

"I'll make you something to eat while Magnolia does your hair," Mom said and bustled out of the room.

"Thanks." I did up the shoes, and Mags had me by the wrist, towing me down the stairs before I'd properly straightened. I winced.

"What?" She frowned and lifted my hand, looking at my bruised skin. "How the hell did you get that?"

"It's nothing you need to worry about."

She scowled.

"Mom will only worry. Go grab my gold cuff bracelet, would you?"

She huffed but did as I said. There was no way I was telling my family what happened last night. They were worried enough already. Mags sucked at keeping secrets but could be bribed with the right inducement.

She rushed back and handed the cuff to me, and I slipped it on before heading downstairs.

"Who did that, Wills?" she asked, her amber eyes huge.

I didn't want her concerned about me. Mags should be enjoying her final year of school and having fun with her friends, not dealing with all of this. "I had a little disagreement with someone, but they're not going to be a problem anymore."

"You mean you..." She dragged her thumb over her throat dramatically.

I forced a laugh. "I didn't kill anyone." No, Warrick did that for me.

"Fine, I'll keep your secret, but it'll cost you," she said and flounced off ahead of me.

I hit the bottom of the stairs, and Iris was there, ushering me to the table. I sat and Mags got started on my hair while Iris and Roe painted my nails. Mom put a sandwich in front of me and Else shuffled over and put a glass of wine beside it.

"Looking good," Else said. "Almost as good as Daisy did when she wore it."

I smiled at her. "You and Gran will always be the great beauties of this family."

She cackled. "Don't you forget it."

Cora was there as well, and she smiled at me. "I hope you don't mind me being here. Else said I could come and see you all dressed up for the ball."

"No, of course not," I said.

Cora was basically one of the family. She and Else had formed a bond almost as soon as she moved in next door.

"I've only ever been to one ball," she said. "Definitely nothing as fancy as the Keeper's ball, with all those important, powerful witches, but it was so fun to get dressed up." Her gaze became distant. "My sweet Emily never got to go to one."

Emily had been Cora's only daughter and Brody's mom. She'd been raising Brody alone before she got sick, and Cora missed her terribly. "I'm sorry, Cora."

"She's never far from my thoughts." She drew in a deep breath and forced a smile. "Ignore me. You never know, you might have a good time."

"Honestly, if I could, I'd trade places with you in a heartbeat," I said, staring longingly at my dinner.

"A lot of people would kill for a chance to be in your position," she admonished. "Make the most of it, my girl."

"Of course. You're right," I said, feeling rather chastised and guilty after what she'd just said about her daughter.

I liked a clear head, especially heading into uncertain situations, but today had seriously been a glass of wine kind of day. Roe, being the caring, considerate one of the family, noticed and lifted the sandwich to my mouth so I could take a bite, followed by a sip of wine. "Bless you," I said.

She grinned, and I grinned back. There was even some color in her cheeks. Seeing her like this, I couldn't help but feel some hope that maybe she might turn a corner.

"So where's Ren?" Mags asked as she twisted a lock of my hair and pinned it back, then grabbed her heated hair curler.

Best to say it quick, like tearing off a bandage. "He's with the hellhounds."

The room stilled.

"What do you mean he's *with the hellhounds*?" Iris said.

"He's fine. He's training with them. He wants to learn to fight and they're the best males to teach him."

"He's fighting them?" Mags shrieked, always the dramatic one, and tugged my hair.

"Bald isn't exactly the look I had in mind for tonight." She quickly eased up. "And you don't need to worry. Lothar, the male in charge of training him, is..." What? What could I say to put my family at ease. "A really good guy, and an excellent fighter. I promise, Ren wants to be there." I hoped that was true, all of it.

"I can't believe he left you," Roe said.

Iris frowned. "Yeah, he was so worried about being here to be your backup, he wouldn't just leave. Maybe they're forcing him to stay. Maybe he told you he wanted to be there, but really..."

"Warrick said he'd help while Ren's training," I told them grudgingly. "That's why Ren was cool with it."

Again, silence filled the room.

Then Iris hooted. "Oh man, I bet you hate that."

Mom smiled. "I think it's wonderful."

"Don't get any ideas," I said to her.

Roe smiled down at my hand as she painted one of my nails but said nothing.

"So what time is he getting here?" Else asked.

"He's not. This is just a ballroom full of witches trying to one-up each other, I don't need backup for that." I winced when Mags started on my hair again.

"It's not just witches. The trials are a big deal, and we have allies from many different walks of life, allies who often get caught up in our drama while we're completing our tasks," Mom said. "Many are invited as a gesture of goodwill. This is exactly the kind of thing you should tell him about. You never know who'll be there."

Nope. That would not be happening. "I'll call him when I leave," I lied.

Else eyed me, a look on her face that said she knew I was full of shit, and Mom beamed like it was the most romantic thing she'd ever heard.

I ignored all of it. After my time at the den, I was in serious need of a little space from the hellhound alpha.

Finally, after a lot more fussing and a mascara wand in the eye, they were done.

"You look hot," Else said.

"Hotter than any of those rich bitches," Mags added.

I grabbed my keys and the gold clutch Mom shoved into my hand after slipping my lipstick and phone inside, and I headed for the door. The invitation sat on top. Good thing, since I had no idea where I was going.

"Watch your back tonight," Mom called after me.

"Give 'em hell," Else yelled.

Hopefully, I wouldn't need to do either of those things, because I had no plans of staying there longer than necessary.

I almost expected to find Warrick waiting for me outside. Thankfully, there was no surly hellhound there when I reached the Morris. I climbed in, started her up, plugged the address into my phone, and headed out.

The drive was uneventful, which was a nice change.

The event was being held at the Grand Valencia. The witches' council had booked out the entire place, so the only humans here were staff. The building was beautiful, built in the 1920s, and had that whole art deco vibe in spades. Lots of glass and gold and gorgeous tile. It also had an upscale hotel and boasted a Michelin star restaurant and two massive ballrooms.

The valet rushed out as I pulled up. When I handed him my keys, he screwed up his nose. "If you scratch her, I'll break your fingers," I said, wiping that look off his face.

Some people didn't appreciate classic beauty.

I glanced up at the massive marble entrance. Warm light spilled out onto the steps, shining through the prisms of crystal dangling from giant chandlers just inside the door. It danced and glinted across the white marble, making it look like everything was under water and adding to the feel of outrageous opulence.

I'd never felt more out of place in my entire life.

Straightening my spine, I carefully gathered up my dress, trying not to crease the silk, and headed up the stairs. Several people stopped midconversation, turning my way. An older witch I'd never met went as far as elbowing her companion so they wouldn't miss the show. My family avoided these people, these kinds of events, and it was clear a few people had obviously assumed I wouldn't attend.

Don't let them see how nervous you are.

Ignoring the wild fluttering in my belly and the tingle of unease down my spine, I walked through the wide doors, across the massive foyer, and through to the ballroom doors. An attendant held out his hand for my invitation.

"Willow Thornheart, of coven Thornheart," he called, reading it out loud.

The room seemed to still, drinks pausing on the way to painted lips, conversations stopping, all so they could look my way.

I wasn't fond of attention, especially not from these people, but I had to play the part or get eaten alive. The Thornheart name was old, and because of that, well known. My great grandparents had enjoyed the finer things and had moved in these social circles, thus the reason Gran had needed a dress like this for her engagement party.

But my grandmother had defied them in the first place by marrying my grandfather, and refusing the suitor they'd chosen for her. And when my grandfather hadn't bent to their will like they'd expected, my grandparents had been cut off. Even after my grandfather died, they'd pretended Mom and Gran didn't exist.

Gran had left this life behind and she'd had no interest in coming back to it.

The fact we were as powerful as we were but chose to stick to ourselves, to *snub* them, still pissed a lot of them off.

I carried on, not allowing my step to falter, and took the stairs down to the main floor, focusing every bit of my energy on not tripping and falling on my face.

I reached the floor and, ignoring the overt stares and whispers, headed to a table laden with champagne flutes.

Someone coughed as I passed, and I was pretty sure they said whore. Nice.

Some of the witches here had decided my family thought we were better than everyone else, unable to comprehend that we didn't give that first fuck about status and money. Now they were desperate for a chance to knock us...me, down a peg. That wasn't happening tonight, not if I could help it.

I grabbed a glass of champagne and took a deep sip when what I really wanted was to down it and grab another. I hadn't mixed with any of these people in a very long time, not since Mag's moon goddess initiation two years ago, where all the young witches were pranced around and forced to pretend to "make friends," but really it was a superficial load of crap, like tonight, where parents tried to find their sons and daughters influential connections.

Mags had insisted on doing it with her friends, but we'd been given the same treatment as tonight. Mags had felt it and withdrawn, hadn't talked to anyone during the event, and it had solidified the we-think-we're-too-good-for-you narrative in everyone's eyes.

"Willow, is that you?"

A beautiful Japanese woman walked up to me, her hands held out, and smiled warmly. I smiled back at the first welcome face I'd seen here. "Asuka."

"It's so good to see you." She pulled me in for a hug and I squeezed her back, probably a little more desperately than I would have liked, but I was so glad she was here.

Asuka's family had moved to Roxburgh when she was fifteen. We'd been friends until they moved to the other side of the city and she'd changed high schools after her mother had taken her place on the witch's council. Her mahogany gaze took me in. "You look stunning. How have you been?"

"You look like you should be on a runway. And same old, you know, except for the part that I'm here." Asuka had always known this was her destiny, and she'd taken the honor very seriously, training for the trials to come all her life.

I, on the other hand, had partied and goofed off because I could.

She grinned. "I've missed you."

"I never did forgive your folks for taking you away. So I hear congratulations are in order. Who's the lucky guy?" I'd heard through the grapevine she'd gotten engaged, but since I didn't run in her circles these days, I was short on facts.

Her smile slipped. "No congratulations needed, not anymore, anyway."

"I'm sorry, I didn't realize…"

"It's fine, really. He's a good man but was more my parents' choice than mine."

Some families were all about finding ways to gain more power, like my great grandparents had been, and an advantageous marriage to a Keeper was one way to do that. I personally thought it was fucked up, but what did I know?

"So how did your final trial go?" she asked, sympathy and curiosity in her eyes that kind of rubbed me the wrong way. I mean, it was to be expected, she knew as well as everyone else here that I was runner-up in this situation.

"I'm actually still in the middle of my task. You?"

"You haven't completed your task?" Her head tilted to the side. "So you're a bit behind everyone else then."

Awesome. I didn't let the stress that shot through me show on my face, at least I hoped I didn't. "Mine's a bit of a mess, honestly. I've…"

"You know we can't talk about that stuff with each other," she said, her gaze moving to something over my shoulder. "My father's waving at me to join him." She sighed. "We'll catch up later?"

I smiled, trying not to let my inner freak-out show on my face at what she'd just said, and hugged her back. "I'd like that."

"And don't worry, whatever it is, you've got this," she said and strode away.

I finished my champagne. *Screw it.* And grabbed another. This was going to be a four drinks kind of night, maybe five. I glanced around the room, feeling like a spare prick at a wedding. Else was right, there weren't just witches here, there were shifters of many and varying breeds, and a couple of vamps…and a dhampir.

Ronan stood on the other side of the room. Ronan was my

friend Luna's brother, and Luna was mated to Gunner, one of the knights. The dhampir was talking to several other males. Someone stepped back—

Glowing golden eyes hit me from across the room.

Warrick.

He took a step forward and my heart smacked against my ribs.

God, he looked gorgeous. His hair was knotted at his nape, and he was dressed in a black-on-black suit that was beautifully tailored and sculpted to his wide shoulders and thickly muscled thighs. The shirt under his jacket was undone at his throat, revealing his tan, muscled neck.

It was the most civilized I'd ever seen him dressed, and still it did nothing to smooth out those incredibly rough edges. There was no mistaking him for anything other than what he was.

Rebecca's words from earlier entered my head. There had been other bodies buried where Jane had been found. A lot of them. I didn't truly know what Warrick was capable of. I didn't know him, not really. But I did know he would tear the head off one of his own brothers without a second thought if he believed they'd crossed him or tried to take what he considered his. Had the hounds put those other bodies there? Were they responsible for them? Was Warrick?

My gaze shifted back to his and my belly swirled.

Shit.

CHAPTER 12

Willow

"Willow," a male called behind me.

Tearing my eyes from Warrick, I turned.

Tall, broad, and still tanned from holidaying on his boat, stood Clayton Whitlock. He was even more handsome now than he'd been in high school. I'd thought myself in love with him back then. He, on the other hand, had suffered from no such delusions.

Now he was the witch all the teens swooned over. Including my baby sister. And he worked hard to keep his followers happy. Mags had shown me the picture he posted earlier tonight, one of those bare-chested, only-in-a-towel shots taken in front of a bathroom mirror. Under it had been the hashtags #goingtotheball #princecharming #lookingformycindy.

He presented himself as the rich playboy of the witch world. Regularly posting shots of himself by the pool, at parties, or behind a big desk like an important businessman, when everyone knew it was his mother who had taken over the businesses when her husband, Clayton's father, died.

His smile was wide and genuine as he closed the space between us and took me off guard, giving me a quick hug. I returned it, pulling away would only draw more attention. I'd wanted to hate him all those years ago, I really had, but I could never quite manage it. I'd actively avoided him, though, for a lot of years, but there was something about him that had always been so...charming. Something he'd seriously tapped into as he'd gotten older.

"God, Wills, you're a sight for sore eyes," Clay said, still holding my shoulders, and beamed. The guy had a great smile, and he knew how to use it. His gaze drifted over me. "You look amazing."

"Thanks." Warmth brushed over my skin like invisible hands, making me shiver, and it had nothing to do with Clayton. I was being watched, and I knew exactly who by.

That smile was still on his face when he tilted his head to the side. "You never returned my calls."

"No," I said, smiling right back, and offered no more.

His hands slipped from my shoulders, and he slid them into his pockets. "Okay, I see I have my work cut out for me here."

As nice a guy as he was back then, and probably was now, we weren't friends. We didn't socialize or hang out or even text every once in a while to catch up. If he was calling, he wanted something, and whatever he was selling, I wasn't in the market for. "What is it you want, Clayton?"

He huffed out a laugh. "Still the straight shooter."

I didn't answer. I didn't need to.

The smile lost some of its polish. "I ah...have something I'd like to discuss with you."

"I worked that part out for myself, Clay."

He glanced around us. "This isn't really the place. Will you come to the house tomorrow?"

"What's this about?"

He looked up, and I followed his gaze. An older woman stood on the balcony edging the ballroom, and she was watching us. His mother, the formidable Olive Whitlock. He looked back down at me. "It's a…delicate matter."

I had no idea what this could be about. I didn't even know the guy anymore, not really. But finding out could be in my best interest, especially if his mother was involved. "Fine, text me your address and I'll try. But I can't guarantee anything."

His relief was obvious. "I'd appreciate that."

I glanced over his shoulder and Warrick was still on the other side of the room, his gaze was bright and locked on me. A gorgeous woman in a skintight silk gown stood with her friend, an equally gorgeous woman in an equally gorgeous dress, and they were looking at him like he was god's gift to womenkind—he was ignoring them completely.

I couldn't really blame them, because in that suit, he kind of was.

Had I really just thought that? I hadn't eaten much that day and the second glass of champagne was obviously going to my head. Or was it my third?

Clay hung around for a while, attempting to make small talk before he finally excused himself. I sipped my drink and looked around for food, and instead, spotted Sapphire Eldridge. She sat at the far end of the room, surrounded by a gaggle of witches and several familiars. Sapphire was a *very* distant cousin of Gran and Else, on the other side of the family, so not a Thornheart, but she acted like we were an extension of her coven and as such liked to keep tabs on us, much to Mom and Else's annoyance.

They were not fans of the Eldridges.

As soon as her eyes caught mine, she waved me over with an impatient hand.

Great. Just great.

Plastering a smile on my face, I went to join her, even though it was the last thing I wanted to do. She shooed everyone away when I reached her. The woman was formidable, a seriously powerful witch, and anyone who purposely pissed her off was an idiot, plain and simple.

"Sit, girl," she said to me, and her familiar, a diminutive, surly, dark-haired woman, a bird shifter of some kind, dragged a chair over for me.

I sat.

"Your tasks, your trials," she said, not beating around the bush. "I've heard nothing of substance about you, and I'm not happy about it. I like to know what's going on. A witch was killed just this week during her trial, and I did wonder if it might be you." She pursed her lips. "But here you are."

I wasn't sure how she wanted me to answer that. "Nope, not dead."

She scowled. "People know of our connection—it's distant, yes, but it's still a connection. If you fail in this, if you shame me, I will not be pleased, not at all."

I took another sip of my drink. "I'll be pretty upset myself."

"Don't be flippant, girl. I wasn't pleased when you were chosen as Keeper, but here we are. Nothing to be done now." Her creep of a son, I wasn't sure which one since he was an identical twin, moved closer. He'd been watching from the sidelines up until that moment, but obviously didn't like being left out. Which meant this was probably Isaac. The guy's picture was in the dictionary under mama's boy.

He was good-looking, a skilled witch, the more powerful out of him and his brother. He wasn't the Keeper for his coven, though; his older brother by seven minutes, Elmer, had taken that honor.

"Willow," he said, dipping his head, a smile spreading across his face. "You look lovely."

"Thanks, Isaac."

His lips curled up. "I'm flattered you know the difference

between me and my brother. Not many do. I hear you're still on your second task? You won your first trial, though, yes?"

Asuka obviously hadn't wasted time spreading that around the ballroom. No, we didn't spend time together anymore, but I still considered her a friend. I could admit her sharing what I told her, here of all places, stung.

"Yes, and yes," I said, not elaborating. "That's a nasty-looking cut on your cheek, Isaac. Run into some trouble during yours? Oh sorry, I forgot, Elmer's your Keeper, yes?" I should shut up, especially since it seemed I was on the back foot in a lot of ways, but the champagne had loosened my tongue.

"Elmer's doing exceedingly well," Sapphire said, then her calculating gaze slid between me and her son. "Are you married?"

"No." I didn't like that look on her face. "And I have no intention of ever entering the state."

"You don't believe in love?"

"Not particularly." That wasn't exactly true, more I wanted to avoid it at all costs.

"Good, because marriage has nothing to do with it..." I opened my mouth and she shut me up with a look. "It's a way to strengthen, to grow, to ensure one's power is all it can be," she said, and a small smile curled her lips.

It was the first time I'd seen the old bat smile. It was terrifying. I had no idea how this woman could be related to us. She was rotten to the core. "I'll keep that in mind," I said, and somehow I stopped myself from saying a cleansing spell to flush away her bad energy.

I needed another drink, and when a waiter offered one to me, I took it and downed almost half.

"You have that wonderful cemetery, don't you, Willow?" she said, and her gaze slid to her son again, conveying something that had him straightening from his slouch against the wall. "And as unsuited to this role as I think you are, I have eyes and ears all over this city and know what a powerful witch you are, Willow

Thornheart. It obviously comes from our side of the family. It's only fair and right that we benefit from that as well."

It was my turn to straighten. "Now hang on a minute..."

She smacked her walking cane on the floor, silencing me. "I'm proposing a union between you and Isaac. I'll speak to your mother. She always was a meek, weak-willed woman, I don't see her refusing."

Had she really just said that to my face, right here in the middle of this ballroom? "Thanks for the offer," I said through gritted teeth, "but I'll have to decline."

Her expression didn't change. "I'll give you some time, but this will happen. Once I make my mind up about something, I can't be deterred." Her gaze sliced to Isaac. "Dance with the girl."

He immediately closed the space between us and held out his hand. I wanted to slap it away. I didn't want to give the terrifying old crone the satisfaction of doing what she'd demanded, and I also didn't dance, but she was right, nothing deterred her from going after what she wanted, or the lengths she had been known to go to in order to get it.

I needed to cut this line of thinking off at the pass. I didn't trust her not to use magic to get what she wanted. One minute I'd be living my life, the next I'd be married to her wet mop of a son with no idea how it happened.

I had hex protection, Mom had tattooed the spell on our hips when we were infants, but one could never be too careful. There were ways around it if someone was motivated enough and willing to dabble in dark magic to get it.

Downing the last of my drink, I took his hand and let my cousin lead me to the dance floor. Yes, he was a very distant cousin, but still—gross. He pulled me into his arms and started to move.

I stepped on his foot. Hard. "Sorry. Two left feet."

He smiled, or more grimaced.

"So, did you know she'd planned that?" I asked him.

He opened his mouth to lie, then shut it and nodded. "When you became Keeper, she deemed you worthy. Not worthy enough for Elmer mind you, she has loftier goals for him, but she thinks we'd rub along nicely."

I couldn't decide if he was being sarcastic or he was just that much of a dick. "And how do you feel about being married off to some random witch, your cousin, no less?" He thankfully kept the dancing uncomplicated, but as we turned, Warrick came into view across the room. His gaze wasn't bright anymore, it was dark and seriously unhappy.

Isaac's blue gaze moved over my face. "I agree with Mother, it would be advantageous for both of us. Alone we are powerful, but together we'd be unstoppable. I'm more powerful than Elmer, and everyone knows it. I should be Keeper. But this way if he fails, we still gain power even if it's not through my brother."

I shouldn't be surprised by this, some of the covens were on a never-ending search to increase their power, but I still had trouble believing what I was hearing. "You're willing to marry me, even though you don't really know me, for more power?"

His gaze dipped, moving over my body, and I didn't like the look in his eyes when they came back to mine. "You're a beautiful woman, Willow. Do you find me handsome?"

"You're all right," I said, because this guy was obviously used to being flattered and I wasn't going to boost his already massive ego.

He chuckled, knowing exactly how good-looking he was. Oh yes, he knew all right, and he thought I should be flattered by his attention, that maybe I was and playing coy. I'd never played coy in my entire life.

"No, we wouldn't be a love match, but I'd want a true marriage, a partnership. And that includes sharing a bed."

This asshole was beyond cocky. "So you'd be a faithful husband?"

"Sure, why not? If that's what you want." He smirked. He was lying through his teeth. "But we can revisit the topic in a few years. I can't imagine getting bored of fucking you, but who knows how either one of us will feel in the future."

"So true." I shouldn't be letting him think I was even entertaining this whacko idea. I should be dissuading him, but he was just so goddamn arrogant I couldn't help myself. "So you guys are rich, right?"

His grin widened; he thought he had me. "Very."

"I want kids."

"Me too. Genetically our children would be attractive and extremely powerful."

I felt someone move up behind me, someone big enough to cast a dark shadow over us. The shadow moved over Isaac's face, like the moon being eclipsed by something bigger and darker.

That actually took longer than I thought.

Isaac frowned and stared over my shoulder.

"This is my friend Warrick," I said without looking back. I didn't need to. "He's alpha of the hellhounds. He also has a bad habit of killing anyone who touches me."

Isaac released me instantly and stepped back. Warrick crowded my back, his thick arm circling my waist, and he tugged me against his front. "Fuck off," he said to Isaac.

Isaac's eyes widened, then he looked down at me. "Willow?"

"Best you do as he says, he's kind of unpredictable," I said and watched as Isaac's face turned red with rage. If I was trying not to piss off Sapphire, I'd gone the wrong way about it. That'll teach me to drink copious amounts of champagne at one of these things.

Judging by the look on Isaac's face, he wasn't giving up yet, though. And he proved it by opening his mouth. "Now hang on a minute, we'd be a good match..."

"You're kidding, right?"

His gaze flicked to Warrick again, then back to me. "You need to think..."

"I don't need to do a damned thing. I'll never marry, and if I did, it wouldn't be to you." Warrick's arm tightened around me and he growled a warning. It lifted happy little tingles all over my skin. Nope, I really shouldn't have had that third glass of champagne, or was it four? I couldn't remember now.

"You're making a mistake, a big one," Isaac said and strode off.

Warrick's beard brushed my neck, and then his lips were against my skin. "Watching you with that fucking cockroach has made me very unhappy."

"How unhappy?"

"I crave the scent of his blood and the sound of his screams while I tear him to pieces, one limb at a time."

His deep voice rumbled right through me and I shivered. I should push him away, but I couldn't make myself do it. "That's seriously unhappy."

"Yeah."

"He wants to marry me," I heard myself say. "Their family and mine are both powerful. A mutually beneficial union, apparently. They want access to what we have." Everyone wanted our cemetery. It was coveted by nearly everyone in this room.

His tongue flicked my earlobe, and I shivered. "I'll kill him first."

"You're serious, aren't you?"

"Yes." He breathed deep, scenting me. "Come home with me. Let me pleasure you, dove. I'll show you why I'm the male you should choose."

I wanted to say yes—badly. But even seriously tipsy I knew I shouldn't. "That's not a good idea."

"No, it's an excellent one." One of his hands was curled around my side, the other resting on the curve of my belly. His fingers flexed against the delicate silk. "Just once, that's all I need to have you craving only me for the rest of time."

Warrick was immortal; he had the rest of time. I, on the other hand, did not. I laughed, even as heat curled under his wide palm. "That's pretty arrogant."

"I have reason to be."

"You're that sure of yourself?" I needed to stop talking, to stop thinking about what he was offering.

"Yes." His lips brushed my jaw. "I told you before, we worship our females."

A scream echoed through the ballroom.

And it was followed by a howl so mournful, so terrible, it lifted the hair on the back of my neck.

CHAPTER 13

Willow

WARRICK STRODE TOWARD THE EXIT, and I rushed after him.

Someone screamed again, outside this time, and we ran, tearing out to the front of the hotel—

Blood.

Oh goddess. So much blood.

Body parts, gore, scattered around the valet drop-off area.

I spun to Warrick. "Edric?"

The alpha's jaw could have been carved in stone as he dipped his chin. "He took out a family of owl shifters last night, two of them just kids."

"What?" I felt sick. "Why didn't you tell me?"

Fire danced in his eyes. "You ignored my calls."

That's exactly what I'd done. *Idiot.* "Right...sorry. So why did Edric come here. of all places?"

"Because I'm guessing there's enough of him still in there, still fighting it," Warrick said and yanked off his jacket. "He wants me to stop him."

In seconds, Warrick was naked, uncaring of our audience, shadows and moonlight highlighting every muscle on his warrior's body. Without another word, he shifted, exploding into a massive hellhound, red eyes, maw big enough to bite me in half, and thick shaggy black fur.

"Warrick..."

He took off across the beautifully manicured garden, through the golf course, and into Wolf Hill Woods, the north end of the Roxburgh State Forest that bordered the grounds.

Shit. Kicking off my shoes, I ran after him, ignoring Clayton calling my name.

As soon as I burst through the tree line and into the woods, the blade strapped to my thigh under my dress, heated, vibrating almost violently. Danger, this area was full of it. Yanking up my dress, I grabbed my blade and followed the howls echoing from deep in the forest.

For generations, this area had been controlled by wolf shifters. Then a few years back, when the last pack to reside here thinned, their numbers dropping far too low to defend it, demons overran the place, attacking relentlessly until the wolves finally left. The knights of Hell had always left this place to the wolves, since they didn't want anyone encroaching on their territory, and with all the demon activity in the city for the knights to contend with, especially in recent times, this place had been seriously neglected. Thankfully, I'd heard rumblings of a new pack slowly reclaiming territory. I had yet to meet any of them, but I'd seen smoke coming from high on the craggy hill, the hill that gave this place its name.

There were no wolves around now, though.

I searched my surroundings as ice slid down my spine, growing more intense with every step I took.

There was evil here, only a short distance from hundreds of

people, from a fancy hotel. I'd been around a lot of demons—sick, twisted individuals—but what I felt here was on another level. These were some seriously dark beings.

My blade grew hotter in my hand.

Something was about to happen. I turned in a slow circle.

A shriek so high it made my ears ring filled the woods a moment before a demon ran at me. My adrenaline spiked and my muscles tensed. I lifted my hands, manipulating the breeze moving through the trees, sending it at the demon in a short, hard blast, knocking it off its feet. It sprang back up and I let my blade fly. With a thud, it wedged into its eye. He kept coming.

Throwing out a hand, I called on the tree beside it. Roots punched up through the soil and coiled around the demon's legs, and the decent-sized rock I fired at its head knocked it to its knees. The roots coiled tighter, pinning him down while he shrieked.

I strode forward, yanked my dagger from its eye socket, fisted its greasy hair, and buried the blade deep in its neck. Gritting my teeth, I dragged the blade around its throat, cutting through skin and tendons, hacking until I was able to remove its head and toss it aside. The demon turned to ash almost instantly, and I spun around, searching for more.

A vicious growl echoed through the forest, startling birds from the trees. *Warrick*. I rushed on, running toward him.

The sense of being watched prickled my skin. There were many creatures here, hiding, waiting for their chance. If they weren't attacking, they were scavengers, the kind of demons who ate what was left of someone else's kill.

A clearing loomed up ahead, and I pushed aside the pain of my cut and grazed bare feet as I rushed toward it. It was surrounded by pines, and glossy white and black stones defined the area. The full moon lit the whole place up—and in the middle, two enormous hellhounds squared off against each other.

The larger one was head down, teeth bared, red eyes sharp and steady on their prey. *Warrick*.

While the other, Edric, foamed at the mouth, pink from the blood of his recent victims, eyes crazed and confused.

He charged, and Warrick snarled, exploding into action. Their bodies crashed together in a bone-jarring collision before they rolled, smashing into a tree, making the ground shake.

Edric sprang back to his feet and ran off, Warrick making chase.

I took a step into the clearing—

"*Sooo* preeeetty. *Hmmm*."

I turned as the owner of that creepy voice, a dark and misshapen creature, revealed itself. A forked tongue darted out, tasting the air—then it took a step closer.

"Taste good," it said in its weirdly pitched voice.

Some demons were more humanoid in appearance, and others, like this one, were not. The demons in the surrounding woods had been here a very long time, the gene pool limited, and demons like this one were the result. They couldn't walk the streets, they couldn't blend in, so they hid in the shadows and watched for opportunity.

"*Yessss*, tastes *soooo* good," another voice said.

I stepped back as a second demon glided from the shadows, and my blade let me know what I could see with my own eyes—shit was about to get ugly. Yes, I'd handled one demon while not completely sober, but two—I wasn't so sure I was up to the task. Especially since my powers were feeling rather depleted.

"Girl *mine*," the first one said and slithered closer.

"No, she *mine*," the other said and did the same.

Fucking hell. All I could do was wait for one of them to make their move. I didn't want to exhaust my magic unless absolutely necessary.

"*Mine*," the first one shrieked and ran at me.

I let my blade fly, nailing it between the eyes. The demon

dropped, flailing around, and I threw out a hand, calling the blade back to me. It wriggled, working its way out of the demon's thick skull.

The other one cackled. "*Sheee minnnne*," he said in a loud, singsong voice.

Then he ran at me, right as the blade finally worked itself loose, the hilt landing in the palm of my hand a second later. I drew back, about to let it fly again, when a huge black shadow exploded across the clearing at a speed that should be impossible and knocked the demon to the ground. Warrick. Without pause, he bit off the demon's head and spat it out, his massive jaw and long serrated canines making quick work of it.

One moment the alpha was in his hellhound form, ten times my size, the next, he was a very tall, very naked male. He looked down at the demon's ashy remains with disdain. "No, fucker, she's mine."

I stood stunned as he turned to me, eyes no longer red but vibrant gold.

My gaze moved over him, and that's when I saw the gaping wound across his stomach. "Oh my god." I rushed to him, dropping to my knees and applied pressure, while blood steadily pumped out. "Don't move. We need to stop the bleeding, then get you out of here." I tore strips of silk from my dress and wrapped them around his thickly muscled waist, tying it off firmly—

A branch cracked behind us and I shot up, spinning around and blocked him with my body, my knife gripped in my bloody hands. Nothing stirred, nothing emerged from the shadows. I reached out with my magic and the cold evil had faded, just a shade of what it had been. "Must've just been an animal. I think we're safe for the moment."

"What are you doing, dove?" Warrick rumbled behind me.

I scanned the tree line again. "You're injured. If you keep losing blood like that, I'll have to drag you out of here, and right now we're easy prey."

Big hands landed on my shoulders, and he turned me around. "You're protecting me?" he asked, his expression impossible to read.

"Well...yes." I motioned to his bound stomach.

"You think I need protecting?" he said, chin dipped, eyes bright in the moonlight flooding the clearing.

I looked down at his stomach. "You're injured."

He fisted the blood-soaked silk.

"Warrick..."

And tore it off like it was tissue.

I cursed and dropped to my knees again, bringing up my hands. "Why are you like this? So damned stubborn. I know you're strong, you don't need to prove it to me by bleeding to death..." My words died in my throat. It was almost gone, the deep gash across his stomach was now just a long scratch. I looked up at him, stunned.

"We heal fast."

I looked back down, truly shocked. "I've seen fast, but this is...*holy shit*."

A wide, rough palm cupped my cheek, tilting my head back, forcing me to look up at him.

"I'm the one who protects," he said in a gruff voice.

He stared deeply into my eyes, head angled down, his long dark hair falling forward. I tried to look away, but he wouldn't let me.

"You were worried about me," he stated in a low rasp that set off sparks in my belly.

I quickly pulled away and looked down again. "I didn't want to get stuck lugging your huge ass out of here, that's all."

"Because I'm yours as well," he said. "You feel it."

I didn't answer because I didn't want to think about it, about the way I felt. It was a waste of time. He didn't feel tender emotions, didn't understand them, and I sure as hell did. He was immortal, and I most definitely wasn't.

This thing that swirled and pulsed between us was utterly hopeless.

A recipe for emotional devastation—mine.

His abs tightened and the muscles in his monster thighs flexed —and his cock, that had remained flaccid up until then—began to grow and harden. I should look away, I needed to look away, but couldn't. He was huge, long and thick and...*right there*. His breathing grew choppy, harsh, and I didn't dare look up.

Blood from the wound had trailed down, dampening the dark hair surrounding the thick base of his cock, had dripped down the shaft and smeared his thighs.

Adrenaline still pumped through me, my heart pounding in my chest. It was dark, and there was no one around. The evil had gone, and it was just him and me and the moonlight. It felt like another world, like it wasn't real. My blood-slicked hand lifted to that impressive cock before I had time to second guess it.

And ignoring the voice in my head telling me to *stop this now*, I curled my fingers around him. There were so many reasons not to do this, but I needed this, this moment, so badly it eclipsed every bit of the common sense, of harsh reality I'd been clinging to.

Air exploded through his clenched teeth. "Dove..."

The way he said it, so deep and full of desperation, of need, made something swirl low in my belly, and I couldn't stop myself from gripping him more firmly.

I glanced up at him then, and his hungry gaze bore into me as if he were waiting for me to stop, as if he expected me to realize what I was doing and pull away.

I didn't do either of those things. I stroked him from base to tip, the blood coating my hand and his cock easing the way and forcing a harsh groan from him—and the look on his face, god, it was...utterly breathtaking.

I kept my mouth shut. I didn't want to talk. Talking would only make this real—I wouldn't be able to pretend this wasn't really happening, that it was a dream, or some alternate version of reality.

And honestly, this moment couldn't be any more fitting. This violent, potent male, hard cock slicked with his own blood, thrusting into my hand in the woods under a full moon...

How many times had I thought about him in some variation of this exact scenario? More times than I cared to acknowledge. I didn't want to think about how good it felt to finally be touching him like this, or how much more of him I wanted to touch.

Curling the fingers of my other hand around him as well, I stroked him again. Warrick widened his stance, the muscles in his thighs jumping, and he growled low.

The wild sound had my belly quivering and my thighs squeezing together.

"Turn around," he gritted. "Hands and knees."

My inner muscles clenched, but I shook my head. No, I couldn't give myself to him, not here, not like this. If I did that, it wouldn't be a shadowy dream anymore, it would be too real, too much.

I stroked him faster, gripped him tighter, and he snarled, thrusting into my hands.

"Can smell your pussy, dove. Offer it to me," he demanded, his voice deeper, rougher, more urgent.

I didn't answer, and he thrust his fingers into my hair and tilted my head back, making me look into those beautiful golden eyes again. I couldn't speak, not when I saw the pleasure intensify on his face, the raw, untamed hunger.

I shook my head again. *No.* I couldn't do that, I couldn't give him that.

His fingers flexed in my hair, and tension, longing, lined his handsome face. "Keep your eyes on me."

He wasn't going to push me for more. Because Warrick would never hurt me, not intentionally, he only wanted to pleasure me. I knew that with every part of my being.

And I couldn't look away, even if I wanted to, but that was the last thing I wanted. His warrior's body was beautiful, flexing and straining for more of my touch, but his eyes held me transfixed. Spellbound. I wanted to see the way they looked when he came more than anything else.

His lips peeled back, revealing clenched teeth, his canines, sharp, extended. He fisted my hair tighter; the strands tugging at my scalp, and he came, shooting across his tight abs, and the sound he made was almost one of rage.

His chest was pumping, and through it all, he never looked away from me, not once.

Then finally, when he stopped pulsing in my hands, he hooked me around the waist, his other arm still keeping a hold on my hair, and brought me to my feet.

I tried to step back, but he held me fast, and when he dipped his head and I tried to pull back a second time, he wasn't having it. That hold was relentless, not painful, but made it clear I wasn't going anywhere. And I hated that his rough handling of me, that edge of the untamed, turned me on even more.

Then his mouth came down on mine in a hard, brutal kiss. His tongue swiping inside, feeding me a deep growl, one I was pretty sure was filled with frustration.

And the force of that kiss left me weak, breathless.

Finally, he eased back, touched his lips to mine once more, then lifted his head. "Denying me hurts us both."

His words hit me like a physical blow, and I opened my mouth to say something, to protest, but he kissed me again, robbing me of words.

When he broke the kiss, he stared down at me, the need still there, barely diminished. "Let me touch you, dove. I need to make you come."

I swallowed once, twice, self-preservation kicking in and gathering momentum. What the fuck was I doing? "No," I rasped, finally finding my voice. "Nothing's changed."

He stilled, though I didn't miss the tremor moving through his fighter's body or the look on his face that could only be described as fury. It was kind of...terrifying. "Nothing's changed?" he repeated.

"I drank too much wine," I said lamely, and my face heated. Truthfully, adrenaline had well and truly burned up any alcohol left in my system, and that wasn't why what happened had just happened, it was because this thing between us was growing stronger, more intense by the day, and seeing him injured like that, believing he was truly hurt for those few minutes, had caused my defenses to momentarily weaken.

The muscle in his cheek jumped. "The next time you touch my cock, I will fuck you, understand?" he said, his lips hovering just above mine, voice so deep I felt the words as well as heard them.

I nodded, and my nipples tightened, my traitorous body liking those harsh words, the threat I heard in them, when it was the last thing I should be feeling.

His gaze raked over me before his nostrils flared and he breathed deep, drawing in my scent. My face got hotter, and he watched me, lids lowered, eyes utterly predatory and filled with molten heat. He could smell how much I wanted him, of course he could. And for a moment, I thought he was going to kiss me again, but he released me this time and straightened.

I scrambled back, and he watched me do this, eyes narrowed, before he finally turned away and stalked back the way we came.

I followed, trying not to limp too much and draw Warrick's notice. I really had done a number on my feet, and I thought that might just piss him off more.

The moonlight glinted off one of the stones surrounding the clearing, and that's when I realized where we were. It was where the wolf shifters brought their females to mate, and why the wolves and witches of this area had always had a good relationship. Many, many years ago, in exchange for the pack's loyalty, a witch had enchanted this spot. When a wolf found his true mate, invisible walls lifted, creating a hidden oasis for the pair to consummate for several days and nights.

What would that be like? I glanced up at Warrick and heat curled low in my belly, along with an urge to run to him that grew incredibly, terrifyingly strong.

Instead, I kept my distance—and my mouth shut—because I could see he was hanging by a very thin, very fragile thread, and I sure as hell wasn't going to push him to breaking point.

I wasn't ready to face the consequences.

What the hell had I done?

CHAPTER 14

Warrick

MY DOVE STAYED behind me as we walked through the woods, and I was alert to every breath, every sound, every subtle move she made.

I was closer to the edge than I'd ever been, and if she touched me just once more tonight...

I sucked in a steadying breath and growled low when the scent of her need reached out to me. My female was wet and achy and still she turned me away. No female had ever refused me. I knew I could be intimidating, my size alone could frighten them away. So I let them come to me, like Willow did tonight, and if one made their interest known and I offered to fuck them, they enthusiastically accepted.

But after my dove touched me, she wouldn't let me do the same in return.

I didn't understand. She confused me, was driving me to madness from wanting her.

She wanted me too. I was in no doubt about that, yet she continued to deny herself. Deny us both.

By the time we reached the Grand Valencia, the moon had slipped behind the clouds. I scanned the area. The place had been cleared out, cleaned up, and locked down. The aftermath of death, all evidence of the horror show that had taken place, hidden from the humans who worked here, their minds wiped clean of the memory.

I could still smell the blood in the air, though, and the beast surged closer to the surface, growing more alert.

Willow cursed, and I turned to her. She was looking up at the darkened hotel.

"What is it?"

She planted her hands on her rounded hips, her torn, blood-stained dress clinging to every inch of her smooth flesh. I wanted to bite her and leave a mark, cover her in my scent so every male knew she belonged to me.

"Warrick? Did you hear what I said?" She shook her head and scooped up the delicate heels she'd been wearing, slipping them back on.

I wanted to fuck her while she wore those shoes.

"Warrick?"

Dragging in a breath, I made myself focus on her words.

She sighed. "I dumped my purse when I took off after you. My phone, the keys to my truck were in it. Someone probably took it inside."

"I'll take you home." I strode to my bike, yanked a pair of jeans from the saddle bag, and tugged them on, leaving the suit I'd stripped off earlier in a heap on the ground. I'd never have reason to wear it again. I'd only forced myself into the fucking thing so I could be here tonight. So I was here to protect my dove.

She paused. "It's fine, I'll call Iris."

I held back a vicious growl, my anger rushing forward again.

"You don't have a phone, remember?" I swung my leg over the seat and started my bike, the engine roaring to life.

Still, she didn't move.

"Get on my bike, Willow. Now." Fury ignited in her green eyes, and she opened her mouth to fire more attitude at me, but I got in first for both our sakes. "I'm not a man, I'm a hellhound, I'm an animal, and we do not like being denied. So don't fucking push me, not tonight." I tried to breathe through the feeling growing inside me, not just the urge to claim what was mine but something else, a feeling I didn't understand. Fuck, there was an ache in my chest and the urge to rub at it was overwhelming.

"Not a fan of what you're implying, Warrick," she said, the hilt of her blade slipping into her hand.

I fought the growl trying to crawl up my throat. "No?"

She shook her head.

"I fought one of my brothers tonight, a loyal brother I have to hunt down before he murders anyone else, and then put him down. The animal in me doesn't like that idea, and that part of me is also struggling to understand why my female, who smells ripe for fucking, who *finally* touched me, still won't submit to me. There is no reasoning with that side of me, do you understand? I'm not some weak, pathetic human you can play with. I'm at breaking point, female, and if you turn and walk away right now, the beast will break free, that's how close to the edge I am. That's not me trying to scare you, that's just what will happen. So either you get the fuck on the back of my bike, or I'll pick you up and put you on it."

She stood motionless for several long seconds, eyes razor sharp on me, then she gripped her blade tighter and the muscles in her arms tensed.

"You going to try and kill me, dove?"

Her eyes narrowed. "I haven't decided."

I took in her stance, the tension in her beautiful body. "What is your blade telling you?"

"That you meant what you said."

Her gaze became distant, hollow, and a slight tremor moved through her. I fucking hated it. I wanted her fire, not her fear. But I wasn't human, I was a fucking animal, and I didn't play by human rules.

I waited to see what she'd do. That blade in her hand was no ordinary blade, she could wound me badly, maybe even kill me if she moved fast enough after she threw it.

"I don't want to hurt you, dove. That's the last thing I want."

She studied me for long seconds. "There were more bodies found with Jane's...at the location she was found, a lot of them. Did you and your brothers put them there? Are you responsible for all those deaths?"

I stared at her as every muscle in me tightened. Did she truly think I was some stone-cold fucking killer? That I'd murder inno-cent humans for a bit of fun? "Jag found them." I tapped my nose. "Hard to miss that much death. He buried Jane there, and I tracked the fucker responsible for the other bodies—it wasn't hard, the scent of his victims, their fear, it saturated his home, then I ended him so he couldn't hurt anyone else. It seemed the best solution. They will assume she was one of his kills, and like Jane's mother, those people had family looking for them."

She blinked. "You killed a serial killer?"

"Yes."

"Human?"

"Yes."

"Have you done something like that before?"

"Yes."

Her chest expanded, and then...she moved to the bike, paused for a moment, eyeing me, then finally climbed on behind me.

Thank fuck.

Her arms came around my waist, but the dagger stayed in her tight grip, the point of the blade pressed to my stomach. I let her, if it made her feel safer. Still, helplessness pulsed through me because I didn't know how to make her understand. I couldn't make her see that every part of me wanted to protect her, not hurt her.

Why did she keep refusing me? Why did she keep denying us both, when it was obvious she wanted me just as fiercely?

The ride to her family's house was torture. Her pussy snugged up against my ass, her tits, hot and soft against my back. The way her thighs tensed against mine with every corner we took.

I wanted to take her to my den, my room, *my bed*, not here to this house. She didn't belong here, not anymore.

Rolling to a stop, I waited for her to climb off, then did the same. I should stay back, keep my hands to myself, but that was impossible right then. I advanced on her, and when she retreated, I gritted my teeth. "Stop."

"No, you stop," she bit out, her face flushed.

I didn't stop. I closed the space between us, ignoring the dagger in her hand because she would either stab me or she wouldn't. I was positive she didn't want to kill me, and another taste of her lips was worth a second slice to the gut.

Hooking my hand around the back of her neck, I stilled her, but instead of claiming her mouth like I'd planned, I locked eyes with her. Confusingly, something stronger than lust, something I couldn't name, gripped me in that moment. "Tell me you're not afraid of me, dove." I couldn't bear that she might truly be frightened of me.

She licked her lips. "My dagger's telling me you're a threat, Warrick. I think fear is healthy for me where you're concerned."

I gritted my teeth as the strange pain in my chest intensified at her words.

Didn't she know? Didn't she understand—I would lay waste to this entire city to keep her safe.

Willow

The vibration of my blade was low. The beast, not the man, could hurt me, but he didn't want to. I knew that deep down, I did. But the threat was there all the same, and I'd be an idiot to ignore it.

"I would never purposely harm you, but I want you, dove, and when I'm this close to the edge, one push and I would take you like an animal, rough and driven by need."

A shudder moved through me. The things he just said should repulse me, scare me, but they didn't. No, what I felt was the opposite. He wanted me and he'd made no secret of that, and he was warning me not to push him when he was like this. "You've been in your animal form around me before, you had control."

"The form I take makes no difference, the beast is in here." He thumped his fist against his chest. "And in here." He tapped the side of his head. "We are one at all times."

"Right." That made sense, but it also made me realize just because he was standing in front of me looking like a man, he wasn't one, and never would be, the beast was always there.

"You're still afraid," he rasped.

I nodded. There was no point lying. He could sense it.

His hand coasted down my bare arm, his fingers curling around my wrist. He lifted my hand that still held the dagger and put the blade to his throat. "I would rather you slit my throat now, dove, than harm you. My strength in all things, including control over the beast, is unsurpassed. That is why I'm alpha. But sometimes I am driven close to the edge, and when that happens, I will always warn you, like I did tonight. I would never intentionally hurt you or frighten you, and the part of me that is capable of it only wants to get closer to you. I just want to get closer to you."

He'd never said anything like that to me in all the time I'd known him, and I didn't know how to react, what to say. It was easy to turn down the gruff male telling me he wanted to fuck me, but this was something else entirely. "Understood," I whispered. "Thank you for sharing that with me."

He stilled and scented the air. "You're injured."

"It's just my feet, they…"

He lifted me off the ground, surprising me, and planted me on the hood of Iris's car. My ankle was in his hand a moment later.

"Warrick, it's fine."

He growled, ignoring me as he brushed the dirt from the bottom of my foot.

"Honestly, it's…"

He spat in his hand and rubbed it over the damaged skin. I shut my mouth and watched him, his absolute focus as he tended my wounds. It should gross me out, but it didn't, it made my belly flutter and my heart clench.

Stupid goddamn heart.

He repeated the whole spit and rub routine on the other foot, his hold firm yet gentle. "They should be better by morning." He glanced up at me, his thumb stroking my skin. "I can feel you trembling. You still think I'd harm you? You don't believe me."

I was, and yeah, that fear was still there. But the fear wasn't about him physically hurting me, not anymore. God, I couldn't do this. I couldn't give into this force between us. It had disaster written all over it, but I didn't want him beating himself up over this either. "I believe you."

"Then leave with me. Spend the night with me, dove."

The way he said it had my heart fluttering. "That would be a huge mistake, Warrick. I can't ever let that happen. I don't want it to happen," I made myself say.

A muscle in his jaw jumped, then in a movement so fast I could barely follow him, he tugged me forward, his other arm banding around my waist, and hauled me up off the car and against him. Fitting my body tightly to his, he buried his face against my shoulder and dragged his nose along my throat. His lips following up to my jaw, and he sucked before lifting his head.

I stood immobile in his arms as his gaze raked over me. Then he breathed in again like he had in the woods, deep, letting his eyes drift shut for a moment, a rough sound vibrating through his chest. When they opened, the hunger in their depths made me quiver all over.

He licked his lips and his mouth curled up on one side. "Keep lying to yourself, if it makes you feel better, but your body sure as fuck doesn't agree." His fingers slid deeper into my hair and his lips were just a breath from mine. "Say yes."

My gaze dipped to his mouth without my say-so. "You need to go."

His jaw did that tightening thing it often did around me, then he released me as quickly as he'd grabbed me. He made a harsh, frustrated sound and walked away, swaggering back to his bike, and swung his leg over the seat. He was angry, it surrounded him like a red haze, his aura letting me know just how unhappy he was with me.

Then, firing the bike to life, he roared away without a backward glance.

I collapsed against the side of Iris's car. *Holy shit.* How the hell was I going to survive this? After tonight, and what Edric did, there was no doubting we were stuck working together. But that kind of intensity was more than I knew how to deal with.

"That you, Wills?" Iris called.

"Yeah." I rounded the corner and found my sister standing in the cobbled courtyard, Nia at her side as always, her big brown eyes alert, and Brody with them, looking more than a little disheveled.

My sister's mouth dropped open when she got a look at me. "Are you okay? Pictures from the ball are all over Nightscape. There's some of you and Warrick as well."

Shit. "Edric showed up."

Brody looked around wildly, as if he expected to see the giant hound walk out of the shadows.

I looked down at myself and guilt and sorrow hit when I took in the state of Gran's utterly destroyed gown. "I'm okay, but let's go inside, I have a lot to tell you," I said.

"No shit," Iris said, sounding just like Else. Then she grabbed my hand and pulled me inside. Nia and Brody following.

Later the next morning, after repeating almost every detail of what happened last night to my family—omitting the bloody hand job and pretty much everything Warrick said or did—Iris dropped me off at my truck before she headed into work. And yes, thankfully, my purse had been at the hotel reception.

They'd all seen the pictures and read the gossip posted on Nightscape. I'd logged on this morning. There were pictures of Warrick, of him naked, of him shifting, a clip of me running after him into the woods. And that was all I needed. Sapphire Eldridge was probably humiliated by association and happy I'd turned her creep of a son down.

The only reason so few witches who had attended were out for blood was that "no one of consequence" was killed, just the help. Jesus.

And though I had a feeling I'd regret it, I'd just turned into Clayton Whitlock's driveway, the house looming up ahead.

Though "house" was too paltry a word.

They may not be as powerful, magic-wise, as they wished they were, but their bank balance wasn't lacking, that's for sure.

Else and Mom had given me a little Whitlock history lesson before I left this morning. It turned out they'd had a string of bad luck in the past. Their cemetery had been all but destroyed during a flash flood, bodies washed away, never to be found again, setting them back centuries in the power stakes. And this house looked new because it was; the one before had burned down in a fire. Then Clayton's father, Albert, had been killed in a car accident and his mother's familiar had drowned in their pool this summer.

That was some seriously bad luck. It was almost like they were being punished for something.

I pulled the Morris to a stop out front of what only could only be described as a mansion, right as my phone beeped. I smiled when I saw Ren's name.

We spoke several times a day, because not having him around the last few had been tough on both of us.

Ren: Warrick's in a foul mood. What did you do to him?

Willow: Pass. How you doing?

Ren: Good. Feeling stronger.

Willow: How many new bruises?

Ren: I'm fine, Wills. Don't worry about me. Is Warrick helping you like he promised? Or did you send him away? Is that why he's pissed?

As if anyone could make Warrick do anything he didn't want to.

Willow: No idea why he's pissed. Everything's fine, I promise.

I didn't lie to Ren, but if I told him the truth now, if I told him what really happened between the alpha and me, Ren would walk right out of the clubhouse or worse, confront Warrick.

The front door opened, and Clayton walked out as my phone buzzed with another text from Ren. I put it on silent and shoved it in my back pocket to reply to later.

Clay smiled as he jogged down the stairs.

He was in tan trousers and a navy dress shirt, the sleeves rolled up, casual for him. He also looked extremely nervous. "Clayton," I said as I opened my door.

"Willow." He grabbed my hand. "I'm so glad you made it."

Yep, he was nervous all right. His hands were clammy.

"Come in. Cook made us some morning tea."

I took my hand back and followed him up the stairs and

through a grand entrance, on feet that were completely healed from the night before, thanks to Warrick.

I shivered, remembering the way he brushed my skin with his fingers, then got pissed off with myself and shoved it out of my head.

The foyer Clay was leading me through was white marble and there were two statues, one of the mother's pet serpent and the other, a woman looking into the distance, her hair blowing around her face.

"They're beautiful, aren't they?" he said, watching me check out his home.

"Yes, lovely." The click of heels had me turning. Olive Whitlock, Clayton's mother, walked down a curved staircase, her shrewd amber gaze moving over me. Her lips pursed. Not a fan of leather pants then?

"The one of the mother's serpent has been in our family for hundreds of years," Olive said. "Our line has been taking part in the trials for a very long time." She stopped in front of me. "This is your first attempt, yes?"

Apparently, the claws were out. "That's right."

She smiled, her gaze moving over me again from boots to hair before coming back to mine. "I hear you're yet to complete your second task?"

"And where did you hear that?"

She lifted an elegant shoulder. "We talk. The more prominent families, I mean, we stick together. Come." She strode off, expecting me to follow her like an obedient dog.

"You mean, you gossip," I corrected, reluctantly trailing after her.

Clay winced a little, his expression apologetic.

Olive laughed, the sound was rusty, as if she didn't find much to laugh at these days. Considering everything the family had been through in recent years, that didn't surprise me. "I suppose you're right."

We entered another impressive room, but that was the point, wasn't it? The Whitlocks wanted me to see how rich they were, how well connected. They either wanted to intimidate or impress me. I wasn't quite sure which they were going for yet.

If they knew me at all, they'd know that wasn't going to happen—on both fronts.

Olive sat, perching on the edge of her chair with all the regalness of the queen herself. Jesus, it even kind of looked like a throne. Clay sat on the love seat opposite and aimed that easygoing smile of his at me. I took the chair beside it, and the smile slipped before he rallied.

"So, what's this about?" I didn't owe them anything. They may be rich, but again, if they knew me, they'd know that didn't mean anything to me. There was no coven hierarchy despite what families like this one had tried to create. As far as power went, I was stronger than both Clay and his mother put together, and they both knew it.

Olive leaned forward and motioned to a coffee pot and a plate of finger foods, ignoring my question. "Would you like something to eat or drink? The coffee is imported from Italy. It's exquisite, you really should try it."

"I'm fine, thank you. I actually have a busy day ahead so if we could cut to the chase."

This pissed her off, and the false but brittle smile dropped in an instant. "How's your sister..." She glanced at Clay, brow arched in question.

"Rose," he said politely.

Everything inside me froze.

"Yes, Rose. I hear she's unwell?" Olive said.

Clay turned to me. "Yes, people have been talking. They say you've been unsuccessful with treatment."

My blade remained still, cool, at my side, no warning telling me there was imminent danger—I almost wished there was, because I had a strong and sudden urge to reach for it anyway. "My sister is none of your business."

"Oh, of course not," Clay said, flushing. "We were merely concerned. We were friends once, you and I, good friends." He offered me a charming yet sympathetic smile, and I wondered if he spent time practicing it in the mirror. "I care about you and your family."

I smiled back, and by the way his eyes widened slightly, I knew it looked as violent as I felt. Bringing up Roe felt a lot like a threat. "We haven't spoken in years, Clayton. I honestly haven't thought about you in all that time, and pretending that you care about me and my family is, quite frankly, horseshit." I stood. "I don't have time for whatever this is—"

"Wait," Olive said. "Please, sit back down."

I turned to her. "I'd rather not."

She sighed. "Look, the only reason we brought up your sister is that we have the resources, access to incredibly rare relics and ingredients through our business, anything you need. Her illness is worsening, yes, and by all accounts, possibly derived from magic. We have the connections, people who could help you search, *research*, for the cure you need, anywhere in the world. We can afford the manpower that would take." She crossed her legs. "We could help you, help Rose, immeasurably. Let us help you, Willow."

Clayton stood, moving closer. "I'd like nothing more than to help your sister, Willow."

My family was constantly searching for answers, and I had people searching in other parts of the world already. "I have it covered."

"I'm sure you do, dear, but we could cast a much wider net."

She was right, of course. My family's funds, our resources, were limited. "And what is it you'd want in exchange for all this help? I assume your offer has a price, yes?" That was the real reason I was here after all. They wanted something from me.

Her gaze sharpened. "Of course. I knew you were intelligent."
Condescending cow. "What do you want?"

Olive looked to Clayton and he quickly stepped forward. "We have a history. We were friends once...more than that. I messed up, but I was young, stupid, I hurt you..."

"Not as much as you think you did, I assure you."

That easygoing smile returned. "Right, of course."

"Spit it out, Clayton." Though I had a feeling I knew what he was about to say.

"We...I'm proposing an alliance."

Goddess, not again. "What kind of an alliance?"

He closed the space between us, took my hand, and looked deep into my eyes. "Marriage. You and me. Your power is impressive, Willow, and your family's cemetery is coveted by every coven in America. But our power is not to be sneezed at either. I think we're closely matched..." *In your dreams.* "...and our family has money, influence, connections. Our children would be formidable, unbeatable."

I couldn't believe this was happening again. "Well, aren't I the popular one? That's two marriage proposals in twenty-four hours."

Olive shot to her feet and Clayton's smile dropped completely. "You're engaged?"

"No."

They both released sighs of relief.

"I have no intention of marrying, not for any reason."

Olive's hands curled into fists. "How very selfish of you. This conviction of yours, you consider it more important than your sister's life?"

"Mother," Clay said, tone chastising, then he turned back to me. "Will you think about it, Willow? Despite the obvious reasons this alliance would be beneficial, I think we'd get along very well together. I'm not after a marriage of continence. I want a real marriage, a true partnership. We'd be good together."

Was he serious? "As lovely as this has been, I'll be leaving now." I strode out, and Clayton's quick steps followed me.

I jogged down the stairs and to my truck.

"Willow, wait."

I pulled the door open.

"I'm sorry for that. We ambushed you. My mother and I, we both want this alliance, just for different reasons."

A laugh burst from me, surprising us both. "If you're about to tell me you're in love with me..."

"No, of course not." He shoved his fingers through his hair. "But if an alliance is in my future, I'd rather it be with you."

"Why would you do that? Christ, Clayton, a marriage of convenience, really?"

He shrugged and slid his hands in his pockets. "You've obviously heard about my family...our losses. I believe someone is out to get us, Willow. I care about this family, about the future of our coven. We need power and to increase our coven's numbers." His head tilted to the side. "I want to save my family, and I believe you can help me do that. I've always cared about you." He flashed me one of those handsome grins. "You're incredibly beautiful, even more so than when we were in high school. Being with you, sharing a bed with you, wouldn't be a hardship. And I do believe love could grow between us if given the chance."

I opened my mouth to tell him it would never happen, but he got in first.

"Don't say no, not yet. Just think about it. The offer's there if you change your mind. I know how much you love your sister. We could really help her, Wills."

There were so many things I wanted to say. Instead I got in the Morris, slammed the door, and got the hell out of there before I punched him in the face or burned their fugly new mansion to the ground as well.

I'd find a way to help Rose, I would, and without selling my soul to the Whitlocks. And passing this task, winning my trial, increasing my family's power, strengthening our magic, was the best way to accomplish that.

Something hot and tight, something that gripped like jagged claws, bit into my stomach.

Fear, real and raw.

I couldn't lose my sister. I couldn't lose my Roe.

I wouldn't survive it.

CHAPTER 15

Willow

I STEPPED out of the shower and looked at my ribs. A couple of the vines had stretched out, creeping closer together. Tracing one of the thorny tendrils with my finger, I breathed in deep when sharp fear tried to push forward again. Time was running out.

Fear only paralyzed, it got in the way of getting things done.

I didn't have time for fear. My family wouldn't come out the other side of this with their powers intact if I gave in to fear. And Roe wouldn't get any better.

Since my discussion with Clayton four days ago, I'd been either holed up in Else's library or online while I was at the shop, researching, learning everything I could about malevolent souls, hoping there might be something that could help. So far, I'd found nothing I didn't already know.

And at night, I searched the city for any sign of them. Nothing. And no sign of Edric since his fight with Warrick, only the bodies he left behind. Torn to shreds without mercy.

I felt the weight of every single casualty. This was my task, it was my job to send those souls back to where they came from, and if I didn't find a way to stop them real fast, more people would die.

I assumed Warrick was having as much trouble as me.

The hellhounds' alpha hadn't called, so I could only assume. It wasn't like he needed to call to check up on me, though, the male knew where I was at all times, and more than once over the last couple of nights, I'd clocked him shadowing me. Okay, I'd *felt* him before I'd seen him. God, the weight of his stare was like black velvet across bare skin, lifting goose bumps all over me, causing heat to swirl through my entire body.

He hadn't approached, though, or announced he was there, so I'd pretended I didn't see him. It was better for both of us that way...that's what I kept telling myself, anyway.

He'd made a promise to provide backup and he was keeping it, even if he was doing it from a distance, which only made me feel like more of an asshole, honestly.

I'd seriously angered him the night of the ball with my complete and utter loss of self-control. Yes, the male was obviously used to getting his way, and no, I didn't owe him anything, but I'd seriously thrown out some mixed signals in those woods. He wasn't human or witch; he wasn't just a man, and he didn't play by those rules.

He was an alpha, a hellhound, created in the fires of Hell by Lucifer himself. I needed to remember that, and I needed to heed the warning he'd given me.

I shook off thoughts of Warrick, because I needed to find Edric, now.

When souls lingered after a person's death, it usually meant unfinished business. Since brutally murdering a bunch of innocent people seemed to be the only goal, it had become clear that these souls weren't stuck here, unable to move on, but had been summoned here from Hell, or some other unpleasant place, by a twisted individual.

The pure evil that had emanated from the one inhabiting Edric had sent icy tendrils through me just being near him. If I was right? Souls like that usually picked up where they left off—doing all the evil, twisted things they had done before they died.

Which meant, right now, Edric and the other one still on the loose were probably out there, hurting people.

But there would be no sending them back if I couldn't find them.

Pulling on a pair of leather pants and a long-sleeved shirt, I went to my room and shoved on my boots, slid my dagger into the sheath at my hip, grabbed my jacket, and headed downstairs to the kitchen. If I could find Edric, I could question the soul and make it spill its secrets—namely, where it was from, and most importantly, who brought it here.

Magnolia was standing by the kitchen table.

"Hey," I said, taking my phone from my pocket.

She had her black hair down, wavy around her pale face. Her amber eyes were surrounded by black eyeliner and her full lips were deep red. She was wearing black ripped jeans, chunky black boots, and an oversized black T-shirt with the name of some band I'd never heard of printed on the front. She'd always preferred to wear black, even when she was young. She'd leaned into it more the last couple of years though. She and Bram looked like a goth prince and princess when they were together.

Bram, currently in his human form, stood at the counter behind her. Staying close to Mags as usual, even while he made himself a snack.

"Another night out hunting?" Mags asked.

There was something in her voice that had me looking up from my phone. "Yeah." Her lips flattened. "You okay?"

She gripped the back of one of the chairs. "Let me come with you. I want to help. Iris and I have been talking and we're worried. Don't get me wrong, I know you've got this, but we hate seeing you go through it all on your own, Wills."

Bram was suddenly at my sister's side. I hadn't even seen him move, but now his dark eyes sliced to me, waiting for my answer.

He didn't say anything, he rarely did, but he didn't need to, not in this. It was all there in his stare. Ren and Bram were alike in a lot of ways. Bram didn't want Mags to put herself in danger, and if she did, anyway, he was going to be right there with her. But then that was most familiars.

"Don't freak out, B," Mags said without looking at him, sensing his movement, knowing what he would be thinking and feeling it without him saying a word.

And of course, my sisters were worried about me. I hated this. "I wish you could, but you know that's not allowed." A witch could get help, but only outside their family and coven. Things got messy when family got involved, so the mother had forbidden it a very long time ago.

Her jaw tightened. "It's a fucking stupid rule."

"I know, but I promise I have help." I held up my phone. "I was just about to call Warrick." As much as I didn't want to, Edric had tracked his alpha to that ball, so it was only logical that it could happen again, and I'd do anything, even spend time with Warrick, if it helped my family and Ren not to worry.

Mags crossed her arms. "Go on then, call him."

My baby sister didn't believe me. I held up the phone, showed her the number, and hit call. Yes, I could fight. I'd slayed demons, lots of them, but that didn't stop me from being scared every time I went out there. Every fight I risked my life. One of these nights, I might not make it home. And I kinda liked living. My family counted on me, they needed me, so safety first, always, and yeah, backup was always welcome...even from a possessive, dominant alpha hellhound who wanted me in his bed.

My sister smirked and moved to the counter, Bram following, and they got back to making their snack, sandwiches by the look.

The phone rang several times and kept on ringing. Maybe he saw it was me and wasn't going to answer—

"Yeah."

I paused at the harsh note to his voice.

"It's me."

"I know."

Okay.

Usually, he'd answer with a growly, "Dove." Yep, I was right, he was seriously pissed off with me. *Awesome.* He was totally going to make me beg for this.

I pushed on. "So, time's running out for me, and I really need to finish this. I'm heading out tonight, looking for Edric. I thought maybe you'd want to tag along?" *Ugh.* I sounded like an idiot.

"Not your fucking lap dog, Willow."

This was worse than I thought. And *Willow*. He rarely called me that. Was he...had I actually *hurt* him? *Don't be stupid.* He didn't have a soul, he'd told me that himself. He wasn't capable of love, didn't believe in it, or even deep feelings, something else he'd shared with me, so how could my rejection hurt him? His male ego was bruised, that's all this pouting was about.

"I know that, Warrick, but we had a deal, right?"

"Yeah, we had a deal. Doesn't mean I'll just let you lead me around by the dick because you finally decide to call. You sure as fuck haven't worried about our deal the last few nights."

"I knew you were there."

"And yet you pretended that I wasn't."

"Okay, just..."

"Not in the fucking mood to chase your ass around all night."

"Are you serious?"

"Deadly."

"You think I'm leading you around by...I'm not doing that—"

"Do not leave your fucking house, female."

I glanced at my sister and Bram, who were both watching me

while eating their sandwiches. I smiled and rolled my eyes, giving them a thumbs-up, pretending that Warrick was just being Warrick and all was well, so Mags didn't worry. Then I swiped my keys off the small table by the door and hustled down the hall and out of the house. "I can't believe you're throwing a tantrum over... what happened between us," I said.

Silence.

"Warrick..."

"A tantrum?" he said, his voice pure grit.

"Yes, a tantrum. I gave you a hand job, alpha, I thought you enjoyed it. But you're acting like I stole the cookies from your lunch box right before recess."

More silence.

"Warrick..."

The line went dead.

"Hello?"

Nothing.

I stared at my phone in shock.

He hung up on me. He'd actually hung up on me.

Muttering under my breath, I climbed in the Morris, fired her to life, tore down the driveway, and out onto the road. *Unbelievable*.

Okay, maybe what I'd done had been uncool. But I had a little bit on my damn mind. God, I thought human males took rejection badly. The hound took sulking to a whole new level. It wasn't like I needed him. I was capable of looking after myself. I had been for a hell of a long time. I had magic, and my dagger, and that was all I needed.

Just as long as Warrick didn't tell Ren about our conversation, we'd be fine. Because Ren knew me better than almost anyone, which meant he'd know I wouldn't just sit around at home because Warrick told me to.

But then Warrick would have already realized it himself by now, the great big freaking stalker.

The question was, would he do anything about it?

Twenty minutes later, I climbed out of the truck at the edge of Wolf Hill Woods, the last place we'd seen Edric, and pulled on my jacket. Muttering a protection spell, I slung my satchel across my chest. The spell was simple yet effective, and witches in my family had been using it for generations, something we all recited every morning.

The spell wouldn't make me invisible or untouchable, but it did put luck more firmly on my side. I could seriously use all I could get. Anything stronger would defeat the purpose, which was to get Edric as close as I could, then try to coax the spirit to chat.

I was also wearing an onyx pendant. The stone wasn't as effective as getting naked and covering myself in the Thornhearts' special spiked oil, like I had at the hellhound den, but it was fairly effective at protecting against your average, everyday spirit. Smaller layers of protection would work better in this situation, since I still needed to attract those malevolent bastards.

I paused at the tree line when the growl of a motorbike engine echoed in the distance.

Apparently, the furious, furry one had changed his mind.

I wasn't in the mood to argue or trade scowls, or...whatever. My belly squirmed as visions of what we'd done, *what I'd done*, last time we were here flashed through my mind.

I shoved them the hell away and headed into the woods. Nope, I wasn't hanging around to wait for him. It wasn't like he'd have trouble tracking me.

Dried leaves crunched under my boots, the shadows closing in as soon as I walked deeper, and my knife was vibrating at my hip before I'd even taken half a dozen steps. And not a gentle nudge either, it shrieked. A full-on red alert.

There was a crash, and a demon ran at me full-speed. Taking my blade in a loose hold, I aimed and let it fly.

The blade embedded in her throat, and she fell to the forest floor, clawing at it. Warrick would be right behind me, so I didn't expend the time and energy of removing her head when he could do it with his bare hands. It was also too dangerous to stay still for any length of time, so instead, I sliced through the tendons in her legs to slow her down, and carried on.

Another came at me about three minutes later. This one wasn't a demon, though, it was something else. Some kind of goblin maybe? I honestly didn't know, but it meant to kill me. So, pressing my palms together, I called to the earth beneath me, then jerked my palms apart. The earth opened in a jagged split beneath the goblin's feet. He fell in up to his thighs and I brought my hands back together with a loud clap, the split earth closed, trapping it there, growling in fury. By the time I reached the clearing where Edric and Warrick had fought, I'd taken down two more demons and some other creature I couldn't name, leaving a trail of blood and groaning bodies behind me.

Still, no Warrick.

But then, he was probably doing what he had the last few nights, staying back so he didn't have to actually talk to me. Whatever, if he wanted to act like a spoiled child who wasn't allowed to play with his favorite toy, so be it.

I strode to the middle of the field, put my fingers to my lips, and whistled. "Edric! You out there?"

"Jesus Christ," a male voice growled.

I turned, but it wasn't Warrick, it was Ren.

"What the hell are you doing here?"

"Providing backup since you've somehow pissed Warrick off enough that he refused." He strode toward me and a grin curled his lips. I couldn't help but grin back and pulled him in for a tight hug. He dropped a kiss to the top of my head. "Missed you, Wills."

"Missed you too, foxy." Warrick wasn't coming. I mean, he'd said it, but I hadn't actually believed him.

A surprised laugh escaped him at the nickname I used to call him. We were ridiculous. We hadn't even been apart that long. But we didn't do that. We didn't purposely stay away from each other. I squeezed him again. "You feel bigger."

"I am bigger," he said, that grin still there.

"Gotta love those shifter genes. Lift some weights for a few days and you turn into the Hulk," I teased. But joke aside, physically, he had seriously transformed.

"It's been a week actually, and Jagger has me doing some serious reps," he said as he scanned the edge of the clearing.

"How's the training going?" There was a bruise on his jaw and another on his cheekbone.

"Really good. I feel..." He shook his head. "It's a good feeling, you know? I'm still learning, but I don't go down as easily as I did a week ago."

I wasn't sure I liked the sound of that. "Are they being dicks to you?"

"Nah, they're hard on me, but they're fair. And Ronan's been teaching me a few things as well. The male's so cold and controlled, I've never seen anyone fight like that before."

"Ronan's there?" This seriously surprised me.

"Yeah, he has a room at the den. He comes and goes. I don't know how it happened, but he's tight with the hounds."

My friend Luna didn't know where her brother had been living. I would definitely be giving her a call later.

"So we're looking for Edric?" Ren said.

"Yeah, though I'm not sure you should be out here, Renny. It's not safe."

He snorted. "I think I'll be okay. I followed your gory trail of mutilation all the way here, remember?"

I smiled. "True. I'm getting better, more in tune with my dagger every day."

"Nice..."

A howl echoed in the distance, and it definitely wasn't Warrick. Yes, I knew the difference.

I spun toward the eerie sound. "Stay close to me," I said and snatched a bag from my satchel. Stabbing the corner, I made a tight, thick circle of salt and cemetery dirt around Ren, then another beside him around me. "Whatever happens, Ren, promise me, you'll stay in the circle."

He nodded as he drew a hunting knife from the sheath strapped to his thigh.

"I know I should be pissed that you came out here, but I missed you so much, I'm just happy to see your pretty face." I stepped out and in front of my circle.

"Hey, I'll accept handsome, or even hot, but I draw the line at pretty."

There was a tremor to his voice that he tried to hide. He was nervous. Nerves were good. A little fear was healthy. Cockiness, that's when you ran into trouble. "So noted." My blade was vibrating like crazy now, and I spun it slowly between my fingers.

The howl came again, louder this time.

"Move back, Wills, get in your circle," Ren said.

"Not yet, the spirit won't be interested if I'm behind the salt. If I can get him close enough to wound him, I might be able to question him."

Ren made a rough sound. "This isn't just some demon, it's an evil-as-fuck spirit inhabiting a hellhound. They're twenty times stronger and more viscous. Get back into your circle, Willow."

"I've got this," I said and braced when the giant hound exploded through the tree line and ran at me full speed.

Edric was a massive hound, and the spirit occupying his body was taking full advantage of all that speed and strength. He was coming in fast, but I needed to time it just right, too far back and he could dodge the blade when I threw it, not something that ever happened at a closer range. The adrenaline spike hit, letting me know it was time, and I let my dagger fly. I watched it arrow through the air, glinting off the moonlight.

Edric jerked right, and it glanced his massive, shaggy shoulder, then spun off into the long grass.

Fuck. I backed up and aimed my hands at the ground. It shook, the earth splitting beneath him. He bounded out of the way and kept coming.

I tried to call my blade to me as I backed up to my salt circle, but pain sliced down my leg and I stumbled before I could reach it. *What the hell?* It was followed by a repeated stabbing sensation that knocked my legs right out from under me. I cried out as my legs lost all strength.

"Willow!" Ren started toward me.

Fuck.

"Get back!" I screamed at him and threw out a hand again. My blade flew toward me, and finally, the hilt hit my palm. I tried to scramble back, but my legs were useless. I quickly drew back my arm to throw the blade again, but Edric was too close. I cried out as he ran over me like a freaking truck. Agony slammed through my body.

The hound spun as Ren ran for me.

"No!"

Edric snarled and smashed into us both, knocking Ren several feet away, then he prowled toward Ren, sniffing the air. I called my blade and threw it again, visualizing where I wanted it to land, and it sunk into Edric's tree-trunk-sized thigh.

He roared and turned back to me.

"Get in the circle, Ren, now!" I held out my hand for my blade once more. It flew back, but Ren wasn't moving. Edric turned to me, stalking closer, limping now. He was foaming at the mouth, eyes blazing red, and I held out my blade. "Come closer and I slit the hound's throat and I won't stop slicing until I've taken his head. You won't easily find another vessel as strong as this one," I said to the spirit living inside Edric.

He stopped in his tracks, and I'd never seen a hellhound in its beast's form smile before, but I was positive that's what I was looking at now. He had no intention of backing down. He dipped his head, preparing to charge. I jerked my hands up, reaching for the trees, the forest floor, with my magic, and a hail of dead branches, debris, and several rocks flew at him on a flurry of violent wind, smashing into him with force.

Edric jerked back as the wind whipped around us, his body taking hit after hit. He roared, then turned, and with a powerful move, exploded across the clearing and vanished back into the woods.

I released the wind and scrambled to Ren, who still wasn't moving. "Ren...Renny, talk to me?" He was shaking, his entire body quivering.

A muffled sound reached me.

I frowned. "Ren?"

And then the sound became clearer.

Giggling.

A deranged, twisted sound that had my heart thumping against the back of my ribs. He spun suddenly and grabbed me by the throat. His eyes were black, no trace of the soft gold or his gentle heart that could be seen whenever you looked into them.

Instead, pure evil stared back.

He was possessed.

I gripped his wrist, trying to wrench it away, but he was too strong.

"Get out," I rasped past the tight grip he had on my throat. "Get out of him. Right the fuck now!"

"Or what?" A voice that wasn't Ren's answered, "What will you do?"

This wasn't the spirit who Edric was housing, this was someone else. How many had been piggybacking in the hellhound? No other creature was strong enough to hold several spirits at once. No wonder they'd been drawn to the clubhouse.

Grabbing the onyx around my throat, I shoved it against Ren's face and tried to choke out the spell to exorcise the spirit from him. But the words were indecipherable. He squeezed tighter and tears slid down my face as I gripped my blade tighter. I didn't want to hurt him.

But he grabbed my wrist before I could aim for his arm or leg, somewhere that wouldn't kill him, like he'd read my intentions. Twisting it behind me and up, his legs wrapping around mine and squeezing impossibly tight. Using all the new impressive fighting skills the hounds had taught Ren, locking me in a hold I couldn't get out of.

I was going to die here in this field—at the hands of my best friend.

He stared down at me, gaze wild, excited, as he watched his own hand slowly strangling the life out of me.

I'd failed him.

I'd failed my family.

I'd failed the people who had died at the hands of these spirits.

And I'd never get the chance to make it right.

Warrick's dark eyes, his rugged face, filled my mind, and the regret grew even deeper, the pain in my chest fiercer. I wanted him. I needed him.

Black spots danced across my vision—

A snarl broke through the blackness, then Ren was torn from me. A terrifying roar came next, and my fox was tossed halfway across the clearing.

I fell back, gasping for air, twisting toward Ren, searching for him in the long grass.

He sprang back to his feet suddenly, and without a backward glance, sprinted into the woods.

Then Warrick was there, looming over me.

That rugged, handsome face all I could see, and those dark eyes were filled with fury.

CHAPTER 16

Willow

WARRICK GRIPPED the steering wheel of the Morris in those huge hands, the big silver rings he sometimes wore catching the moonlight every now and then.

No one drove this truck but me. But I'd been shaking so hard by the time we reached it, Warrick had steered me to the passenger side without a word and lifted me into the seat.

Ren was gone.

We searched for hours, wandering through the forest. Nothing. Not a single sign of him. Warrick couldn't track him or Edric. Their scents weren't the same, anymore. They seemed to change and morph when they were possessed, making it impossible.

My sweet fox was out there somewhere right now, and that spirit could be making him do terrible, terrible things, things he'd never recover from. I bit back the sob trying to crawl up my throat. I should have sent him back as soon as I saw him. No, I should have taken him back out and driven him home myself.

Oh goddess, what would I tell his parents? Sally and Calum were like family to me, and I'd *promised* them I'd look after their son when I became a Keeper.

I gripped the door handle and tried to draw breath.

"Dove."

"It's my fault." I stared out the window and fought back my scream of helplessness. My throat felt raw. "I told him to stay in the salt circle, but his instinct to protect me..." I swallowed convulsively, acid trying to crawl up my throat. "He saw I was in pain and...I should have seen it coming, I should have..."

"A man makes his own decisions. The fox chose to follow you out there, and he chose to ignore your orders to stay put."

Warrick didn't understand. How could he? He didn't love, he didn't know what it was to *really* care about another being. He understood loyalty, but that wasn't the same. He didn't even have a soul; how could he ever understand? "It's happening again," I said, unable to keep the words inside me. I felt untethered, spinning out of control, the kind of fear I'd only ever experienced once in my life, and it gripped me so tight, it was all there was.

"What's happening again," he said, voice sharp.

"When Azel hurt me, when he cut me..."

Warrick jolted at that monster's name, his big body jerking like he'd been struck by lightning. "Dove," he said.

I ignored him and carried on, I had to get this out. I don't know why, but I had to purge the horror, the fear. "I remember lying there, his breath brushing my cheek as he leaned over me and carved WITCH into my back. He laughed, but he was so angry, so incredibly angry. I'd never heard a sound like that before. I broke...when he threatened my family. I was in so much pain and he was in my head, breaking me from the inside out, stripping back layer after layer, crushing my spirit, my will to live, to fight.... so much, that I gave up my friends. I've never felt like that before..." My hands shook in my lap. "He took me to the knights' compound and I dropped the ward protecting them. I've never felt weaker or hated myself more." I curled my fingers into fists. "I should have let him kill me before doing that... I should have..."

Warrick growled, loud and harsh, the sound ripping through the cab. "No," he barked. "You did what you had to do."

"I failed, Warrick. I failed all of them, and it's happening again. I'm failing." I sucked in a ragged breath. "Ren is gone. What if I don't...what if I lose him forever?"

His fingers curled tighter around the Morris's steering wheel, but he said nothing, because Warrick didn't lie and he couldn't promise that Ren would be okay, that he'd come home.

Finally, we reached the crossroads, and he indicated the turn that would take me back to my family. My stomach churned. "I don't want to go home."

Still, he said nothing, just turned in the opposite direction and headed toward the hounds' clubhouse, and I let him. I was being a coward, but I couldn't face my family after what I'd done, not yet.

Ren's parents, though, I needed to tell them now. Before I completely sunk into my pain and was utterly useless. I forced myself to hit Sally's number. Warrick remained quiet beside me as I tried to explain to Ren's mom what happened. She cried, and I made more promises I wasn't sure I could keep.

Warrick pulled up outside the clubhouse, and I followed him in.

He strode through the main room, down the stairs and into his room, shutting the door behind us. I stared at him, and tears stung my eyes, but if I cried, I wouldn't stop, because I'd lost Ren, because we were going to lose everything, and I didn't know how to stop it.

"Dove," he said so low it rolled through me like a tremor.

I didn't want to think. I didn't want to think about Ren out there somewhere, or that I might never get him back, even if he did survive this. I couldn't. I'd break if I did.

I locked eyes with Warrick. "Fuck me," I whispered.

His expression didn't change, but his eyes darkened before he shook his head.

I strode toward him. "You want to, you've said it enough times." I pressed my hands to his chest and tried to shove him toward the bed. He didn't budge. "What? Now you're acting all chivalrous? You either want to fuck me or you don't."

I was behaving like a crazy person—well, I fucking felt crazy. Out of control, and so desperate to get out of my own head space, so full of horrors and fear, that I pushed on, moving closer, pressing my body against his huge, hard one.

"You don't want this," he said.

I reached down and cupped his hard dick through his jeans. "You told me the next time I touched your cock, you'd fuck me." I lifted a brow. "Don't chicken out on me now, alpha."

"You don't want this," he repeated.

I squeezed him hard, wringing a groan from him. "Don't tell me what I want."

"Fine." He grabbed me, lifted me, and tossed me on his bed, then he came down on top of me, pinning me with his large body. He looked at my mouth and licked his lips.

"Well, what are you waiting for? All those females you fuck, they want more, right? Show me what I've been missing."

He cupped my jaw, his gold eyes locking with mine. "Your emotions are all over the place, I can feel them." His expression darkened. "The shit you said on the way here..." He growled under his breath. "You're in pain, dove, and you'll hate yourself, and me, if we do this."

"Why do you care how I feel?" I fired at him. "You don't know what the hell you're talking about. You don't even understand emotions."

"I didn't say that."

No, he hadn't, I'd made an assumption. But I didn't care, I wanted an escape, and he could give me one.

"I want you," he said. "You fucking know I do, but not like this."

I tried to shove at his chest, but again, he didn't budge. "Then let me up."

He shook his head.

"Warrick, let me the hell up."

"Not letting you up until you've calmed down. You still want me to fuck you in the morning, I'll let you bounce on my dick all you want."

"You really are a giant assho..."

He pressed a thick finger to my lips. "Quiet."

I stared up at him, my fury shooting higher, so much so, heat fired through my veins, igniting my skin. I fought, shoving and kicking.

He held me in place easily.

I shook my head, dislodging his finger. "Get the fuck off me."

"No, but keep throwing the attitude. I like it, makes my dick even harder."

I hissed up at him like a demented wild cat. "I've changed my damn mind, you can keep your dick to yourself."

"Liar. You want my dick so bad right now, I can smell it." He scented the air. "Can damn near taste it."

I screamed in outrage and tried to shove him off again.

Again, he didn't budge. Instead, he grabbed my hands and pinned them over my head by the wrists. "Best you keep still, shut the fuck up, and go to sleep, or I might forget how emotional you are and fuck you, anyway."

If I could, I would have punched him. A broken hand would be worth it. "Fine," I bit out.

"Fine what?"

I stared up at him, looking into his eyes, and the way he watched me back...was that concern? No, of course not. Now I was imagining things. "I'll sleep, but I'm covered in mud."

"So."

"So, can I at least take a shower?" *Let me up so I can kick you in the nuts and get the hell out of here.*

"No."

"No?"

He shrugged his wide shoulders. "I don't give a shit about mud."

"Well, I do."

He shrugged again, brought my hands down, rolled away, and pushed me to my side, then he rolled back in behind me. A muscled arm banded around me, keeping me pinned against him. I felt him kick off his boots.

There was no way I could get off this bed unless he let me, and suddenly I didn't care. I was exhausted right down to my bones. With the last of my energy, I kicked off my own boots, because it was obvious he wasn't letting me go anywhere tonight, even if I had the energy to leave.

The light went off.

"How did you do that?" I asked.

"You're not the only one with powers, dove."

I figured he had them, I'd just had no idea to what extent. "What else can you do?"

I felt him shrug. "A lot of things. Not as much as you."

The look in my fox's eyes, eyes that had no longer been his own, filled my head. "Where do you think Ren is right now?"

He was silent for several moments. "Don't do that."

I blinked into the darkness. "Do what?"

"Come up with stories in your head. We'll worry about that shit when we find him. Then we'll deal with the aftermath, whatever that is."

I swallowed, and the sound was audible in the dark room. "What if...he's like Maddox and runs away? Or what if what that spirit forces him to do is too much for him and he goes feral?"

"A shifter goes feral, we put them down."

The words were blunt, harsh, but his tone had gentled. I

squeezed my eyes closed and kept them that way. I knew this, I knew what happened to shifters that lost control of their inner animal. Ren was strong, though. I had to believe that, or I'd lose it.

Warrick's warmth, his strength, soaked through me as if it were trying to fill the gaping hole inside me, leaving no room for the pain.

And somehow, in his arms, the anxiety and turmoil was just a little bit more bearable.

———

I was laying in long grass, eyes closed, the sun beating down. *So warm.*

Crickets chirped, while birds perched on headstones and sang their morning song.

The cemetery had always been a place of peace for me. Some would find that weird, macabre, but I didn't care. When I lay here, it was as if I were being embraced by the women, the amazing witches, that had come before me. I always felt recharged, energized after I spent time here.

A dark cloud drifted over the sun, taking the warmth with it.

The birds and crickets quieted.

Thunder rolled across the sky.

I sat up, looking around, shivering as an icy chill lifted goose bumps on my skin.

"One by one," a voice called, traveling to me on the breeze.

"Hello? Who's there?"

A dark figure stepped out from the trees lining the cemetery. I didn't know them, they shouldn't be here, they shouldn't be able to enter our most sacred place.

"One by one," the dark figure said again.

I scrambled to my feet. "Who are you? What do you want?"

The figure slowly walked closer. They were small, draped in a dark cloak so large that was all I could see of them. A red fox trotted up and sat at their side.

"Ren?"

But Ren didn't move. He looked at me with eyes that weren't his own, eyes that didn't know me.

A shadow hovered behind him, growing larger. "Come here," I called, "come to me." Ren turned and walked back into the woods, and that strange shadow drifted deeper into the cemetery. "No, please, Ren. Come back."

"One," the dark figure said and lifted a hand. "By one," they finished and lifted their other hand. The billowy sleeve of their cloak slid back as they lifted them higher, and tangled in the skinny fingers of their right hand was a tumble of chestnut hair, the left was wrapped in pale gold waves.

I stumbled back, screaming, falling to my knees.

Iris and Rose stared back with dead eyes, their decapitated heads clutched in the stranger's hands. The cloaked figure laughed and kicked something.

Another head, this one rolled to a stop beside me. Beautiful black hair, thick and wavy, covered the face, and I brushed it back with a shaking hand.

Magnolia.

I screamed again.

"Wake up," a voice said, echoing all around me.

The dark figure dropped the heads and walked toward me, a long, bloodied knife in their hand. "One by one," they repeated. The strange shadow followed.

"Wake up, dove," the voice said again, against my ear this time.

I jolted and gasped, my eyes shooting open.

"Dove?" Warrick said, voice so low I felt it.

My face was wet, and I was shivering.

"Your skin's like fucking ice," he said.

My throat hurt and a sob escaped before I could stop it.

Warrick wrapped his arms around me, rubbing those hot, rough-skinned hands over my skin, and I couldn't bring myself to push him away. I needed it. I needed to be held so badly.

The cold slowly washed away, my body drawing warmth from Warrick, letting it soak through me.

"I'm okay," I said, because the last thing I wanted to be in front of this male was weak or vulnerable.

"You were screaming, Willow, crying. You are not fucking okay. Why are you so cold? Why can't I get you warm?" His voice was gruff, and yes, definitely filled with concern.

"It was just a...a bad dream, that's all. And I'm starting to warm now." But it wasn't just a dream, was it? I squeezed my eyes closed. It felt too real. Ren turning from me...the contorted looks on my sisters' faces. They were dead. Oh goddess, they'd all been dead. They filled my mind again, and I snapped my eyes open.

Warrick didn't question me, but I got the feeling he wasn't buying my bullshit. I was too shaken to try to convince him otherwise, though, the lies wouldn't come.

We lay there in silence for a while, and as I slowly calmed, as the dream drifted away along with the ice under my skin and in my veins, I became more and more aware of the male surrounding me.

The way he'd held me, so...tenderly. He'd wrapped me securely in his strong arms, offering me support, and it felt more than just physical. One arm was across my middle, the other banded across my chest. One of his thighs was between mine, his front pressed to my back, his groin against my butt, and his bearded chin was on my shoulder.

It should feel restricting.

It didn't.

He was warming me.

Comforting me as if he thought he could make it better if he could just get close enough.

And I liked it...way too much.

"You must think I'm pathetic." I swallowed several times. "Weak."

He made a rumbling sound. "Seen you hack off a demon's head, dove. Several times."

"You've also seen me cry," I added.

"Also seen your dress torn, covered in my blood, crouched in front of me ready to take on an entire forest of creatures to protect me."

There was a smile in his voice. "You're never going to let me forget that, are you?"

The hand on my chest slid up, and he pressed a finger to my lips like he had the night before. His mouth came to my ear. "Enough," he said roughly.

I didn't try to pull away this time, no. A shiver slid through me at the dominant tone of his voice.

"No one has ever put themselves between me and danger, dove. Not ever. I'm alpha, that's my job. But you did that." His lips moved against my ear, and he breathed deep. "So no, not fucking weak, sure as fuck not pathetic."

"Warrick..."

"You're the strongest female I know, Willow."

His finger traced my lower lip, and before I could stop it, my tongue darted out to taste his salty skin, needing it, craving it.

He stilled, his sharp indrawn breath loud in the quiet room.

I turned in his arms, and he let me, not stopping me this time. Not when I rested my forehead on his wide tattooed chest, or when I pressed my lips to his incredibly hot skin and kissed him there. Then a second time.

His blunt fingers thrust into my hair, and he tilted my head back, looking down at me with question clear in his eyes.

I stared back, needing him so badly at that moment there was no way he could miss it.

And I knew for sure that he hadn't when his nostrils flared, and on a rough sound, he leaned in and kissed me the way only Warrick could. Fiercely.

His mouth covered mine, hungry and demanding, his tongue delving deep, claiming, wild, leaving me breathless. One of his hands dropped to my ass and he squeezed, making me squirm. I couldn't hold in my whimper, my thighs clenching as the ache inside me intensified.

He kissed along my jaw, down my throat, a low, rumbling growl rolling from him almost constantly now. "You need me to get you off, don't you, dove?"

"Yes."

"You think you're ready to be fucked, but you're not. It doesn't matter what I said, what I wanted in the woods, I was wrong. So I'm gonna use my fingers this first time," he said.

I wanted to protest. I wanted him inside me already. We'd been dancing this dance for so long. Too long. I opened my mouth to beg for it, but he kissed me again in that all-consuming way, filled with hunger and dominance and need.

The hand on my ass slid around my hip, and with a sharp tug, he tore the front of my pants open. I gasped into his mouth as he dragged my destroyed pants and underwear down my thighs.

I kicked them aside and spread my legs for him as his hand slid back up, grasping, massaging my skin, making me squirm. I was so impossibly wet and achy, so empty, I was close to tears from how much I needed him.

Near mad with lust, I reached for the front of his jeans, but he grabbed my wrists and pinned them over my head with one hand. Then the other was sliding between my legs, pressing against my slick flesh, making me arch and groan into his touch.

"Fuck...this hot little pussy," Warrick gritted out. "It knows who it belongs to, doesn't it, dove?"

I nodded before I could think better of it. I'd say anything, do anything, for him to make me come at that moment, but deep down, I knew he was right. My body had never responded to anyone the way it did him. And that was one of the reasons I'd tried to ignore this fire between us.

We had a connection I couldn't explain. And as much as I'd tried to deny it, he wasn't the only one who felt it.

It did scare the hell out of me, though.

He slid his middle finger over my needy flesh, and all thought scattered as he grazed my clit, but he didn't linger, he dipped down lower and dragged his finger through my wetness before coming back up and giving me what I needed, circling my clit.

"Look at me," he said.

I forced my eyes open, staring up at him heavy lidded. I bit my lip and rolled my hips desperately, all control shot to pieces.

His glowing golden eyes bore into mine as he dipped back down and pushed a thick finger inside me. I arched deeper and cried out, so close to the edge, to coming just from that alone.

A tremor washed through me.

He slid his finger out and back in with a grunt. "Yeah, we're gonna have to work you up to fucking, dove. This tight little body isn't ready for my cock, not yet."

His thumb brushed my clit again, and I shook all over. What was he doing to me? How was this possible with just his finger?

He dragged it out and pushed back in, adding a second, and I cried out when he went deeper. I was writhing beneath him, straining against the hold he had on my wrists above my head, where he pressed them into the mattress.

He dragged his lips along my throat, my jaw, while the fingers between my legs thrust faster, deeper. I spread my thighs wider, wanting more, rocking against his hand, so wet now, the sound of those thick fingers fucking me filled the room. My skin was hot and sweaty, my breathing coming in pants, mixing with Warrick's own harsh breaths.

"Come for me, dove," he grated against my ear. "Let go."

The rasp of his voice lifted goose bumps all over my skin as I worked myself down on his thrusting fingers, the feeling inside me building, until it flew through me, filling me, breaking me into a million pieces.

My mouth dropped open in a silent cry, and Warrick covered my lips with his, kissing me, swallowing my desperate sounds as I spasmed and clutched at his fingers.

He didn't stop until I collapsed back against the mattress, desperate for breath.

Oh shit.

He pressed more kisses to my neck, my jaw.

His fingers were still deep inside me, and I squeezed my thighs around his thick wrist, not even ashamed that I was silently asking him to stay where he was—inside me.

Because I wanted more.

I needed it.

CHAPTER 17

Warrick

HER THIGHS CLENCHED around my forearm as if she thought I was done with her.

Fuck.

No.

I knew what she was doing. My dove was using pleasure to forget her pain, like she'd tried to last night.

Only now her emotions were less volatile and more focused. She wanted this, needed it from me. I'd finally been able to give her pleasure, to make her come, and if that's what she needed, I sure as fuck wasn't finished making her feel good. Soon enough she'd be back to her tasks, the next trial, to worrying about her family and the fox. I wanted to make her feel good, to take her mind off all that shit, even it was just a short time.

Carefully, I pried her thighs apart and slid my fingers free of her tight pussy, gritting my teeth when she whimpered. Fuck. The driving need of the beast thrumming through me had every instinct in me roaring to take her, to finally make her mine. I fought it back and, instead, lifted her off the bed.

"Where are we going?" she asked, sounding almost groggy.

The sound of satisfaction in her voice pleased me, filled me with pride. I'd made her come hard, and I intended to do it again. "Gonna clean the mud off, dove."

In the bathroom, I removed the rest of her clothing, and possessiveness swelled in my chest that she'd allowed me to do that for her. As if she knew it was my right, as if she'd finally accepted that she was mine.

Turning on the shower, I moved quickly, getting what I needed, not wanting to give her time to change her mind, to run from me again. I felt her eyes on me, watching my every move, and as soon as the water was warm, I closed in on her again, the beast taking the lead for a moment, all but herding her into the stall.

She didn't protest, no, she sighed as the hot water hit her skin. I quickly stripped out of my clothes and climbed in, and her gaze drifted over my naked body hungrily.

I liked the way she looked at me, especially when I was naked and she wasn't trying to hide her lust. Not that she ever truly could; the scent of her need filled my senses, drove me wild every time we were together. Backing her up against the shower wall, I grabbed the soap, lathered it between my hands, then ran them over her shoulders, her arms, washing the dirt from her skin.

"You don't need to do that," she whispered, looking up at me, eyes wide, *fuck*, vulnerable like an abandoned baby dear. I wanted to haul her into my arms and hold her to me, to protect her from everything that hurt her, to keep her safe in this room with me for the rest of time. I'd never felt this way in my life and the power of it was a staggering force inside me. "Warrick?"

The husky note to her voice when she said my name made my scalp tingle and my cock throb. "I want to do it."

I lathered my hands again and slid them over her shoulders a second time, then around her delicate throat, washing away the dirt streaked there, then back down.

Her breath hitched as I slid my hands over her full tits, soaping up her sweet little nipples, so tight and desperate for my mouth. I worked them between my fingers first, and she gripped my biceps to hold herself up, a groan slipping past her lips.

"I haven't tasted you here yet, dove," I said as I washed the soap away.

"No, you haven't," she said.

No resistance, full surrender.

It would be so easy to take advantage of that, to take what I wanted, but I would never do that, no matter how much the beast in me howled for it—for her. If I did that now, while she was in pain, I would lose her forever. Yes, she was the strongest female I'd ever met, but here, now, she seemed almost fragile, breakable. My dove needed me to take care of her. And I wanted that, too, and surprisingly, it was even stronger than my need to fuck her.

Anything else would end up hurting her, and every part of me abhorred the very idea. Instead, I took her mouth in another kiss. My dove liked the way I kissed her. The scent of her arousal increased every time, but it was more than that. When Lucifer created us, he'd given us heightened senses that went beyond scent, sound, touch, and taste.

The reason hellhounds were so good at fucking was our ability to register pleasure. We knew when a sexual partner enjoyed what we were doing.

It was the same with all emotions, really. Which meant, although I hadn't experienced a great many myself, I understood them.

Which was how I knew it made her happy when I kissed her, in a way that went beyond the physical. It was something I'd never felt before, not in myself, and not in others, maybe because I'd never once sought anything beyond the physical before. The females I'd bedded in the past hadn't been interested in anything other than getting off.

But I felt it now, this strange warmth, it settled in my chest, in my lower stomach, and it was a *good* feeling. It made me want to get closer to her.

So I kissed her throat, something else she liked. I didn't need to use my senses for that, though, her whimpers and the way she gripped me tighter as if she were afraid I'd leave her wanting, told me just as easily.

Dropping to my knees, I wrapped my arms around her tiny waist and sucked a nipple into my mouth. Her fingers delved into my hair, holding me there, and I sucked greedily, feeding off her pleasure even as my own throbbed deeper, more fiercely.

My cock was impossibly hard now, an ache in my balls, a desperation to rut that had me locking my thighs so I didn't thrust into thin air. I licked and sucked her nipple until she was writhing, then I shifted to the other and did the same until her scent was so strong it filled the shower stall. Until her need was so intense that I knew she'd come for me almost as soon as I put my mouth on her.

Finally, I worked my way down her taut stomach, to where it was rounder, softer, below her belly button, and hungry female that she was, she opened wider for me.

I growled low at the sight of her glistening and swollen, primed for the taking. "Haven't tasted you here either, dove."

She moaned. "Please."

At her soft plea, I all but fell on her, gripping her thighs and pushing them apart before swiping my tongue through her folds. A snarl escaped when finally...fucking, *finally*, I knew her taste. I threw her thighs over my shoulders, her body sliding up the wall as I gripped her ass, wanting more, wanting inside her in any way I could.

I couldn't get enough. I would never get enough.

Savage lust throbbed through me, and my hand dropped to my

cock, gripping it tight. She tasted better than I'd ever imagined, and I lapped at her like the hungry dog I was, so desperate for her, for more. Her legs shook and she cried out, tugging on my hair, rubbing against my mouth in her frenzy to come.

I tugged on my dick faster as I ate at her, fucking her with my tongue, then finally giving her what she needed and sucked her slick little clit. She screamed, her cries echoing off the walls as she came against my mouth. I licked her all up as she trembled, wringing every last shudder from her, and kept going, not stopping until she screamed again, coming on my tongue a second time.

When her body went soft and pliant, I lowered her legs and stood. Holding her up, I tilted her head back and devoured her mouth while I stroked my dick hard and fast. It wasn't going to take long, not after that, not with my tongue in her mouth and her taste passing between us.

I broke the kiss, my breath forced roughly past my lips with every vicious tug of my fist.

She looked down, realizing what I was doing, and immediately reached for me. I grabbed her hand and pulled it away. "No."

"What? Why? Let me..."

"No," I said more harshly. "You got a pass last night because you were hurting, but I meant what I said, you touch my dick, I fuck you. I meant it, the beast in me sure as fuck meant it, and we both know you're not ready for that. Not here," I said and tapped the side of her head. "And not here," I growled and cupped her sweet as fuck pussy. She was too fucking tight, I'd need to work her up to my cock with my fingers, and she'd need to come a lot more than she had this morning. "And despite how badly I wanted you in the woods, you were right to turn me down."

"Yes, you're really big, but..."

"No," I said again, then fisted her wild red hair and locked eyes with her as I planted my feet wide and fucked into my fist. "Look, dove, look down at my cock, watch me come."

I'd held off what was about to happen in the woods, I couldn't now, not after making her come, not after tasting her...tasting my mate. My animal instincts had kicked in, setting off a response that had lain dormant inside me my entire life, waiting, waiting for her. My mated brothers had explained the feeling or tried to, but I hadn't been prepared for it.

Fuck. Heat coiled in my gut, pulsing deeply along my shaft, an ache building in my balls and down my thighs.

My body had been fooled by Willow's scent, so thick around us, and her taste still on my tongue, that it believed I was inside my female, that there was a chance to breed her. "Watch," I said again, but I didn't need to.

She already was, and her pink tongue darted out to swipe over her lower lip. I watched her face, her reaction as I got closer. She was panting again and her eyes widened, lips parting.

I glanced down, but I knew what she was seeing, my cock growing bigger. I hissed, watching as the veins bulged thickly along my shaft, the head darkening, widening.

"Warrick?" she whispered.

"It's so our females are locked in place, dove. It's so we're as deep as we can get when we come." I didn't tell her it only happened with our mates, she wasn't ready to hear that yet, even though deep down she knew the truth. I groaned, my balls drawing up. "So you can't get away when I pump my seed deep inside you."

I expected fear, or worse, revulsion.

What I got was the opposite, and that look of hunger on her face tipped me over the edge. I slapped my hand against the wall, leaned in, and emptied myself on her stomach, hissing and groaning as my come splashed her smooth skin.

When there was nothing left, I hooked the back of her neck with one hand, holding her in place, and pressed the other to her belly, smearing my seed there, then higher, over her tits, marking her with my scent. Even if she used soap, it would still be there.

My brothers would smell it, any shifter around her would sense my claim on her.

The thought pleased me greatly. I stared into her eyes. "That's why, when we fuck, you need to be ready for me, in every way."

She didn't argue, just nodded slowly. She'd tried to deny it so many times, but she knew we were inevitable. She knew it now. And there was no turning away from this, not anymore.

I reached for the shampoo, squirted some in my hand, and turned her around, and she instantly tilted her head back as I worked it through her hair.

If she was worried about having me inside her after witnessing what she just had, she didn't say. Still, I worried. "You'll like it, dove, the way I fuck you, I promise you that," I said, trying to reassure her.

But again, she didn't deny it, or tell me it wasn't going to happen—no, a sexy little quiver moved through her, and I had to bite back a snarl of triumph, even as I was filled with contentment, because nothing had ever felt better in my long fucking life than being in this shower with Willow.

I'd made my dove come and now I was tending to her other needs.

It was only a matter of time before I made her mine in every possible way.

Before I claimed my mate.

CHAPTER 18

Willow

THE HOUSE WAS quiet when I walked in.

I knew it would be. Iris was out with Brody, and Mom, Arthur, and Else had taken Rose for a drive to pick up supplies for the shop. I wasn't sure where Mags was, with Bram somewhere, no doubt.

Kicking off my heels, I turned on the kettle. The funeral was rough. Rebecca had no family to speak of, and Jane apparently had only a few friends. I'd held Rebecca's hand the whole time, her pain like a bleak gray cloud around her, the horror she still felt over the way she believed her daughter died, rolling off her in waves.

I'd slipped some calming herbs in her tea, but it'd barely made a difference. Twice I'd nearly taken her aside and told her the truth. Jane's death was horrific and heartbreaking, but at least it'd been quick, not the gruesome, drawn-out murder Rebecca believed it was. Knowing her child hadn't suffered would ease her pain.

And then I'd seen Maddox. He'd been on the other side of the cemetery, watching from a distance as Jane's coffin was slowly lowered into the ground, the small stuffed bear Rebecca had placed on the top going with it.

He'd seen me and walked away before I could go to him, his howl echoing from a distance several minutes later, so mournful and broken it brought tears to my eyes.

I'd texted Warrick, told him where I'd seen his brother, then left. The urge to run to Warrick, to seek comfort from him, had been strong, so much so, it kind of frightened me. And after what we'd done that morning, it would've been easy to go to him, but I couldn't allow myself to get emotionally involved.

There was no point catching feelings for a guy who couldn't return them. That was just asking for a flying kick to the heart, and I wasn't that much of a masochist.

But resisting the physical attraction between us was something I couldn't do anymore. Maybe that made me weak? Probably. But I wanted him like I'd never wanted another male. And I'd been having no-strings relationships my whole adult life, why would this be any different? What could possibly go wrong?

My brain flashed up one disastrous scenario after another. I shoved those images back, and all thoughts of Warrick from my mind, and instantly guilt worked its way back in.

Maybe I should have stayed with Jane longer? Her neighbor had been at the funeral and had offered to drive her home. I'd hugged her goodbye, and she'd been so broken. I drew in a steadying breath. It was selfish, but it'd been a struggle being around that kind of pain, that kind of loss.

I took down a mug, my eyes sliding to the herbs and tonics, the oils and elixirs that Else had prescribed Rose.

They weren't helping.

Nothing was helping.

If I lost her—

I squeezed my eyes closed as tightly as I could, praying to the mother to give me the power of healing—though Cora was a healer and nothing she'd tried had helped—or the power to stop time then, anything to make sure we never lost our Rose.

A scream came from upstairs, followed by a bellow.

My blade was in my hand a moment later, and I sprinted up the stairs. The scream came again, filled with panic, with pain.

Magnolia.

I rushed into her room.

Mags was on the floor, Bram clutching her to him, terror in his eyes. She was covered in blood.

"What the hell happened, what's…" My voice trailed off as a wicked slice appeared out of thin air across her thigh, like an invisible blade slashing her flesh. Oh goddess, she was covered in them.

She screamed again, while Bram watched on, eyes wild, clutching her tighter, trying to staunch the blood.

"A hex doll," I rasped—the stabbing pains I'd felt in the woods, the reason Ren left the safety of the salt circle. I hadn't thought about it again, but someone had attacked me, it was the only explanation, and now they were attacking Magnolia, only this was so much worse.

"Downstairs," I yelled at Bram and ran down ahead and into Else's work room.

I was searching for what we needed when Bram ran in carrying Mags. She screamed again, another slice appearing, this time across her shoulder. Bram roared. Whoever was doing this, they weren't just doing it to scare her. All it would take was a slice across her throat and we'd lose her.

Iris ran in, Nia barking at her side. "What the hell is going on…Magnolia!"

"Hex doll," I said, trying desperately to keep it together.

"How? We're protected…"

"The darkest kind of magic." Terror slid through me, and I

saw the same in Iris's eyes. "Quick, I need unbleached linen, rosemary, and matches." Iris jumped into action, and I finished grabbing the oils and one of Else's special elixirs.

"Put her on the floor, Bram."

He shook as he lowered her to the ground.

"You need to stand back."

Bram did as we asked but stayed close, shifting in his big boots as he watched Iris sprinkle rosemary on the stone floor around Mags in a wide circle.

"We've got you, Mags," she said. "Hold on."

Magnolia jerked as another slice appeared high on her chest, close to her throat, *too close*. Whoever was doing this was having fun; they wanted her to know they were going to kill her, and they wanted us to know it too.

Iris handed me a wide strip of linen, her eyes meeting mine as we began tearing it into thinner strips. "Thread and needle, linen so fine, save our beloved, sever this bind," we both chanted as we walked around her, tearing strip after strip, laying them end to end.

I handed Iris the blended oil, and I popped the cork from the elixir as we continued to chant, emptying our bottles on the linen, soaking it. When they were empty, I snatched up the matches. Lighting one, I crouched down and set fire to the fabric circling Mags. It ignited instantly, the flames rushing from one strip to the next.

Fear transformed Mags's face, and her hand flew to her throat.

"No!" Iris screamed.

The final piece of linen caught, breaking the connection to whoever was in control of the hex doll, and Mags collapsed back. Bram rushed to her, jumping the circle, and hauled her into his arms as her hand fell away.

I grabbed for the shelf beside me, my legs shaking so hard, they were close to giving out. Blood leaked from a new slice at the side of her throat, but it was small, not life-threatening.

Thank the mother.

Iris dropped to the floor, covered her face with her hands, and sobbed.

I grabbed more rags from Else's stash, handing some to Bram, the both of us holding them to the deeper of Magnolia's cuts, to stop the bleeding. Though, I didn't think any of them were life-threatening either.

I cupped Magnolia's face. "Mags?"

"I-I'm okay," she rasped.

I wasn't, and I never would be again. Someone had just tried to kill my sister.

We'd been a split second from losing her.

"Who'd do this?" Iris said, looking up at me, her hand buried in Nia's fur, seeking and giving comfort. "Why?"

"I don't know." I had no answers. Magnolia was no threat to anyone. "But we need to get her stitched up. Go get Cora, Iris."

Iris did as I said, and I held the rags more firmly to the deep cut in Mags's thigh. Cora was a decent healer, and she'd worked as a nurse in a human hospital for a lot of years. Taking Mags to a hospital would only send the police to us, though, and there was no explaining this. We had to take care of this at home.

My sister clung to Bram, who looked like he wanted to commit murder, his dark eyes going between Mags and searching the room, but there was no one to direct his rage at, not yet, and I felt that down to my soul.

"It's going to be okay," I said to Mags, but I had no idea if that was true. What the fuck was going on?

She nodded, trembling, probably going into shock.

I didn't understand this. This wasn't part of my task. It had nothing to do with the malevolent souls in Roxburgh. The mother didn't mess with a Keeper's family or their coven. I couldn't see how this was connected at all.

A few minutes later, Cora rushed in, carrying a bag, and cried out in alarm. Brody was right behind her, his arm around Iris, who was still seriously shaken.

"Back up," Cora said, all business, and got down on the floor. "I need to see the damage."

She tried to shoo Bram away, but he wasn't having it. In the end, I stood and got out of her way. I watched on as she cleaned and sewed up the worst of the cuts, using one of her healers' spells to numb the pain, then Bram carried Mags to the kitchen and laid her down on the chaise by the window so Cora could treat the rest.

"Thank the goddess you were here," Cora said.

Iris's eyes grew huge. "We could have lost her." Exactly what I'd been thinking. "I was out with Brody and you were at the funeral," she said to me. "Else, Mom, and Roe are out for the day. None of us were supposed to be here, only Mags and Bram. Whoever did this must have known we'd all be away. They wanted her here without any of us to stop it."

Iris was right.

And I didn't know what to do. I was the one they looked to when things turned to shit, and I had no answers. I'd been so caught up in what happened to Ren, so deep in my own misery, then distracted by Warrick, I'd forgotten about the unexplainable pain I'd felt in that woods and I'd left them all vulnerable.

"We need to make sure no one else is at risk." I gripped the back of a chair, watching Cora sew a slice down Magnolia's arm. "I'm pretty sure I am. Something happened in the woods last night...well, a couple of things actually."

"What? What happened?" Iris asked, pulling away from Brody.

"Ren was with me...he followed me out there. I had him in a salt circle, and he wasn't supposed to leave it. Then Edric, the possessed hound, came at me, and before I could get in my own circle, I felt stabbing pains in my legs. I'm pretty sure Mags isn't the only one who has a hex doll with her name on it. They were just a little subtler about it in my case."

"Christ, Willow," Cora said. "You could have been killed."

"Is Iris safe?" Brody said, tugging her in closer to him again.

"I don't know," I said honestly. "We'll do the same ritual we did on Mags to the rest of us, then Else can make something extra to protect us, to stop it from happening again."

"And Ren?" Mags asked, trying to sit up. "What happened to Ren?"

I turned to her, my heart lodged in my throat. "He was possessed. He attacked me and ran away. Warrick and I searched for him most of the night. There was no trace of him."

"No," she whispered and gripped Bram's arm when he immediately moved closer to her. Ren was their friend as well, their family. This hurt them too.

Bram aimed his dark eyes my way. "Can I help?" he said in his incredibly deep and rough voice. "I can search the woods?"

He could fly above the forest, covering ground faster. "Yeah, that'd be really good. Thanks, Bram."

He dipped his chin.

"Why aren't you still out there looking for him?" Mags said, voice filled with fear and accusation.

My heart had never felt so heavy. "We tried, there was no sign..."

"If something happened to Bram, nothing would stop me from searching for him. He's your familiar, he's supposed to be your best friend."

"Mags," Iris said.

"No," Mags said, hands shaking. "Why are you like this, Wills? You're so damn distant, so cold, you never let us in. You never let him in. Do you even care?"

"Magnolia," Iris said more sharply.

She was hurting, in shock after what happened, I got that, but her words cut me down the middle. I was actively not thinking about what might be happening to Ren right then. My heart couldn't take it. It felt like someone had torn it to shreds. "His scent changed when he was possessed, tracking him has been extremely hard, Mags. Warrick has some of his brothers looking for him, their tracking skills are unsurpassed. I assure you, I'm looking for him."

And she was right, I did keep my family at a distance sometimes, but only to protect them. That had been my role in the family for as long as I could remember. It started with me trying to shield them from the men who'd come in and out of mom's life. My mom would get so lost in her feelings, in the idea of love, she missed all the red flags, over and over again. I'd pushed my sisters closer together, while I held back, always watching, always alert, making myself the barrier, trying to deflect the pain from them.

I'd felt like I had the weight of the world on my shoulders, but I'd never meant to hurt them, or make them feel like I didn't care. I'd only wanted to keep them safe.

Her face dropped, and I hated it. "Mags..."

My phone rang, and I bit back a curse, pulling it free. I checked the screen. An unknown number. A queasy feeling hit my stomach. "Hello?"

"Willow, I...oh god..."

"Clayton?" His voice was shaky, broken, barely recognizable.

"I'm sorry, I shouldn't be calling you, but I didn't know who... who I could trust."

"What's going on?"

"It's my mother, someone...someone killed her. She was, Christ, Willow, they cut her to ribbons. They slit her throat."

CHAPTER 19

Willow

I took in Clayton's house as I pulled up outside the next morning. He'd wanted me to come here last night, but I'd had my own family to take care of, and when Mom, Else, and Roe got home, we'd had to perform on them the same ritual we had on Mags.

Then we'd been up all night walking the perimeter of our house, strengthening our wards. No one was getting to them again.

Mom had been beside herself when she'd seen Mags, then Rose had collapsed, looking paler, sicker than I'd ever seen her. I'd hoped...we'd all hoped that maybe it was a hex doll making her sicker, but after the ritual there'd been no change, and the hopelessness I'd felt had been mirrored in the faces of my family.

Mags was doing as well as could be expected this morning. Bram had slept on the floor in her room last night, and Cora and Else were treating her wounds to prevent infection. Else had an excellent salve that sped up healing and reduced scarring, something that we all used a lot, considering how often we cut ourselves spelling.

That wouldn't take away the scars she would carry on the inside for the rest of her life, though. When I'd checked on her this morning, she'd been subdued, and the light that had always shone from Magnolia had been seriously dimmed. My fingers curled into a tight fist. I was going to find the monster who did this, and when I did, I was going to end them.

And how the hell are you going to do that?

I rubbed my hands over my face and forced myself to breathe, because I felt like I was drowning. I needed to protect my family, keep them safe from whoever wanted to hurt us. I didn't know what they wanted, why they'd done this, or if it was connected to what happened to Clay's mother, because her injuries sounded so similar.

And if I didn't pass this task *and* my next trial, all the gifts that had come to our family from trials past would be revoked. We'd still be witches, but our powers would be greatly reduced. We'd be sitting ducks. The covens could come for us, for our cemetery, and we'd be as helpless as lambs.

My eyes stung, and I choked back a sob.

And, on top of all these problems, I needed to find Ren.

The door was pulled open, and I jolted, spinning in my seat, my blade in my hand a second later.

Warrick stood there staring down at me.

His bike was behind the Morris. I hadn't even heard him drive up, lost so deep in my own thoughts. "What are you doing here?"

He rested a hand above the door. "Just came from your house, dove."

"So you know that someone attacked Magnolia?" My voice was husky from fighting back goddamn tears. I hated crying. It solved nothing. It helped nothing. Feeling sorry for myself sure as hell wouldn't help the people I loved most in this world.

"Yeah, and you've already got enough shit to deal with. I can't stop an attack that involves witchcraft, but I can keep them phys-ically safe. I sent some of my brothers to your place. They'll cover all of you until we know what the fuck is going on."

I blinked up at him, and my heart smacked against the back of my ribs, then I was moving, flying out of the truck and wrapping my arms around him. "Thank you," I said against his chest.

We could ward the house, we were still powerful witches, for now, anyway. We'd been taking care of ourselves for as long as I could remember. But I wanted all bases covered, and sometimes straight-up brute strength was what you needed. And as much as I hated owing favors or relying on anyone else, when it came to my sisters, to Mom and Else, my pride didn't matter. I'd take all the help I could get. "You don't know what a relief that is."

One of his thick fingers hooked me under the chin, and he tilted my head back. "Anything you need, dove, just ask. And if anyone comes for your family again, one of my brothers will shred them into bloody pieces."

I grinned up at him, knowing that my smile looked more than a little wobbly. "Aww, you old sweet talker you. Now you're speaking my language."

The grin he laid on me in return made my damn knees weak. "Enough of the old."

"Aren't you like a thousand years old?"

He chuckled and then shrugged. "Give or take a few hundred years."

That chuckle seriously did things to me. My gaze dropped to his lips—

"Willow?"

I turned to see Clayton coming down the stairs. He looked as though he hadn't slept in days, eyes bloodshot, hair disheveled, clothes wrinkled.

"Be nice," I said to Warrick, then ducked under his arm and strode toward Clay.

Warrick stuck close, and for once, I was more than okay with it. I had no idea what I was about to walk in on. This could be some kind of trap, for all I knew. Maybe Clay was behind it all, maybe this was some twisted ruse?

Now you're just being paranoid.

Probably, but I couldn't afford to trust anyone right now. My gaze slid to Warrick. Apparently, the hellhound alpha was an exception. I hoped like hell I wouldn't live to regret it, but every one of my instincts told me I wouldn't, that I needed to trust him. He may not have a soul, but his aura...god, it was all warmth, deep oranges with glowing reds and yellow sparks floating around him, like embers floating up from a fire.

Yes, he'd been created by Lucifer and had lived most of his life in Hell, but there was nothing evil about him.

"Come with me," Clayton said and strode back to the house.

I glanced at Warrick and his brows lowered, his head tilting back, scenting the air. He stopped me with a hand to my stomach. "Something's dead in that house," he said.

"Clay's mother was murdered here last night, but I assumed he had her body removed."

"She's still here."

Oh god.

We followed Clay inside, up the grand staircase, and down a long hall. He stopped in front of a door, staring at it for several long seconds, then finally, he reached out, gripped the handle, and opened it. He reached in, flicked on the light, and slowly walked in.

I paused at the threshold, the sweet, sickly scent of death hitting the back of my throat instantly. Clay stood at the end of her bed, his expression blank. Olive Whitlock lay in a sea of white and pale pink bedding drenched with blood, some dry and rust colored, some still vibrant red.

"Who would do this?" he asked, his entire body shaking. "They tortured her, cutting her over and over again until she was too weak to move...then they sliced her throat." He slid his trembling hands into his pockets. "I'd been at the office all day. I came home and found her. There was no sign of a break in or forced entry, nothing..." He cleared his throat. "I should have been here to protect her, I should have..."

I walked into the room and stood beside him. Olive was tangled in her sheets, her face a mask of horrors. She'd writhed in pain before she'd died. She'd screamed in terror.

My stomach churned.

I could have come home, like Clay had, and found Magnolia like that.

The cuts were exactly the same as the ones on my sister, just a lot more of them. Had they somehow known I'd gotten back early? Were they watching the house? They'd gone for my sister's throat far sooner than they had Olive's. "Why is she still here, Clay?"

"I..." He turned to me. "I didn't know what to do, Wills."

I touched his arm, and Warrick took several steps closer. "Have you been in here with her all night?"

He nodded, shaking harder.

"Come on." I led him from the room, shutting the door firmly behind us, and back downstairs to the sitting room. I poured him a bourbon from the liquor cabinet and handed it to him. He downed it and slumped back against the couch.

"You need to call Sal," I said.

Sally Macanroy, Ren's Mom, was the only mortician witches in Roxburgh used. When something like this happened, a magic-related death, they took care of the bodies so we didn't draw attention from the human police. As far as justice went? If there was foul play, the victim's family needed to gather evidence before they could appeal the witch's council. If the council approved their claim, they could then seek restitution. The most common was financial. But some chose a life for a life. Others...got more creative.

He nodded and took out his phone, but his hand was shaking

so badly he had trouble calling up the number. I reached for his phone. "I'll do it."

"Thanks."

I quickly called Ren's parents and asked them to come and collect Clayton's mother.

"I'm so sorry for dragging you into this," he said to me when I ended the call. "But recently...well, Mother had lost a lot of friends. And along with all the other fucking awful shit that's happened, we found ourselves rather isolated."

"How did she lose friends?"

Clayton blinked down at me. "You didn't hear?"

I shook my head.

"My trial," he said, waiting for me to catch on.

"I've heard nothing."

He sat forward, his throat working. "I was paired with Johnston Avery. His family is large and powerful, and everyone assumed he would beat me, and easily. There was a marriage counting on it. John was promised Asuka if he won. A joining of two magically powerful families." He gave me a look, but thankfully didn't mention the similar deal he'd offered me. "But I won, and the marriage was taken off the table. We've been blacklisted, ostracized, they said I cheated, and some believed the lies." His mouth twisted. "Mother was humiliated. I may not be as flashy as some witches, but I am a lot more powerful than many realize. I sure as hell don't need to cheat. They underestimated me, they always have, that was their mistake."

So that's why Asuka's engagement ended. "I didn't know." I gave his arm another squeeze. "I've been so busy with my own task, I had no idea what was happening with everyone else. I'm sorry, Clay." I'd left the ball so quickly, I hadn't noticed if people were treating Clay and his mother coldly. I didn't get it, why the hell would someone want to be part of that?

Clayton's eyes flashed, and he shot to his feet. "Avery did this. He murdered my mother."

"I'm not so sure." I stood. "My sister was attacked as well, and in a way almost identical to your mother." I gave him the details and watched his reaction closely.

He sat up straighter. "Is she all right?"

I studied him, searching for a sign that he wasn't telling me all he knew. But there was nothing, and after seeing him in his mother's bedroom, I couldn't believe he'd done it. There was no missing how much pain he was in. His aura looked like Rebecca's.

"A hex doll?" he asked.

"I'm sure of it. I managed to break the bind before they slit her throat..." My heart raced faster at the memory, my palms growing clammy. "But they meant to kill her." Hex dolls were created using hair or nails, sometimes fabric cut from the victim's clothes then a spell was used to link the doll with the victim. After that, any damage inflicted on the doll was felt by the person whose image it was created in.

"I don't understand," Clayton said. "Why would the Avery come after your sister?"

"They have no reason to, not that I'm aware of. I'm not convinced they're the ones who killed your mother, Clay."

Warrick and I stayed with him until Sally and Calum arrived, and I promised to call Clay as soon as I knew anything, and he promised the same.

I was walking out when Sally stopped me, pulling me aside.

"Have you seen my boy? Or heard anything?"

She looked exhausted, beside herself with worry over Ren, and I hated that I had nothing for her. "I'm sorry, Sal. I will find him. I promise you that." I shouldn't be making promises, but I couldn't take the agony in her eyes, eyes identical to Ren's.

She squeezed me in a tight hug. "I know you will, Wills. You'll bring our boy home." Then she walked into the living room to speak with Clayton, and I rushed out, because suddenly I felt like I was suffocating.

"You touch him too much," Warrick said when I reached the bottom of the steps.

I drew in a steadying breath, trying to avoid hyperventilating. "His mother has been murdered. I was comforting him."

Embers danced in his eyes. "I didn't like it, dove."

Seriously? What did the guy want from me? I couldn't deal with his jealousy. He'd offered me sex, that's all. Nothing more. I appreciated all he was doing for us, but that didn't mean he could act this way. I didn't care if it was some possessive animal instinct thing. I wasn't an animal, and I couldn't deal with his crap on top of all the other crap I had going on. "You'll just have to get over it." There was so much more I could say, but I didn't have the emotional bandwidth for it right then.

He growled, and I ignored it, climbed into the Morris, and headed out.

CHAPTER 20

Willow

My mind raced as I headed toward home. None of this made sense. Someone had hexed my sister and me. There were malevolent spirits loose—on a killing spree—and those spirits had something to do with the task the mother had set me. And now Clayton's mom had been brutally attacked and murdered, her injuries identical to the ones inflicted on Mags.

What the fuck was going on? It wasn't just us being targeted now, but the Whitlocks as well? I didn't see the connection.

Sally's face flashed through my mind, and I gripped the steering wheel tighter. I needed answers, something, anything. I didn't know who was behind the attack on Mags, or Olive's murder. I also didn't know who was responsible for letting the spirits loose. The list of shit I didn't know was fucking ridiculous, but what I did know was both involved using the darkest, most twisted kind of magic there was.

And I was willing to do anything for even the smallest clue at this point.

The closest I'd come was that dream while I was at Warrick's den. If I could just see who was behind that cloak. If I could go back to that dream state and instead of giving into the fear, tear away that cloak, I'd see who was behind trying to hurt us, I was positive.

So when I reached the next crossroads, instead of heading for home, I turned toward Shadow Falls. Warrick turned as well, following me. I was sure he was fuming and wanted to tell me to go home, but you couldn't use a phone while riding a motorcycle, lucky for me.

I needed him with me for this, anyway, someone to watch over me while I was under.

Thirty minutes later, I pulled the Morris off to the side of the road and parked. Warrick rolled in behind me a second later and was kicking down the stand of his bike when I climbed out of my truck. By the look on his face, he was still brooding.

Awesome.

"What the fuck are we doing here?" he said, striding toward me.

I planted my hands on my hips. "You're not going to like this, but I'm going to need you to suck it up and trust me, okay?"

"You know I fucking trust you, but if I'm not going to like it, that means you're about to do something that could get you hurt. I'm not cool with that."

I smiled up at him and was sure it looked as strained as it felt. "That's why you're here, alpha. To protect me."

His eyes narrowed, not buying it.

I slung my satchel over my head and started toward the trail. "I'll explain while we walk."

"Where are we going?" he asked as we hit the rocky path.

"A place called Shadow Falls." I glanced up at him. "There's a reason this place is free of demons and other creatures that might try to attack us, and why the land looks so barren…can you feel it?" Very little grew here, and when it did, it didn't last long. There were ancient trees that had managed it, but just as many that didn't and were gray, spindly, dry shells.

His wide shoulders bunched, the muscles in his arms flexing as he tilted his head back and scented the air. When he looked down at me, his eyes had changed color. They were red. "What the fuck is that?"

A shiver slithered through me, because the deeper we went and the closer we got to the falls, the more I felt it. "The falls have been used as a burial ground for centuries. It's where witches who have gone bad go, the ones who turned to dark magic. They're placed there when they die. Their families, their covens, don't want them in their cemeteries because they'd sour the soul and taint the magic. So their families bring them here."

His hand came down on my shoulder, stopping me. "I don't fucking like this. Why are you here?"

"Because whoever is behind all of this is using magic that is forbidden. The night I stayed with you, that bad dream…it wasn't just a dream, it was a vision, I'm sure of it. I need to go back there, to that place in my mind. It's called shadow seeking, and I can only do it here at the falls."

His brows lowered, and he planted his hands on his hips. "How dangerous is this?"

I bit my lip.

"Willow."

"As dangerous as you can get." There was no point lying. He needed to know, because it would be him stopping things if the worst-case scenario was about to happen. "If I'm under too long, I might never wake up again. The shadows can claim you, confuse you."

He cursed viciously, his fingers flexing against my shoulder. "And you're sure you can get answers doing this?"

"Yes, but timing is everything." I winced. "Only there's no way for you to know what's happening while I'm under, and the things that are happening to me there can affect my body here. So basically, if I appear to be under serious distress, it's probably best to wake me, otherwise, you need to let it play out, but no longer than around thirty minutes. The longer I'm there, the harder it will become for me to distinguish the vision I'm in from the real world. Witches have been known to stay in their visions, not realizing that's what they are, until they eventually die of old age. Others stay too long and can't get back or are killed by whatever sent them shadow seeking in the first place."

"That's too big a risk," he bit out.

"That's why you're here. You won't let me get lost there, right? Which means there's nothing to worry about." I started to walk again, and he cursed some more.

I almost expected him to physically stop me from going through with this, to pick me up and carry me back. He didn't. Warrick did trust me, and he respected me. No matter how much he hated what I was about to do, he believed in my abilities, and that meant something.

The sound of the falls reached us long before we saw them, growing louder as we walked.

Finally, we rounded the path and there they were. Furious white foam exploded high from a rocky outcropping, a torrent of fury forced down into the blue water below before snaking away through the barren land poisoned by dark magic.

I pushed forward when everything in me wanted to turn around and run the other way. The evil surrounding this place was so thick it was stifling. Warrick had to feel it, too, but he said nothing and kept following me.

The water came down with such velocity that it was hard to see the gap behind the falls themselves. But there was a cave hidden behind all that water, and I walked along the rocky path, a narrow lip in the rock that led to the cave. It was cold and loud, the water a moving wall between us and where we'd just come from. It felt like a different world in here.

I turned slowly as Warrick closed the space between us.

"Christ," he said, taking in the stone walls.

The witches who were brought here were wrapped and placed on ledges dug out of the wall itself like ancient bunk beds. Their dark magic pulsed around us, drenching the small space. I didn't know how deep it went, the darkness seemed to swallow the cave, hiding its secrets. I didn't want to uncover them. I had no need to.

I could do what I needed to right here.

"Now what?" Warrick asked.

He was so close to me his body brushed against mine as if he were afraid to put distance between us, like he thought I was about to be snatched away.

I lifted off my satchel and moved to a small, raised dais, placing my knife on the white stone. "A blood spell, and I need to lie here while I do it." There was no missing the blood already staining the stone. Blood from the witches laid to rest here and witches who had come to this place like me—some for good, some for not so good, purposes. I didn't let myself think about that either.

I stripped quickly and set my clothes by my bag on the floor and climbed up. The stone was rough and cold, hard against my bare skin. Warrick watched me do this, jaw tight, eyes flickering like there were flames dancing there.

"Why the fuck are you naked again?"

There was no hiding how much he didn't like this. "Because that way you'll see any injuries that I get in the dream state. Only wake me if it looks serious." Visions of the dream I'd had flashed through my mind, my sisters, all of them dead. How real it'd felt. "I might scream and thrash. Ignore it. Ignore any bruises that might appear on my skin as well. Broken bones, blood, that's the only reason to wake me."

He bit out several words in that coarse language I'd heard him use when he was talking to Maddox. I assumed it was more cursing.

"How do I wake you?"

"Lift me off the dais and I'll be dragged back. Ready?" I asked.

His jaw tightened. "No."

"It's going to be fine. Just don't let me stay under longer than thirty minutes."

He didn't answer with words, just dipped his chin, his expression carved in stone. My blade was gripped in my hand, and I made a long but fairly shallow cut along my forearm and watched as the blood bubbled to the surface then slid down to pool on the stone. The dais warmed under me almost instantly. I handed the knife to Warrick and closed my eyes.

"Crones of Shadow Falls, I offer you this gift of mortal blood from coven Thornheart. In return I ask that you take me into the shadows of my mind and help me seek the ones who would harm me and mine."

I repeated the words over and over. The stone beneath me grew hotter, and the dais began to vibrate beneath as if the ancient rock hummed. A rumbling sound reverberated through the space, and shadows gathered at the edges of my mind, closing in more and more until I was surrounded by the kind of darkness I never knew existed. So black and cold and dense, there was no way of knowing up from down.

I was suspended in nothingness, in horror, in fear. I opened my mouth to scream, but no sound came out, then the crone's hands, so many hands covered my mouth, my eyes, tugged at my hair, pulled on my arms, my legs.

They were going to kill me, they were going to—

Something cool brushed my feet.

The hands released me, vanished.

I blinked several times. Home. I was home again, laying in the grass. I got to my feet. The cemetery. Mom was with Art, weeding the herb garden. Else, Mags, and Rose sat in the long grass, Roe's cheeks pink, smiling, laughing at something Iris said. Bram sat on a headstone, in bird form, Nia lying beside them. I smiled, warmth filling me, and went to join them.

A small yipping sound had me turning.

A large, orange fox stood just beyond the edge of the cemetery. My fox, my Renny. "Ren!" I waved, overjoyed to see him. I couldn't remember why, but I'd missed him. He'd been somewhere far away from me.

He didn't move, and there was a strange shadow beside him that grew darker. I didn't like it. I wanted Ren away from it.

I waved him forward and headed toward him, but the closer I got, the more different he looked. His soft fur was matted with something, something rusty colored. His gold eyes were black, hollow.

"Ren?"

He shifted forms, and I stumbled to a stop. His body was scarred with cuts and burns and smeared with blood. My gaze darted up to his face. His lips were peeled back, hatred radiating from him. His eyes changed back to gold, the whites bloodshot.

"You did this. This is your fault," he said, his voice moving over me like broken glass.

I winced at the hatred directed at me, the loathing I heard in his words. He hated me. Why did he hate me? Why? It was there in the back of my mind, but I couldn't reach it. No matter how hard I tried, I couldn't reach it.

The shadow curled around him, and he lifted a knife, pressing it to his own throat.

"Ren! No!" I ran for him.

He jerked his hand, slashing through his skin, blood rushing from the long slice. I screamed and ran toward him. He dropped the blade and clutched his throat with one hand and reached for me with the other. I ran faster, but I couldn't reach him, he kept getting farther and farther away.

Finally, he fell to the ground, still, lifeless. I dropped to my knees and screamed as pain like nothing I'd ever felt lashed through me.

Someone called my name, and I lifted my head. Three figures dressed in black hooded cloaks stood before me. Each held a bloody knife in one hand, then as one, they lifted the other hand, each dangling one of my sisters' severed heads. That's when I realized I was still screaming, my throat raw, the taste of blood in my mouth.

I scrambled back, running for Mom and Else, Art. The hooded figures weren't behind me anymore, they stood instead before the rest of my family. They raised their knives and slashed without a moment's hesitation, killing them too. "*No!*"

This wasn't happening. This couldn't be happening.

"One by one," three voices said together, echoing through my mind.

Warrick was suddenly there, and he ran toward them with a roar. They jumped on him, hacking at him with their knives, tearing him apart. *No...oh god, no.*

Then they were right there in front of me, bloody knives in hand. I tried to run, but my limbs were suddenly weighted down. I couldn't move.

Why was I even trying? I stopped. I didn't scream, not anymore.

They could do what they wanted to me. I had no reason left to fight.

I had nothing left.

No one.

The strange shadow floated closer, slowly solidifying as it did.

A face took shape...

That face. A face that still haunted my dreams.

Huge shadow wings unfolded behind him.

"Hello, witch," the monster said. "We have some unfinished business, do we not?"

"Azel," I whispered.

———

Warrick

I gripped the edge of the dais, teeth gritted as my dove writhed. She'd stopped screaming, but the tears she'd been crying still dampened her cheeks.

I couldn't fucking watch her like this. A feeling inside me I'd never felt before expanded in my chest, knocking the fucking wind from my lungs. I didn't know what it was, only that it made me want to snatch Willow up and run with her, far away, and never let anyone hurt or scare her ever again.

A shadow appeared on her shoulder then bloomed into a dark bruise. I growled, the vicious sound bouncing off the walls around me. Fuck this. I wasn't going to stand here and watch while someone hurt her, wherever the fuck she was.

I searched her body frantically for more signs of damage—

A drop of blood appeared at the side of her throat, then trailed down. Suddenly it was an inch long, and I snatched her up, shaking the fuck out of her. "Willow," I roared. "Dove, wake up."

The slice in her skin had stopped, not going any farther, thank fuck.

I held her to me tight, too tight, but I couldn't help it. She blinked, but she didn't see me, her gaze lost, fuck, even the green of her eyes was dimmer. She was still lost in the shadows of her mind. In whatever Hell she'd just been in. Her body shook, and the tears were renewed, falling silently down her face.

"Dove," I choked out and pressed my forehead to hers. "Fight it. Fucking fight it, Willow." She stared blindly up at me, still lost somewhere I couldn't go. The feeling in my chest grew wider, bigger. I didn't know what it was, but it hurt. The pain was nothing like I'd experienced before. "Willow?"

She didn't respond. What the fuck should I do?

My gaze flew over her, searching the blank expression on her face, calling her name, shaking her, trying to wake her. Still nothing.

It was probably fucking stupid, but one thing kept entering my mind. My dove liked when I kissed her, it made her happy. It was all I had, all I could do, so I kissed her softly, lingering there. "Come back to me, precious one," I said against her lips, then repeated it in my own language.

I'd never called anyone that in my life—I'd never even thought the words until her—but that's what she was, she was my dove, my precious mate, and I refused to let her go.

She jolted in my arms and gasped.

Her gaze cleared and flew around the room, then came back to me, and before I could open my mouth to speak, her arms were around my neck, and she was holding on tight, sobbing against my chest.

I held her, trying to get my shit together.

"You're back. You're back, dove. I've got you."

She lifted her head. "There were three of them...and...oh goddess, they killed my family. They're going to kill them, Warrick, all of them."

Fuck. "Did you see who it was?"

She shook her head. "They wore cloaks. I couldn't see their faces. It was...it was so real, I forgot everything else." She gripped my shirt. "They killed my family, they killed you, they killed all of you, everyone I love, and I was so broken that I-I gave up. I sat there when they came for me, and I just gave up." Her eyes filled with terror. "He was there, Warrick...Azel. He was there."

Jesus. I cupped the back of her head and pressed my nose to the top of her head, breathing her in. I'd almost lost her. I'd almost fucking lost her again.

I wanted her the fuck out of here, now. So snatching up her bag, I carried her out of the cavern. She was naked still and it was cold, but I had to get her out of this fucking cave first, away from the evil here, the beings who could have taken her away from me.

I strode out into the darkening forest, and only when that feeling of dread dimmed did I stop, lower her to her feet, and help her dress. I got her underwear and jeans on but paused before I pulled her top over her head. The sight of that cut on her neck, the one on her forearm, had my fucking hackles lifting.

I wanted them gone. I needed them gone. Lifting her arm, I dragged my tongue along her forearm, ignoring her little cry of surprise. I looked at her as I did it again, making sure I wasn't hurting her. She watched me wide-eyed but didn't try to pull away.

"Okay?" I asked as I watched, not about to stop until the healing started.

"You don't need to do that," she said.

I glanced up at her again. "Don't fucking like seeing you bleed, dove. If I can take away your pain, I'm sure as fuck going to do it." She stilled as I slid my hand up between her shoulder blades and cupped the back of her head, then gently angled it to the side, asking without words if I could do the same to her throat.

She gave me a little nod.

I hooked my other arm around her waist as I leaned in, dragging in a lungful of her scent mixed with her blood, and I swiped my tongue over that slice to the side of her throat, just below her jawline. The combination had the animal in me roaring for revenge, for death. I wanted to tear apart whoever had hurt her, and the fact I couldn't, that I didn't know who it was, was fucking with my head.

I licked her again, and she shivered. "Okay?" I repeated against her damp skin.

"Yes."

I couldn't stop myself from licking her one last time, from

wrapping my lips around the short slice and sucking gently. She made a soft little moan, her fingers digging into my shoulders, and I forced myself to lift my head. And when I was sure the healing had begun there as well, I finished dressing her.

She protested when I scooped her back up, and I ignored it, carrying her out of the fucking woods.

When we reached her truck, I put her down and strode to my bike to get her my jacket. Her door closed, and I turned.

"I need to get home," she said and fired the thing to life.

"Wait."

But she was already pulling out onto the road.

Fuck.

Swinging a leg over my bike, I started it and roared after her. There she went, running from me again.

I told her I'd never stop chasing her.

I didn't think she'd believed me, but she would.

CHAPTER 21

Willow

When I pulled up outside the house and parked beside four bikes and a car I didn't recognize, I was still shaken. My mind struggling to decide what was real and what wasn't. What had already happened, and what could happen if I didn't work out who was under those hooded cloaks.

Azel.

Maybe he'd been a figment of my imagination? Maybe the crones had been playing with me—or maybe the people under those cloaks were trying to bring that monster back. To set him free.

I had no idea, but I was sure that what I'd seen was the future, our future if I couldn't stop whoever was behind everything that had happened.

Three witches were working to hurt us. Three, our power number. That, combined with the dark magic they were using, meant they had some serious power behind them—more than I'd imagined.

My door opened before I could do it, and then Warrick was there. He hauled me out, his face in mine.

"I told you to wait. You're in no fucking state to drive yourself anywhere, not after what you've just been through." His hand carefully slid down my arm and lifted it, then brushed my hair back, checking my neck. The slice on my arm was already fading, thanks to Warrick.

"I'm fine," I said, lying through my teeth. But how the hell could I be?

"Bullshit," he said, seeing right through me.

"I'm sorry, okay, I just…" I struggled for anything to add. My only thought had been to get the hell out of there, to get away from the darkness, the awful feeling of dread…the living nightmare the crones had shown me, it was all I could see. I'd wanted to get to my family, to see for myself that they were okay.

Warrick bit off a curse, and then his hand curled around the back of my neck. He dipped his head, pressed his lips to my temple, and breathed me in, almost like doing it comforted him as well. How could that be? This was the alpha of the hellhounds, a male who had limited emotions, was utterly fearless—a male who had lived for a thousand years.

"Warrick?" I said, because he was still holding me, and the longer he did, the more my stupid heart beat faster and the closer to him I wanted to get.

"Shut up," he said gruffly, then finally lifted his head and urged me to get moving toward the house.

"Charming."

He growled. "Haven't recovered from that shit back there, dove. I'm not ready for you to give me attitude, and I'm sure as fuck not ready to spar with that sarcastic mouth either."

I pretended to zip my lips and throw away the key, trying to make light because this sure as hell wasn't normal Warrick behavior, and I didn't know what to do with that, not with everything else running through my mind.

Had seeing me lost in my mind back there truly unsettled him? I didn't think he was capable of being unsettled. I'd been kind of out of it but remembered him holding me tight. I thought he might have been shaking when he helped me dress.

"Come back to me, precious one."

The words drifted through my mind, Warrick's voice, low and full of fear, right before he'd said something in his own language. Had I imagined it? Was it all part of the vision, or had he actually said that to me?

Fender was standing outside the door when I walked around the house, and he gave Warrick a chin lift.

"Thanks for protecting my family," I said to the stoic hound.

"You're War's female," he said simply.

I narrowed my eyes at Warrick but didn't correct Fender. I didn't think that was wise, considering Warrick had just saved me from having my throat slit.

Warrick opened the door, motioning for me to go in, that hot, possessive hold still on the back of my neck.

Voices, a lot of them, came from the kitchen. We walked in, and crammed into the small room was Mom and Arthur, Iris and Nia, Mags and Bram, in his crow form, which was unsurprising since he didn't like being around a lot of people, and Roe, who was sitting at the end of the table. Her cheeks were flushed, and yes, she looked weak, but she was also smiling, her eyes dancing as she watched Else.

My great aunt was standing over a shirtless hellhound, who was currently on his knees, long hair pulled to the side, while Else manned a tattoo gun.

"Um...what the hell is going on here?" I said.

"We can't have these guys here unprotected," Else said,

without looking up. "Those spirits like 'em too much. So I did some digging through my demon texts, found some ancient runes that ward off spirits, worked a spell into the ink, and Bob's your hairy uncle. It's the best protection I can give them while they're away from their clubhouse or when they leave our boundary wards."

"They're not demons, Else," I said, taking a closer look at what she was doing. There were four runes, all about two inches in diameter. This wasn't Else's first tattoo, she and I both did them from time to time. Shifters especially liked spells worked under their skin since wearing charms didn't work all that well due to the whole shifting thing. They tended to lose them a lot. "You think this'll work?"

Else winked at me. "I know it will. And these guys are Hell born, they're as close to a demon as a being can get and not actually be one."

If Else said it'd work, it would work.

"You look kind of like shit. What happened to you?" she asked.

"Nothing, I'm fine," I said and forced a smile.

Warrick stepped forward and took a look at Else's handiwork as well. "You'll do this for all my brothers?" he asked as he grabbed a chair, sat it beside me, and coaxed me to sit without even looking at me, that big hand on my shoulder applying gentle and persistent pressure. He wasn't taking no for an answer.

I sat.

"Sure thing," Else said. "Not a hardship seeing all you boys with your shirts off." She cackled.

Jesus.

Mom laughed, looking more relaxed than I'd seen her in a long time, which told me just how scared she'd been.

Magnolia groaned, and for once, I was glad she was being her usual drama queen, teenage self.

Relic, the male Else was tattooing, looked at Mags and winked. My sister turned beet red. I slapped the hound's shoulder, and he glanced at me. "Don't even think about it."

He held up his hands in surrender, and when I looked up at Warrick, he was grinning down at me, again. Twice in one day, my heart couldn't take it. He was dangerously hot when he was being a broody jerk; grinning, he was sex on a stick and then some.

"My brothers would never touch any of your sisters," he said.

"What about her mom," Mom said.

"Mom!" Iris squealed.

She cracked up and so did the hounds, one of them eyeing her in a way that I did not appreciate. That was all I needed; Mom hooking up with a hellhound.

Arthur frowned.

"Okay, let's move this along," I said. "Who's next."

"Me," a deep voice said, and Ronan stepped forward, unbuttoning his shirt as he walked. The last time I'd seen the dhampir was at the ball. I hadn't had a chance to talk to him then. "Vampire is demon. I'm only half, but it should work on me also."

"Ronan, hey, I didn't expect to see you here," I said.

He looked down at me with that unusual, emotionless deep purple gaze. "You're important to Luna," he said as way of explanation and slid off his shirt, revealing his extremely pale, muscled chest.

Everything was black-and-white to him, there was no gray. Dhampir took emotionless to a whole new level. "Well, thank you."

They didn't feel or express emotion at all. His sister and my friend Luna did *now*, but only after she'd met her mate. Ronan wasn't so lucky, but somewhere along the way, he'd given his loyalty to the hounds and seemed to be accepted by them as well.

He dipped his chin in acknowledgment, folded his shirt, and placed it on the back of Roe's chair. My sister gazed up at him, her cheeks still pink, getting pinker when her gaze dipped, taking in his chest.

Ronan paused and looked down at her as well, his head tilting to the side, studying her. Rose's blue eyes widened a moment before Ronan moved, quick, fluid, and placed his hand to the speeding pulse at her throat. "There's something wrong with you. You're unwell."

Humiliation transformed Rose's face.

"Ronan, brother, no," Relic said.

Ronan turned to Relic.

"This is one of *those* times, my man," Relic said cryptically.

Ronan's brow lifted, and he turned back to Rose. "My apologies."

He didn't know what he was apologizing for, it was obvious from his puzzled expression.

"It's fine," Roe said and quickly turned away, struggling to her feet. I jumped up to grab her when she looked like she'd fall.

Ronan got there first, scooping her up in his arms. "Where would you like to go, Rose?"

"Please...I'm fine," Roe whispered. "I can walk."

"You're not fine," Ronan said matter-of-factly. "You're sick, and you weigh nothing."

I tried to step in, but Mom got there faster. "Just into the living room, thank you, Ronan."

Rose hated how skinny she'd become; she didn't even like to be hugged anymore. Having a gorgeous male like Ronan lift her, touch her, and actually mention her weight, would be utterly mortifying to her. My heart hurt at the pained look in her eyes as they disappeared into the other room.

Ronan returned a short time later, his expression stoic, but there was something in his eyes I couldn't read.

"On your knees," Else said to him.

Iris's eyes met mine across the table, and she looked as worried about Roe as I felt.

Else didn't take long to tattoo Ronan, and by the time the last hound was being inked, the room had cleared out.

When she finally finished, my great aunt looked up at the hellhound alpha standing beside me, flexing her fingers, and winced. "You're next, big boy."

"Your hand's causing you pain," he said. "Willow can do mine."

Else put down the tattoo gun and shook her hand out. "Sounds good to me. My arthritis is acting up."

Warrick's brother left, Else behind him, leaving the two of us alone. "You well enough to do this?" he asked.

"Yes. Honestly, I'm fine." Physically, I felt almost back to normal. Mentally, that was something else, and I was happy for the distraction.

"Where do you want me?" he said.

So many things popped into my head at those loaded words, but I resisted and instead dragged out a chair.

He reached back, tugging off his shirt, and draped it over the back of the chair beside him and sat. I prepared the tattoo machine, filling it with Else's special ink. With these guys, we didn't need to worry about infection, not with their healing abilities, so there was no need to sterilize anything.

I grabbed a marker to draw the runes on him first. His monster shoulder was partially covered by all that thick, wavy hair. It was soft, too. I knew that because I'd had my fingers in it several times now.

I put down the marker and grabbed a hair tie from the bowl on the counter and came back. "I'll need to tie up your hair."

He lifted his chin.

Moving behind him, I gathered it up and put it in a kind of messy bun that looked, yeah, really good. Else had drawn the runes on a piece of paper, and I studied them. They were fairly straightforward, and I tried to focus on drawing them and not on his strong, hard, muscled body. It wasn't easy.

Warrick wasn't the only one with a lot of hair, and mine fell forward, getting in the way as well, so I grabbed another of Mag's hair ties that she always left scattered around the house. But before I could lift my hands to my hair, Warrick grabbed my hand and drew me to him.

"Let me."

He turned me, then pulled me back so I was sitting on one of his solid thighs. As soon as he ran his fingers through my hair, tingles danced across my scalp. I could feel him carefully separating my hair into three sections, and I shivered.

He made a low sound and leaned in, breathing deep. He did that a lot. "Why do you do that? Smell my hair?"

His fingers brushed the back of my neck, and I bit back a moan.

"I'm a hound, dove. I'm sensitive to different scents, and yours is my favorite."

I blinked, stunned. "My scent is your favorite?"

"Fuck, yes."

What the hell did you say to that? And why did I love it so much? I had noticed the couple of occasions I'd slept in the same bed as him, he always had his nose buried against me, usually at my throat.

His fingers brushed my neck again. "What are you doing?"

"Braiding your hair."

He wore his hair braided sometimes—most of the hounds did. My belly did another of those flips it seemed to be doing a lot around him. No male had ever done anything like this for me before, and somehow, it was one of the most erotic things I'd ever experienced.

The gentle touch, the attentiveness, the care the massive alpha was taking, hit me behind the ribs and between my thighs all at the same time.

He held out a hand, his rough, calloused palm facing up...a warrior's hands, and I slid mine over his, my hand and fingers so much smaller than his.

"Hair tie, dove," he rasped.

He wanted the hair tie, not to hold my goddamned hand. Heat hit my face, and I quickly pulled my hand away in humiliation, replacing it with the hair tie. He secured the braid, and I tried to stand, face still burning over my mistake, but he stopped me, those strong hands dropping to my hips, fingers flexing.

He leaned in again, his chest pressing against my back, and pressed a kiss to the side of my neck.

I shivered again. "Ready?"

He gave my hips one more squeeze. "Yeah."

His voice was nothing but a rumble now, and my belly actually quivered. Moving behind him, I turned on the tattoo machine, and the low buzz filled the room. Resting my free hand on his shoulder, I pressed the needle to his smooth skin and started. He didn't even flinch. Not surprising with all the tattoos he already had.

I forced myself to focus on what I was doing and not how tempting he looked sitting here. But by the time I finished the first rune, I was kind of a mess, hot and achy and seriously restless.

I wasn't the only one affected. There were goose bumps all over Warrick's shoulders. He liked the feel of my needle moving over his skin.

"It doesn't bother you at all, does it?" I said, trying not to think about the way he'd looked in the shower, all naked and muscled.

"What?"

"Having a needle repeatedly stabbed into your flesh."

"No." His hands were resting on the table in front of him, and he curled his fingers into fists, then released them. "I've always liked it. But right now, I fucking love it."

"Why's that?" I asked, when I knew I shouldn't because I was pretty sure whatever Warrick was about to say was going to make me want to tear my clothes off and straddle him right here in my family's kitchen.

"I almost fucking lost you today, Willow. I needed your hands on me after that. And now I have them, and I can feel the heat of that tight little body, right there. Can feel your heart beating, and every now and then one of your tits brushes my back...and those slow, even breaths, fuck, I can hear them, feel them." He made a rumbly sound in his chest. "But what's making my dick hard enough to hammer in nails, is the smell of your pussy. It's soaked, dove. And staying still, waiting for you to finish before I tear off your pants and get my tongue inside you, is taking every bit of control I have."

My thighs clenched. God, the things he said. No one had ever affected me the way he did. Even though most of the time I wanted to punch him and fuck with equal measure. "What if what happened yesterday was just a one off?" I said, making a final half-hearted grasp at resistance.

He laughed low and rough, and dirty as hell, not even bothering to reply with actual words. Because I was full of shit, and we both knew it. Let's be honest, at this point, if he wanted me, I was his for the taking.

And now that I knew what was going to happen when I finished concentrating was near impossible. As I worked on the last rune, my slow, even breaths had turned into ragged pants.

My belly quivered, and my nipples tightened, and if I'd purposely let them brush his back more than once while I finished, I blamed him for making me feel so out of control. Maybe I wanted to push him, to feel as out of control as he made me.

Warrick's head was down, his body held rigid. Those thick biceps were rock solid, and his hands no longer rested on the table in front of him but were curled in tight fists, pressing down on his thighs.

With a shaky breath, I turned off the tattoo gun and put it down.

Silence engulfed the room.

Grabbing a damp cloth, I wiped away the excess ink and blood and dropped it on the table. Warrick grabbed my wrist before I could take my hand back, turned in his seat, and slowly pulled me around his body. I ended up standing between his spread thighs.

His nostrils flared, and he reached for the front of my jeans.

"Not here." I backed up a step, and he rose to his feet, chest heaving as he advanced on me. My belly flipped, and I turned, rushing out the door and up the stairs. The thump of his boots echoed on the hardwood floor as he came after me.

I'd never been happier that my room was all the way up in the tower and away from everyone else than in that moment. I shoved the door open and rushed in. Warrick strode in right behind me.

His gaze raked over me, and he kicked the door shut. For some reason, I backed up at the look on his face. It was fierce, wild, all animal. He watched me do it and stalked me until my back hit the wall.

I'd wanted him to lose control, and it looked like I was getting my wish.

He grunted and reached out, tugging on the hair tie he'd put in my hair a short time ago, and pulled it free, then slowly undid the braid. I was breathing hard and fast, an out-of-control feeling inside me building higher with every moment that passed.

Resting his hand at the base of my neck, he cupped it with his long, thick fingers. Not a threat, it was pure possessiveness. His thumb pressed lightly against the pulse thumping madly below my skin, then he leaned in and dragged his nose along my throat and made a sound that had me wanting to tear my clothes off.

Instead, I stood there frozen, heart pounding, so far beyond turned on, I couldn't think, my damn mouth wouldn't work. All I could do was wait for what he would do next—

He dropped to his knees, and gripping the front of my jeans, tore them open. I gasped, and he yanked them down my legs, tugging them right off, my boots and socks with them. Then with another grunt, he tapped my ankle, and I instantly stepped out, following his silent orders, and spreading my legs.

His hand came up between my thighs, and he cupped me over my underwear as he dragged in a breath through his nose.

I whimpered, and he looked up at me. "Yeah, fucking drenched, dove." He tore my underwear off my body, reducing them to tatters, but he paused, his golden gaze moving over me, and he licked his lips as if he were about to feast on his favorite meal.

I couldn't take it another moment. "Warrick…"

He buried his face against my swollen, slick flesh and lashed his tongue over my clit before sucking it between his lips. I cried out, and he grabbed one of my thighs and threw it over his shoulder. My hand went to the back of his head, and I tugged him closer. He sucked more firmly, and I was so on edge, so needy for him by then, I came instantly.

Warrick growled and lapped me up as I made incoherent sounds, desperately holding him to me.

I'd barely caught my breath when he was back at my sensitive clit, licking it with broad strokes, making me quiver and moan, Christ, building me right back to the same desperate state I'd been in when we'd walked in here.

He didn't stop until he took me over the edge again. I groaned helplessly, my hips rocking restlessly as I came a second time.

Before I could catch my breath, he stood, lifted me, and tugged my legs around his waist, then pressed me against the wall and claimed my mouth. The kiss was wild, untamed, and it completely overwhelmed me. I was utterly, willingly, at his mercy.

How was it possible that I wanted more? I wanted more of him.

One of his hands slipped between us, and he rubbed two

broad fingers over my opening. I sucked on his tongue, arching against the wall. He shoved them inside me with a hiss, fucking me with them, fast and deep, hitting me right where I needed him. It was like I hadn't already come twice, I was back to pure all-consuming need.

"You think you can take more, dove?"

"I need you," I said, so beside myself with desperation for this male, I couldn't think straight.

"You're not ready for me," he said and then slowly eased a third finger inside me.

I shook against him. "Oh god, *oh god*."

"I'm wider than that," he said, voice harsh. "A lot wider. I'll hit you so deep you won't know where I end and you start. You really ready for that?"

I was gasping for air now, on the cusp of the most intense orgasm I'd ever had.

"No, you're not ready for me to shove my big cock inside you, dove, not the way I'll do it. I'll claim you like the dirty, rutting dog I am. I'll make you mine, Willow, and I'll never let you go. You know that, don't you? That once I've had you, that's it, there's no getting away from me. You'll me *mine*," he said the last with an edge of dominance, possession, god, violence.

"Warrick," I said, and the helplessness, the surrender in my voice, would have alarmed me if I was thinking beyond my need to come, to get closer to this male, for more of what I was positive only he could give me.

Then I was screaming, shaking, coming for him all over again.

When I finally slumped back, exhausted. He slid his fingers free, then pressed them against my swollen flesh, cupping me with that big, rough hand, and stared into my eyes in a way that screamed ownership.

I couldn't look away as he slowly, so slowly, lowered me to my feet. My knees shook, but somehow, I didn't fall.

He stepped back and his hands dropped to the front of his

jeans, popping the button. He yanked down the zipper, shoved his jeans low enough to free his erection, then braced his legs apart.

Taking himself in hand, he started stroking, fast, not trying to tease. Warrick needed to come.

I couldn't tear my eyes away as he lifted the front of his T-shirt, revealing his tight abs, and snarled as he thrust faster into his fist, watching me the whole time. Then the same thing happened that had in the shower. His cock grew longer, thicker, the head darkening and widening.

"You want that inside you, dove?" he asked, flames dancing in his eyes.

I licked my lips, needy and a little afraid all at the same time.

Watching my reaction, he snarled and came, coating his fingers.

He kept stroking until he was done, then shoved his pants back up and closed in on me. I couldn't move, locked in place by the fierceness in his eyes. He lifted his hand, holding a finger to my mouth, waiting. The move was one of pure ownership, and I don't know what came over me, but I gave him what he wanted. I took his hand in both of mine and sucked that thick finger into my mouth, his taste mixed with my own, coating my tongue as I licked it clean.

Nostrils flaring, he cupped the back of my head and his lips peeled back, revealing teeth that were no longer his. They were those of his beast, the hound, canines extended, sharp and vicious. "No fucking backing out now, you know that, don't you, dove?" he said.

I stared up at him, my heart still racing. He meant what he said. The truth of it was in his eyes.

What was I doing with him? I was setting myself up here for serious hurt. I could see the collision coming, the ugly aftermath, but I couldn't put on the brakes. I couldn't stop this.

A tingle danced along my belly.

The vines.

Shoving up my shirt, I looked down. "Oh no."

"What is it?"

"It's too late."

"What are you talking about?"

"The vines, they've joined. I failed. *Oh god*, I've failed..."

CHAPTER 22

Willow

COME TO ME.

The mother's voice echoed through my mind. "I need pants." I ran across the room and yanked my drawers open, then pulled on underwear and a fresh pair of jeans.

"Where the fuck are you going?" Warrick said, stepping in front of me.

"I need to go to Oldwood Forest. The mother, she's summoning mc."

"Why?"

Because she's about to strip us of our powers. "I'll find out when I get there," I said instead. I didn't know if the mother was open to making a deal or some other bargain, but I was willing to offer her my soul, if she was interested, to make sure my family didn't suffer this.

Rose...she wouldn't survive being stripped of what power she had.

"Is this what usually happens?"

My mind spun, and my stomach churned. "I don't know."

He gripped my upper arms. "Don't go."

I wish. But if I didn't go, the punishment would no doubt be worse. "I have to."

I pulled from his hold, shoved my feet in my boots, picked up my blade from the floor where it'd fallen, and jogged down the stairs.

"I'm coming with you," he said, pounding down after me.

I'd say no, but I had a feeling I'd need help getting home once the mother was finished with me. "Fine, but you have to promise you'll stay back."

He grunted.

"I mean it. No matter what happens, you stay the hell back."

"Is that you, Wills?" Mom called from the living room.

What the hell was I going to tell them? *You won't need to tell them anything, they'll feel the mother stripping their power along with yours.* I was going to throw up. "Yeah, I have to go out. Be back soon."

"Is Warrick with you?"

"Yes!"

"Oh good, have a nice time."

I rushed outside, climbed into the Morris, and fired her to life.

Warrick got in beside me. "I don't like this. What the fuck happens now? What will she do to you? Every time you see that bitch, she pumps you full of fucking venom. Not fired up to watch her take a bite out of you, dove."

However badly she'd hurt me in the past was going to be nothing compared to what was about to happen. "I don't know what happens now." I licked my lower lip and was hit with another taste of him. God, I wanted him to haul me into his arms at that moment, to tell me that everything would be okay, so badly I ached. But it wasn't okay. It was the complete fucking opposite of okay. The mother was about to strip my entire family of everything.

"We better get going. The mother doesn't like to be left waiting." Shifting the Morris into gear, I roared down the driveway.

Warrick remained quiet after that, a large silent dark cloud beside me, and since my head was all over the place, wondering what I was walking into, I was okay with that.

Oldwood Forest was about twenty minutes from home. The Roxburgh State Forest split into two and joined with Wolf Hill Woods a hell of a long way from here, and both were currently full of monsters. Good times.

I parked the Morris, climbed out, and headed into the forest. Warrick was right behind me.

There was no moon tonight; it was concealed by dark clouds. The wind was gusty and icy, and it whistled through the trees, making branches creak and dead leaves fly around us before hitting the forest floor.

The animals had obviously found places to hide for the night, and I hoped that included the two-legged creatures that lived here as well. I was tired, worried...scared for my family and what this would mean for us, for our entire coven.

I hadn't just failed Mom and Else, and my sisters. I'd failed my entire coven. Would they kick us out after this?

We made it to the clearing without too much trouble. A demon ran at us about ten minutes after we arrived, and Warrick beheaded it with his bare hands.

The next one, I got with my blade, taking it down, and again, Warrick tore his head off. He certainly was consistent. And I was much obliged. I wasn't sure I had a decapitation in me right then, not when my stomach sank more and more with every step closer to the clearing that we got.

"Wait here," I said to Warrick when we finally reached our destination.

He didn't look happy about it.

"Remember, no matter what you see, you don't leave this spot."

He grunted.

"I mean it. If you walk out there, the mother will be pissed, and she'll take it out on me and my family."

"Not gonna fuck this up for you, dove," he said.

"Thank you." I walked to the center of the clearing.

It was so dark tonight, I had trouble seeing a foot in front of me. When I reached the center, I whispered a spell, lighting a fire in the ring of stones that was already there and quickly took off my clothes, tossing them aside. Then, taking my blade, I sliced the side of my calf and watched as the blood ran down my leg, over my foot, to soak into the dirt.

Dropping my knife, I closed my eyes and lifted my hands. "Mother, please grant me an audience. You requested my presence and I have obeyed."

I didn't know the words for this kind of thing, there was nothing written for it in all our texts.

The wind picked up speed, and a moment later, that familiar rattle reached me.

The serpent was approaching.

I had visions of Warrick exploding from the trees and tearing the snake to shreds. That's exactly the kind of thing he'd do. I almost smiled at the thought. The nerves were obviously getting to me.

Daughter.

I opened my eyes and the huge snake raised up in front of me. Maybe she'd brought me here to kill me? Maybe I'd sucked so bad at being a Keeper that she was going to get rid of me instead. If I could convince her...*beg her*, to pass the position on to another branch of the family within our coven, they might come out of this unscathed.

You passed your task.

Her voice echoed through my mind.

I froze. "What? I passed? But I...I thought I failed...I thought..."

You passed, she said again.

Relief hit so hard, I had to choke back a sob of relief and my knees almost buckled. How? How was this possible? I hadn't sent the souls back. I didn't understand. None of this made sense.

I should keep my mouth shut, but I couldn't stop myself. I had to know. "May I ask what my task was, Mother?"

To keep our world a secret, no matter the cost to you or others.

I blinked into her vibrant green eyes.

Rebecca.

I'd almost told her the truth of our world time and again. *She* was my task? What the fuck was going on? If the malevolent souls weren't my task, then who'd sent them?

"Mother, there are spirits loose in the city. They're the reason I was forced to keep our world a secret. Humans have been killed because of them."

The opportunity arose, a way to present you with your task, how it came about is of no consequence to me.

"You didn't send them, the souls?"

No.

The mother's voice rose, her anger lashing out like a whip. The serpent hissed and jerked toward me. I locked my knees when every instinct told me to run.

You dare question me? Her voice roared through my mind.

"Apologies, Mother," I said quickly. "I didn't mean to offend you."

She hissed again, but the snake seemed to calm. I stayed quiet and waited for her to tell me why she'd summoned me.

That wasn't the final task for coven Thornheart, Keeper.

What? I'd done two, there were always two. "But I've done both—"

Silence.

I shut my mouth.

A Keeper's power comes from not one but many. Your ancestors proved their worth time and again. Your coven thrived and grew in power because of those who came before you. That line was severed when Joshua Thornheart died. This is a new line, untested. You are but one of worth, daughter, and there must be many for a new line to secure their position.

My heart pounded hard in my chest because I knew what she was going to say next.

Each of your sisters must pass one task and one trial to retain your gifts and your Keeper status.

No. "Mother," I rasped. "One of my sisters is unwell and another is only eighteen years old—"

She hissed, and I pressed my lips together.

If they are weak, they will fail. That is the purpose of the trials. As for your youngest sister, she will be given the time she needs.

"When?" I dared to ask.

The next in line will be given time to prepare before she is summoned.

Iris.

"Months?"

Perhaps. Are you ready to receive your gifts?

My heart was pounding, and my head was spinning. I wanted to argue, but angering her would be a terrible mistake. "Yes, Mother."

Remember, you must also win your trial to keep the gifts I bestow upon you today.

This I knew. If I lost my trial, the mother took the gifts back that she'd given to us, and all the past gifts my ancestors had received as well.

The serpent rose up. She didn't strike this time, something flashed in her eyes, then she spun and slithered into the woods without another word. I stood there, naked, shivering, mind racing. God, Mags had foreseen this, hadn't she? After the last time I was here, and she'd been mostly right. Except it wasn't me the mother had plans for, it was them. I shook my head in denial. This wasn't meant to happen. I was supposed to keep them safe.

The thought of any of my sisters coming here, enduring this, the dangers they would face...

Rose...oh god, she wouldn't survive it—

I cried out as pain sliced down my spine. I fell to my knees, my legs knocked out from under me and my mouth opened on a silent scream. Power swelled inside me, then again, the next surging even higher.

The gifts the mother had promised for passing my task were solidifying, strengthening.

It was ours.

My sisters, my mom, Else. Our entire coven. And it would stay ours as long as I passed the combat trial ahead.

"Willow?" Warrick called and dropped down in front of me. "Dove, what's happening?"

I couldn't talk, my back bowing as another surge pulsed through me. I blinked up at him as the pain throbbed and grew.

I screamed, positive I couldn't take another moment—

Then it crashed like a furious wave smashing into rocks before washing the pain away, leaving only the power that drove it.

I gasped as the final wave flowed through me. "It's okay, I'm okay...I passed. Somehow, I passed." I pushed myself up into a sitting position and shoved my fingers in my hair. "I just have to win my trial, then my part in this is over." I'd won the last fairly easily. Yes, I trusted in my abilities, but my next opponent may not go down so easily. There'd already been a couple of deaths, witches who were strong, skilled.

My sisters were untested.

"That's good."

He gave me room as I stood, watching me as I quickly dressed.

"But something's wrong, why aren't you happy? Talk to me."

I yanked my shirt on. "The souls weren't part of my task, Warrick. I don't know who sent them or why. And now my sisters have to go through this as well."

He planted his hands on his hips, his brows dropping, his golden gaze raking over me. "We'll figure it out," he finally said.

I nodded, because I had to believe that as well. "I need to get home to my family."

My sisters would have felt it, the increase in power, and I needed to check on Roe. Had it worked? We'd all been counting on it. More power to go around meant more for Roe. If we were right, then when Iris passed her trial, Rose would get another boost.

Maybe it would be enough.

It had to be.

"You're bleeding."

"It's fine, I'm used to it." I stepped back, and he grabbed my arm.

He shook his head. "The smell of your blood fucks with me. I don't like knowing you're hurt, dove."

"You better be careful, alpha, you'll have me believing you actually care," I said, the words coming out more than a little bitter, my emotions far too close to the surface to temper.

He scowled fiercely. "I don't like seeing you hurt."

Awesome. He didn't like to see me bleed. Not exactly a heart-felt declaration. Best not to get all excited that Warrick suddenly had a functioning heart.

Then he lowered to the ground, carefully lifted the leg of my jeans, and leaned in, giving it the hellhound healing treatment, licking the slice along my calf until it began to seal itself. Then he dragged my jeans leg back down just as carefully and stood. "Now we can go."

I fought back a shiver, turned, and ran for my truck and home.

The Morris skidded to a stop outside the house, and I jumped out and ran inside. Mom was in the kitchen, making a cup of tea, when I rushed in. "Did you feel it?"

She turned, and a gentle smile curled her lips and nodded.

"And Rose?"

She put down the cup in her hand. Her hands were shaking. "No change."

I grabbed for the back of a kitchen chair. *No.* I fought the tears that instantly sprang to my eyes. "Where is she?"

"Resting," Mom said. "This has...it's hit her hard." Her lips quivered. "This was keeping her going, Wills. Hope was keeping her going. I'm afraid that now she'll just...give up."

I walked to Mom and pulled her into my arms, hugging her tight. "We'll find a cure for her. We will."

She gripped my arms and looked up at me. "How? When we don't even know what's wrong with her?"

Heavy boots hit the floor behind me, and I knew Warrick had just walked in.

"Dove?"

"I'm okay, I just...I need a minute," I said without turning around. If I looked at him, I'd be tempted to run to him, to beg him to hold me, to comfort me. And I couldn't let myself rely on him for that.

I heard him retreat, and Mom cupped my face. "He's a good male."

I looked into my mother's soft brown eyes filled with hope that her daughter had found someone, the kind of male that she'd never managed to find for herself. "He doesn't love me."

She brushed her fingers over my cheek, and sadness filled her eyes. "I've had men tell me they love me, then hurt me with their very next breath. Love isn't what someone says, it's what they do. Warrick is protective and attentive. When he makes a promise, he keeps it, there's no BS with him. There will never be that gray area, the shadow of doubt, hovering over you. I'd take that over someone's declaration of love any day, Wills."

She was right, of course, but in my heart I knew I couldn't

accept less from him than everything. I wanted it all. I wanted the big love. I wanted to be loved as fiercely as I would love right back.

Warrick couldn't give me that.

From my experience, not many could, which why I'd chosen to avoid serious romantic relationships and would continue to do so. I kissed her cheek. "I'm going to check on Roe."

She nodded, and the sadness in her eyes deepened. "I'm sorry, Willow."

I paused. "Mom..."

"No, this needs to be said, and I should have said it a long time ago. Because of me, the men I brought into this house, you felt unsafe. You watched out for your sisters when it should have been me. Instead, I put myself ahead of you girls, and I'll never forgive myself for that." She closed the space between us and cupped my face. "You're much smarter than me, my beautiful girl, you don't need to lock your heart away."

My throat felt tight, her words hitting me hard. "Mom, I don't blame you, not for anything."

She smiled a sad smile. "You are the bravest, strongest woman I know, Willow Thornheart, and the kindest."

"Mom..."

"Go check on Roe, honey."

This conversation was hard on her, so I said no more. Instead, I kissed her cheek, and as I turned to leave, Arthur walked in, the concern in his eyes telling me he'd felt my mom's pain and was coming to take care of her. That was love. What Arthur felt for my mother was the purest, deepest kind of love there was. And not just as a friend, or a familiar. Art was *in* love with her, and guilt from her past mistakes had Mom paralyzed, afraid to take another chance on love.

I walked out as Art pulled her into a hug, then I headed upstairs. Rose's room was dark when I walked in. I didn't want to wake her by turning on the light, but I had to see her for myself that she was okay. So I drew the curtain back a little instead, letting the moonlight in.

She was curled on her side, her hands twisted in the covers, clutching them to her chest. Her wrists and fingers were so thin, so damn frail. Her breathing was erratic, and she shifted restlessly under the covers, like she was in pain.

No, our new gifts hadn't helped her. If anything, she looked worse than before.

We needed help.

We couldn't wait for a miracle anymore. None was coming.

I'd put every resource I had into finding a cure, into figuring this out. Our last hope had been the trials. The boost in power. It hadn't worked. Now we had nothing, and we were running out of time.

There was someone who could help, though, someone who had the money to spread a wider net, someone who had overseas connections, who was literally in the business of witchcraft relics, spelling ingredients, and research. Clayton. He and his mother may have lost some friends here in Roxburgh, but the Whitlocks' business was global and highly successful.

He could help. He was our last...our only chance at saving Rose.

And if I was going to be with someone who didn't love me, at least this way, there was no chance of me getting my heart broken.

Pulling my phone from my pocket, I quickly sent Clayton a text asking if he was free to meet the next day, before I lost my nerve.

Any sacrifice was worth it to save Rose. I'd do anything to save her.

Anything.

I slid Roe's covers higher.

I would not lose my sister.

CHAPTER 23

Willow

I WOKE with a start and blinked into the darkness of my room. I was alone. Completely. There was no scent of pine and leather or motor oil lingering. Warrick hadn't been here.

I sat up.

Something felt...wrong.

Shoving off the covers, I climbed out of bed and threw on some clothes, slid my blade into the sheath at my hip, put on my boots, and rushed from the room.

I opened the doors to my sisters' bedrooms as I went. All were fast asleep, and Mom had drifted off in a chair at Rose's bedside.

I took the stairs as quietly as I could. Else was tucked up in her room as well.

Relic was in the kitchen when I walked in, and he didn't look happy. "Where is he?"

"Edric," Relic said. "War went to clean up."

This was not good. Not good at all. "Where? What happened?"

Relic studied me for several long seconds, deciding if he should tell me, then shrugged. "State forest, the east side. Edric wiped out a group of campers."

Fuck.

"How long ago did Warrick leave?"

"Not long."

"He went alone?"

Relic looked pissed. "Yeah, and he pulled rank. Said it was his mess to clean up."

Which meant Relic's hands were tied. You did not ignore the alpha of a pack's orders, and in some cases, it was physically impossible, depending on the animal.

I rushed to Else's workroom, quickly and quietly loaded my satchel with what I needed, and headed out in the Morris.

I didn't know if Warrick would find Edric, but if he did and they fought, the spirit might leave and I needed to trap it before it moved to someone else, before it caused more damage.

I pushed the Morris to its limits the whole way, my stomach in knots. Warrick was incredibly strong, the most brutal out of his brothers, which was why he was alpha, but Edric was possessed by pure evil. That alone made him beyond dangerous.

I cursed and planted my foot harder on the accelerator. The sense of urgency grew. He needed me. Somehow, I knew Warrick needed me, and it drove me forward.

I finally saw his bike and skidded to a stop, then throwing on my satchel, I gripped my blade and ran into the forest. My gut told me where to go, and I was positive I could smell his scent lingering among the trees. Pulling out a flashlight, I shone it at the forest floor, and sure enough, large hound prints were pressed into the soft soil.

I rushed on.

This part of the forest was frequented by humans, the trees

and undergrowth not as dense, giving very little cover, so demons, especially, tended to avoid it. I tramped on until I saw firelight flickering up ahead.

"Stay back," Warrick's gravelly voice called through the shadows, sensing my approach.

There was no way in hell I was doing that. I strode to the edge of the campsite and froze. There was barely anything left of the campers. They'd been torn to pieces.

Warrick closed in, naked and fierce. He looked me over, and his nostrils flared. "You shouldn't have come here. You're still recovering and Edric's close by."

"I'm fine, and him being close is exactly why I should be here," I said and lifted off my satchel. "We need to stop him from doing this to anyone else."

"The sprits weren't part of your trial, they're not your problem anymore," he said. "This is too dangerous."

I ignored that and took what I needed from the bag. "You've seen what I can do. You've seen me fight. I know you feel protective over me, but that doesn't actually mean I need your protection. And task or not, I need to end this. One of them has Ren, or have you forgotten?"

He growled, watching as I quickly mixed the body oil we'd used before. "The tattooed runes should be enough to protect you." I looked up, and he didn't look happy. Nothing new there. "You think you can hold him down long enough for me to exorcize him?"

"Yes."

"Is he watching us now?"

He lifted his chin, scenting the air. "Yes. He's stalking us."

Fuck. "I better move quickly then."

A few minutes later, I was naked in a salt circle, rubbing oil all over my body, and we had a plan. Edric howled close by, very close, and goose bumps lifted across my skin.

He was about to make his move.

Warrick had been pacing around me, still in his human form. At the sound of that howl, he stopped, and with his broad back to me, tilted his head to the sky and howled in return, the sound filled with warning, with rage, communicating what would happen if he came closer.

Chest pumping, preparing for the fight, he looked at me over his shoulder. His face was a mask of fury, still mostly man, but his hound's muzzle elongated his jaw, and his canines were extended and impossibly sharp. "Do whatever you have to do to keep yourself safe," he said, his voice blending with the beast. "And if it looks like he's winning, run and don't look back. Call Relic."

I dipped my chin and he turned away. *No fucking way*. If he looked like he was losing, I was using my blade, and I'd make damned sure he didn't lose.

A rustle came from the right, and Warrick collapsed onto all fours, his body exploding into his hound form—

Edric burst through the trees and Warrick charged him. Their bodies collided with a horrific sound. They tore at each other, rolling around the clearing, massive jaws gnashing, claws tearing. I didn't wait, I grabbed my bag of salt and Thornheart cemetery dirt and sprinted to the edge of the campsite, then stabbing a hole in the bag, ran it around the perimeter, to trap the spirit inside, like Warrick and I had planned.

Warrick slashed at him and Edric sprang away, making a run for the edge of the clearing right as I closed the circle. He came to a jarring halt, flying backward, falling heavily to his back.

I sprinted for my smaller salt circle, leaping over body parts and scattered camping equipment, sliding in gore and blood. Edric got to his feet and spun, his red gaze locking on me as I made it to safety.

He snarled and charged me. Warrick slammed into his side, knocking him down, and they went at each other again. I lowered myself to my knees and started chanting, saying the words of the spell that would draw the spirit from Edric.

He fought harder, making a sound that lifted the hair on the back of my neck, thrashing against Warrick. I raised my voice as I lifted my hands, the words coming faster, louder.

Edric roared; it was earsplitting and filled with anguish. All Edric, not the spirit.

I snatched up the urn and used the small hand brush I'd brought to sweep away a section of salt, then held out the urn in front of me. Wind whipped around us, the roar coming from Edric mirrored by the soul now searching for a new host and only finding one.

The dead rat in the urn shrieked, and I slammed on the lid, screwing it tight. "I've got it." I turned to Warrick, and my heart smashed against the back of my ribs.

Both males were on the ground and had shifted back. Warrick stared down at his brother, and Edric's harsh breaths burst through gritted teeth.

"Talk to me, brother," Warrick said.

The other hound fisted his hair, then smashed his fist into the side of his own head. "Kill me," he snarled.

Warrick shook his head. "You're safe now."

Edric grabbed Warrick's shoulders. "What I did...what I've done. Women...children. I killed them all, their screams of fear, of agony, they're in my head. Kill me. Please."

Warrick searched his gaze, and I could tell he was going to tell him no.

"I'll kill again...I'm barely holding on," Edric rasped, eyes flashing to the brightest of reds.

He was about to go feral.

Warrick's expression was made of stone as he pressed his open palm against Edric's chest, right over his heart. "I'll send you home, brother."

Edric nodded.

Without pause, Warrick grabbed each side of Edric's head and twisted, snapping his neck with one brutal move. Then he stood and opened his clenched fist. Flames danced on his palm and shot from his hand, setting Edric ablaze before he had a chance to heal enough to reawaken from the merciful death Warrick had given him.

Warrick turned to me then, his eyes bright gold. "Get back, dove."

I quickly gathered my things and rushed to the edge of the campsite, watching as Warrick burned it all, hellfire spitting from his hands, incinerating human bones to nothing but ash.

Then he strode toward me. He was covered in bite marks and scratches, but they were already healing. His chest was pumping hard, his body held rigid.

As he passed by, I grabbed his hand. "Warrick…"

A muscle in his jaw jumped. "I have to go."

He tried to move again, and I stopped him a second time.

He snarled and shook his head.

I wrapped my arms around him. He may not have a soul, he may not think he was capable of love, and maybe that wasn't what this was, but he was hurting. He felt this. Deeply. He'd just killed one of his brothers and sent his soul back to Hell, and he was in pain. Anger, grief radiated from him like intense black waves. He didn't move, just remained rigid in my arms as I squeezed him tighter, the oil on my skin mixing with the blood on his.

The need in me to ease the pain he was feeling was so impossibly strong that I slid my hands over his broad shoulder and looked into his eyes. Shadows and light danced across his skin from thc fire still blazing at the campsite, and I reached up and cupped his bearded jaw. "I'm so sorry," I said.

His lips peeled back, incisors still extended, and he growled. The look in his eyes was one I'd never seen before, pain, confusion…god, fear. My hound's default emotion was anger, it was the only one he truly understood. He didn't know how to process all he was feeling and had reverted to the basest part of him.

His beast.

I lifted my other hand to his face, my oily, naked skin sliding over his, smearing with more of his blood. His hand shot up, and he grabbed my throat. Like the last time he'd done it, it wasn't to intimidate, it was pure possessiveness. His thumb moved to my fluttering pulse, and he shook his head, warning me off.

He could never be mine, for a lot of reasons.

But I cared about him, enough to know I couldn't just settle for animal need with him. It couldn't just be sex, not for me. My beautiful, vicious, soulless hellhound couldn't offer me more than that, though, and knowing that was all we shared would eventually shatter my heart into a million pieces.

Unlike him, I'd grow old and frail. I'd die. How long would he want me once I was wrinkled and gray. I didn't want to know the answer to that.

I would only ever be a blip of time in his immortal life. He and I, we were never meant to be. It was impossible.

But I could give him now.

Because there was no moving on with my life without knowing what it was like to be with him, to give him all of me and have him give me all he was capable of in return. So I ignored his warning and urged him down as I lifted to my tiptoes.

With a tortured snarl, he released my throat and snatched me off my feet, his mouth slamming down on mine. I wrapped my legs around his thick waist, and he stepped forward, my back making contact with a rough tree trunk. He attacked my mouth, a kiss so brutal, so full of need, all I could do was hold on and surrender to it, surrender to him.

The hard, thick length of his cock was pressed between our stomachs, and he rocked against me, grinding it between our slippery, sticky bodies. One of his hands slid down between my breasts and he cupped one, lifting it as he dipped his head, sucking a tight nipple into his mouth.

I threw my head back and cried out. It was too much already. The base of his cock rubbed against my clit as he thrust between us and tugged harder on my nipple. I came, unable to hold back, shuddering against him.

I'd barely got my breath back when he shoved two fingers inside me. I groaned, my thighs shaking. "I want you."

His growl was vicious. "You're gonna get me." He pressed his forehead to mine, flashing sharp white teeth, and added a third finger, then continued to use them to fuck me deep and fast. "Promise me you're ready, dove? Promise me."

I nodded, gasping as his thumb did a devastating circle around my clit, as his fingers deep inside me worked my G-spot.

Oh goddess.

I screamed again, coming a second time. I was still fluttering around his fingers when he yanked them free, lifting me away from the tree and spinning me so my back was to his front.

He brushed my hair to the side and his mouth touched my ear as he gripped the back of my neck. "Hands and knees, dove."

I shuddered, my entire body quivering with need, somehow still turned on after already coming twice. He applied pressure to the back of my neck, and I dropped to my knees, then down on all fours.

Warrick came down behind me, his massive body covering me completely, his mouth back at my ear. "You need to relax and accept me." He gritted his teeth against my skin. "It's going to feel like too much, but you can take me. You just need to let me in." His hand covered my breast and he squeezed. "You gonna let me in, Willow?"

At the sound of my name on his lips, my heart went wild in my chest. My body was aching, my pulse racing, desperate for what was about to happen, what we'd been building up to for so long. "Yes," I rasped.

"The first time I fuck you will be like the animal I am, it's what I need, what the beast in me needs." He dragged his tongue up the side of my throat and nipped my ear as his hand slid down my stomach and between my legs, cupping me possessively. He pressed his middle finger in, making me moan. "You'll get off on it, dove, you'll love the way I fuck you."

I shuddered again. "Warrick." There was no missing the hunger, the desperate need, in my voice. I was basically begging for him to give that to me, and I didn't even care.

"I'm here, dove," he said. "And I'm not going anywhere." His other hand went to my hip, while he rubbed, circled, between my thighs, spreading my wetness. My hips rocked against his fingers all on their own, seeking more. His hand left me, and I heard him spit before he was back, rubbing my pussy again. "Oil?"

"I don't need it." I'd never been so wet.

"Trust me, it'll help," he said and squeezed my hip again.

"In my bag." There was a rustling, the sound of the lid opening. I looked over my shoulder and watched as he dripped the oil on his hand and rubbed it over his huge cock. My inner muscles clenched with need.

"Brace," he growled.

I did as he said, digging my palms into the softly packed earth, then the head of his cock was against me. He pressed forward, sliding in an inch, and my head dropped, hanging from my shoulders as a low groan left me.

His big, rough-skinned hand rubbed up and down my back. "Can feel you clenching, dove. Don't fight it."

I blew out a breath, forcing my muscles to relax, and he slid in another inch.

"Fuck, that's it. Made for me, every fucking part of you was made for me." He growled and pushed in more.

I gasped for air, balancing on a precipice between pleasure and pain, wanting to pull away and push back all at the same time. Warrick decided for me. One hand on my shoulder, the other on my hip, he filled me, sliding in to the hilt.

I clawed at the forest floor, so full of him, surrounded by him, his heat, his scent, a writhing mix of pleasure and pain, I felt like I was spinning out of control.

Then with a snarl, he let go of my waist, hooked his arm under my hips, lifting me higher, and slid out. I was shaking uncontrollably and involuntarily jerked forward, not sure I was ready for him to fill me again. But he hauled me back, sliding all the way in once more, and I cried out.

This time there was less resistance, this time the pleasure outweighed the pain. He did it again, and I came with a high-pitched scream, the orgasm hitting me out of nowhere.

Warrick roared, all beast now, and fucked me faster, harder. "My dove loves the way her hound fucks her. Rough like an animal in the dirt."

"Yes."

"The way you feel..." He hissed, then barked out words that were more like harsh sounds, his language, and the same thing he'd said in the shower after he'd licked my scratched thighs and again in the cave when he'd been trying to wake me. "So tight, clutching at me." He nipped at the side of my neck. "I'm losing my fucking mind, female, finally being inside you."

He wasn't the only one. I rocked back, shoving him deeper, and Warrick seemed to snap. If I thought he was fucking me before, I'd been wrong. All I could do was surrender to it, to him. His strong arms held me in place as he tugged me back, slamming forward, taking me like he'd promised.

It was too much, all of it, too intense. "I'm going to come," I said. How was that possible?

"Wait for me," he ordered.

I wasn't sure I could. I could feel him growing larger inside me with every thrust, and if he wasn't holding me up, I'd be flat on the forest floor. When he rocked back the next time, I was tugged back as well. Oh god, he was locked in place like he'd told me.

He groaned. "Don't move." Then I felt his teeth at my shoulder, his canines breaking skin as he held me tightly to him, rotating his hips and pulsing inside me, deep and strong. Each throb of his cock heightened my pleasure and the heat of his seed flooded me, setting off my own orgasm. The bite didn't hurt, it warmed, tingled, somehow took me higher.

Finally, he released my shoulder and his roar echoed around the forest, startling sleeping birds from the trees, while I cried out helplessly, surrendering to the pleasure—to him.

His hips continued to rock until he wasn't locked in place anymore, until he could slide in and out of me again, and all the while, his hand coasted up and down my spine, soothing, comforting.

He licked my shoulder several times, over his bite, making me shiver, then he slid out, and still behind me, he gripped my jaw and turned my head. "My dove," he said, and kissed me, deep, calming.

I'd never heard that tone in his voice before, and it warmed me. God, I was barely conscious. Warrick laid me on the ground, and I heard him gathering our things. When I could move, he helped me dress, then lifted me off the ground, holding me to his chest.

"I can walk," I said.

He pressed a kiss to my lips and held me closer. "I know."

Then he carried me out of the forest.

CHAPTER 24

Willow

I DRIED OFF, then stared at my naked reflection in the bathroom mirror. I barely recognized myself. My hair was wild, my eyes bright, lips swollen. My gaze traveled lower, taking in the now colorful thorny vines decorating my skin. Bruises from fighting, and other things—I looked down at my hips, at the massive hand-prints marking my flesh where Warrick had held me tight.

I liked them, the bruises he'd given me. I liked the way they looked on my skin.

And I liked him—more than liked him—but how I felt didn't matter. There were bigger things at stake.

I turned and looked at my shoulder. His bite had completely healed, only two dark pink marks remained where his canines had sunk deep. He'd marked me.

Marks like these, they were what Rebecca would have seen on Jane's shoulder. The marks Maddox had given to Jane, his mate. I shivered, then shoved the thought from my mind.

That's not what this is.

Of course, it wasn't.

Last night, he'd brought me home, laid me in bed, and left.

That said it all, really.

I mean, I assumed he went to talk with his brothers to let them know what happened with Edric. But he hadn't come back. I'd laid awake waiting for him for hours. I guess I should be relieved he hadn't returned. It made what I had to do today a lot easier. I told myself that, anyway.

We'd had sex, *that's all*. That's all it was. I swallowed hard when my stupid heart clenched in denial. I ignored it and reminded myself that Warrick spoke of animal attraction, of his need for me, never affection, never more than the physical.

At least there was no chance of pregnancy since I was on the pill, and with the way the hounds healed, they didn't have diseases of any kind.

Quickly dressing, I checked in on Rose before I left.

She was propped up in bed, a mountain of pillows behind her, and Mom was feeding her oatmeal. My sister was struggling to choke it down.

"Hey," she said when she saw me, her voice as weak as the rest of her.

I strode in and dropped a kiss on top of her head. "I have to head out for a while, but if you're up for it later, maybe we could watch a movie?"

She smiled up at me. "I'd...I'd love that."

I forced a smile in return when all the while I was shattering on the inside seeing her like this.

Warrick wasn't downstairs either when I got there.

"Yo," Relic called after me. "Where you going? War will want to know what you're doing."

"Just lunch with a friend. I'll be back in a couple hours." Then I walked out, got in the Morris and tore out of there.

The alpha would know where I was, of course, but hopefully, if he thought I was just with a friend, he wouldn't come looking for me. Him showing up was the last thing I needed.

The restaurant Clayton chose for us to meet was frequented by the who's who of our world, and an uneasy feeling hit me as soon as I walked in. Had he chosen this place for a reason?

Of course he hadn't, he was grieving. Could I be anymore paranoid? I doubted he'd given the location a second thought.

I spotted him across the room, and he stood, lifting a hand, waving me over.

When I reached him, he pulled me in for a friendly hug and pressed a chaste kiss to my cheek. "Wills, I'm so glad you asked to meet."

"How have you been?"

His easy smile dropped. "Not so great, if I'm honest."

"That's to be expected. You lost your mom."

He dragged in a shaky breath. "I miss her, a lot."

I squeezed his hand. There was no missing the truth to his words, his aura spoke volumes. There was pain but also anger. All completely understandable. But with these families—the ones with power, money—it wasn't the norm to share how you felt or show it. It was seen as a weakness. "I'm so sorry, Clay."

He dipped his chin and visibly pulled himself together. "So I assume you invited me here because you have some idea who hurt her?"

"I'm sorry, no. I have no idea who hurt your mom or Magnolia. But I promise, I won't stop until I do." Though right now, I wasn't sure how I would do that. They were using dark magic to cover their tracks—and breaking every one of our covenants in doing so.

Clayton's brows lowered. "Oh, I just assumed..." He cleared his throat. "Well, I appreciate you taking the time to check on me."

I chewed my lip and sat straighter in my chair. "There's another reason I asked you to meet with me, actually."

His head tilted to the side, his blue eyes meeting mine. "Oh?"

You're doing this for Rose. Just say it. "The offer you made, is it still on the table?"

His mouth opened, then closed, then opened again. "Of marriage?"

Everything in me recoiled at the idea, but then I thought of the way Rose had looked this morning, and I pushed on. "Yes."

Color hit his cheeks and his eyes widened. "Truly? I just assumed...I saw the pictures on Nightscape. I thought you and the hound..."

"This has nothing to do with Warrick." I couldn't talk about him, not with Clayton, not at all. If I did, I'd run out of here and never come back.

"Okay."

"Rose is...she's really sick. We need help, Clay. That was the deal, yes? You said you'd get your researchers to help her?"

He nodded. "Absolutely." He reached out, covering my hand with his. "I will put everything I have, every resource, money, research into finding a cure for her." He gave my fingers a squeeze. "But I don't just want a marriage of convenience, Willow. I want a real one. I want us to make a real go of things."

"I can't give you that, not yet. Maybe not ever. I'm sorry, but if we're doing this, I want us to be honest with each other." We were both getting something out of this—he, power and access to our cemetery, me, money and resources. As far as I was concerned, that was enough.

"I believe love can grow, if we both give it our all," he said. "My parents' marriage was arranged and they grew to love each other. It can be the same for us, if you're willing to try."

"I'm not sure I believe in love," I said, even as something deep inside called me a liar.

"That's because you've never been in love, Wills. I hope to change your mind about that." A smile spread across his face.

"I'm not playing coy, Clayton. I'm not here to lead you on. This is a business transaction first and foremost."

He took my hand again. "Will you at least promise not to close that door?"

It wouldn't change a thing. I knew it down to my bones. There was only one male I wanted, would ever want. "Fine," I said. It was a lie, and I didn't feel good about it, but if that's what he needed to hear to do this, so be it. "So you're saying yes? You'll help me, you'll help my sister?"

He smiled. "Yes. It's a yes to both."

"Even if this thing between us is never what you want?" I couldn't help pushing. I didn't want this to be an issue later on. "Even if we just end up remaining friends and nothing more?"

"Yes," he said. "But you will remain open to more?"

"I said I would."

"That means we live in the same house; we work at getting to know each other again. That we attend functions as a married couple. To anyone looking, that's what we are. And I get full access to your cemetery. This marriage is supposed to be mutually beneficial, after all."

I nodded, my stomach in knots. "Of course. How soon?"

"Rose is that unwell?"

"Yes."

His eyes filled with sympathy and determination as well. "As soon as our engagement is announced, I'll get the ball rolling."

"Thank you. I just nccd a fcw days. I want to tcll my family first."

"Would you like me to be with you?"

This news was not going to go down well, not any of it. "I think it's best if I do it alone."

"Okay," he said, then waved for a waiter.

We ordered lunch. I wanted to leave, but it seemed rude, considering I'd just agreed to marry him, even if it was in name only.

The food arrived, and Clay ordered champagne.

He smiled at me. "We're celebrating, right?"

"What are we celebrating?" a smooth voice said behind me.

I turned in my seat and Isaac Eldridge stood behind us, a polite smile on his thin lips.

"This is a private party, Eldridge," Clayton said, gaze darkening. "And you'll find out soon enough."

"Clay," I bit out.

Clayton drew in a shaky breath and smiled at me. "Apologies."

Isaac's dark gaze slid to me. "If this is what I think it is, you chose wrong, sweetheart."

Jesus.

"If you've finished, we'd like to enjoy our lunch in peace," Clay said to him.

Isaac didn't look away from me, and something slithered up my spine. "Give me a call if you change your mind." Then he winked and walked out.

"Goddamn it," I said and shoved my chair back.

"Don't leave," Clay said. "Stay, ignore that asshole."

"He knows, Clayton. It will be all over the city, all over Nightscape by the end of the day. I need to talk to my family."

He stood. "You're right. Sorry, I didn't handle that very well."

"It's…it's fine. But I need to go."

He pulled me into his arms, and my instinct was to shove him away, but I forced myself not to. Recoiling in public at your fiancé's touch probably wasn't the best way to keep him on your good side. Yes, I was using him, but he was using me as well. I was doing this for Rose and Rose alone.

He pressed a kiss to my cheek. "I'll call you later."

I nodded and got the hell out of there.

My phone rang as I parked outside the house. Pulling it out of my satchel, I checked the screen. My heart seized.

Ren.

"Ren? Is that you?"

Some choppy breathing echoed down the line.

"Ren?" Had the spirit released him?

An awful laugh filled the space between us. No, not him, it was the monster living inside him.

"Let him go," I gritted out. "Release him."

He giggled, then someone screamed, and the line went dead. *Goddammit.* I couldn't even find him through his GPS because he'd turned it off when he went to train with the hounds, just in case his mom looked him up and freaked out.

Squeezing my eyes closed, I bit back a cry of rage, of fear, of utter hopelessness. My best friend was missing, possessed by an evil fucking spirit, Rose was sick with a mystery illness, someone had tried to kill Magnolia and was possibly planning to free Azel's soul from Hell—the monster who had tortured and almost killed me—and I didn't know what to do, how to stop any of it.

Nothing was fucking working—and the shadow seeking had given me nothing but nightmares. I'd contacted the knights, since Azel rising would affect them as well. But they assured me he was still in Hell, where he was supposed to be.

But for how long?

Shoving my door open, I climbed out.

Music traveled from Bram's tree house, and I heard Mags laugh from inside. The carefree sound hit me hard, and suddenly I was finding it hard to breathe. She trusted me to keep her safe, they all did, and I had no idea how to do it, other than keep them here, and never let them leave, secure behind the wards I strengthened daily with the help of Else.

I wasn't ready to tell them about Clayton, but now I had no damn choice. Isaac would more than likely be blabbing all over the city, or his mother would be anyway, in her outrage.

Laughter and voices traveled from the kitchen, and I slipped past. I needed a moment, just a few minutes, to gather my thoughts. I walked past Roe's door and peeked in. She lay on her side, frail, eyes closed, asleep.

Tears stung my eyes, and I rushed past and shut myself in my room, the weight of everything crashing down on me. I fought against it. I had to be strong for them. One thing at a time. One step at a time.

There was a tap at the door. "Dove?"

I took a step back, looking for a place to hide. I couldn't face him right now. The door opened before I could make an escape, though, and Warrick walked in, huge and untamed and utterly gorgeous. My stomach zapped, and my heart fluttered as his gaze ate me up.

"You're back. You told your brothers about Edric?"

He nodded.

"That must have been hard."

He grunted and advanced on me, and before I could get the words I needed to say out of my mouth, his lips were on mine. He kissed me in the way only Warrick could, possessive, hungry, giving, and demanding everything in equal measure. No games, just need, raw and honest.

When he lifted his head, a rumbling sound came from his chest and he dipped his head, his nose moving along my jaw, my cheek, and his head jerked back. "Someone touched you. Put his mouth on you," he said, rubbing a spot on my cheek with his thumb like he was trying to rub Clayton's kiss away.

"Yes, a friend of mine. We met for lunch."

His brows dropped. "Your scent is different, dove, I can smell your fear. What the fuck is going on?"

I didn't want to have this conversation with him. There was no doubt in my mind that he'd be angry, but what else could I do? I had to put my family first, not whatever this thing between us was. This wasn't real. This was heat and sex and desire, nothing more.

Liar.

I closed my eyes and breathed through the pain filling my chest. He'd moved closer, backing me up, and I forced myself to look up at him as he trapped me between the wall and the heat of his body. He pressed his hands to the floral wallpaper on either side of me, caging me in. "Talk, dove. Now."

I pressed my hands to his chest and looked up at him, needing him to understand, for him to make this easy on me, because I was cracking down the middle, and I didn't want to shatter in front of him.

He scented me again and his nostrils flared. "You saw Whitlock."

"You remember his scent?"

"He smelled like desperation and money and too much cologne, still does." His eyes narrowed on me. "Why did you meet with him?"

Say it. *Say it*. You're doing this for Rose, for your family. "Clayton...he wants to align with a powerful family, and Rose...she's, she's so incredibly sick. We need help, and he can give us that help..." I drew in a steadying breath. "We agreed to help each other out."

"You're talking in riddles, female. What are you saying?"

"I've agreed to marry him."

Warrick jerked back, his face contorting, then he snarled, his eyes flashing to red and staying that way. "Like fuck. You are mine, I told you how it was. I told you what would happen when you gave yourself to me. I will tear that fucker's head off before I ever let him come anywhere near you, do you hear me?"

His fury set off my fight-or-flight instincts. I didn't reach for my blade, though, because he wasn't going to hurt me, I knew that with everything in me. "If you kill him, it will hurt me. You said...you promised not to do that, not ever."

His chest pumped, nostrils flared, and I watched, my pulse racing, as his incisors slid down, his mouth and jaw trying to reshape into his beast. "You became mine on that forest floor," he said, voice melded with his beast. "You think I'll just let you go?" He tilted his head back and roared.

"Stop," I said, shoving at his chest. "You need to stop." Tears stung my eyes, and I fought them back. "This is how it has to be, Warrick, how I want it to be, and I need you to accept it. I need you to walk away."

"You don't want him, this is some fucked-up deal."

My hound, who didn't play games, who said it like it was, expected the same from others, and if I didn't lie to him now, he would never let me go, and he would go after Clayton.

I'd lose Rose.

So with every bit of internal strength I had left, I stared back into his gorgeous eyes and told him what I needed to. "It's more than that."

He stilled, taking me in, and he took an abrupt step back. His eyes stayed locked on mine. "You want this male?" he rasped.

"Yes, I want him. I've loved him since we were in high school." More lies.

He was back in front of me in a second, his expression twisted with rage, and goddess, hurt. "No."

"Yes," I said, voice as strong as I could make it. "What you and I shared was just sex, animal attraction, like you said."

"Dove..."

"Please, I need you to leave." *Before I break down in front of you, before you see for yourself how I really feel about you.*

"Go," I said, and shoved at him. He didn't budge.

"No."

"It's over," I said, my throat raw from holding back my tears. "Leave."

He roared again and slammed his fist into the wall, punching almost right through it, gaze wild, confused.

It was like the night before, as if my hound was struggling to process what he was feeling, as if he didn't understand what to do with it all. Or maybe it was as simple as he didn't like to lose. It was easier to believe the latter, the former meant he might actually care for me, really, truly care, and I couldn't handle that. That would break me.

I didn't move, didn't speak as he straightened, his eyes still locked on mine.

Finally, he leaned in, and I expected him to call me a bitch, to fire that anger at me, like a lot of guys did when they didn't get their way. Instead, he leaned in, his big body shifting closer, and he buried his face against my throat and breathed deep like he always did, as if he were seeking comfort from me. I squeezed my eyes closed, pain lancing through me.

I loved him.

I was *in* love with him. With this wild, untamed male who didn't know how to love me back.

It finally happened, the thing I'd spent my entire adult life trying to avoid, and as predicted, it was a complete and utter fuckup.

Then he lifted his head and stunned me by tucking my hair behind my ear with a gentleness I didn't know he was capable of. "I'll leave, but my brothers stay until you're safe. You know where I am if you need me."

Then he turned and walked out.

CHAPTER 25

Willow

I MADE my way down the stairs on shaky legs. After that confrontation with Warrick, my emotions were wrecked, but there was no stalling. I needed to be the one to tell my family before they heard about Clayton from someone else.

Mom was at the counter mixing cake batter, and Else was lining a cake tin when I walked into the kitchen. Mags was back, and she was sitting with Iris at the table, talking. I could see the lights on in the tree house through the kitchen window—Bram was still at his place—and the low hum of the TV in the other room, a familiar gardening show, told me where Art was.

I leaned against the wall for support. "Do you guys have a minute?"

"Does it have something to do with the thundercloud I saw over the alpha's head when he stormed out of here?" Else asked.

I curled my fingers into a tight fist, my blunt nails biting into my skin. "Yeah, it does."

Else limped to the table and took a seat. "I'm thinking I better sit for this one."

"What's going on, sweetheart?" Mom asked.

I hated the look of concern on her face. I never wanted to be the cause of her distress, she'd been through enough in her life, and with Rose sick, the last thing I wanted was to add to her worries.

"It's good news," I said to her, and did my best to force a smile.

"Well, that's a lie," Iris said and sat back on her chair.

Mags snorted. "You really think you can pull the wool over our eyes? You look like you've eaten a bad burrito."

I couldn't deny I felt sick to my stomach. "Okay, so maybe it's not wonderful news, but what I have to tell you will benefit the whole family, but especially Rose."

Mom grabbed for the counter. "Have you found something, a cure?"

I grabbed her hand and pressed a kiss to her shaking fingers. "Not yet, but..." I looked at my sisters, Else, then back to Mom. "I've agreed to marry Clayton Whitlock."

"What the hell for?" Else said. "You don't even like that twerp."

"He cheated on you!" Iris said. "He's a pig. I can't believe you'd chose that guy over Warrick. The huge hellhound alpha who thinks you walk on water and your turds smell like flowers? *Warrick*," she said again with more emphasis, like I needed reminding who he was.

Mags shot to her feet and winced when her stitches pulled. "You've been seeing both of them?"

I lifted my hands. "I know you're all confused and worried. Clayton is a good guy. We were young when we first went out. Things happen. And no, we haven't been seeing each other. And this isn't a love match—"

"No shit," Else said.

"It's a mutely beneficial agreement. He marries into a magically powerful family and gets access to our cemetery—"

"No." Mom gasped. "You can't be serious."

"This can't be happening," Mags said and dropped to her seat.

"And he puts his considerable funds, connections, all his recourses into finding a cure for Rose," I finished.

The room went silent.

Mom sat heavily on the chair beside Else, then looked up at me, and there was no missing the conflict in her eyes.

"You really think he can find a cure?" Mags said, voice broken.

"Yes."

"No," Rose said and walked through the door, her voice stronger than I'd heard it in a very long time.

"Sweetheart." Mom rushed forward and tried to help her into a chair.

Rose shook her head, brushing her away, and held onto the doorframe. "You will not do this, Willow, do you hear me?"

"It's okay, Roe—"

"No, it's not," she said, her voice losing some of its strength. She gripped the doorframe tighter. "You always said you didn't believe in love, but it exists, and I think you've recently worked that out for yourself. You're in love with Warrick."

I took a step forward. "Roe, please…"

She shook her head. "I'll never get that. I know that now, I've resigned myself to it, but I won't let you throw away your chance at happiness on some…wild-goose chase."

"You don't know that," Iris said. "Whitlock is loaded. He can help."

"I said no." Then her face softened, because this was Rose, the kind one, the gentle one, and being assertive like this didn't come easy to her. But when she looked at all of us, what I saw in her eyes had my heart constricting in my chest. "I'm tired," she whispered. "I'm so…very tired. I've been living like this, in limbo, in pain, weak, for so long. I don't want to do it anymore."

"Roe," Else choked. "Honey, we won't let you give up."

"I'm not giving up, Else. But I've had time to come to terms with it. There is no cure for this. We've been searching most of my life. No amount of money"—she looked squarely at me—"no sacrifice, will change that."

Mom rushed to her, and Rose let her help her to a chair.

"You love me, and I love you too. So much. And I'm so...so angry that I won't be here to see all the good things you have coming...but I've accepted it." Then she took her knife from the pocket of her robe. "That's why I need you to swear you won't do this, Wills. I want a blood oath that you will stop this now. I want one from all of you. I can't rest until you do."

I shook my head. "Roe, no, I can't..."

"You will," she said and looked at Mom. "You know I'm right. Don't let her do this."

Mom closed her eyes, and when she opened them, tears streaked down her face. The truth, the stark, awful truth we'd been denying with everything we had, was right there. Rose was dying, and there was nothing any of us could do to stop it.

"Do it," Mom said to me.

"No," Mags said, tears running down her face.

Rose took her hand. "It's going to be okay, Mags, I promise." Then she cut herself.

And with tears running down our faces, we all did the same. We swore we wouldn't sacrifice ourselves to find a cure that we all knew deep down didn't exist.

Then Mom helped Rose back upstairs.

Else passed around the healing balm and gave my shoulder a squeeze. "Go on, go to your hound."

"He doesn't want to see me."

"Of course he does," she said and walked out.

I had to get out of the house, but not to go to Warrick. I was pretty sure he'd tell me to get lost if I went to the club-house tonight. Instead, I went searching for Ren. I drove around for hours, searching all his old haunts, like I had many times since he was taken from me. His favorite places to go, to eat, to party, but there was no sign of him, and no one had seen him.

My stomach was in knots, and my heart hurt, and when it was finally time to head for home, I knew that wasn't where I was going. I'd been lying to myself.

Going to Warrick was a terrible idea. I should stay away. All the reasons we couldn't be together were still there. But I needed him. I wanted him so badly I shook.

He'll probably refuse to see you.

Probably, but I had to try.

The gates of the hellhound clubhouse were closed when I arrived, but they'd opened the bar. Light and music spilled out, lots of cars out front. I guess now that all the hounds had been inked with Else's runes, there was no reason to keep the place shut anymore.

I grabbed my phone and shoved it in my pocket. Clayton had been disappointed when I called him on the way here and told him I'd changed my mind, there'd been no missing it. But he'd taken it better than I'd expected. Thank the mother for that, I couldn't handle another confrontation tonight.

I peered at the clubhouse through the fence, it was dark, quiet. They were no doubt all at the bar blowing off some steam.

I locked the Morris and walked in. People milled around, drinking, laughing, some danced.

The hounds...not so much. They stood in small subdued groups around the room, quietly sipping their beers. They may have limited emotions, but they'd just lost one of their brothers in a fucking awful way, and they were feeling it.

I glanced down at the cut on my arm, and the pain grew and built inside me. I'd made a blood oath tonight to let my sister die.

We had no idea how much time we had left with her, and I was grieving.

I was grieving for Rose, and I was grieving for Ren, because he was strong, stronger than he'd ever believed, but after seeing the way that spirit had affected Edric, I knew my sweet fox would never be the same again.

God, I felt like I was coming undone, like I was about to unravel right here in front of everyone. My heart was in my throat as I searched the room for Warrick. My need to be close to him growing into a desperate ache. I turned, scanning the rest of the room, while my mother's words filtered through my head.

Love isn't what someone says, it's what they do.

I was in love with Warrick, I was sure of that now. And no, Warrick didn't feel the same, he'd told me himself he wasn't capable of it, and that male was a man of his word—but he did care, in his own way, I truly believed he cared for me beyond animal need.

He'd promised me loyalty and devotion, and that was more than a person could hope for in this life, right?

People touted love as a reason to trust, throwing the word around willy-nilly, then turned around and took a dump on that person with their next breath. Romantic love didn't automatically equal faithfulness or commitment. I'd seen that with my own eyes so many times.

I didn't need Warrick to love me back, I just needed him to be loyal and trustworthy, and he'd proven himself to be both more times than I could count.

A tingling sensation slid across my shoulders. He was here, he was watching me. I turned and my gaze collided with his. He stood with two of his brothers on the other side of the room. He leaned against the end of the bar; his fingers curled around a squat glass of amber liquid.

Warrick didn't move, didn't acknowledge me, just watched me and waited.

I'd had a protective wall around me most of my life. I didn't like showing weakness of any kind. I'd viewed love as emotional weakness and I'd never let myself go there. I'd never let anyone I'd dated know that I cared, or that I might need them, even for a moment.

That part of me wanted to lift my chin and stand my ground, it wanted me to force him to come to me. But he'd been doing that already, he'd shown up every time I needed him. He'd made it clear that he cared the only way he knew how, and now it was my turn to do the same.

And I was terrified.

Without allowing myself to chicken out, I strode toward him. He tracked me, but still, he didn't move and his expression didn't change. My heart was in my throat, every part of me afraid that he'd turn me away, that he'd tell me he'd given up on me. Going into battle was less intimidating than this.

I stopped in front of him. "Hey."

He said nothing, just took a sip of his drink. Out of the corner of my eye, I saw Jagger and another hound walk away, and I was thankful for it. Yes, he told me to come find him if I needed him, but he wasn't going to make this easy on me, and he proved it by looking away from me. I deserved that.

I curled my fingers around his forearm, and the muscle bunched beneath my palm. "Warrick."

He gave me nothing.

"Please...will you look at me?"

His gaze slid to me, hard and unfeeling, and I wanted to shrivel in on myself. He was giving back what I'd given him, and it hurt like hell.

It would be so easy to run, to save myself from the possibility of rejection, of humiliation, but I loved the stubborn bastard, and if I didn't try, if I gave up on us, I'd never forgive myself.

"I'm sorry," I said.

Still, I got nothing from him, just that hard, cold stare.

Desperation slammed into me, and I ducked under his arm that rested on the bar. My chest brushed his and his scent filled my head. I gripped the sides of his shirt at his waist. "Please, Warrick," I rasped, pressing my head to his chest. "I'm sorry. I didn't mean anything I said. I was scared, and I was trying to fix everything, and I pushed you away. I don't want Clayton. I don't want anyone else."

His chest expanded, and he leaned forward, trapping me between him and the bar.

I tilted my head back and looked into his golden eyes. "I just want you."

His fingers thrust into my hair and his head dipped closer, so close his forehead touched mine. "Say it again."

"I want you," I whispered. "Only you."

His mouth slammed down on mine, and he kissed me like the animal he was, not holding anything back. I curled my arms around his neck, and he hauled me off the ground, throwing my legs around his waist and prowled across the room. Everyone was watching us, I felt their eyes following, and I didn't care. I didn't care who had witnessed me begging for Warrick to forgive me. I was in his arms, and he was kissing me, and that was all that mattered.

He walked out the back of the building and across the yard to the clubhouse, through the doors and down the stairs, taking me belowground to the den. He kicked his bedroom door shut behind us and a moment later, we dropped to his bed.

He covered me with his body, looking down at me. "Thought I'd lost you," he said, low and harsh.

I gripped the sides of his face. "I was trying to help Rose. Clayton offered to help if I married him, but I never wanted him. I fucked up. I'm so sorry."

His eyes darkened. "You're mine now, dove. I let you go, and you came back. That means you're mine. No going back now."

That should scare the hell out of me. It didn't. "And you're mine."

His nostrils flared. "Yeah, I fucking am." Then he yanked at the front of my jeans, undoing them, and tore them down my legs. He tossed them and my boots aside as my hands dropped to the front of his pants and I undid them with shaky fingers, then pushed them down to free his cock.

His hand dropped between us, cupping me, fingers sliding through my folds, checking if I was ready for him. I was more than ready.

Warrick bared his teeth. "Pussy so fucking wet. You want me, dove, you will always want me and I'll always want you."

"Yes," I said and rubbed up against him.

With a vicious animalistic sound, he hooked my knee over his arm, holding me open wide, then reached between us and took himself in hand. He glided the head over me, and I arched against him, trying to get him where I needed him so badly.

"You know why, don't you, dove? You know why we can't stay away from each other?"

I did, but I'd been too scared to even think it.

"My dove was made for me." He held both sides of my face, hands shaking, and stared into my eyes. "I've waited a thousand years for you, Willow. You have no idea, none. My life was nothing but rage and pain and fire. I never even let myself imagine leaving Hell," he growled. "And I sure as fuck never dreamed a female like you could exist. First time I saw you, all this fucking gorgeous red hair, eyes full of fire, and a heart full of courage, I knew you were mine."

I stared up at him, struggling to breathe. He was decimating that wall I'd lived behind one word at a time.

"You make me whole, dove. I don't need a soul, because that's what you are. You're my fucking soul." Then he said to me those same harsh words in his language he had several times before.

My eyes stung and I fought back the tears. Warrick was my

lifeline, my everything, and over the coming months, I knew he'd be the one to keep me sane when my world felt like it was falling apart.

He deserved the truth. He deserved everything from me.

I smiled up at him, cupping his bearded cheek. "And you're my heart."

CHAPTER 26

Warrick

MY DOVE STARED up at me with tears in her eyes, and I struggled to fill my lungs with oxygen. *Her heart? Me?* A brutal, demanding animal who struggled to find fucking words around this female, and she called me her heart?

For the first time in my life, my lack of soul, my inability to give her what she deserved—to understand and return love—tormented me.

"Kiss me," she whispered.

I fell on her mouth like a beast starved, giving her what she asked for and taking what I needed in return, kissing her hard and deep. I didn't understand what was happening inside me, what I was feeling, but it was a fucking good feeling, and I tried to show her with that kiss, because I sure as fuck didn't know how to tell her in words.

From this moment on, she was never leaving my side. I'd

spend every moment of my life making sure she knew she came first, in everything, always.

Her leg around my waist tightened, and my cock ached to get inside her.

"Please," she said against my lips. "Take me."

I'd fucked her hard on the forest floor, from behind, the way we always fucked, but this time I wanted to look at her when I moved inside her. I wanted to see in her eyes how I made her feel, and I wanted her to see the same in mine.

"Legs spread wide, dove," I said.

She was small, but she could take me, nice and deep, I already knew that. I still needed to be careful, though. Hurting her in any way would destroy me.

She moaned and writhed beneath me, desperate for me to fill her, and I had to grit my teeth against the urge to slam deep inside her. Opening the bedside drawer, I grabbed some lube and shifted back. Her hands grabbed at me, her hips rolling. She reached for my dick, and I pulled away.

"Please," she said.

She was fucking dripping, but I wasn't risking it. "Don't want to hurt you." I quickly lubed up and tossed the tube aside, and when I came back down on top of her, she immediately wrapped herself around me like she couldn't get me close enough.

My fucking head spun with how much I wanted her, how good it felt for her to want me too. Reaching between us, I led the head of my cock to her, and angling my hips, I pushed it inside her.

She tried to lift her hips to take more of me and I pinned her down. "Be still," I said through clenched teeth. She had no idea what she was doing to me or how thin my control was when I was around her. "If I slam deep like I want to, I will hurt you. So for now, you take it how I give it to you," I said, damn near spiraling, I was so close to the edge of my control.

Her pussy fluttered around me, and I hissed and pushed in

another inch. My dove moaned and arched again, taking more, ignoring me completely.

"*Fuck.*"

Shaking like hell, I slid out a little, then back in, giving her more, and she fucking writhed. It was impossible to take it slower, and I pinned her down more firmly. "Look at me."

She did, her lids lowered, lips puffy, cheeks pink.

"You want it all, dove?"

"Yes...give it to me," she said, her heels digging into my back.

With a growl, I slid home, slow and even, giving her every hard inch. She groaned and clawed at my back, marking me. *Fuck yeah.* "That what you needed?"

"Yes," she rasped. "I need it."

That was all I could take, I fucking snapped and started moving, fucking my sweet, little dove, with hard, deep strokes. Taking her like she desperately wanted me to. Like I needed to.

The curve in my cock hit her like it was made to, sliding, rubbing her deep inside, and in minutes she was digging her nails deeper into my flesh and screaming, coming around my cock, gripping me so tight my vision blacked out. I wanted to make her come again. The sound of her pleasure was addictive to me.

She was still shaking when I lifted her up, still buried deep inside her, and sat back on my shins. Her arms slid around my neck, those supple thighs around my waist. I gripped her round ass and moved her on my dick. She took over, though, fucking me harder than I had her.

My female was *taking* me.

After I left Hell, I realized I never wanted to be owned ever again, but Willow owned every part of me. I'd give her more if I had it to give. She could have me, all of me.

"Warrick," she said against my shoulder, then sunk her teeth into my flesh, screaming and shuddering as she came a second time.

Her teeth marking me, her pussy grasping me so fucking tight, over and over, there was no holding back. I swelled inside her, locking her body in place, and shot hard and deep, filling her with my seed. Gripping her hips, I held her down on me as she spasmed around my pulsing length, so she didn't try to pull away and hurt herself.

I slid my thumb over her clit as I continued to come, and fuck me, she came a third time, ringing more pleasure out of both of us.

Finally, she slumped against me, holding on as I finished emptying myself inside her, coming longer and harder than I had before.

My cock still had her locked in place when I gently cupped her face and tilted her head back when I took her mouth and kissed her lips softly. The swelling of my cock slowly ebbed, so I could move again. I didn't pull out, though, I wasn't ready for that yet. If I had my way, I'd stay inside her all night.

When she lifted her head, she gave me a lazy smile. "Jesus, we're good at that."

I grinned, a different kind of pleasure filling my chest. "Yeah, we are."

"We really should do it more often," she said, eyes sparkling.

I chuckled, more warmth filling my chest. "That's what I've been trying to tell you." She laughed softly as I lay her down, still inside her, and held her to me. "But first you need to sleep, dove." When I'd gotten past my own fucking confusing feelings, when she'd walked into the bar earlier, I'd sensed her pain. She was worried about her sister and the fox, and if I could ease that for a little while, that's what I'd do.

I planned on doing it for as long as she'd let me.

"Warrick?"

"Yeah, dove?"

"What did you say before?" she whispered into the dark room. "In your language. You've said it to me before."

I curled my arm around her more firmly. "Precious one. It

means precious one."

Willow

I was on my knees, and I looked up at my alpha in the steam-filled shower stall. His eyes were predatory, unwavering as I took him deeper into my mouth. One of his hands thrust into my hair as his lips peeled back, revealing all those straight white teeth. His other hand hit the tile wall as if he needed the support to hold himself up.

It was a sight to see, that hard mask Warrick always wore cracking for me. He was magnificent. Naked and wet, every sinewy, muscled inch straining, bulging with the effort of holding himself in check.

"Dove," he snarled, and his hips rocked forward.

Warrick liked a little pain with his pleasure, so I squeezed and tugged on his balls, currently in my hand, and he groaned low, his tree-trunk thighs shaking.

I felt him start to thicken in my mouth, and he quickly pulled out before he could hurt me. I wrapped both hands around him in a tight grip and he thrust into my hold.

"Tits," he gritted out. "On your tits."

I stood, and he pumped his hips harder, cursing as he came on my breasts and stomach. When he was spent, he leaned forward, head bent, resting on my shoulder, breath sawing in and out of his mouth.

"You're beautiful when you come," I said.

His hand dropped to my chest, and he rubbed his seed over the mounds of my breasts, down over my stomach, then lower, between my thighs. "Don't hold a candle to you," he rasped. "My beautiful mate."

I moaned as he worked my clit, quivering. *Mate*. It was the first time either of us had said the word out loud. I expected to freak out, but instead, warmth bloomed in my chest. This, here with him, felt so incredibly right. Gripping his shoulders, I tipped my head back, and he gave me what I silently asked for. He kissed me.

He kissed me like the alpha hellhound he was, like no one else ever had.

One of his thick fingers slid inside me and I moaned into his mouth. A gritty sound vibrated from him in return.

"Always so wet for me, dove."

"Yes."

"Because this"—he pushed in a second finger—"was made for me."

He dragged his thumb over my clit, and I was close to the edge of sanity in moments.

"My perfect little witch, every part of you was made just for me."

Yes.

He fucked me with his fingers, faster, deeper, and I gripped his biceps to hold myself up.

"One day soon, I'm going to take you away to my cabin and I'm going to keep you naked and fuck you every way it's possible to fuck. Outside. In the dirt. Under the moon. By the lake, in the lake. I'm going to fuck you over the table after I've fed you, and in the shower after I've washed your hair. You want that, dove?"

I nodded, it was all I was capable of at that point. Then he dipped his head and sucked my nipple into his mouth and lightly bit down. I bucked against him and screamed, coming hard, clutching at him as if I never wanted him to leave me—and terrifyingly, that was the truth.

Because that's exactly what would happen, only it would be me leaving him. Mortality was a bitch.

The thought of losing him now wasn't something I could bear.

"Fuck," he said when I collapsed against him. "My beautiful dove."

He slid his fingers from me and lifted them, slipping them into his mouth, tasting me. Then, without a word, he grabbed a washcloth and worked it over me before he proceeded to wash my hair.

"Will you still want me...when I'm old?" I whispered, the words wrenched from me. I'd never felt more vulnerable in my life.

He stilled.

"You're immortal, Warrick. I'm not. I won't look like this forever. I'll grow old, and frail, and weak." I turned and looked up at him. "I'll die. You'll outlive me, like your brothers did their mates."

His face contorted. "Will I still want you?" he rasped.

I nodded.

He took my face in his large hands. "You are the only female I will ever want, you have been since I first saw you. From now until the end of eternity, you will be my mate, whether you are in this world or the afterlife." He brushed his thumbs over my cheeks. "You will always be perfect to me. You will always be my dove. Tell me you believe me? Because I never want to talk about you leaving me ever again, Willow. Never again."

"But it will happen."

He shook his head. "I can't talk about that, can't fucking think about it, Willow. Tell me you believe me? That you know I'll always want you?"

"I believe you." How could I doubt him?

He kissed me, his lips hard against mine, holding me to him for a long time.

Finally, we'd climbed out of the shower, and he was drying me when my phone rang.

I rushed into the bedroom, rummaging for it, and checked the screen. *Ren.* I hit the call button.

"Ren?" I knew it wasn't him, or maybe the reason he kept calling was that a part of him was breaking through, trying desperately to reach out for me. Like Edric had sought out Warrick.

"Help me, Willow," he said. "Oh god, please, help me."

I gripped the phone tighter at the sound of his voice, tears filling my eyes. "Tell me where you are." Had the spirit left him, had it moved to another host? "Ren?"

"Come get me, please..."

"Please, Ren, tell me where you are?"

"*Help me! Help me!*" he said again, only the voice had turned mocking, then he giggled.

"Why are you doing this? Let him go. *Please, let him go!*"

The sound of a horn blasted in the background, it was loud and long—and familiar.

There was more giggling, then he hung up.

I turned to Warrick. "I think I know where he is."

Warrick snatched his jeans off the floor. "Let's go."

It was dark, fog thick and low as we hit the harbor. The smell of the ocean filled the air along with the smells of the city. There were two main areas down here: the thriving new harbor, where massive cargo ships berthed at the pier, and the old harbor, comprised of rundown warehouses and some original buildings that had been occupied by shipping companies back in the day. The new offices had been moved closer to one of the major trucking companies, and the original area had been left to rot.

Ren had been fascinated by the old buildings and their history. History had been his favorite subject at school, and he'd written a paper about this place and the families who started out here. I'd helped him with it. He'd gotten an A.

Maybe he *was* somehow getting through. Is that why he'd

called? Had he been hoping I'd hear the foghorn? Maybe it had been Ren at the beginning of the call asking for help before the spirit took control again? Or had it just been a trap?

It was eerily quiet as we walked through the old shipping yard, where timber, drums, and pallets were left scattered around, and old shipping containers left to rust.

I glanced up at Warrick. "Anything?"

He tilted his head back, sniffing the air again, and started to shake his head, then froze.

"What is it?"

"Blood...death."

Fuck.

"This way." He jogged toward a warehouse, and a sick feeling gripped my stomach as I followed. He walked along the side of the building and lifted a hand for me to stop when we reached the back corner. He peered around the side. "The scent's stronger here. Stay put."

"No."

The muscle in his jaw jumped. "It's gonna be ugly."

I knew that, but nothing, no one, would stop me from going to him. "Ren's my family."

Warrick's gaze hardened, but he nodded, knowing better than to try to stop me, and we slipped around the side of the building.

The moon was full, shining down and revealing the carnage.

So much blood and death.

Ren had no control over his actions—the spirit and not him had done these things—but he'd been there, he'd witnessed it all. He would have watched his own hands cause this horror. The screams of his victims would forever be in his head.

My Ren would never be the same.

"We've got to bring him home," I whispered.

"You're not getting anywhere near him. It's too fucking dangerous," Warrick said.

I patted my satchel. "I have my salt. He can't get past it." I took a length of thin silver chain from my bag. "And this, it's like the urns we use. Silver binds the spirit, and this has been melted and imbued with a few other things that will make it more effective. Else's been working on it since the first spirit attacked. She said, if we can wrap it round him, the spirit will be trapped inside Ren. Then we can get him home and I can exorcise it."

He took the chain from me, but he wasn't happy about me being here.

"He's close." I didn't know how I knew that, but I felt him, I was sure of it. "If you stay out of sight, he'll come to me."

Warrick's brows lowered. "What are you planning?"

"If I'm right and Ren is somehow getting through, possibly influencing some of the spirit's actions, maybe without it even knowing, I think he'll come if he sees or hears me. This is the first chance we've had since he was taken. I don't want to fuck it up, so let's keep it simple. I'll stand in the open and call him, distract him, then you rush him and take him down. I want my fox back, and I'm not leaving here without him."

He hooked one of those massive mitts behind my neck and tilted my head back. "Stay in your fucking circle, you hear me? You risk yourself for any reason, I'll be fucking pissed off. Nothing is more important than your life."

I swallowed and stared into those fierce and gorgeous eyes of his. "You're pretty important to me as well."

He gave me a squeeze. "Glad to hear it, but I'm harder to kill."

"True."

"Just do as you're fucking told for once and we won't have a problem."

"Roger that."

He grinned, dropped a hard kiss on my lips, and disappeared into the shadows like a freaking ghost.

The quiet closed in, heavy, eerie. Warrick was somewhere watching, but suddenly I felt very much alone. Just me and the evil fuck who was living inside my best friend. I grabbed a bag of salt from my satchel.

"Renny? I know you're there," I called. "Why don't you come and talk to me?" I sliced the bag with my blade and turned in a slow circle, surrounding myself with a thick line of salt and cemetery dirt. Shoving the empty bag in my pocket, I straightened. "I know you're there. You want to come closer, don't you?"

A scrape came from behind me, and I turned as something shifted in the shadows.

"I can see you," I said.

There was a giggle, and he moved quickly, sticking to the shadows in front of the warehouse. There was no mistaking him for anyone but Ren, his height, his broad frame, but the way he walked, the way he held himself, that wasn't my fox.

"Come find me," he called in a strange voice, pitched higher.

"I'm not going to do that," I said as I strained to see him in the darkness. "You have to come to me."

Another creepy giggle. "No, that's not how the game works. You come find me."

"And what happens when I find you?"

Silence.

"What happens?"

Another scrape and I watched him edge farther along the building. "I cut you. I cut and cut until you can't move anymore, and then I keep on cutting."

My heart beat harder, faster. "I don't want to be cut, so I think I'll stay right here."

"You have to come and find me!" he called, now with an edge of anger in his distorted voice, nothing like Ren's, not anymore—a twisted version of it that sent shivers down my spine.

"Tell me your name and maybe I will."

He moved again, slowly circling me, coming closer to the shrubs and iron fence where Warrick was hiding.

A pair of red eyes flashed behind Ren, and I knew he was

getting ready to pounce. I had to keep Ren focused on me.

"Are you going to tell me your name? If you want me to play, you have to tell me." Whoever had possessed Ren seemed younger, or at least childlike and utterly sadistic.

"Your Elswyth knows who I am," he said. "She knows me very well."

I froze. "You know my aunt Else?"

Another giggle. "We used to have fun, she and I. Her screams made me laugh and laugh. I'll make her scream again." Ren stepped out of the shadows, and his face twisted into something from a nightmare. "She'll bleed for me," he said with a roar. "Now come here, bitch, it's your turn to scream."

Warrick moved, readying to strike.

Ren stopped and started to turn around.

Shit. "How about you try to catch me," I called.

Ren spun back toward me as I stepped out of the salt circle.

He instantly came for me, running at full speed in my direction. Warrick exploded from the shadows behind him, thighs bunching, arms pumping. Ren was almost at me when I took a step back, back into the safety of the salt as Warrick tackled him to the ground.

Ren screamed and fought as Warrick trussed him up in the silver chain. In a matter of seconds, he was bound tightly, and I fished zip-ties from my bag and handed them to Warrick, who secured his wrists and ankles, while Ren screamed threats.

I grabbed the scarf I had in my bag, and he snapped his teeth at me, trying to take a bite as I shoved it in his mouth, gagging him. No way was I listening to this asshole all the way to the house. "We need to get him home. Somehow he knows my aunt." This whole situation was getting more messed up by the minute.

Ren stopped thrashing instantly, and he smiled around his gag, eyes lighting up with glee. He wanted me to take him to Else.

Who the hell was he? What had he done to my aunt? And why the fuck was he here now?

CHAPTER 27

Willow

REN WAS STRAPPED to a chair in Else's workroom, and the spirit inside him was seriously pissed off.

"Bring me Elswyth!" he screamed as soon as I removed the gag. "You promised me Elswyth, now bring her to me."

Iris and Mags stood behind me, and Warrick hadn't left my side. I crouched down in front of Ren. "We didn't promise you that." Else wasn't home, thankfully. We wanted to find out more about this guy before she stepped foot in here. They had a past, and it was pretty fucking obvious that past was horrific. "If you want to see her, you need to answer some questions first."

He spat at me, and I dodged the loogie just in time.

"Tell me who summoned you?"

His face screwed up in a way that was not Ren, then he snapped his teeth at me.

"What's your name?"

He said nothing.

His gaze slid around the room, light sparking in his eyes. "Is she listening? Is she hiding somewhere, listening to me?"

"Maybe," I lied.

His gaze slid back to me, with eyes that weren't my fox's, and he stared hard, like he was trying to set me alight from the force of his rage alone. Then he tilted his head back and yelled, "I know you're listening, Else. Stanley screamed, he begged me not to hurt you. He begged for your life right until he stopped breathing."

Stanley? Else's familiar. He'd died when he was twenty-one and Else was nineteen. He'd been the love of her life, she'd told us that much, and she'd never loved anyone the same since. She never told us what happened; she couldn't even bring herself to talk about it all these years later.

"You killed her familiar?" I rasped.

He grinned. "I tortured him. He lingered for days before I finally chopped him into little pieces."

"Who the fuck are you?" I rasped.

The door opened, and Else walked in, Mom right behind her, looking frantic. There was fear in Else's gaze, real fear, something Else seldom let anyone see, no matter how bad things got. She was one of the strongest women I knew.

"This is Edward, my sadistic weasel of a cousin," she said. "He killed my Stan, then tried to kill me." She patted her prosthetic leg. "But I wasn't the one who died."

Ren's head jerked back. "Who are you?"

Else limped to her workbench and unraveled a length of string, then sliced her palm, balling up the string in her hand to soak up her blood. She was trembling as she came closer. "You don't recognize me, Ed?"

He thrashed in the chair, fighting his bindings. "Why would I recognize you?"

"I know I've aged, but surely there's still some of the girl I was left? Why don't you look into my eyes, Ed? Look into your cousin's eyes."

He stopped his thrashing and stared at her with his black gaze, confusion slashing across his face.

"It's been a while, Ed. I had hoped never to see you again, but here we are."

"How?" he whispered.

"Haven't you wondered why your magic doesn't work?"

His eyes went wild. "I thought you bound them, didn't you? You were always jealous of my power...so you..."

She shook her head. "You were the one who was jealous. I was the powerful one, and Stan saw right through you. He knew you wanted to hurt me."

"I got rid of him," he said with glee. "I took him from you, to break you. Then I was going to kill you—"

"But I killed *you*," Else snarled.

The room went silent. Ed had no idea how much time had passed, or that he'd died fifty-three years ago, or that Else had killed him. *Shit*.

"No," he said, fighting against his ropes again. "You're lying."

She went to the other side of the room and snatched a mirror from one of the drawers and brought it back. She held it in front of him.

"Why are you making me look in a mirror?" he said, staring at himself.

"This is not your face."

His eyes darted frantically over the reflection staring back. "Yes, it is," he roared.

The mind will make you think all kinds of things if you want to believe it badly enough.

"You were never this good-looking," Else said. "Another reason you were jealous of Stan. You always were an ugly little weasel, inside and out."

He hissed and snapped at her.

"You set your trap for me and left me overnight," she said. "You planned to come back, to torture me like you did Stan." She slid her blade free from the sheath she wore hanging from her waist. "I took my own leg, freed myself, and when you came looking for me to finish the job, I buried this knife in your heart. I sent you to Hell. That's where you came from, Ed, and where we're going to send you right back."

"No," he said, thrashing harder, fear filling his gaze. He shook his head furiously. "No. You're lying."

"But first you're going to tell me who summoned you." Else lifted her fist, still holding the blood-soaked string, and pressed it to her lips, whispering a spell before she unraveled it, then began wrapping it around one of Ren's arms.

Smoke rose from his skin, the bloodied string burning into it. I cried out, and I tried to rush forward. "You're hurting Ren!"

Warrick hooked me around the waist, holding me back. "Wait," he said against my ear.

The silver was still binding the spirit to Ren, which meant the spirit could feel pain, but so could Ren. If someone became the blood enemy to a coven, the blood of those witches could literally be used as a weapon. Something Else had obviously done. She kept wrapping more around his arm, and Mom stepped forward, her eyes closing, hands outstretched, whispering a spell that would cause more pain. Ren arched, veins in his neck bulging, and screamed. Iris pulled Mags in tight, hugging her as Ren continued to scream in pain. I wasn't sure I could take much more. Mom went to Else's workbench and unraveled more string, making a slice in her own palm.

Else leaned in. "Who summoned you?"

He hissed, nostrils flaring, and shook his head.

She started again, Mom joining in, and I couldn't bear it. I knew why they were doing it—whoever did this had targeted Mags and me. But seeing Ren suffer like this was tearing me apart.

"Stan cried when I told him I was going to kill you next," he screamed. "So I took his eyes."

Else swayed, then straightened and drew her knife. She was

going to stab Ren. Warrick released me and grabbed Else, lifting her off her feet, and carried her out of the room.

Everything went silent. Mom stood beside me, a look of shock on her face. Biting back tears, I turned to Ren—no, Ed. "Who summoned you?"

He clamped his mouth shut.

I lifted my hands and whispered a spell that I never had before. It was used by witches as a torture device, attacking every nerve ending in the body. I'd been told it felt like being sliced by razor blades from the inside out. Ren threw his head back again and screamed. Acid crawled up my throat.

"Tell us!" I yelled.

When he said nothing, I stepped back. "Fine, you can go back to Hell."

He stared at me, and then something flashed through his eyes, a flicker of a memory, and he started to freak the fuck out. "No! No, I can't go back there. Don't send me back there."

"Then tell me what I want to know."

He was shaking so hard his teeth chattered. "I think...a woman." He squeezed his eyes closed. "A woman's voice. That's all I know, I promise. That's all I know."

"Where did you hide Stan's body?" That was the only other thing Else had told us about Stan, that she didn't know where he was. She'd never gotten the chance to say goodbye to him.

He bared his teeth. "I drove him out of town and threw his body into Hunters Ravine."

I had to ask just one more thing. I didn't know if the image of Azel I'd had while I was shadow seeking was real or something my mind conjured, but I had to ask. "Do you know a fallen angel named Azel?"

No recognition showed on Ed's face at the mention of that monster. "No."

Relief shot through me. "Prepare the oil, Iris." I slid off my shirt. "Mags, get the urns."

Ren's head swung around the room, watching us. Ed knew what we were doing. He was a witch, or had been once. "No. No, I told you what you wanted to know. I told you the truth. That's all I know, I promise, it's all I know."

Mom moved in and took his face in her hands. "You deserve to burn in Hell for eternity, Ed. And we're going to make sure you do." Then she gagged him again and we got to work.

I'd done this a couple of times just recently, so it didn't take long for us to gather what we needed, only this time we wouldn't just be getting the spirit out of Ren and holding it, we'd be sending Ed, and the other two we had trapped, back to Hell.

Art and Bram were with Warrick, and I told them to stay with Else and Rose, but Else walked back into the room a few minutes later, calm and focused. She wanted to be here to see Ed go back to the torture and horror he deserved, and I didn't blame her. I looked at Ren, and there was still no trace of him when I stared into his eyes. I felt that loss down to my soul.

"You don't have to do this," I said to Mags. "We've got it covered."

She was behind one of the shelves, finishing with the oil. Mags was still young and hated any spells that required her to get naked; it was bad enough around us, let alone someone else. I got that. I'd been in the same boat as her. It was humiliating. Nothing made you notice your flaws, or changing body, more acutely than having to stand naked in front of someone, but eventually, it also made you accept those things and learn to either love them or not give one shit about them. It just took some time.

"No, I'm helping. I want to send that fucker back to Hell," she said as she walked out.

Our Mags was utterly gorgeous. Shorter than Iris, Rose, and I, and curvier as well. Her thick, wavy, black hair was pulled forward, covering her full breasts, and my heart gripped at the sight of all the long cuts, the rows of stitches, against her pale skin. I held out my hand and she gave me a determined look as she took it, giving it a squeeze.

The five of us stood around Ren, Iris, and Mom, holding the other two urns containing the souls I'd already gathered. They placed them on the floor by Ren's feet, and Else laid salt down in a circle around them, then nodded to Mom and Iris. They unscrewed the urns and the rat corpses exploded out, hissing and backing away from the salt, running around Ren's feet.

We joined hands, and Else began the chant. "What was summoned will be returned. Hell, take back these souls so dark, remove it from the mortal realm, never to return." We all followed one by one, oldest to youngest, a chorus of voices all repeating the spell over one another, an unbreakable chain, a wall of words and magic flowing through our voices.

We grew in speed and volume, and Ren threw his head back and roared, the rats running in circles, shrieking.

The floor within the circle began to swirl and glow.

Ren thrashed harder, blood coming from his eyes, his ears, his nose. I wanted to snatch him out, I wanted to stop his pain, but I couldn't do that. Not yet.

The floor glowed brighter, brighter still, then there was an explosion of heat and an orange light, a boom so deep, it shook the ground beneath us.

The dead, rotting rats fell limp.

Ren slumped in his chair.

The awful noise stopped, the heat and light dimmed until it was gone, and the stone floor was back to the way it had been.

The door flew open and Bram ran in, chest heaving, eyes full of fear. "Mags..."

"I'm okay, B," she said.

He froze, his eyes sliding over her, then widened. He quickly dipped his head and ducked back out, shutting the door behind him.

I rushed to Ren, dropping to my knees. "Renny?"

He didn't move, his eyes squeezed shut.

I dipped my face lower. "Ren, please."

His eyes opened, and I sucked in a pained breath. The agony, the desolation, the horrors there were more than one being could contain. I reached for him, and he jerked away, stumbling to his feet.

Lifting my hands, I took a step back. "It's me, Renny. You're safe now."

He shook his head. "Stay away from me."

My heart shattered. "It's me, it's Willow."

"I know," he rasped and looked at his hands. There was dried blood on them. He stumbled farther away from me. "The things I've done, Wills...the things he made me do..."

"That wasn't you," I said and took a step closer. "None of it was you."

His eyes widened in fear. "I can't be here...I can't..." He shifted, turning into his fox, and tore from the room. I snatched the robe Mom held out to me, shoved it on, and went after him. I ran out the door and down the hall, then out the front door.

But there was no sign of him.

He was already gone.

Still, I wandered into the field next door, a place he loved to run when he was younger. I called for him until my voice was hoarse, but he didn't come. I dropped to my knees and buried my face in my hands and sobbed until big, muscled arms wrapped around me from behind and I was lifted to my feet. Warrick held me close, he held me up, giving me all the strength he could.

"I've got you," he said against my hair.

"He's gone."

"He needs time."

"What if...what if he hurts himself, what if he..."

"Don't," Warrick said. "Give him time to get it all straight in his head."

I wasn't sure that was possible. Edric chose death over living with what he'd done while possessed, over turning feral. A hell-hound, a thousand years old.

How was my gentle, sweet fox going to get through it on his own? Without me there to help him?

Warrick gave me a squeeze as if he were trying to take the pain and hurt from me, and when I was in his arms like this, I almost believed he could. For a short time, anyway.

I lifted my head and Warrick brushed away my tears, then took my hand to lead me inside.

As I turned, I spotted a familiar envelope sticking out of the letterbox.

I slid the thick folded parchment free and opened it. It was from the council, a time, date, and location scrawled on it in blood.

"What is that?" Warrick asked.

"My trial, it's tomorrow night."

CHAPTER 28

Warrick

I HELD MY DOVE TIGHT, her small body shaking against me. She was fighting the emotions hammering her, trying to be strong. She didn't need to do that, not with me. They radiated from her, I could sense them, identify them, even if I couldn't feel them myself.

I wanted to growl in frustration because I didn't know how to help her.

"I failed Ren," she said into the darkness. "I failed *everyone*. I couldn't protect them, and I can't protect my sisters from what will happen if I lose my trial."

Rolling her to her back, I looked down at her in the moonlit room. "Why the fuck do you think you're the only one who can protect your family?"

She stared up at me. "I'm the oldest, and the trials..."

"You're still carrying that fucking guilt over what happened at the knight's compound, but that was not your fault, female. You were up against a twisted fallen angel. He tortured you; he cut you." My voice rolled out, rough and full of rage. "You endured hours of torture." I grabbed her precious face in my hands. "*Fuck*, Willow, stop goddamn punishing yourself. No one here, no one in your family, expects you to protect them. That's all you. You put that on yourself. When you go out there tomorrow night, you need to do it with that shit out of your fucking head. Thinking about what will happen if you fail will fuck you up. It will take you back there, to a time you felt powerless. And you are not power-less, dove, you are so fucking strong."

Her eyes grew shiny.

"If you cry, I can't be held responsible for my actions. You think I'm protective now? Cry in front of me and see what happens."

She gave me a wobbly smile, one of her small hands cupping my jaw. "Who knew you were so wise. You're not just a pretty face after all."

"I knew," I said, biting back my own smile. "You think I'm pretty?"

"Oh, definitely. It's those gorgeous eyes you have. They make a girl swoon."

I grunted, my heart beating like a fucking jackrabbit in my chest. "But do they make you want to fuck?"

She threw her head back and laughed, and my heart didn't just beat fast, it fucking flipped in my chest. Finally, she sobered and looked up at me, wrapping her arms around my neck. "Kiss me already."

My mouth was on hers a split second later, giving her what she needed, what she wanted, and knowing that I could give her that filled me with contentment. A couple of my brothers were mated, and they were obsessed with their females. I thought I under-stood, but I'd had no fucking clue until now, until Willow.

I would do anything, give up anything for her, to be with her.

She was my world, and knowing there was someone out there

trying to hurt her was making me insane. Until I got to tear them to pieces, I wouldn't rest.

My dove wrapped her legs around my hips and rubbed against me, and my ability to think disappeared completely. She was all there was. She was everything.

"I need you," she whispered against my lips.

I growled and eased inside her. "You have me," I whispered back.

Willow

Blood Hill Grove was shrouded in mist as I walked along the torch-lit path. Warrick right behind me. Mom and Art, Iris and Nia, Mags and Bram following. Else was home with Rose, several hounds there with them for protection. They'd assured me no one was getting past them, and I trusted them.

Light shone brightly ahead. A massive clearing that was hidden by the mother's magic and only revealed for the trials that lay in front of us. Witches and their familiars from different covens were already there, gathered around the massive space.

"What happens now?" Mags asked.

She hadn't been at my first trial, but she was nineteen now, she'd helped us send Ed and the other spirits back to Hell, so when she insisted on coming, there was no way I could deny her. She deserved to be here; she'd earned it.

"At the allotted time, I walk out into the clearing and learn who I'm going up against." And I had a bad feeling about it. Something dark and ugly twisted in my gut, a warning maybe.

"You've got this, Wills," she said, but there was no missing the worry in her eyes.

"Thanks, Mags." For once, I couldn't reassure her. I couldn't promise everything would be okay.

I glanced around at the faces surrounding us. All the rich and prominent families. I had no doubt they wanted to see ours get taken down.

"Dove?" Warrick said, obviously sensing my unease.

"Something's not right. Just...keep an eye on my family for me?"

He went into full-on alert, those golden eyes becoming even more intense as he scanned the area. "They're here?"

He meant our faceless enemy. "I have no idea. This place is protected during the trial. The only place a witch can use magic is inside the clearing. Me and whoever I'm fighting get locked in, so no one can get hurt outside it, at least not until it's over. Just don't let anyone get close to my family."

He dipped his chin as the alarm on my phone chimed.

It was time.

Mom caught my eyes. *You got this*, hers silently said. My family was good at hiding their fear when they needed to, but I knew them too well. Despite my entire family collectively refusing to even talk about the prospect of me not walking out of here at the end of this, they weren't quite managing to hide that fear tonight.

Certain spells were frowned upon, some, the covens agreed never to use. No, we didn't fight to the death anymore, but "accidents" sometimes happened. More often than they should. I handed Mom my blade—no weapons were allowed here, knives, swords, guns, etc., were a no-no, but smaller things that could be used for spelling were okay. Our main weapon must be our magic, which made it difficult for witches like us, who often used blood to spell.

I turned back to Warrick. He stood tall and strong behind my family. I caught his gaze, and he gave me a nod. I did the same. Getting back to him, to my Mom and Else, my sisters, to Ren, wherever he was, was all that mattered. And I planned on doing whatever was necessary to make sure that happened.

Last time I won by not letting my emotions get the better of me, by playing it safe and sticking to simple spells that were effective instead of the flashy ones used by my opponent. That's all I had to do to get through this.

Silence filled the space as I kicked off my shoes and walked out onto the field and waited. I turned in a slow circle.

No one made a move to join me.

Time ticked by, only seconds remained before they'd forfeit. I was starting to think they were a no-show when people moved opposite me on the far side of the clearing.

Elmer Eldridge walked out, Isaac's twin brother, joining me in the middle.

The edge of the clearing shimmered, locking everyone else out, and locking us in.

I heard Mom's gasp behind me and I bit down my curse. My distant cousins would not tolerate losing this fight, especially not to me. I'd turned down Isaac's proposal, and Sapphire would not have taken that well. Elmer's dark eyes slid to me as he unbuttoned the cuffs of his shirt and rolled them up his forearms, vines similar to mine twisted and tangled around them.

I looked into the crowd and, sure enough, Sapphire Eldridge and Isaac stood close by. Sapphire's eyes were hard, boiling with rage and hatred. I glanced back at my family. Clayton was there now. He stood beside Mags and gave me an encouraging nod. Warrick didn't look pleased, but I was happy for another witch on our side. Especially if things didn't go my way tonight.

I turned back to Elmer, and as I looked into his eyes, I knew that tonight I was fighting for my life. The Eldridges wanted me out of the way. They wanted what we had, and since I wouldn't give it to them by becoming Isaac's wife, they were going to come after it another way.

It all suddenly became clear.

Sapphire was a distant cousin. She had to know about Else's past, what happened to Stan. It was them. The *three* of them, they were the cloaked figures in my dream. It had to be. They'd summoned those spirits to get in my way, sent obstacles to prevent me from completing my tasks, hurt Mags to throw me off my game. All in the hopes that if I was desperate, I'd accept Isaac as my husband. All for power, for a claim to our cemetery that didn't fucking belong to them. They'd seen me with Clay at the ball and were more than likely watching me. They must have killed Olive as a warning or a way to scare Clay and get him to back away.

They'd hurt my sister. They'd hurt Ren.

Rage filled me as Elmer and I circled each other.

I dug my toes into the earth, bit down hard on my tongue, and spat blood on the ground to soak into the dirt. With the spilling of my blood, my magic flared.

Elmer struck first, firing a bolt of lightning at me, and I managed to duck it. His coven drew on fire, man-made and created by nature, and he was going to hit me with everything he had.

The ground shook as I called tree roots to the surface. Elmer cursed as one tangled around his leg. He blasted it with another bolt, and I ran as he aimed the lightning at me again. The ground shook as more roots exploded one after the other from the ground, blocking him, shooting up, twisting, creating a cage around him.

Forked lightning shot out of the sky, and I dove out of the way, the earth growing scorched behind me. Oh yeah, he was trying to kill me all right, and judging by the gasps and cries from the witches and their familiars surrounding us, they knew it as well. But there was nothing anyone could do to stop him.

He couldn't get closer, trapped in my cage of roots, but then he gripped the branches, exploding the ones right in front of him and sending flaming splinters of wood at me. I tried to avoid them, but several sunk into my thigh, another into my shoulder, burning me as it sunk deep.

I cried out, running as fire shot across the ground as if following a line of gasoline, coming right for me. He was going to burn me alive.

Someone screamed.

Mags.

No.

I would not let this fucker kill me in front of my family. I was stronger than him, stronger than the whole Eldridge coven put together.

Then Warrick's voice filled my head, telling me the same. And I swallowed my panic and stopped in my tracks, braced, and sent a wave of power into the ground. The earth exploded in front of me as if a mini bomb had gone off, stopping his fire in its tracks.

Elmer lifted his hands and began muttering a spell. The sky cracked and clouds gathered. He was going to try to fry me by peppering the clearing with enough lightning that there would be no escape.

Not fucking happening. I could pummel him with rocks and boulders and knock the fucker out, but I decided to go one better. I slid out the needle I had threaded onto my bra strap and whispered my own spell as I poked my finger, coating the tip in blood. "Thread the needle, thread the needle, lip and tongue, lip and tongue." I repeated the simple yet gruesome spell over and over, and Elmer screamed, his cries cut off as invisible thread began sewing his lips together, preventing him from finishing his spell.

Sapphire stood behind him, screaming something at him, Isaac at her side, fury dancing in his eyes.

Elmer turned red, and I lifted my arms and threw every ounce of power I had into calling the wind, and the trees and roots, the shrubs and vines. The wind grew more and more fierce, blowing out whatever fire he managed to summon, like a giant extinguishing a candle. The roots and vines continued to grow around Elmer more and more, locking him in deeper.

And when the invisible shield around the clearing dropped, I knew it was over.

A trial was over when the mother deemed it over. No, she wasn't here in a physical sense, but she was here, all around us. And she'd deemed me the winner.

I'd won.

Iris ran at me, hugging me, jumping up and down. The rest of my family swarmed me as well, their joy filling me up.

Sapphire marched into the clearing with Isaac and stood in front of Elmer's cage of branches. She raised her hand, turning it all to ash in a matter of moments, her magic no longer bound now that the battle was over. Elmer stood there, his lips now freed, red-faced and furious.

Sapphire strode toward me. "How dare you..."

"You should stop talking before you say something you'll regret. You made a mistake, coming after my family, and I promise you will live to regret it," I said.

"Come after you? We had no idea we'd be fighting you tonight," she ground out.

"As soon as I have proof of what you did, I will make you sorry."

Sapphire's eyes blazed. "I have no idea what you're talking about."

"You're lying..."

Elmer lifted his hands behind her, aiming them at me and Iris, and screamed a spell that had been forbidden for centuries, a spell so foul and torturous even the most sadistic witch would think twice before using it. I grabbed my sister, tackling her to the ground.

Elmer's spell hit the witch behind me.

He dropped to the ground, screaming as his skin bubbled and burned, as his body ate at itself from the inside out, liquefying him while keeping his vital organs intact until the very end, so the recipient of the spell suffered through every moment, every second of the horrific torture.

Elmer stumbled back a step, a stunned expression on his face.

Warrick rushed to us, checking we were okay, then he spun on Elmer. The witch tried to back up, turned to run, but Warrick was on him in seconds. He didn't bother with words; he wasn't interested in fighting. No, he tore the other male's head from his shoulders, turned around, and roared at the stunned bystanders, Elmer's decapitated head dangling from his fist. His red gaze slid to a horrified Sapphire and Isaac before looking at the crowd surrounding us.

"If any of you ever come after my mate, or her family, you are declaring war with me and my brothers, and we will hunt you down and tear you to fucking pieces."

No one said anything.

"Do you hear me?" he roared.

Witches nodded, some cried, then they all rushed to leave. I stood there, pretty shocked myself. If we weren't outcasts before, we sure as hell were now. I guess it was a good thing we preferred it that way.

My silent and seriously stunned family followed the crowds, leaving Sapphire and Isaac in the clearing with Elmer's remains.

"Thanks," I said to Warrick when he walked up beside me. "You do realize you can't just tear off the heads of everyone who tries to hurt me."

He hooked me around the back of my neck, in that possessive way of his, and looked down at me, his expression fierce. "Yeah, dove, I fucking can."

My savage little heart lit up.

Who could argue with that?

CHAPTER 29

Warrick

I FISTED the sheet with one hand and buried the other in my dove's hair. Her soft, wet mouth was working my dick, her hand cupping my balls, and I had to grind my teeth to stay in control, to stop myself from flipping her over and driving into her from behind.

Her other hand went to my thigh and her nails dug in. It was that little bite of pain that flicked the switch in my brain. I reached down and hooked her under the arms and dragged her up my body.

She straddled me and I felt her slick and molten against my stomach. I didn't have to say anything, she reached back, positioned me, and took me inside the heat of her welcoming body, stretching around me easier now that I'd had her several times.

My beautiful mate moved on top of me, her wild red hair all over the place, her cheeks dark from her own need. Fuck, I was

love is, dove, or if I'm capable of feeling it. But I do know I will kill anyone who hurts you, that I want you, that I will always and only want you. And that not having you by my side for the rest of eternity is an eternity not worth living."

She looked down at me. "As far as declarations go, I'll take that over a mere I love you any day of the week."

I gave her a squeeze, and she pressed a gentle kiss to my lips.

"I can't believe my trial is finally over. But I can't bear to think of my sisters being forced to fight. I have no idea how it's going to work. The coven trials are every two hundred years. Theirs are special cases, though, so I assume the mother will choose their opponents? But then, who would want to risk losing their powers when they've already secured them?" Her gaze became distant.

"Maybe she'll pit them against one of the losing covens? Like a second chance, a way to get back the power they lost."

"That'd make more sense." Determination filled her eyes. "If you're right, and one of the losing covens gets a second chance, the last person I want one of my sisters fighting is Isaac. He and Sapphire will be after blood. They'll be more determined than ever to come after us. But we know who wants to hurt us now. I'll get my proof and I'll take it to the council. I won't be happy until they're exiled from Roxburgh."

I gave her another squeeze and pressed a kiss to her shoulder. "You want me to send them on their way?"

She smiled and rested her head on her hand. "I think I have it covered, thanks." Her gaze grew distant again. "I knew the Eldridge's were power hungry, but to come after us the way they did…"

I tucked her hair behind her ear. "They'll think twice before doing it again." And if they do come after my dove, or any of her loved ones, I'll kill them as well.

"You're thinking about killing them, aren't you?"

I grinned, flashing my canines.

"I don't think that will be necessary. They got your message."

I pulled her down on my chest and she didn't fight me. She lay on top of me, my dick still buried deep inside her, and let me hold her. "They fucking better have. Now sleep, dove. You look wiped."

She nodded against me and I held her tighter, listening as she drifted off.

Whatever came next, I was going to be here for her, no matter what. My dove would never face anything alone, not ever again.

Willow

I rolled over, reaching for Warrick. Cold sheets met my hand. I opened my eyes and looked around my room. His clothes were gone, his boots no longer by the door where he'd kicked them off.

I got out of bed and walked to the bathroom, but when I opened the door, he wasn't there. Sliding on my robe, I jogged downstairs to find him, but he was nowhere and neither were any of his brothers.

Something was wrong, I felt it deep in my bones.

I ran outside.

His brothers were gone as well, all of them, their bikes no longer parked outside our house.

He never said he had somewhere to be this morning. Why hadn't he woken me to let me know he was leaving? I ran back upstairs and called his phone but got no reply.

By lunchtime, I was feeling seriously antsy. I passed the time with Rose, then made the family lunch and stopped by Ren's place, just in case. Still no sign of Warrick. By dinnertime, I was close to losing my mind. I'd been calling him all day and had left a bunch of messages.

Something wasn't right. I didn't know what it was, but I had this strange feeling inside me, like something was missing, like there was this gaping hole right through the center of me.

Maybe they'd found Maddox? I tried to convince myself that was what it was, and Warrick would call when he could. But by midnight, I was jumping out of my skin. "I'm going to the club-house," I said to Mom.

"Me and Nia are coming with you," Iris said.

Usually, if there was even a sniff of danger, I'd tell my sister she had to stay here, but I couldn't do that anymore. I needed to stop treating my sisters like they weren't capable. They were, and they'd be tested on that in the near future. They needed to learn how capable they were for themselves.

We headed out and pulled up outside the clubhouse's chain-link fence thirty minutes later. I climbed out. The bar was dark and shuttered, the big roller doors of the garage down, and none of the hounds appeared to open the gate. It was padlocked, which was usual, but the clubhouse was dark, no sign of life whatsoever. There was always someone keeping watch, lights on somewhere.

Striding to the back of my truck, I grabbed the bolt cutters from my toolbox and cut through the lock.

Iris watched me, Nia at her side. "This is weird, right?"

"Warrick wouldn't vanish on me like this. He wouldn't just leave." Fear swirled inside me, doubt trying to surface, and I shoved it back down. He wouldn't. He promised me. He said he'd never leave me. The chain fell away, and we shoved the big gates open, got back in the Morris, and drove up.

No bikes here either and no hounds came out to check who I was, or why someone had breached their territory. Nothing. Not even a whisper of sound. I opened the clubhouse door. It was dark and I couldn't see anything. I reached for a light switch and couldn't find one.

Iris switched on a flashlight beside me and shone it around the big space—

The big, empty space.

Everything was gone, the tables and chairs, the bar—they were all gone.

I strode to the door that led to the hall behind the main room, my heart beating so fast I felt dizzy. The stairway that led to the underground den was gone as well.

I spun and ran to the door that led straight to Warrick's quarters and yanked it open.

It was a closet. I stepped in, running my hands over the walls as if they would magically disappear, as if this were some Narnia shit and I'd keep walking and end up in Warrick's room. And he'd be there waiting for me.

But that didn't happen.

Because it was gone. It was all gone, as if they'd never been here. Like they didn't exist.

"He left," I said.

He's left me.

Iris gripped my shoulder. "No, he wouldn't. He wouldn't just leave like that." She frowned and turned, looking into the shadows, shivering. "Can you feel that?"

"What?" There was no danger, my blade was still at my hip.

Iris hugged herself and Nia whined. "I'm not sure, I've never felt anything like it."

I forced myself to calm the hell down and reach out with my senses. Power, so strong, it lifted goose bumps all over my skin and vibrated through the room. It had faded, only an echo remained, but it was still there. I couldn't place it, had never felt anything like it before either.

The hellhounds were a fierce pack, brutal fighters, and incredibly powerful, I couldn't imagine an enemy strong enough to do this, to make them, everything, vanish into thin air.

It had to have been the hounds themselves. "The hounds have powers of their own." I turned slowly, taking in the empty room again. "They would've had to have used them to return this place back to the way it was. I think that's what we're feeling?"

"Maybe," Iris said and ran her hand over Nia's side. "I don't know. I don't understand any of this."

Neither did I. All I knew was the male I loved had vanished into thin air, without so much as a goodbye.

———————

"Any word?" Mom asked when I walked into the kitchen.

I shook my head and poured myself a coffee. It'd been three days and still not a call or a text from Warrick. I was exhausted and worried, and also pissed the hell off.

I sipped my coffee and leaned on the counter. Iris sat on Brody's lap at the table, Nia at her side. Bram was beside Mags. He was still sticking close to her after what happened, but then he always stuck close to her, and Mom had just finished loading the table with food.

"Come and have some breakfast, Wills."

I couldn't eat, I couldn't think, and forget about sleeping. I hadn't slept since Warrick vanished.

"So they just left, the hellhounds?" Brody asked, looking confused. "They just up and left town?"

Iris gave him a sharp look, but Brody missed it completely.

"Yep, they just up and vanished, like they'd never been here," I said and sipped my drink. He was coming back, I knew he was. Warrick didn't lie, and he promised he wouldn't leave me. I believed him.

"Are they coming back?"

Iris said something under her breath to him and he pressed his lips together.

Did they all think he'd left me? That things had gotten too serious, too real, or he wanted a change of scenery? "He wouldn't just leave without telling me."

"Of course," Mom said.

But judging by the note in her voice, she was starting to have doubts.

"He'll call," Iris said.

Mags frowned. "Of course he'll call. Warrick loves Willow. You saw what he did in that field. He'll do anything for her."

"He's a hellhound, Mags," Brody said. "Nothing more than an animal. They're territorial over what they think is theirs, like a lion in the wild fighting over a lioness." He shrugged. "But when mating season's over, they move on. His loyalty is to his own kind, females are disposable."

Iris slugged him. "Brody!"

The guy looked genuinely confused. "What? What did I say?"

"Warrick wouldn't leave her unless he had to. And he's not just some animal. He's *in love* with her, right, Wills?"

Everyone turned to me and my face heated.

"Wills?" Mags said again.

I curled my hands around my mug tighter as Brody's words morphed with something Warrick had told me, something I'd put to the back of my mind. It suddenly all became clear. Brody had been right, partially, anyway.

I knew where he was.

And I knew whose power had saturated the clubhouse when Iris and I were there.

"I'd return if Lucifer asked it of me. My loyalty is first and foremost to my king. My creator. He comes before anyone."

Warrick's deep voice filled my head, his answer when I'd asked him if he'd ever return to Hell.

"We've all seen the way he looks at you," Iris said.

"Like she's a slab of prime beef," Brody added.

I felt like I was suffocating all of a sudden.

"You're really starting to piss me off," Mags said and shot to her feet.

"Your wounds," Bram muttered and eased her back into her seat.

Iris got off Brody's lap. "You're being a dick."

He stood as well, looking pissed off. "I'm the only one willing to tell her the truth. He got what he wanted then he fucked off, like the animal he is."

I gripped the edge of the counter.

"Go," Mom said. "And I don't want to see you for a few days, Brody."

"Mom!" Iris cried.

He muttered under his breath and stormed out.

"Your boyfriend's a douchebag," Mags fired at Iris. Bram grunted his agreement.

"He doesn't think before he speaks sometimes, that's all," Iris said, watching after him.

"He's never said it," I said to the room, my heart racing.

Everyone stopped talking and turned to me.

"He never told me he loved me. He said he wasn't capable of it."

No one said anything.

"I know where he is," I rasped.

Mom stood. "You know?"

"He's in Hell with Lucifer."

"How do you know that?" Mags said. "Did he text you?"

I shook my head. "It just took me a bit to figure out. But that's where he is. I'm positive of it."

Without the ability to feel love, there was nothing keeping him here with me. He understood loyalty more than anything else, and he'd said it himself, Lucifer eclipsed everything and everyone, and that included me.

He'd cared about me, I didn't doubt that, and whatever this was, he hadn't been given the chance to say goodbye, I believed that as well. Because the male I knew wouldn't just leave without an explanation, but he still would have left.

He still would have left me.

Iris stood as well. "Wills..."

"I ah...I have some things to do." I strode out to the front yard, around the side of the house, and away from everyone because I was about to hyperventilate.

I fucking knew this would happen, didn't I? I knew letting myself fall for him was a fucking stupid thing to do, but I did it anyway. This was my own fault. I'd let myself believe that maybe, just maybe, if I loved him hard enough, fiercely enough, that he'd learn to love me back.

"Willow?"

I turned and Iris walked over to stand beside me. She said nothing, just pulled me into her arms, holding me against her tight. The roles were usually reversed, it was usually me being the strong one, the one doing the comforting. Now, I turned in her arms and let her hug me because this fucking hurt.

And I only had myself to blame.

CHAPTER 30

Willow

Ren wasn't at his house. I didn't really expect him to be.

I'm sure Sally and Calum checked the basement apartment every day as well, but I couldn't stay away. I allowed myself to hope—the alternative was unacceptable. I couldn't even think about him never coming back.

I'd brought food with me, stocked his fridge and cupboards with his favorites, just in case he did go back to his house. It was all I could do.

He'd shifted into his fox when he'd run off, and I got the feeling he planned to stay that way for a while. When he was in his animal form, he'd told me, his emotions were more contained; he went deeper into his animal side, his main concerns running, hunting, and sleeping.

If that helped him deal with everything he'd been through, I was more than good with that. I just hoped he came back to me soon, because I missed him, and I couldn't lose him—not him too.

When I got home, Mom and Rose were on the couch. Rose was asleep, her head on Mom's lap. Mom ran her hand over Roe's long blond hair and gave me a sad smile. I couldn't fucking bear it.

"Where are the others?" I whispered.

Art walked in and carefully put a hot chocolate down in front of Mom and held his up, silently offering me one as well.

I shook my head and gave his arm a squeeze. Art was honestly one of the best men I knew. "Thanks, Art, I'm good."

"You look tired," he said. "You need your rest."

Art didn't talk much, but when he did, it was about something important to him. He loved and cared about all of us. "I'll head up to bed soon."

"Iris is in her room, Brody brought her home," Mom said, answering my earlier question, and she didn't look pleased about it. "Else is in her workroom, and I think Magnolia's with Bram. Would you mind checking on her? She hasn't been herself lately. I think she's struggling with everything that's been happening." She looked down at a still sleeping Rose. "There's been a lot."

"Yeah, of course." I said my good nights and headed up to Mag's room to check on her first, but she wasn't there, so I ducked outside and around to the backyard.

Bram's tree house wasn't completely dark, so I took the ladder up to the door and knocked. When he answered, he looked like he'd been asleep. His hair was disheveled and he was in only a pair of shorts.

As soon as he saw me, he went on alert. "Is Mags okay?"

"She's not with you?"

"No."

"Have you seen her tonight?" I tried to stay calm, but my heart was already racing.

"She said she wanted an early night." He aimed his dark eyes at me, now filled with alarm. "I think she's...she's keeping something from me."

"Why do you think that?" They never kept anything from each other.

The pain on Bram's face was acute. "Just a gut feeling. She said she'd met with a friend a couple days ago, but I think it's a guy."

What? "She's seeing someone?"

His throat worked. "I don't know, not for sure. But she hasn't been herself and it's not just the attack."

His pain and worry grew, altering his aura, turning it varying shades of green and indigo. "Why would she keep this from you? From her family?" That wasn't Mags, my baby sister was an open book. She wore her heart on her sleeve, and she sucked at keeping secrets.

He looked at me through thick, black lashes. "I don't know."

The panic grew inside me. Someone had attacked her, had been targeting our family. Disappearing like this wasn't smart, it was dangerous. Mags knew better. She didn't do shit like this. What the hell was going on? I pulled my phone from my back pocket and hit her number. It went straight to voicemail. I left her a message. I had GPS tracking on the whole family, and they could track me as well in case of an emergency. I clicked open the app. I didn't like invading my sister's privacy, but with the way things were right now, I needed to know where she was.

"What is it?" Bram asked.

"She's turned off the GPS. You're sure she hasn't told you anything, anything at all?"

The muscles in his forearms flexed, and his expression grew focused, fierce as he shook his head.

Shit. "Text me if she comes here?"

"I'm not sitting around here waiting. She lied to me again, something's wrong. I need to find her." He walked to the edge of the balcony and shifted, taking flight and disappearing into the night sky.

I scrambled down the ladder and strode across the yard, calling Mags again as I went. Still no answer. *Goddammit.*

When I walked into the living room, it was empty. Art would have carried Rose back to bed. I didn't tell Mom about Mags, it would only worry her, and she needed sleep. She constantly looked exhausted lately, not surprising since she slept in a chair at Roe's bedside most nights.

I paced around the house, the temptation to get in my car and go look for her was overwhelming, but I had no idea where to look. I'd been caught up in my own stuff for so long, I didn't know where she hung out anymore or who her closest friends were. Bram would though. He had a better chance of finding her than anyone.

As hard as it was, I forced myself to stay put in case she came home or called Iris or mom instead of me.

My phone beeped and I snatched it up.

Mags: I'm with a friend, stop calling. I'll be home soon.

I stared at her message with my heart in my throat. Thank the goddess. I typed back my reply, sharing how not happy I was with her lack of communication, and slumped on the couch. We would be having a serious talk when she got home, and I planned to be right here waiting when she walked in.

My mind spun with Warrick and Ren, with Mags and this mystery friend—with the Eldridges and what they'd tried to do.

Something didn't feel right, like I was missing something, something vital. But Art was right, I was tired and worried, and yeah, heartbroken. My thinking capabilities were at an all-time low.

After texting Bram to let him know I'd heard from Magnolia, I grabbed the remote, and I flicked on the TV to wait for her.

I jolted awake at the sound of smashing glass.

Smoke.

The house was full of smoke.

I ran to the kitchen, still groggy, coughing. Flames engulfed the cabinets and the curtains above. I grabbed the fire extinguisher and attacked them. Yelling for everyone to wake up.

Another crash came, a low *boom* as more flames ignited in the living room. We were under attack. I banged on Else's door and sprinted up the stairs. Smoke had traveled up here, too, and was already thick. I yelled, banging on doors. Mom and Art rushed from her room, both only half dressed. This would have made me immensely happy if someone wasn't trying to burn down our house with us in it.

Bram ran out of Mag's room.

"Is she in there?" I yelled.

He shook his head.

Fuck.

"Get Rose."

He took off across the hall and I went to Iris's room and threw the door open. Nia started barking. Iris was a heavy sleeper, but at the sound of her familiar's distress, she woke coughing.

"Quick. We need to get out, the house is on fire."

I helped her up, and we stumbled out into the hall. Art handed us wet towels, and we covered our faces and rushed down the stairs. Flames blocked our way, and I aimed the fire extinguisher at it and cleared a path. Art took off into Else's room, and a moment later, he appeared with her tucked into his side. Bram strode forward, Rose wrapped in a blanket in his arms, and kicked the front door open.

We ran out.

"We're sitting ducks out here. Someone's gotten past our wards," Mom said. "Everyone to the cemetery."

Bram rushed ahead, and I moved to the back, my blade in hand, searching the shadows as we ran along the tree-lined path to our family cemetery. The wards were stronger here because no one else needed access but us. It was the safest place we could go.

Mom rushed to one of the benches, and Bram set Rose beside her. She was unconscious. "Roe," Mom murmured. "Wake up, sweetheart."

A fire siren wailed in the distance as Bram strode up beside me, Iris, and Art. Else, wrapped in one of her woolen shawls, rushed to help Mom with Rose.

"Can you see anything?" I asked Bram. It was dark and the fog was thick, but he had excellent vision in whatever form he chose.

"Nothing," he said, scanning the perimeter, and quickly stripped off as he continued to search. Then he shifted and exploded into the sky to get a better look.

The fog remained thick around us, but as the clouds cleared from in front of the moon, I could see shadows along the edge of the cemetery, trees and shrubs—

Something moved.

Someone was standing there.

"Who's there?" I called out.

Iris frowned and squinted. "Brody? Is that you?" She started toward him.

"Iris, are you okay? Your house..." He stepped forward onto the grounds. He was one of our trusted friends who we'd allowed a certain amount of access to us, more than almost anyone else.

As she got closer, though, his face changed, darkened. He lifted a hand, his lips moving.

Fuck, he was spelling.

I threw up my own hands, rescinding his access to the cemetery, but it was too late. It stopped him, throwing him back out, but not the flash of light, like an electrical current, that had shot from the tips of his fingers, aimed straight for Iris.

She stood frozen in obvious disbelief before she was thrown to the ground. She screamed, Nia running to her, standing over her, snarling and barking at Brody.

"Iris!" I ran to my sister in shock.

She clutched her face, her eyes filled with betrayal and pain. Fury rolled through me, and I straightened, facing off with the fucking prick.

Cora stepped forward.

What the fuck was this?

She smirked, looking like another person completely. I couldn't believe it. They were our friends.

But Cora wasn't alone—

Clayton was with her.

And he had Magnolia.

Warrick

I waited outside the door to Lucifer's quarters again, Jagger at my side.

It finally swung open and Ursula, one of his handmaids, stood there. She gave us both a lazy head to toe. "You two again?"

"I need to speak with Lucifer. It's important." Somehow, I kept the barely restrained fury from my voice.

We'd been back in Hell for several days and hadn't been permitted to speak with the king of Hell once. His handmaids wouldn't let me in. The beast stirred. I was close to pushing my way in. Not a wise move, I knew that, but my control was slipping by the minute. I'd been a free male for a fucking long time, and I liked my freedom a fuck of a lot, we all did. I thought if Lucifer ever called us home, I would return without question. I was wrong. This, being back here, wasn't going to work for us anymore.

But most of all, I needed to get back to my dove. Right fucking now.

"Who's out there?" a deep male voice called.

"Warrick and another one. The alpha wishes to speak with you," she drawled.

"Well, send them in, for fuck's sake."

Had she been barring us from him for her own entertainment? Jagger growled, obviously coming to the same conclusion. My beast pushed forward, and I was close to grabbing her throat and shaking the fuck out of her.

The handmaids were warriors, and she didn't miss my intention. She shook her head and lifted her ax, smirking. "I wouldn't do that if I were you, hound." Then she shoved the door wide and stepped back.

We strode in, taking in the large room. Everything was black and silver and crimson. There was a large couch covered in cushions, and Lucifer sat back on a massive armchair that looked more like a throne, a black cat with vibrant green eyes on his lap. He stood when he saw us, putting the little beast on his shoulder. He held out his fist, and biting back my scowl, I gave it a pound. Jagger did the same.

"War, Jag, it's been too long."

I gripped my hands behind my back, fighting a snarl as the sense of urgency rising inside me had me close to exploding into my animal form and tearing Hell apart to get home.

"My king," I said and dipped my chin.

"So you guys like your new digs? Your old quarters were kind of shit. Thought I'd give them a spruce up."

Our old quarters had most definitely been shit, but no improvements would make me want to be back here. "Yes, and we appreciate it."

Lucifer sat back down and motioned for the couch. "Urse, get them a drink, would you?"

Her eyes narrowed. "Not your servant, Lucifer."

Lucifer sighed. "Please? As a friend then?"

She tapped her chin as if she were considering it. "Aw okay

then, since you asked so nicely...*not*." Then she strode right out the door.

He grinned at her retreating back before his gaze returned to me. "She really is a pain in the ass, but she can slaughter ten men with one swing of that ax." He shrugged. "So anything else you and your brothers need, just say the word and you got it."

"Can I speak freely, my lord?"

"Shoot."

"Why are we here?" There was some growl to my voice this time, but there was no holding it back.

Lucifer's head tilted to the side, gaze sharpening. "I'm back in Hell, that's why."

"We've been on earth a long time..."

"Yeah, and while we've been gone, the demons down here have been fucking running amok. I need help keeping them in line, and I need you and your brothers to do that for me when I'm not here. I occasionally pop back to earth." He relaxed in his chair and stroked his cat. "Why? Do we have a problem?"

Lucifer may joke around at times, even seem easygoing on occasion, but he was the king of Hell, of darkness. He was capable of things that would horrify even me, and I'd seen him angry more than once. It wasn't something I was fired up to see again. But it was a risk I was willing to take to get back to my dove.

"Yeah, there's a problem."

Lucifer put his cat on the floor carefully and sat forward. "I'm all ears."

"We left Hell when you did, and we made a life for ourselves aboveground. We had no intention of ever coming back here."

"I see." He was quiet for several long seconds. "I really need you here, War. I need loyal soldiers. There are demons here who preferred my son's way of running things. I need eyes and ears, and I need brute strength."

Lucifer's son, Diemos, had been in charge of Hell in Lucifer's absence, in fact, he'd managed to lock Lucifer out. There'd been a battle and a lot of shit had gone down, but Lucifer was finally back where he belonged and looking to set things right—with our help, obviously.

Fuck. I needed to make him understand why we couldn't stay. "My female is aboveground. Two of my brothers also have mates and pups, and are now separated from them. We owe you, my lord, you created us, you have treated us with respect and generosity, and we will always be loyal to you, but we cannot stay here."

Lucifer was quiet again, then finally, he stood and paced away then back. "This is a serious problem for me." He grabbed a glass that was filled with red wine and drank deeply. When it was drained, his gaze returned to me. "You got any ideas? Because I need loyal soldiers, lots of them."

"Could you create more hounds? That way you'll have an army here and on earth." I didn't even know if that was possible, but he'd done it once before, right?

"I could, but they would need to be trained, they would need leadership." His head tilted to the side again and then his face lit up. "How about, you stay long enough to train them? Then all you have to do is pop back regularly to make sure shit is running smoothly? Maybe some babysitting when I'm aboveground."

I didn't want to stay here, not for any length of time. I wanted to get the fuck back to my dove. "How long would we need to stay?"

Lucifer held my gaze, and his eyes turned hard, icy. He was done negotiating. He was accommodating us, giving us what we wanted, but that came at a price, and if we pushed, if we pissed him off, he might never let us go back.

"I can create full-grown hounds in several days," Lucifer said. "But they'd be as helpless as newborn babes. I'll need you here for several months, at least."

I turned to Jagger, and my brother looked about as thrilled as swelling inside her already. I brushed my thumb over her clit to get her there faster. "Feel good, dove?"

"So good."

Her head dropped back as she rode me harder, her soft hair brushing my thighs, tits bouncing, and I was overwhelmed with a feeling so fierce and deep I gasped. I'd almost lost her tonight. She'd almost died horrifically right in front of me, and there'd been nothing I could do about it.

I hooked her around the waist, my other hand going to the back of her head, and I dragged her down, taking her mouth, needing her closer. Still, it didn't feel close enough. "Don't ever leave me," I said, the words torn from somewhere deep inside me.

She moaned against my lips. "I'm not going anywhere, alpha."

But she would—one day I would lose her. Willow was mortal. Pain smashed into me at just the thought of her not being here with me. I'd never felt anything like it, but I recognized it instantly. Why the fuck hadn't Lucifer made us like the knights? Their females became immortal as well when they mated.

I hated those fuckers right then.

I gripped Willow's ass and thrust up into her until I'd grown too thick to move, locked in place inside her. I wanted to pull her inside me, to protect her, to keep her safe, and make sure she never left me. She rolled her hips, shaking and crying out, coming around me. Her muscles clamped down, and I barked out a harsh cry as I came deep inside her.

We clung to each other, breathing hard.

"I love you," she whispered.

Fuck. How would I ever deserve it, her love? I had no idea, but I would keep trying, with everything in me.

I clung to her tighter, as warmth filled me, like it often did now around my dove. Another feeling I had never experienced before, until her. She had me feeling so many new things, things I wasn't sure how to name. I didn't know what this was, but it scared me and felt vital all at the same time. "I don't know what

I felt, but he sensed Lucifer losing patience as well. Jagger dipped his head, giving me his agreement.

Something occurred to me, and I decided to push for one more favor. "We will stay as long as you need us to train them, my lord, but when we go back, can you return us to the same time as we left?"

Lucifer grinned. "Yeah, War, that I can do."

And just like that, the ice melted. Lucifer got what he wanted and that's what mattered.

We stood to leave, and I opened the door. Jagger walked out, then Lucifer spoke again. "Your female, she's the witch, yes? Willow?"

I turned back. "Yes."

"She's a worthy female."

Jagger gave me a nod and headed to our quarters, and I moved back into Lucifer's rooms. "She is." He'd met my dove or at least seen her fight. She'd been there when he took Hell back.

"You'll have many strong sons with her, I have a feeling." He winked. "A few daughters as well, I'd wager."

The organ pumping in my chest seemed to swell and grow warm. "I hope so."

"I appreciate your sacrifice, War. I know it'll be hard to be parted from her, but I will forever be in your debt."

The king of Hell didn't say that shit lightly, and I wasn't going to let it pass. "Then may I ask for another favor?"

"It seems I'm in a good mood. Ask."

"Our mates are mortal, is it possible..."

"You want them to have immortality as well?"

"Yes, and our children, not just our sons but daughters as well."

"Done," he said as if it were nothing, as if he hadn't just given my brothers and me an eternity of happiness.

"Just one more thing?" Yeah, I was totally fucking pushing it, but I had to try. "Willow's sisters, she wouldn't want to be parted from them, and one of them is sick…"

"Yeah, you are fucking pushing it," he said like he was reading my mind, and he more than likely was. "But why not. Only if they find mates, though. Both parties will be granted eternal life, if that's what they want. As for the one who's sick, her fate is already set. I can't meddle there. The fates are vindictive bitches and would focus their evil bidding on me. I'm not down with that. I'm not saying *she won't* live a happy life mated for eternity, but yeah." He gave me a wince. "Don't bet on that one."

Fuck. "Thank you," I said and took a step back, ready to leave because Lucifer's patience would run out sooner rather than later.

"I reward loyalty, War. And you and me, we go back a long fucking way. I created you, you're one of my children, and I consider you a friend." He tilted his head to the side again, studying me. "Which is why I know there's something else. Now's your chance. Ask it."

Lucifer was definitely in my head. I knew it because there was a question that had been occupying my mind since I first saw Willow, and it was obviously loud enough that the king of Hell couldn't ignore it. "I don't have a soul, right? So can a soulless animal like me…" Fuck, this was hard. "Can we…are we capable of love? Of feeling it, expressing it?"

Lucifer scooped up his cat again, and she smooched his face. "No being spawned in Hell has a soul, brother, and that includes my own grandson, Zenon. The difference between you and him is he doesn't know it." A small smile curled his lips, flashing straight white teeth. "And no one has loved another the way Z loves his Mia, and don't get me started on Zephyr, my great grandson. No child has ever had a more devoted father."

"So I can, I can give that to Willow?"

"You and your brothers were created full-grown, not raised up. You didn't have the same familial connections as humans or shifters, or whatever the fuck else, to begin with. But you became your own family, over time. Yes, I gave you the ability to sense emotions, Warrick, but the reason you *understand* them is because you are capable of them yourself." He stroked his cat, looking down at her with adoration in his eyes. "Even those of us with the blackest of hearts are capable of love, if given the right motivation."

I left a short time later, and it was like a fucking light had been switched on.

I was capable of love.

Yeah, I fucking was.

Because it suddenly became so fucking obvious. I loved my dove with everything in me.

And I was going to work day and night to get back to her.

To get my eternity with her.

CHAPTER 31

Willow

FLAMES SURROUNDED THE CEMETERY.

The smell of smoke and burned flesh filled my head. My heart was a lump of coal in my chest.

Warrick hadn't come. I'd called for him. I'd called until my throat was raw, and still, he never came.

Now they were gone.

They were all gone.

Their charred bodies scattered around the cemetery like crumbling statuary—Mom and Else clinging to Rose, Art with his arms around all of them, trying to shield them to the very end. I turned in a slow circle, numb, so fucking numb, while ash floated on the air around me like falling snow. My Iris was curled on the ground, Nia at her side. A sob crawled up my throat when my eyes finally landed on Mags and Bram, his body covering hers protectively, while she clung to him.

Clayton promised me he'd let her go, that he'd spare her if we surrendered. He'd lied. He'd fucking lied.

He grabbed my hair, fisting it, and shoved my head back. I let him. I had nothing left. Nothing. He'd already bound my powers with the dark magic he'd given himself over to. He'd been too strong. He'd overpowered us.

"Kill me," I said.

He smiled. "Oh no, that won't do." He clicked his fingers, and a frightened man I'd never seen before rushed forward, Cora at his side. "Say hello to the nice man. He's about to bind us for a lifetime of wedded bliss." His smile widened. "I can't claim all this power if we're not married, now can I, darling."

A short time later, I became Mrs. Clayton Whitlock without even uttering an *I do*. The minister didn't seem to need one. It probably had something to do with the huge wad of cash Cora handed him when it was done.

I wouldn't survive this. I didn't want to.

My death was the only way to stop it—and I would stop it.

Warrick

It had been six months of literal Hell, and as I strode through the massive chamber surrounded by fire, by souls screaming in agony, I knew I was finally going home to my dove.

Gus walked beside me. The young hound was only six months old but looked mid-twenties, by human standards. The new pack of hellhounds had come a long way in a short time, but then we'd been highly motivated to get them to this point.

We moved farther into the chamber, and Gus lined up with his brothers. "I'll be back," I said to them. "Until then, Jagger is in charge. Do as he says."

"Yes, alpha," they all said in unison.

Jag had agreed to stay here for another couple of months, with me coming back for short visits every couple of weeks. Once they were ready to go it alone, I'd spread my visits out to every month or when Lucifer was away from Hell.

I strode over to Maddox, who was staying as well. He'd been brought back when the rest of us had. Mad was still struggling with what happened, his loss, and had no desire to return above ground. I didn't think that would change for a long while, if at all. We clasped hands and the pain in his eyes as fresh as it had been the day he lost his mate. "There'll always be a place for you, brother, when you're ready."

With another nod, Mad strode away, and I joined my brothers gathered across from our new hounds, and where Lucifer stood shooting the shit.

"You ready to go home?" he asked me.

"Fuck, yes."

He chuckled. "I'll try not to take that as an insult." He lifted a hand. "You should get back around the time you left, it's not exact, so any trouble, just call." He lifted his cell phone and waved it about.

Boots shuffled, my brothers as anxious to leave as me.

"Right, catch you on the flippity-flip," Lucifer said and clicked his fingers.

We started to fade, then *poof.*

We were home.

CHAPTER 32

Warrick

I WAS in Willow's room.

She wasn't.

I'd been torn from her bed months ago, but my dove wasn't here now.

My brothers were nowhere to be seen. I had to assume they'd been sent back to where they'd been as well.

I strode into the hall. The house was dark, the air wet and acrid. It was silent except for the sound of dripping coming from downstairs. I rushed down and water squelched under my boots. What the fuck was going on?

Storming through the house, I checked the living room, the kitchen. There'd been a fire. *Fuck*. I rushed outside, and the sound of distant screams filled the night. They were coming from the cemetery. I sprinted along the path to get there.

I reached the edge of their family burial grounds and frantically searched for her in the darkness.

Then I spotted her.

Willow.

She was on her knees, Clayton Whitlock standing in front of her holding a blade, Willow's blade.

Defiance lit her gaze, and she moved so fucking fast, snatching up a jagged-looking rock from the ground. Then she attacked him.

One moment her blade was in Whitlock's hand, and the next, it was buried in my dove's chest.

Clayton yelled in outrage, and Willow slumped to the side, blood covering her chest. *No.* I exploded into my beast form and ran for her—

My body collided with the ward surrounding the cemetery, barring me from getting to her. My dove didn't move, she lay on her side, eyes wide, lifeless.

Roaring, I ran at the barrier over and over again, but I couldn't get through, I couldn't reach her.

She blinked and extended her hand for me—

Then she stilled.

She was gone.

I roared again, Clayton turned to me then, and his wild gaze locked with mine.

My phone rang, the only sound filling the silence.

Lucifer's words filtered through my head.

The wrong time, Lucifer had sent us too far forward. Hands shaking, knees close to giving out as grief ate me up, I yanked out my phone.

It was the king of Hell calling. I stabbed my finger down on the call button.

"Yo! So I think I made a mistake?" he said before I could speak.

"I just watched my female being slaughtered," I choked out.

"Ahh...so I did mess up?"

"Too far forward." I checked the date on my phone. "By a couple days."

"I'll try again. Hang tight." He disconnected, and I tried to breathe, but I couldn't take my eyes off my dove lying fucking lifeless, brutally slaughtered on the cold ground.

What the fuck had happened here?

Clayton started toward me, stopping several feet away, still behind the safety of the ward.

"I'm going to kill you," I growled.

"Why the fuck do you care? You left her." His lips curled up. "She called for you, you know, and you never came."

She'd called for him. He roared in fury, in pain.

Clayton's expression darkened. "Then she forced me to stab her, ruining my plans. That won't stop me, though." He glanced back. "We didn't even get to consummate the wedding...although, she'd still be warm. Would it be wrong if I..."

"You will know what it feels like to have your limbs torn from your torso."

"Oh, I'd like to see you try that." Clayton frowned.

I looked down at my hands, I was fading. I looked back up at Clayton and grinned, then I was gone.

I was back in Willow's bedroom, and again, she wasn't there. I exploded out of the room. Same fucking night. Only it had to be earlier because the house was still on fucking fire. I looked in the open doors of the bedrooms as I bolted for the stairs—empty—then exploded through the fire and sprinted outside.

Clayton fucking Whitlock was about to die.

Willow

Clayton stood behind our ward surrounding the cemetery, unable to pass or get to us. He held Mags tight and pressed his lips to her cheek, looking at me. "I had a feeling you'd flake on me, Wills, had to have a backup plan. And she made it so easy for me, she came right to me all on her own." He nuzzled my baby sister. "Meet my fiancée."

Mags was shaking, and she tried to wrench away. "Oh, no you don't," Clayton said.

Her lips trembled. "I-I'm so sorry, Willow," she said. "Rose...I just...I wanted to help Rose..." Tears streamed down her face.

She'd broken her blood vow to Rose to try to save our sister.

Clayton smiled and looked at Cora. "I told you I could do it. I told you I could get you what you wanted."

Cora smiled. "Yes, you did. I'll admit, I underestimated you. But you've more than proven yourself worthy of my Emily."

Emily? What the fuck was she talking about? "Let Magnolia go," I said. "Please, just let her go."

"Why would I do that?" Clay said. "She belongs to me now. Through her, I have access to all of this. What's hers will be mine, and all that. And seeing as she'll be the only member of this line of the Thornheart family left alive by the end of tonight, it means we get it all, right, Cora?"

Cora was watching him, eyes calculating. "Right."

"We've treated you and your little shit of a grandson like family, and this is how you repay us?" Else said to Cora, disgust lining her face.

I looked from Cora to Clay. "Why are you doing this?"

"Because I deserve it; I deserve power and respect," Clay said, eyes bright with fury. "My parents treated me like I was nothing my whole fucking life. I was a disappointment, not powerful enough for them, not smart enough. The handsome idiot, the face of the family business, but nothing more. No one respected me because of the way my own parents treated me. I should have been in charge of the company. I should have taken over from that fucking prick after I killed him, not her. Now I'll show them, I'll show everyone."

"You killed your father?" I asked, but I knew the answer, it was written all over his deranged face.

"He was weak, and he'd ruined my life."

He sounded like a spoiled child. "And what about your mother and her familiar, did you kill them as well?"

He shrugged. "I had no choice. Mother's familiar suspected me of knocking off the old man. It was his own fault, really. As for mother, I'd only planned to scare her, but then..." He shrugged. "I guess I got carried away. But in the end, I showed her, I showed both of my parents how powerful I really was."

And he'd used dark magic to do it, in a way that blocked my blade from sensing his true intentions. And I knew, without doubt, he'd done the same to win his trial, breaking every one of our laws, our covenants. "Is that what you were trying to do to Magnolia? Scare her? You almost killed her as well."

"I saw the pictures on Nightscape, you running after the hound. Hurting her the same way as mother gave us a common enemy, made you sympathize with me, and it worked for a while, didn't it? You agreed to marry me." Mags struggled harder and Clay shoved her to Brody. Mags cried out when Brody wrenched her arms back, holding her tight enough to bruise.

My pulse thundered in my ears, fear for my sister a tight coil in my stomach. I couldn't attack, not all of them at once. And there was no way they hadn't protected themselves. "And you think Cora can give you the power you want?" I asked Clayton, genuinely puzzled.

Fury lit Cora's eyes. "Who do you think summoned those souls, who do you think summoned Edward? *Me*, I did. You're not the only powerful one in this family, Willow."

"Diana?" Else whispered.

"Finally, you've worked it out," Cora said. Hatred darkened her features, making her almost unrecognizable. "When you killed my brother, you took everything from us. Our families severed ties, we were cast out of coven Thornheart. I've been waiting so long to get back what should have been mine."

"You think our coven will welcome you back if you kill us? Do you think the witches' council will let you get away with it?"

"They won't know. No one will know. Everyone will think your family died in a house fire."

Something occurred to me. "You killed Joshua, didn't you?" I said to Cora. Joshua Thornheart, the male who was meant to be the Keeper of the Thornheart line. "You thought Brody would be chosen as Keeper in his place."

Cora hissed. "I had to try. It should have been my line, not yours. But it's fine, I'll get what I want a different way. I just have to remove the obstacles in my way, one by one."

One by one.

She'd said that in my dream, she'd been one of the three hooded figures.

Cora, Brody, and Clayton.

"With this cemetery and its power, I'll bring my family back. I'll bring Ed and my Emily back."

"That's why you summoned Edward? You want your family back?"

She smiled. "Yes, and Emily will be next."

"We already sent Edward back where he belonged," Else said.

Cora curled her fingers into a fist. "Not for long."

"Your brother's a monster. You were only a baby, Cora. You don't know what he was. You don't know him. If you'd told me who you were, I wouldn't have held Edward's actions against you. I would have helped you."

"You're lying," Cora yelled.

"What are you going to do?" I said, trying to keep them talking, trying to come up with a way to save my sister, to get her away from them.

"The first two souls we summoned were to throw you off your true task, Willow, and, of course, practice before I brought Ed and Emily back. You were supposed to fail your task, and in desperation to keep your family safe, accept Clay's proposal. Ed would continue to possess Ren and Emily would possess you. My daughter would become the Keeper. The only thing that's changed is now I'll have to find a new vessel for Ed."

This whole thing was completely twisted.

"How did you know Clayton would help you?"

Cora smiled. "We met through a mutual friend, someone with the same interests."

Dark magic.

And I'd bet anything the "mutual friend" was someone Clayton did business with. Someone who had access to all manner of dark and ancient spells and relics.

"So Clay got greedy, killed his parents and made a deal with you? He'd marry me, Keeper of coven Thornheart, and then you'd summon Emily, she'd possess me, you'd move into our house and take over my life. Am I right so far?"

Clayton said nothing, eyes glittering.

"And what happens to the rest of my family?" My heart thudded against the back of my ribs because I already knew the answer to that.

Clayton smirked. "Maybe we could work something out?"

He was lying, nothing would stop him from going after what he wanted, not after everything he'd done to get here. "I'm listening," I said, trying to stall him.

"I mean, Magnolia could get the job done well enough, but it's really you I want. Okay, yeah, you won't really be you anymore, you'll be Emily's vessel, but you've got all the power, Wills, it's fucking hot, and I've worked too hard to end up with second best. Say you'll marry me, and all of this ends."

I didn't believe that in the slightest. "What if I say you can have the cemetery, you just have to let Mags go and we all walk away." Else squeezed my hand and nodded. We'd find a way to get our home back if we lost it tonight. I just had to get my family away from here in one piece.

Clayton studied me, eyes wild. "Nope. We need one of you for this to work."

"Fine, then take me, like you planned, and let Magnolia go."

"Throw me your blade and drop the barrier and I will. And if you even attempt to kill any of us with that knife, Magnolia will die before you can call it back to you."

I looked at Else and fear filled her eyes. I just needed to get Mags away from them. I was powerful enough to stop these assholes. I just had to get my family away from here without any bloodshed, then I'd come back and slaughter them all.

I threw my blade, and it sunk into the soil by his feet. Triumph transformed Clayton's face, and I was instantly hit with unwelcome memories from a year ago. Of another time that I was forced to drop a ward protecting people I cared about. I started to shake.

"It's okay," Else said. "We don't have a choice. Do what he wants, and let's get our Magnolia back."

She was right, we had no choice. I was going to make them pay for this. I nodded and lifted my trembling hands, stomach churning, heart pounding, holding them out, palm down, fingers spread, and I uttered the words to release the ward.

It dropped and Clayton smiled wider and stepped forward, then turned to Brody as the ground began to shake. "Kill her."

No!

Brody lifted a blade—

A roar echoed in the distance, and Brody paused, turning to look. It was just a split second, but before he could turn back, something dark gathered behind him. Bram in his shadow form. Brody's head twisted unnaturally, the snap loud in the night, and he dropped to the ground. Bram instantly scooped up Mags and sprinted for us.

Clayton hissed, hands aimed at the ground. A deep fissure

appeared in the earth, and I threw out my hands and yelled the words to bring the ward back up. Clayton flew backward, expelled from the cemetery like he was attached to an elastic bungee.

Cora, who had bent over her dead grandson, then stood, rage contorting her face as she aimed all her power at the ward. Clayton scrambled to his feet, and face lined in fury, joined her. He lifted something gold and ancient looking—a wide, thin disk, a talisman of some kind—and yelled words I could barely hear, repeating them over and over.

His voice rose in volume.

Azel.

Oh god, he was calling on Azel.

Their combined power increased and smashed against our ward with greater force, and impossibly, it began to thin.

They were both so strong, stronger than they should be. Dark magic flowed from them, clawing and biting at the barrier, the kind of evil magic you sold your soul for. And with our blood running through Cora's veins and her knowledge of the spells we used to ward, they were going to get through if we didn't do something quickly to stop them.

I shoved my feet deep in the dirt and fired back with everything I had. Else grabbed my hand, her long white hair whipping around her. Mom joined in, and Iris stumbled to her feet and rushed to my side and took my other hand, then Mags.

Clayton laughed and crouched beside Brody. Shoving him to his back, he dug his dagger into the dead male's chest, wrenching his rib cage open and removing his heart. Cora faltered but didn't stop with her attack.

"We'll bring him back, too," Clay said to her.

The magic of the dead was incredibly dangerous and immensely powerful, which was one of the reasons it was forbidden.

He coated the talisman with Brody's blood, hung it around his neck, and took a bite out of Brody's lifeless heart before speaking in a strange tongue. Instantly, dread and terror swirled around us like a cloud laden with horrors and power. He was calling on Azel, a monster so evil, so vile, that if he succeeded in the summoning, we'd be lucky if any of us survived.

Clayton would know what happened to me over a year ago. Cora would have told him what Azel did to me, what he tried to do to my friends. And she knew the fallen angel was incredibly powerful, able to help them reach deeper into the dark magic they'd sought. Angels were always listening, it was part of the job description, even fallen ones, even if they'd been sent to Hell, if you knew how to reach them. Clayton would have had access to everything they needed to achieve that, including that talisman.

And they'd succeeded.

I needed to stop them, now. But attacking Clayton and Cora with my powers wasn't an option, not when I was using almost everything I had maintaining the ward.

The wind whipped more fiercely, and the trees beside Clayton shuddered, a dark hole opening in the wide trunk, something awful moving in the darkness.

Azel.

Gripping the edge, his ghostly form struggled. He dug black claws into the trunk, wind whipping and biting at him as he tried to claw his way out of Hell. Clayton's eyes filled with excitement as he continued to chant.

Oh god, Azel was going to free himself.

His head, torso, and hips were out.

Clayton turned to him and raised his arms in the air, calling with everything he had, face red, veins bulging.

"Azel won't help you get your family back, Cora, he'll kill you," I yelled.

"You're lying!" she screamed. "We made a deal. He made a deal."

"Azel doesn't give a fuck about your deal."

She shook her head frantically. "This is your fault. If you'd handed yourself over to us, we wouldn't have needed him. You did this." Hatred filled her eyes. "I curse you and your entire family."

Azel turned to me and grinned, then his spirit began to fragment, being sucked into Clayton.

He was coming, and he was going to kill us all.

Fear took hold, and my magic faltered, the ward almost dropping. I cried out in defiance, in anger. "No!"

No, I would not let them do this.

There was only one way to counter that kind of darkness—with light.

So tilting my head back, I screamed words I had never said before in my life but had read many times in Else's library. "I invoke coven Thornheart, mothers, daughters, sisters past. I call on Betsie Thornheart, Lilly and Rosemary."

"I call on Selene and Elizabeth," Else called.

"I call on Agnes and Morag," Mom added.

Iris squeezed my fingers. "I call on Delilah and Elsbeth."

"I call on Prudence and Daisy," Mags finished.

The ward shimmered, strengthening as the ghostly figures of our ancestors appeared around us, including our beloved grandmother. One by one, they raised their hands and aimed them at the ward, at Clayton and the yawning portal in the side of the tree, at Azel almost completely free, his spirit being slowly dragged into Clayton.

The hole started narrowing, and Azel's spirit twisted and writhed in place.

Warmth bathed us, power surging all around us. Light danced around the thick trunk and the portal kept narrowing.

Azel was suddenly sucked back, pulled from Clayton completely, and dragged back to Hell. Clayton screamed in outrage.

A howl rang through the night. Closer this time.

Then a hound, my hound, exploded from the trees, knocking Clayton to the ground, and tore him to pieces.

The tree closed immediately. The darkness, now drowned in light, lifted.

Then Warrick shifted, standing naked and covered in Clayton's blood. He turned to Cora, who was backing up in terror, but Ren strode forward, blocking her. He was dirty and naked, and even in his human form, he was all animal. My Ren was still gone from his eyes as he bared his teeth, stopping her in her tracks.

Warrick snarled, lifted a hand, and crooked a finger at me. "Get the fuck over here, dove."

Then I was running to him.

He caught me up and kissed me.

He kissed me like only Warrick could.

CHAPTER 33

Willow

WARRICK'S ROOM WAS SILENT, the whole den was. I snuggled closer to him, and his arm tightened around me.

Everything was back, as if it hadn't vanished at all. Warrick had explained what happened, how long he'd been gone and how he got back.

It had been a lot to take in.

But right now, we were here, and we were safe. All of us. Warrick had made room for us here in the clubhouse while we waited for the repairs to be finished on our house. Thankfully, it was mainly just the kitchen and living room that needed the most work, though all the carpets needed to be torn out and replaced due to smoke damage. Warrick was taking care of that as well— his brothers were working on the repairs now—and I was more than happy to let him.

It'd been three days since the attack. Rose was stable for the time being, but there'd been no improvement. Iris wasn't talking much, and there was now a black star-shaped mark on her face from Brody's attack that seemed to be permanent. Mags was still blaming herself for all of it, and Bram barely left her side. She'd broken a blood vow when she went to Clayton for help. It didn't matter that it was to try to save Rose, there would be consequences for her, but none of us wanted to think about that now. And Mom and Else were sticking close to all of them, Art as well. He and Mom were together now, and they weren't trying to hide it. Apparently, he made his move the night the hellhounds came to our house. Honestly, it was about time.

And my Renny, he was still staying away. Though, a couple of the hounds had seen him running in Wolf Hill Woods since he'd shown up at the cemetery. I'd been out every day looking for him. I'd left him food, clothes, some of his favorite books, and a few little things that I hoped reminded him that I loved him, and that I was here whenever he was ready to come back. He had a phone as well. I'd left one out for him two days ago with my number programmed into it, and it'd been gone when I went back. I'd been calling and leaving him messages. Just updates on how everyone was and sharing memories, some of the fun we'd had over the years. I hoped it helped him to not feel as alone. It was helping me. Now all I could do was wait and hope he came back to me.

Warrick's arms tightened around me. "What's going on in that head of yours?"

We hadn't had a lot of time to talk about everything the last few days. With so much going on, we'd collapsed into bed every night and just clung to each other. And honestly, I hadn't been ready to talk. I was now.

Resting my arms on his chest, I lifted my head and looked into his eyes. "It was bad, wasn't it? When you came back at the wrong time?" I'd had this...I don't know, a darkness following me, and I couldn't shake it.

"Yeah, dove, it fucking was."

"We were dead, weren't we? All of us." I don't know how I knew, but it was like this shadow I couldn't shake. As if the emotional pain I'd felt in that first reality had been so acute, so incredibly bad, it had left a permanent scar on my soul. It was the strangest feeling, as if I knew I'd felt terrible pain and grief, but I couldn't actually remember it.

His throat worked. "You can't ask me about that, dove. I can't talk about it, okay?"

Not a no, because I was right.

The moment Brody held the blade to Magnolia's throat filled my mind, then the sound of Warrick's howl in the distance. It had distracted him, if only for a moment, but it was enough for Bram to kill the little piece of shit. That was the moment that changed the outcome of that day. I was sure of it. Warrick had saved us all.

"I love you," I said, looking into his eyes. I didn't need him to say it back. He was the best man I'd ever known. I didn't give a fuck if he had a soul, or if he wasn't capable of feeling the way I did. The way he was looking at me right now was so much bigger than those three words could ever be.

Those roughened hands of his lifted and he cupped my face, like he often did, one of them sliding back into my hair. "I love you, too, dove."

I froze.

"I fucking love you, Willow."

Tears swelled in my eyes, and I dropped my head to his chest, breathing heavily. He dragged me higher, and I pressed my face against his throat.

"Was too fucking dumb to understand what I was feeling, that I was capable of it. Lucifer explained some things to me, but yeah, it only took one day away from you, with no guarantee that I'd ever get back to you, to realize I'd been wrong." He turned his head, pressing his lips to my hair, his hot, rough-skinned palm rubbing up and down my back. "You're my entire world, dove. So yeah, I fucking love you." He gently cupped my face again, making me lift my head so he could look at my face. "I love my mate."

I blinked, and he was nice enough, not to mention the tear that escaped and slid down my cheek. "You need to stop being sappy now, alpha, I can't handle it."

He grinned. "It's your fucking fault, female, so get used to it."

"Will you love me when I'm old and withered and you're still all young and hot?" I tried to make light of it, but it hurt, knowing that one day I would have to leave him. That we'd only get my lifetime together.

His thumb brushed over the apple of my cheek. "You won't get old, dove." His throat worked again, and his eyes grew shiny. "And you won't ever die. You are my eternity, Willow, and I am yours."

I stared down at him in shock. "What?"

"Lucifer granted me a boon. Well, a couple actually."

He proceeded to tell me about my sisters, that if they found mates, I'd never have to lose them either. "And Rose?"

His expression grew serious. "He made no promises for her. It's up to fate, her path is already mapped out. I'm sorry."

Then I'd just have to find a way to change her fate. Because I wasn't losing her. I wasn't losing any of my sisters. Their trials were coming, I just had to make sure they found their mates first. "I think that perhaps we should keep this to ourselves for now, at least until they need to know."

His hand slid down my back and he squeezed my butt. "Agreed." Then he gripped my thighs and spread them.

And instantly, I wanted him, I always wanted him. "I need you," I said. "I need my mate."

"Then take me," he growled and kissed me.

I did.

EPILOGUE

Iris

Six months later

The chatter around the dinner table was lively, it always was when the hounds were here. Well, Warrick was here with Willow, and he'd brought a couple of his brothers and Ronan with him. The hounds were loud and big and filled the room, not leaving space for anything else, and not just in the physical sense.

And everyone soaked it up enthusiastically. Anything for an escape from the dark cloud hovering over us.

It was only a matter of time before our world was thrown back into upheaval.

I glanced across the table, but unlike his friends, Ronan sat quietly and observed. I'd noticed his deep purple gaze shifting to and lingering on Rose more than once. He did it a lot when he came here and always with this puzzled look on his face. I didn't know what the emotionally void dhampir was thinking, but something about my sister drew his attention.

Nia pressed her nose into my palm, and I glanced down.

Iris sad.

I kissed the top of Nia's head. "I'm okay, Ni."

No, Nia couldn't speak, not using actual human words, anyway. But animals were intuitive, they picked up on how someone was feeling, like a predator could sense fear in its prey. That intuition came from the animal as a kind of vibration, and one of my powers was translating that vibration. So even though Nia, or any other animal for that matter, didn't think in human words, my mind translated what they were putting out in a way I could understand it.

It was a fairly new power. I'd always had a special connection with animals, but the communicating thing had been growing stronger slowly over the last year.

She whined and rested her head on my lap. *Sad.*

I gently ran my hand over her head and down her back and made myself calm down. Just like I could pick up how she felt, she could with me, and I hated my girl to worry.

"She's a beautiful dog," Relic said.

I glanced up and smiled, and the hound's gaze slid to my damaged cheek, then to my lopsided grin. I inwardly winced and forced myself not to cover it with my hand. I did, however, tip my head so my hair fell forward. "Yeah, she is."

"Iris," Willow said, nudging my shoulder from her seat beside me.

I made myself smile and lifted my gaze. "Yeah?"

"You doing okay?"

"Yeah, of course."

"If you need to talk..."

"I'm fine, Wills."

Willow didn't look convinced.

"I am, I promise," I lied.

Warrick's big, scarred fingers were curled around the back of my sister's neck, even while he spoke to someone else. He was a good male, one of the best, and I loved my sister had found that kind of goodness in her life.

She nodded, but the look in her eyes told me she still didn't believe me. Thankfully, she didn't push. "Relic's cute, huh?" she said under her breath instead.

I sighed. "Seriously, Willow, you need to stop with this."

Her hand covered mine. "It's been six months and...I want you to be happy."

"I don't need a male for that."

"I know...I was just..."

"I'm not ready. I'm not sure I ever will be."

Willow seemed obsessed with finding us, me especially, a man. She wanted us mated for some reason, in a way that bordered on obsessive. Oh, she thought she was being subtle about it, but I knew why they were bringing Warrick's brothers here all the time.

"So where's Mags?" Wills asked.

"The tree house. She's there most of the time these days, sleeps there most nights as well."

Willow glanced out the window toward Bram's tree house. "Do you think they're together?"

"No. She's still struggling with...a lot of things that happened. Bram makes her feel safe, you know." Bram was also desperately in love with Magnolia, in a way that was heartbreaking to witness. And our baby sister didn't seem to have a clue.

Like Mom and Art had been before. Now they were sitting pressed together, holding hands. Seeing Mom happy like that, both of them happy, filled my heart with warmth.

"Have you seen Ren?"

Sadness filled Willow's eyes. "A couple of times, but he's still not ready to come back." Her gaze became distant. "He's so different, Iris, and not just the way he looks. You wouldn't recognize him."

I squeezed her hand as Warrick leaned in and kissed the top of her head, sensing her pain.

Mom moved to Rose, crouching by the chaise she was napping on, and brushed her hair back. She didn't like to miss out but tired so quickly. "Do you want some tea, sweetheart?"

Rose didn't stir.

"Rose?" Mom shook her gently.

Still nothing.

"Rose," Mom said more sharply, fear clear in her voice.

Ronan shot to his feet across the table, and Art rushed to Mom's side. I sat frozen, watching in abject terror as Mom tried to wake my frail sister.

Rose finally moaned softly and blinked up at Mom, and the relief was so strong, I had to bite back a sob. Art scooped Roe up in his arms and carried her out of the room, Mom right behind him. Wills squeezed my hand, but neither of us said anything. This wasn't the first time this had happened, and not knowing how much longer we had with Rose was a constant fear in our hearts.

Suddenly all the people, the noise, it was too much.

I had to get out of here.

Willow had turned to Warrick, and they were talking in hushed tones, and Nia was asleep. My girl had been extra protective since that night in the cemetery, and by the end of the day, after following me literally everywhere, she struggled to stay awake.

So careful not to wake her, I slid out of my chair and quickly left, then kept on walking out into the night.

As soon as I hit the yard, I sucked back a desperate breath. It wasn't enough, though, and as my gaze slid to Cora and Brody's house, the house where I'd spent so much time, my breathing grew fast, panicked.

Spinning away, I strode down the path to the cemetery, walked through it, and out the other side to the field. It backed onto a small, wooded area that we'd often explored as children.

Tonight, the whole area was bathed in moonlight, the wildflowers that grew here sleeping, their petals closed, waiting for the sun to return. I looked up at the night sky, soaking in the mild night air, the peace of this place, and concentrated on breathing through the panic.

How would I ever be able to trust my own judgment again? Brody had destroyed that. He'd been the worst kind of monster, and I'd not seen it.

Goddess, I felt untethered. Disconnected from myself, my family.

My hand lifted to my cheek and ice-cold skin met my palm. The dark magic Brody had used on me had altered me permanently. Half of my right cheek was blackened, his spell manifesting in a star shape of cold, lifeless flesh, the nerves and muscles damaged beyond repair.

They were dead.

Like I was supposed to be.

How many times had I laid in his arms? How many times had we whispered I love yous in the dark? It'd all been a lie, all of it. He'd never meant a single word. He'd used me, and I'd been blind to it.

I froze as something shifted through the trees ahead of me.

I tried to see through the shadows but couldn't make it out. I should run back to the house, get Warrick and his brothers to come and check it out, but I couldn't move.

No, that wasn't it, something compelled me to stay.

The spring breeze grew in momentum, carrying a low growl right to me.

Still, my feet remained rooted to the spot.

A living shadow, as dark as the darkest night, prowled closer, weaving through the ancient oak trees, then to the edge of the clearing.

Huge and black, with glowing green eyes.

A wolf.

I reached out as it watched me, searching for the vibration, trying to hear what it wanted, to learn why it was here. Nothing. I got absolutely nothing.

Not animal. Or at least not *only* animal.

Shifter.

One of the wolves from the new pack that had recently moved to Roxburgh, I guessed. The pack had all but eradicated the demons in Wolf Hill Woods the last six months, reclaiming territory. We'd yet to meet any of them, though, and given the close relationship witches and the local packs had always had in the past, we'd assumed it was only a matter of time.

He didn't come closer or try to communicate, though. He waited, like he was expecting some kind of reaction from me.

Maybe for you to stop staring at him like a startled rabbit.

I lifted my hand. "Hi."

The male bared his teeth.

Well, shit. That couldn't be good. He wasn't foaming at the mouth, at least. So he wasn't feral. But he also wasn't happy.

"I welcome you," I said, trying again, making sure he knew we were no threat to him or his pack mates.

He made a low sound, his big, boxy head shaking from side to side, then he suddenly shifted.

I took a startled step back. The male was incredibly tall, his body muscled but lean. Solid thighs, broad shoulders, sculpted chest and abs. His hair was black like his fur, slightly overgrown, and hung around his ruggedly handsome face in messy waves. It did not soften him one bit. And those vibrant green eyes hadn't left me, not for a moment.

Oh, and he was still baring his teeth.

"You seem upset," I said stupidly.

"You think?" he said, voice like roughened granite.

"Why don't you tell me what you want, and I'll try to help you?" As far as I knew, this was the pack's first attempt at contact since they got here, and the last thing I wanted was to offend them or screw this up. We had to live in the same city, and we needed access to Wolf Hill Woods and the surrounding forest. We couldn't afford to make them our enemy.

He laughed, and it was dark and mocking as his gaze raked over me as if I were a slug he'd just stepped on.

My hackles rose instantly. "Something funny?"

"Don't treat me like I'm a fucking idiot, witch. I sure as hell won't fall for your tricks a second time."

"A second time?"

He growled.

"What the hell's your problem?"

"You want to know my problem?" He flashed a vicious smile. "You need me to refresh your memory?"

What was with this guy?

"Iris!" Willow called from the cemetery.

The wolf drew in a breath, his wide chest expanding, and he lowered his head, shaking it.

"Back here!"

"Roe's asking for you," Willow said, getting closer.

"I'm coming," I said, not taking my eyes off the male in front of me.

"You and me, we're not done," the wolf said. "I promise you that."

Then he shifted and ran off.

I stood there, heart racing.

Who the hell *was* that? And what did he want with *me*?

I got the feeling I was going to find out whether I wanted to or not.

ABOUT THE AUTHOR

Sherilee Gray is a kiwi girl and lives in beautiful New Zealand with her husband and their two children. When she isn't writing sexy contemporary or paranormal romance, searching for her next alpha hero on Pinterest, or fueling her voracious book addiction, she can be found dreaming of far off places with a mug of tea in one hand and a bar of chocolate in the other.

To find out about new releases, giveaways, events and other cool stuff, sign up for my newsletter!

www.sherileegray.com

Broken Rebel

Beautiful Killer

Ruthless Protector

Glorious Sinner

Merciless King

Boosted Hearts:

Swerve

Spin

Slide

Spark

Axle Alley Vipers:

Crashed

Revved

Wrecked

Black Hills Pack:

Lone Wolf's Captive

A Wolf's Deception

Stand Alone Novels:

Breaking Him

Printed in Great Britain
by Amazon